Reflections of Blue

Abbey K. Bowen

CONTENTS

ACKNOWLEDGMENTS

To my parents and Logan. Thank you.

Chapter 1 – Another Summer at the Farm

Things weren't always bad. Even though in the early 2000s, Uncle Ford's traditional lifestyle coupled with my inability to afford modern technology made life on the farm feel somewhat antiquated at times. It wasn't until the fourth or fifth time I was sent to live with him that everything really took a turn for the worse. I had just turned eighteen, and it was the summer before I was supposed to start college.

Although my uncle was much younger than my dad, he inherited the strawberry farm—without protest—after their parents died. It was located in a small town in Northern Wisconsin, and I stayed there on and off throughout my teens.

My dad wasn't a bad guy; he just lived a nontraditional life that many people couldn't relate to. He married his high school sweetheart, Sarah Faith, right after they graduated. The way Daddy talked about her made it clear that he'd been deeply in love with her. According to him, she had flowing blonde hair and striking green eyes that "could buckle the knees of any boy." But, unfortunately, Sarah Faith's time on this earth was cut short a few years into their marriage. She died after a brief battle with cancer.

She was the only love my dad had known his entire life, and he'd been so devastated by her loss that he'd promised himself he would never fall in love again. He'd kept that promise too, for a long time—over twenty-five years. He never talked much about all that time he spent alone.

Eventually, however, he met my mother, Johanna. He saw her from across the grocery stall, picking apples up to investigate for ripeness. He later told me that he felt some kind of cosmic pull, and he couldn't stop his feet from walking right up to her.

According to my mom, he clumsily introduced himself and offered her his sweaty hand to shake. Then, after some light chitchatting, he mustered up the courage to ask her out. As far as I know, they were a couple from that day on.

That's not to say their relationship did not have to overcome adversity and skepticism from others. When my parents met, my mother had just turned twenty, while my dad was in his forties. Outsiders looking in would see her, a young woman who'd recently immigrated from Argentina, and him, an older white man who made a decent living for himself, and say that they were interested in each other for all the wrong reasons. Call me ignorant, but I genuinely don't believe that was the case. My parents were always incredibly affectionate and warm toward each other, so I never had any reason to doubt their love.

Although, being with my mom also came with other personal challenges for her middle-aged husband. She was so young when they married, and she basically had her whole life ahead of her. She wanted more than anything to have children, and she wanted to have a lot of them. This meant that my dad was a first-time father well into his adult life. He was forty-six by the time I, their eldest, was born. I guess they struggled for over five years to have more, but then my siblings started coming like a blue moon—every two years or so. But after their fourth child was born, there was a four-year break, I don't know if it was planned or not, before the twins arrived. My father was in his sixties by that time.

Unfortunately for him, all of that would require him to work well past the typical retirement age, something I think he was trying to avoid by giving up any right to the farm.

Over the years, his body just couldn't keep up with the labor-intensive jobs that were plentiful in our town. Years and years of abuse—kneeling on concrete to fix machines, hauling heavy equipment off of trucks, etc.—had really done a number on his physical health. Plus, during the summers, all the young, able-bodied college kids would come back to work. When the weather started turning nicer, and he inevitably got laid off, Mama would try to supplement their income by taking on odd jobs. But, for reasons I didn't understand at the time, she never went after any type of long-term, gainful employment. Regardless of what she could find—usually cleaning the homes of wealthier families—it was never enough to support my younger siblings and me.

I always knew the circumstances around my time at the farm had to do with money, but I didn't fully understand how bad things got. I also never felt like we lived in poverty growing up. But it became evident to me that we were raised in some state of destitution when I learned that I would be sent away because my parents couldn't afford to feed all of us three meals a day. They didn't have to worry about this when us older kids were in school, as we received comped breakfast and lunch five days a week. I didn't realize that all the other students weren't afforded this same benefit. Looking back, I'm thankful for my naivety.

Since I was the oldest, and probably ate the most, I guess it made sense to my parents that I was in the best place to be moved in and out of the house during the summers when money got tight.

That June, right after my high school graduation, my dad lost his latest factory job after only a few months due to "the company's downsizing," an excuse he had heard dozens of times. The real reason, and he knew it, was because it took him twice as long to make a product, and the younger employees could run circles around him. So, they were naturally more valuable to the employer.

As usual, I was sent away again to live on the farm. I never entirely "moved out" of my tiny suitcase because I knew there would always come a time when I would need to fill it up again. Because of this, I was ready to leave in under five minutes.

Daddy always asked our neighbor to drive me to Uncle Ford's. I don't know if it was because he was too sad to see me go or too ashamed to face my uncle. Either way, I said goodbye to my family. I think we were used to this to some degree, but it was still a challenging interaction for all of us. I could always hear Mama muffling her tears as I climbed into the backseat of our neighbor's pickup truck. I looked away from them to discreetly choke back a few tears of my own, and then I plastered a huge fake smile on my face as I turned and waved. I was never angry at my parents for sending me to Uncle Ford's. I knew they were doing what they needed to do for our family. It was just hard, never knowing how long I'd be gone. Sometimes I was there for only a few short weeks, and other times I was there for the entire three months.

I had only been away for a little under a year. So, it wasn't much of a shock to my system when I was driven, once again, down the dusty road that led to the farm.

As we approached, my uncle was in his typical position—leaning against the big oak tree in the front yard with his arms crossed, a leg resting on the bark, and a toothpick in his mouth.

I jumped out of the truck and silently walked toward him. *Here we go again,* I thought to myself as I forced another fake smile—the kind of smile where your lips fold in on themselves, and your mouth looks like a flat line. I knew he didn't want anything more than that from me, and that's all I was in the mindset to give.

Similarly, Uncle Ford appeared less than enthused that I was back. He blew the toothpick onto the ground, rolled his eyes, and shrugged. "Hi," he muttered through a clenched jaw.

He didn't say anything else but motioned his head toward the house. He then turned around, and I followed.

We walked together on the grass in awkward silence. At one point, I caught a whiff of the horse's stables, and I was surprisingly comforted by it. Uncle Ford had no interest in engaging with me during my stays at the farm, so I viewed the animals as my friends.

I thought about my favorite mare, Maple. When I went back home the year before, she had just had surgery on her eye; she'd lost partial vision after contracting an infection.

"How is Maple's eye?" I asked my uncle. I knew he shared my affinity for her and the other horses. In fact, they were all he cared about, next to successful harvests and himself, of course. I knew this because the horses weren't essential in producing the strawberries, although he sometimes used the younger ones to cart larger quantities across the property. But that was rare. So, he had them primarily for companionship. Plus, he'd paid the money for her to have surgery in the first place when most people probably would have just had her put down.

"Fine," he barked back.

I could tell he felt guilty for failing to detect the infection early on. However, all the blame was not on him. I also hadn't noticed any sign of discomfort, despite spending a considerable amount of time around her.

Finally, after several uncomfortable minutes, we reached the front door. I walked into the kitchen and was surprised to see a younger man sitting at the table.

"Hi!" he said with enthusiasm and an accent I didn't recognize but immediately guessed was European.

Without thinking, I shot a curious look at my uncle. The stranger must have sensed my confusion because he said, "I'm Janusz! I'm—"

Uncle Ford quickly cut him off. "He's from Poland. He's come here to stay on the farm for the summer." He held his palm out toward me. "Janusz, this is Seraphine, my niece. She will be living here for the time being. She won't be in your way. Right, Sera?" he asked rhetorically, lightly shoving his elbow into my ribs.

Now wearing his own look of curiosity, Janusz stood to shake my hand. He had to grab at it a few times as it was dangling lifelessly beside my body. I was too stunned by his appearance to move or speak. I'd been prepared to enter the same dark dwelling with the same dark energy. But instead, this man standing to greet me had the broadest smile I had ever seen. Adding even more appeal to his face were three or four rows of laugh lines that permeated from his infectious grin.

His positive aura seemed to change the entire farmhouse, and I had to look around a few times to convince myself that I had, in fact, been there before. In place of the ominous cobwebs that once clung to the walls were actual pieces of art. And instead of the dirty old farm equipment that wouldn't fit in the barn, there were plants on the floor. They were strategically placed by the windows that let in the most light—which was even more amplified now that baby blue curtains were hung and open to welcome the long beams of sun. *Since when did Uncle Ford care about interior design?* I wondered to myself.

As far as his guest's appearance—in contrast to my uncle, who was naturally muscular and relatively stout—he was tall and slender. He had tan-colored skin and dreadlocks that reached past his shoulders. He was also considerably younger than Uncle Ford. He appeared to be in his early thirties.

Besides random family members from time to time, the only people I'd ever seen on the farm were paid workers. So, I had no reason to believe he was anything but that.

Plus, I knew it wasn't rare for immigrants to help around the farm—as I had met several before—but I had never known my uncle to hire anyone so seemingly unfit for carrying the heavy bushels of berries. Most of his other employees had bulging muscles that could be seen even under thick cotton shirts. Stranger yet, this person was also the first farmhand I knew of allowed in the farmhouse. Nonetheless, invited to stay overnight.

It was common in the farming industry to have a high employee turnover rate, and my uncle's farm was no exception. As a result, he was understandably uneasy about strangers wandering around in his home. So, he had set up portable toilets and drinking fountains along the property to negate the need for anyone to come inside.

However, I wouldn't dare ask Uncle Ford about the special privileges he gave his newest hire. I knew from my previous experiences living with him that my uncle preferred that I not ask questions I didn't have the business of knowing the answers to. So, I figured it was safest to file all of my recent inquiries under that "none of my business" category.

Up to that point, Uncle Ford was never unkind to me, per se. He was just indifferent. I didn't feel hated by him, but I didn't feel overtly loved either. I was a nuisance that he had to take care of when his older brother was down on his luck. Sure, I helped in the house and around the farm, but I figured there was a reason he never had children of his own—I always assumed he didn't want the extra burden.

I couldn't put my finger on it, but I always sensed a darkness in him. He never acted outwardly happy or sad, and he usually spoke with a monotone voice.

Just like the tone of his voice, but unlike his sudden interest in home décor, Uncle Ford's fashion sense never, ever fluctuated. He always had his jet-black hair gelled neatly to the back, and every day, he wore a white thick-strapped tank top with jeans, a black belt, and black work boots. Curiously, he also consistently had a cigarette behind his right ear, but I had never seen him smoke.

While it was never said out loud, Uncle Ford and I had a mutual understanding. In exchange for temporary lodging, I was to be neither seen nor heard as much as possible.

With that in mind, I carefully tiptoed through the kitchen the following morning to get a bowl of cereal. I frowned when I saw the bland options that I considered only appropriate for elderly people. Nevertheless, I decided what the least disgusting choice was and poured some into a bowl.

I was reaching in the fridge for milk when a large shadow appeared behind me out of nowhere. Caught off guard, I jumped and spilled the flavorless flakes all over the ground. I panicked and immediately began to clean up.

Unlike my uncle, who would have yelled at me for making such a mess, his new roommate said nothing and helped clean the cereal off the ground.

After throwing the now-soiled food away, he grabbed a box of pancake mix and motioned toward the picnic blanket folded on the table. "Wanna watch the sunrise?"

This was the first morning of many that he and I had what we affectionately called a "breakfast picnic."

He prepared the pancakes and brought them out to me. We sat on the gingham blanket during our first meal together and gobbled down our food in relative silence.

I still wasn't sure what his relationship was with my uncle, and I definitely wasn't sure how I was supposed to act around him. Questions were rushing through my brain so loudly that I didn't even hear when he finally initiated a conversation with me.

"Um? Seraphine? Sera?" He waved a hand in front of my face to get my attention. "May I call you Sera?" he asked after I snapped back out of my head.

"Yeah, of course. That's what most people call me. And you said your name is . . . Jah . . .?"

He must have anticipated the difficulty I would have when pronouncing his name because he smiled and quickly said, "You can just call me Jonesy. An American student who came to live with my family nicknamed me that because he said I looked like a famous football player, Cobi Jones."

Given Jonesy's frail body type, I was confused about how he could resemble a professional athlete. I made a mental note to try to look up the soccer player he mentioned on the slow and unreliable internet later that day.

After I finished my chores and had some alone time, I grabbed the old laptop my parents had bought for next to nothing at a garage sale, and I opened it slowly while listening to make sure there weren't any footsteps in the hallway. Then, I typed "Cobi Jones" into my search bar. It took much longer than it would have if I'd made a similar search on one of my high school's fancy computers. But eventually, dozens of images popped up. Sure enough, Jonesy was deserving of his nickname. He had the same skin tone, hair, and broad smile as the man on my screen. Except that Jonesy's eyes were bright blue, not brown. Also, after a quick assessment, I learned that I was right to assume that his famous doppelgänger had a more athletic build than he did. I wondered what Jonesy looked like when he was younger. I smiled at the thought of that version of him.

Although I was still confused about his relationship with my uncle, especially since I noticed that he never joined the workers in the field, Jonesy and I started to bond over the following days on the farm. We mainly discussed me and my life, but I was a vain teenager and didn't mind talking about myself for hours on end. But there were several times I wished the conversation would somehow turn to revolve around him so that I could get insight into his connection with Uncle Ford. Of course, I wasn't going to ask about it randomly. I would worry that he'd tell my uncle if I pried into their business. Sure, he hadn't seemed angry when I made a mess in the kitchen that first morning. But accidentally spilling cereal didn't seem as offensive as being nosey on purpose. However, if he just happened to bring their association up, my uncle couldn't blame me.

While I wouldn't probe too deep into his personal life, one of my favorite things to do was point and make fun of the "happy crinkles" in the corners of Jonesy's eyes when he smiled.

He would chuckle and say, "I got them from laughing at you, *mała perła!*" He called me "little pearl" because of my incredibly fair skin. He first said it during one of our picnics. I was complaining about a boy who had teased me about it. I couldn't remember exactly what was said, but I knew it was something ineloquent—yet still surprisingly hurtful for a young mind to come up with.

As I told him the story, he stared blankly at the ground. Then, after I finished, he looked up, sighed loudly, and smoothed back a few errant braids that had fallen into his face. Finally, he turned to me and said very seriously, "Don't ever trust the words or actions of a man who treats you like anything less than a *mała perła*. Okay?"

Before he told me the Polish translation, I was confused because I knew that *perla mala* could be used as an insult in Spanish. Mama often played music by Raphy Leavitt, a Puerto Rican composer, and she particularly liked one of his albums that featured a song of the same name, "*Perla Mala.*"

My emotions must have once again been strewn across my face because Jonesy clarified with a smile, "Oh! No, no. *Mała perła.*" He was careful to enunciate the "w" sound on the l's. "Not *perla mala*, like in your mother's native tongue."

This was the first time Jonesy mentioned anything about my mother, but I didn't think much of it. I assumed Uncle Ford must have filled him in on my family's background.

Chapter 2 – Raindrops: A Welcome Interruption

It didn't take long for me to realize that Jonesy, unlike myself, seemed relaxed and almost carefree around my uncle. Sometimes, after I had resigned to my bedroom for the night, I would watch as they talked under one of the trees visible from my window. Jonesy was usually lying on a blanket, staring up at the auburn sky through the branches. At the same time, Uncle Ford would rest his back against the trunk and sharpen a random piece of wood. I couldn't help but smile as Jonesy cheerfully picked the disregarded wood shavings out of his long hair and flicked them back toward my uncle. In response, he looked down at Jonesy and raised the right side of his mouth. This, I assumed, was his best attempt at a smile. But as small as his reaction might have seemed to the outside world, it was monumental to me. I had never seen the slightest sign of approval on his face before. While I might not have had the fondest feelings toward him, he was still family, and it warmed my heart to see him express some form of happiness.

However, one night, I witnessed a less than cordial interaction between the two of them. They were standing in a dark corner on the stairs leading down to the kitchen. I couldn't quite make out what they were saying, but it was apparent they were both angry.

After a few minutes of arguing, Uncle Ford lost control of his temper and grabbed Jonesy's wrist. I had never seen them engage in such a heated exchange before, and the sight caused an audible gasp to escape from my mouth. Uncle Ford must have heard me because he ripped himself away from Jonesy's body and retreated into the shadows.

Jonesy then turned around and was visibly spooked by my presence. We made eye contact for a few seconds before I averted my eyes, embarrassed to have witnessed their scuffle and trying to play it off like I hadn't. As I looked around, I noticed that the house was starting to look like it used to, and the heavy darkness in the air was returning. The bright colors in the new art now appeared muted, and the plants were starting to wilt. Faint water drops that began to fall on the roof above us accentuated the negativity in the room.

"Uh—" he started to say before looking back up the stairs and bashfully chuckling. I don't know if he was aware that he was doing it, but he discreetly rubbed at the small red indents left on his arm by my uncle's fingers. Before he could attempt to explain what had just happened, we both heard the animals rustle outside. Then, with a sigh of relief and gratitude for the distraction, Jonesy said, "Let's get the horses in the stables."

I walked out before him, and I remember turning back briefly and seeing him rest his head on the window. Half of his face was covered by the curtains—which, in the gloomy weather, looked gray instead of blue. The eye that I could see was mostly closed in defeat, but for one second, I glimpsed its radiant iris through the raindrops sliding down the glass. I hurried over to the horses, hoping he hadn't noticed me staring.

I wasn't resentful of his delayed help. On the contrary, I was happy to give him a little extra time to process whatever he and Uncle Ford were arguing about. And while I wouldn't have admitted it at the time, I also selfishly appreciated a break from the awkwardness that had just been created between us.

After joining me, we quickly worked together to reign in the horses and secure them in their respective stalls. Jonesy and I were standing across from each other at one point, with our attention on separate animals. I gave the silky black tail in front of me two quick brushes and then glanced up at Jonesy, grooming the animal before him. I could tell he was trying to stay busy to avoid engaging with me.

Taking the hint, I kept my mouth shut, finished my duties in the stable, walked into the house without him, and went straight up to my room.

I woke up that night to loud arguing. More accurately, it was one-sided yelling. The only voice I heard came from the mouth of Uncle Ford, but it was distorted and muffled.

So, I walked softly across the room, opened my door just a crack, and pushed my ear into the tiny sliver of light to hear what he was saying more clearly. It was soon evident why it was so hard to make out his words. He was crying.

I felt nauseous with embarrassment from hearing my uncle express such intense emotion, and I didn't want to listen any longer. Instead, I quietly shut the door and walked back to bed. Then, I wrapped a pillow across the back of my head like a hamburger bun to avoid hearing any more yelling and slammed my eyelids shut. I started to daydream about Jonesy being a robust and muscular soccer player eloquently dribbling a ball between his feet, with the sweat on his forehead glistening in the sun. I pictured myself and my family dressed in matching jerseys, cheering him on from the sidelines. With similar images reeling through my mind and completely shutting out the chaos occurring below me, I eventually fell asleep.

The following morning, I figured Jonesy would still be avoiding me, so I didn't wake up with the excitement I had grown accustomed to over the last few weeks. In fact, I stayed in bed for much longer than I usually would. I knew this might come with consequences from my uncle, but I didn't necessarily care. The only "punishment" I'd ever received from him was verbal. I had heard plenty of screaming the night prior, so it wouldn't shock me to hear more.

But I decided to get up when I heard a light commotion in the kitchen. When I finally made my solemn way down the stairs, I was pleasantly surprised to see Jonesy standing by the counter. He had a packed picnic basket in one hand and our blanket tucked under his opposite arm.

"Good morning, sleepyhead!" he said gleefully, like the events of last night hadn't occurred. I wasn't positive what time I'd been woken up by Uncle Ford's yelling, but I remembered seeing the faintest brightness through my closed eyelids as I conjured up my happy fantasies about Jonesy as a superstar athlete.

A tinge of happiness flooded my body as my mind returned once more to the images of an energetic and powerful Jonesy. Then I consciously snapped myself back into reality to see the real-life version of him. Thin and weak.

But he seemed to be faking his good spirits, so I decided to go along with the charade. "Good morning!" I said through gritted teeth and a fake smile.

"Your uncle and I have a surprise for you," he said, flashing a more sincere grin. He then led me outside.

I had slept with my long black hair tied up in a bun, but several pieces had come loose during the night, so I used the back of my hands to clumsily push them out of my face.

With squinted eyes, which were sore as they adjusted to the bright sunlight, I recognized the figures of my parents sitting on the grass. Even though they lived close by, it was rare for them to make it out to the farm. Daddy was always busy working or looking for a job, and Mama was taking care of my siblings—especially her two-year-old twins. So, this really was a surprise. I audibly squealed as I walked toward their open arms. The last twenty-four hours of my life had been so confusing that it was refreshing to see their familiar faces. Uncle Ford was also there, lurking under the trees.

"Ford was just telling me about what a big help you've been around the farm," my dad said. "I'm proud of you, Ser."

I was startled by this unexpected compliment, and I cocked my head to face my uncle. He was wearing a cowboy hat, something I had never seen him wear before. His emotionless face was darkened below it. The hat dipped as he nodded to confirm what my dad had just said. I wondered if he offered this praise to dissuade me from mentioning the bizarre events I'd recently witnessed.

With no way of confirming or denying my suspicions, I changed my focus instead to my mother. First, she and I exchanged pleasantries, and then she extended her hands toward Jonesy. "*Que bueno verte de nuevo*, Janusz," she said, expressing that it was nice to see him again.

I took particular notice that she said "again." I wasn't aware they had met each other before that morning.

Then, as was tradition for my mom—but only for people she truly loved—she kissed his cheeks twice, once on each side, and he reciprocated. Like me, my mom was a petite woman, so it was almost comical to see how low Jonesy had to crouch to reach her. It looked almost as if he had folded himself into a "U."

"*Tú también*, Johanna," Jonesy said as his upper body began its journey upward again. Pushing himself up, he rested both hands on my mother's shoulders for support. She seemed unfazed by this and held his arms to help him stabilize his footing. A kind smile washed over her face as she grabbed his hands and gave him a reassuring nod.

Jonesy and my parents were obviously comfortable around each other, and my parents weren't comfortable around anyone. Not even Uncle Ford. I think they were always worried about being judged for their age and cultural differences, but it was clear they did not have these concerns when it came to Jonesy. He spoke to both of them with familiarity, seamlessly switching from English to Spanish.

I noticed that Uncle Ford seemed unimpressed by the excitement they had about seeing each other. He sighed as he reached for the toothpick in his mouth and emerged from the shadow of the trees. He reluctantly sat on the ground by us and chomped on the shard of wood, moving it from one side of his mouth to the other. He was murmuring something to himself. Either my parents didn't notice this behavior, or they chose to ignore it. On the other hand, Jonesy gingerly patted Uncle Ford's knee, nonverbally acknowledging my uncle's frustration. Besides walking in and seeing Uncle Ford grab Jonesy's wrist the day prior, I had never seen them touch before.

We sat and ate the rest of our meal, entertaining ourselves with light conversation.

"How have you and Sera been getting along, Janusz?" my dad asked.

"You raised a good one," Jonesy replied. "I have really enjoyed getting to know her." He playfully ruffled the hair on top of my head.

His genuine praise made me beam with pride. I took my hair down and smoothed the crazy nest of hair his fingers had created before securing it back up with a scrunchie. "We like to eat breakfast together and watch the sunrise," I said with a smile. "Jonesy has also been teaching me a little Polish." My mom and dad looked at each other with confusion.

Realizing their unfamiliarity with this alternative moniker, he quickly jumped in to add clarification. "Sera was struggling with the pronunciation of my name, so I suggested she call me by a childhood nickname."

My parents nodded, seeming satisfied with this explanation.

"Hmph—" Uncle Ford loudly cleared his throat. "Anyway, Sera, you should probably start your chores. The stables could use a good cleaning."

I knew this wasn't true because I was diligent about tidying them every single day. But since I had gotten a late start to the day, even before having breakfast with my parents, I obliged. I said goodbye to my parents and headed to "clean" the barn. With no apparent task to complete, I wandered toward Maple. Instead of lightly napping in a standing position, she was lying down. So, I made every effort to be as quiet as possible to avoid disrupting her deep sleep. I instead focused my attention on the other horses. After ensuring their stalls were also up to par, I was left with nothing to do but find errant pieces of hay on the floor and shuffle them between my feet.

When that inevitably became uninteresting, I stared across the barn and looked around desperately for anything to arrange or reorganize. In doing this, I caught the image of my parents, Uncle Ford, and Jonesy huddled in a circle talking outside the house. They were too far away for me to hear, but their hand motions suggested that they weren't engaged in the lighthearted small talk we had shared while eating breakfast.

While my dad and Uncle Ford seemed animated in their body movements, Mama and Jonesy stood motionless and simply stared at the ground. *What are they talking about?* I wondered with a frown, wishing I could hear them.

The discussion soon reached a breaking point. Daddy grabbed my mom by the arm and marched to their beat-up station wagon. Mama looked back at Jonesy and Uncle Ford several times as she was being led to the car. My parents got in their vehicle and drove off. Puffs of smoke billowed from the undercarriage, emphasizing Daddy's anger as they sped away. Of course, it was him in the driver's seat. My mom never drove anywhere. She said she was too scared to. This anxiety had rubbed off on me, and I made every excuse not to get my license.

With similar gusto and rage as my father, Uncle Ford stormed into the house, slamming the door behind him.

Jonesy sat down on the porch. I recognized his facial expression, even though I had only seen it on one other occasion while watching the Olympics. It was plastered across the face of an American gymnast who fell off the balance beam during her routine. As she processed the fall, her eyes were wide but not focused on anything in particular; her mouth was closed tightly in disbelief that she had come so far just to fail.

As I continued to watch the real-life scene before me, I realized that I was clinging to a broom resting by the window I was peering out of. My thumbnail was sore from a sliver of wood that had burrowed underneath it as I unconsciously scratched and picked at the handle.

I left the broomstick to rest once more against the windowsill, and I cautiously walked outside to Jonesy's sad, deflated body.

Perhaps it was fortunate that I was focused more on removing the painful debris under my fingernail than on him. I think my distraction made my approaching presence less threatening to him, as I wasn't staring directly at him at any given time.

"Everything okay?" he asked and pointed to my right thumb, which I was furiously picking at with my left index finger.

"Oh, yeah. I'm fine. I think it's just a splinter."

"Let me see," he said. I offered my sore appendage to him, noticing his hands shaking violently as he inspected it. He released my hand a moment later, perhaps embarrassed by the uncontrolled movements of his own. "Try soaking it in warm water for a while. It might loosen up that way." As he said this, he was clumsily scaling the house with his hands behind his back to stand up and walk inside.

"Okay. Thanks, Jonesy," I muttered. Then, with my uncle in the house and out of earshot, I felt comfortable asking Jonesy a little about the tense conversation I had just witnessed. "Are my parents okay? I just happened to look out the window as they left. My dad looked pretty angry." I was careful to ask questions about my mom and dad instead of him. No one could fault me for being concerned about them.

"Oh, don't worry about that. I think they just wanted to get back to relieve the neighbor watching your siblings. Didn't want to overpay the sitter."

I knew he was lying. "They don't pay Mrs. Cardoza to babysit. . ."

His eyes darted back and forth as he panicked to think of a plausible excuse. "Um, I think they said it was someone different. Maybe one of the teenage neighbor kids?"

Once again, I knew he wasn't telling the truth. Mama was particular about who she would leave her younger children with. She told me that she only felt comfortable having an elderly and fellow Latina woman watch over them if she couldn't. My mom barely even trusted my dad alone with them. That's another reason why she rarely made it out to the farm. She didn't want to abuse the kindness Mrs. Cardoza provided by calming the chaos of my siblings for free.

And clearly, she and my father weren't in any financial position to actually pay someone else, even if that was an acceptable option.

But I didn't want to continue pushing Jonesy. His body was already trembling before I started interrogating him. Plus, I trusted that he was at least being honest about my parents' well-being, and that's all that really mattered.

That night, before I jammed my pillow into my ears in anticipation of more disturbance, I wrapped my thumb. Unfortunately, the pain from the splinter had not been relieved by the warm water technique Jonesy suggested. But I managed somehow to drift to sleep.

Either the house remained quiet throughout the night, or my trick worked once again because the next thing I knew, I woke up to the sound of birds chirping outside my window. When I looked at my alarm clock, I was surprised to see that I was awake an hour or so earlier than usual. Since I felt sufficiently rested, I decided to begin my day anyway.

As I started my descent down the stairs, I was shocked to hear my mother's voice. Apparently, the flames had died down from the previous argument because she and Uncle Ford spoke to each other calmly and quietly. I listened carefully but didn't hear my dad or Jonesy join the conversation. I looked back up toward the room next to mine, and the door remained closed, which led me to believe Jonesy was still asleep.

"I understand," Mama said in her beautiful Argentine accent. "But this is his choice. We brought him here so he could live out the rest of his days in comfort."

"That's bullshit, Johanna, and you know it. He could get better if he took the medication. I even have a bottle in the house. He just needs to pull his stubborn head out of his ass, and you and Clark are only encouraging his tenacity!" His voice was still low, but I heard his hands bang against the table.

"Ford, please. You'll wake them up," she murmured, scolding him.

Usually, she would have reprimanded him for using foul language. But she remained relatively silent as he continued to speak. She seemed to be careful not to interrupt his whispered rants, and she let out only the smallest of "mhms" to communicate an understanding of his point of view.

Eventually, Mama and Uncle Ford fell silent, and I heard him turn on his truck to take her home. From the anger I had seen him express toward Uncle Ford, I guessed Mama had snuck away before my dad woke up. I didn't think he would agree with her quietly continuing their discussion.

I made sure the truck was gone before going into the kitchen. I prepared a bowl of cereal, and I ruminated on the conversation I had just overheard. Throughout it, they never explicitly said his name, but they didn't need to. It wasn't difficult to deduce that they were talking about Jonesy and his illness. I had noticed his frail, weak condition on several occasions. But I hadn't gotten verbal confirmation that he was actually sick.

I was also getting more and more proof that Jonesy had a close connection to my parents. My mother basically said it herself when she said that she, and likely my father, specifically brought him to the farm. I was adamant about getting to the bottom of this mystery, but I knew I had to be discreet. So, I carried on as usual throughout the rest of the day.

I woke up early again the following morning, and I saw my uncle in the kitchen violently chopping something into what appeared to be a powder of some kind. I peered around the corner of the wall and watched him in silence. He carefully transferred the powder into a cup I had only ever seen Jonesy drink out of. I recognized it because it had a large "J" on the front of it. Then, clearly pleased with himself, Uncle Ford looked down the hall as if to make sure no one had witnessed what he had just done. He let out a happy sigh and snuck outside.

After I heard the back door handle click, I walked over to inspect the cup. I picked it up and swished the liquid around. Whatever Uncle Ford had put in it, it didn't seem to change the consistency or color. It appeared to be a regular cup of coffee.

I had seen *The Princess Bride* at a friend's house several years prior, and I instantly thought about the poison scene. Then, remembering that he'd told my mom about his desire for Jonesy's health to improve, I shook my head to dispel that horrifying suspicion.

I put the mug down as I stared at the cabinet and continued to recall the conversation between Uncle Ford and Mama again.

"Good morning, *mała perła*!" Jonesy appeared behind me.

When I turned around, I was startled by the harsh reality of the sickness so clearly on display in front of me. The dark circles under his eyes and his sunken-in cheeks were even more visible to me now that I had heard someone say it out loud. Jonesy was sick and apparently getting sicker.

He took the cup from my hands and placed it down. Then, he grabbed another mug out of the cabinet and poured coffee into it for me.

I contemplated whether or not to tell him what I had witnessed Uncle Ford do to the contents of his mug. But it wasn't like I actually had anything definite to tell him. I had no idea what the substance was. Then, before I could make up my mind, Jonesy raised the mug to his lips and took a sip. I held my breath for a second as I waited for his reaction. But, to my relief and surprise, he unceremoniously swallowed the coffee and turned to walk outside.

"Do you have the blanket, Sera?" He looked back at me and smiled. "Hurry! The sun is almost up!"

I grabbed all of our breakfast picnic stuff and raced after him.

Throughout our meal, I couldn't take my eyes off the coffee cup. I watched it each time he shakily raised it to his mouth to take a drink. *What on earth did Uncle Ford put in there?* I wondered over and over again.

As determined as I was to get the answer to that question, I couldn't catch Uncle Ford in the act again for several weeks. In that time, however, I noticed the whites of Jonesy's eyes brighten. His cheeks were also becoming a bit rounder. He was still visibly ill, but he didn't look like he was ready for his death bed anymore.

Oddly, as his physical appearance improved, his attitude worsened. Now, instead of laughing and telling stories, he remained relatively silent during our picnics. I wanted so badly to ask him what was wrong. I had since learned to trust that he probably wouldn't tell my uncle if I did, but he and I had gone so long without talking about such things that even the thought of initiating that conversation made me feel uncomfortable.

Luckily for me, he did eventually, from time to time, offer small breadcrumbs about his declined demeanor.

"I don't know, Sera," he would randomly interject during our morning ritual. (I was "Sera" when he was feeling down, not "*mała perła*.")

"You don't know what, Jonesy?" I would ask. Each time I was more and more hopeful that he would give me an insight into his internal conflict.

"Aagh. Never mind.mYou're too young to understand" was always his reply.

One day, I'd had enough. I needed to know what was going on with my friend. I swallowed my nausea away, stood my ground, and bravely asserted, "Why do you keep bringing it up if you're never going to tell me what's wrong? Even if I'm too young to understand what you're going through, maybe just saying it out loud will make you feel better."

Jonesy let out a sigh, and I could tell that he knew I was right.

"Life is just long," he finally said after a long pause. "It's a lot longer than you think. That's all I'm going to say about it." Then, without another word, he rose to his feet, something I had not seen him do as effortlessly before, and stormed off.

I was disappointed he didn't offer me more, but his absence made any further inquiry impossible. So, I got up off the blanket myself and headed toward the stables.

Life is longer than you think it is. I kept repeating it in my head as I brushed the smooth strands of Maple's long mane with my fingertips. I was also thinking back to Mama's conversation with Uncle Ford. I remembered her saying, "We brought him here so he could live out the rest of his days in comfort." Then, it suddenly hit me. Jonesy didn't want to be getting better. He wanted to die.

This conclusion, however, came with more questions than it did answers.

Chapter 3 – Secrets

After several failed attempts, I finally caught Uncle Ford crushing something up and sneaking it into Jonesy's coffee for a second time. That morning, I crept down to the kitchen, and I saw that his back was turned to me. To my delight, I had peeked around the wall at just the right moment. He rubbed the last of the powder off his hands and into a container before placing it in a drawer and covering it with other supplies.

As he had done the previous time, Uncle Ford did a quick scan of the hallway to ensure his anonymity. Then, once he was sure that he had pulled off this scheme again, he headed outside.

I waited until I was sure my uncle was outside, and then I went to the same drawer and shifted through the various items in it. It didn't take long for me to find the bottle he had tried to conceal. It was made of transparent blue plastic. A white label was stuck to it with Jonesy's full birth name printed on it: Janusz Michalski.

"Oh my God," I said out loud. Finally, it was all starting to make sense. Uncle Ford was secretly medicating Jonesy.

Without making the mental decision to do so, I pushed the bottle into my jean pocket. Then, I walked cautiously up the stairs, keeping a hand on the bottle to prevent the rattling sounds of the remaining pills. Once I successfully made it to my room undetected, I put the bottle in an old jewelry box. My distant aunt had sent it to me from Argentina for my birthday a few years prior. Before that morning, its only contents were fake gold rings and necklaces, which came from Easter eggs that you got after putting quarters into machines outside of restaurants.

I closed the box and brushed my hands together, probably subconsciously trying to wipe the guilt off of them. Then, as I thought about my actions' potential consequences, a wave of remorse washed over my body. If Uncle Ford didn't have the pills, he couldn't give them to Jonesy, and if Jonesy wasn't ingesting the crushed-up powder, he would become sick again. The inner turmoil ate at my brain like a parasite. One moment, I decided I would put them back. The next, I intended to flush the pills down the toilet. Then I changed my mind all over again. To avoid going insane, I pushed the entire situation out of my head, and I went outside to enjoy my favorite time of the day, breakfast picnic.

Again, I couldn't help but watch the mug as Jonesy lifted it from the ground to take a drink. I slightly smiled to myself, knowing now that he was inadvertently taking his medication. But I still didn't understand why he didn't want to be, so I tried to probe him for even the tiniest of clues. While the idea of asking him personal questions still made me feel a little uneasy, my previous outburst, and his eventual inclination to answer me, gave me a little more confidence to do so.

"What was your life like when you lived in Poland?"

"I try not to overthink about the past. Memories are sometimes best left unspoken."

"Okay . . ." I said, deflated. I changed my line of questioning, "So, what would it be like now if you went back? Do you have family there?"

His energy seemed to brighten at the thought of his loved ones. "Yes. My mother, who immigrated from Africa when she was young, and two sisters still live there. My white father left to teach at Oxford a long time ago, and he just never came back." Then, however, just as quickly as it had suddenly brightened, the light inside of him grew dark again.

I felt bad for making him do exactly what he'd said he tried to avoid, thinking about the past. But, to my surprise, he kept talking. "It isn't always easy being biracial in Poland. So, as soon as I was old enough and got my degree, I decided to leave. That was years ago," Jonesy said as he ripped off a bite of toast with his teeth. I noticed that he was taking in long, shallow breaths as if to calm a risen heartrate.

This was the most about his background he had ever disclosed, and I was thankful that he felt comfortable sharing such intimate details with me. But then, I again remembered that Uncle Ford said he had just come from Poland to work on the farm that summer. I had gotten hints before that this was not true. For one thing, Jonesy stayed in the house for most of the day and never worked alongside Uncle Ford's other farmhands. Also, it didn't make sense, given his mysterious history with my parents. My dad was pretty secretive about his past, but I knew for sure he had never been out of the country after marrying my mother. She often complained about his lack of adventure—not like they had extra funds to cross-country travel, but still. I think it irritated her that he wasn't willing to hypothetically search the world with her.

There was still so much I wanted to know, like how exactly Jonesy knew my parents. But I didn't want to aggravate him further. By his exaggerated inhales, I could tell he hadn't yet managed to slow his pulse down. So, I paused my investigation for the day. We ate the rest of our breakfast in silence. After I finished, I quietly got up to tend to my chores.

As usual, I started out in the stables. After that, I roamed around the farm for the rest of the day.

Despite being given a few additional tasks, I managed to finish my work early, and I was still contemplating Jonesy's previous whereabouts when I walked into the house. My body and racing mind stopped when I heard subdued voices coming from the living room. I was really getting tired of walking into conversations that I was not meant to hear, but curiosity got the best of me, and I resolved to amble closer to make out their words. Even when I got as close as I could without fearing detection, however, I still couldn't quite make out what was being said. But I could see the shadows of two figures projected onto the wall.

What started out as two black silhouettes turned into one giant blob as the bodies got closer. I could hear faint sounds of moaning.

"What the—" I whispered to myself.

"Ford, please. No," Jonesy said.

"Why not? Janusz, please. You've been feeling better, and I gave Sera extra chores today, so she should be outside for a while yet."

I wished he were right. Though I was curious at first, I wasn't sure I wanted to continue hearing what was happening. Jonesy didn't respond audibly, but I heard more quiet moaning. The urge to walk away overwhelmed me.

When I was safely behind my closed bedroom door, I began processing what I had just witnessed. "Oh my God!" I screamed silently into my pillow. Never in my wildest dreams would I have pictured Uncle Ford and Jonesy *together*. I wasn't surprised about this only because of their significant age difference; I was also surprised they were compatible because of the drastic differences in their personalities.

However, now that I knew about their relationship, Uncle Ford's constant disdain for life and all of those around him made a little more sense. It was clear to me that he was hiding his true self from everyone. I wondered if my dad knew the truth about his brother.

A few seconds later, I heard the faint sound of Jonesy's feet coming up the stairs. The ominous sound of my uncle's boots soon followed after him. Upon arriving at the spare bedroom, where I was led to believe he slept each night, Jonesy did his best to slam the door. My uncle pushed against it with such force that my walls trembled in reaction.

"Ford. I'm sorry. I'm just not in the mood. It isn't about you," Jonesy quietly pleaded through the slab of wood that remained closed, despite my uncle's efforts to open it. "I just haven't been feeling myself lately."

"So, you only feel yourself when you're sick and tired?" Uncle Ford asked.

"You know that the whole reason I came here was to finally let it all end. I was so tired of fighting against my body for so many years. Do you know what that's like? Feeling your body actively trying to kill you but knowing that you can't ever succumb to it? Can you imagine that inner turmoil? It's a form of torture I wouldn't wish on anyone. That's why Johanna and Clark helped me and found a place for me to stay. I don't know why I'm getting better now. I don't want to be. I just want the pain to end!"

I took particular interest in their conversation after I heard my parents' names. I was right. They had known Jonesy before he came to the farm.

I chewed on my lower lip, remembering the bottle I had stored in my old jewelry box. I was once again torn about what to do with it. Clearly, Jonesy didn't want to take them, but I also wanted him to continue to get better. I decided the best course of action would be to consult with Mama. She obviously had some background information on the situation.

I came up with what I considered to be the perfect plan. I decided I would go to the back of the stables right away in the morning where Uncle Ford's workers, who didn't run errands or stop at home, typically rested on their breaks. This would allow me to speak with someone and give the illusion that I was carrying on with my chores around the horses like normal. Then, if I got a worker to agree to a bribe with the small amount of money I had saved up in exchange for the rides, we would time the pickup on his next break, so his absence on the farm would not be cause for concern.

Satisfied with this strategy, I performed what was becoming my daily ritual of placing my pillow over my ears, which I pressed extra firmly that night, and fell asleep.

Fortunately, it didn't take long for me to break a deal with one of the workers to secretly drive me to and from my parents' house.

I was saving up the money I paid him to eventually buy a newer laptop. But I was far from my goal, and I decided Jonesy was more important anyway.

When I arrived, Mama was sitting on her favorite rocking chair and knitting on the front porch while my siblings occupied themselves in the front yard. She always got up in the early morning hours—I made it a habit of getting out of bed the same time she did so my circadian rhythm would never be off when I inevitably returned to the farm—but I was surprised that my brothers and sisters were also awake. I wondered about that for a moment but eventually decided it wasn't on my agenda to ask about their changed schedule.

I hugged each one of my siblings separately, and after I got to the twins, my shirt was covered with the general stickiness that seems to always be on little kids.

"Mama!" I said as I finally approached her and kissed her on the cheek.

"Oy, Seraphine. *¡Qué sorpresa!*"

I continued for a moment to remove the nasty residue from my clothing. But I eventually decided it was a lost cause and sat down on the chair next to her. She continued knitting what looked to be the start of a blanket, which she often made in her small amount of spare time for church fundraisers.

"I know, Mama. *Lo siento.*" I then explained that I had come on such short notice because I needed to speak with her about something urgent. "It's about Jones . . . I mean, Janusz," I said, carefully and slowly. I don't think I got it exactly right, but she seemed to understand who I was talking about.

"What about him?" Her eyes darted up from the sequence of knots she was making.

I crouched down and put my hands in her lap. I whispered, "Mama, I know."

"Know what, exactly?" she asked hesitantly, avoiding my gaze and returning her attention to the yarn she was working with.

I lowered my voice even further to avoid my siblings from hearing and said, "I know he's sick. I don't know exactly what he has, but I know he needs medication to survive. I also know about the relationship between him and Uncle Ford." I swallowed hard, relieved to have said all of that out loud. "I also know that he doesn't want to get better."

After a few seconds of silence, I continued, "But he has been getting better, Mama."

She briefly looked up to make sure her younger children were out of earshot, then muttered, "*¿Qué?*" Her eyebrow rose in curiosity. That was the first time she'd made eye contact with me since I started talking about Jonesy.

"He's getting better because Uncle Ford has been crushing up pills and secretly giving them to him." I handed her the small bottle. "I didn't mean to, but I walked in on him making pills into powder and slipping it in Jonesy's coffee. Then, a few days later, I saw where he was hiding the bottle, so I stole it after he left the room."

To my surprise, she didn't yell at me for snooping or stealing. Instead, she put the bottle in her pocket and said we needed to tell my dad. Then, she loudly instructed the eldest of my younger siblings to watch the others while we went inside for a few minutes.

"Clark! Sera is here. *¡Mira!*" Mama yelled as she walked into the house.

He stumbled from his bedroom, vigorously rubbing the sleep out of his eyes. "Oh! Hi, sweetie!" he said as he gave me a big hug. "What are you doing here?"

Before I could answer, Mama pulled us both into a room and shut the door.

"Clark, she knows," she whispered. "She knows about everything."

"You mean . . .?" my dad said with his eyebrows elevated in shock.

Mama nodded. "She knows that Janusz is sick and about his relationship with Ford." She put a hand on my lower back and pushed me toward him. I took this as my cue to tell him about the pills. She reached for the bottle and placed it in my hands.

"Uh, Daddy," I said nervously. "I always thought it was odd that Uncle Ford would hire such a slender and frail person to work on the farm. I suppose I always assumed Jonesy was sick. I just didn't want to be rude and flat-out ask him or Uncle Ford. But, one morning, I saw Uncle Ford crush up one of these pills and put it in Jonesy's coffee cup. And it's been working, Daddy. He has been getting better. I don't know why I took them. I guess I was just mad that Uncle Ford was deceiving him like that."

"I see," he said.

"Last night, I saw something happen between him and Uncle Ford, and I connected the dots that they were more than just friends or roommates. I could only see shadows, but it looked like they were embracing, and you know . . ." My face was heating up, no doubt turning red. I had never talked about anything like this with my parents before. "I didn't mean to walk in on them doing anything," I said to justify myself. "I just walked into the house after finishing my chores a little early."

My parents exchanged glances at each other.

I continued, "That same night, I heard them yelling about Jonesy's illness. Jonesy was angry that his condition seemed to be improving when he specifically left someplace so he could, I guess, eventually die at the farmhouse. I'm so sorry. I don't mean to dump this on you and Mama. I just didn't know what else to do. It seemed like the two of you and Jonesy were well acquainted, so I thought maybe you could help me understand what exactly is going on."

Realizing I had left a part out of the story, I turned to Mama. "Oh! I also overheard you and Uncle Ford talking about it the other day. You also said that he had chosen to leave somewhere else to stay at the farm. I swear I don't mean to keep walking in on conversations and scenes that I'm not supposed to hear or see. It just keeps happening. I don't—"

Without responding to me directly, my dad interrupted and asked, "What are we going to do, Johanna? This wasn't the plan. You know this isn't what he wanted." Apparently, my theory that she secretly snuck away to meet with Uncle Ford was wrong. My dad seemed unfazed by a mention of their private interaction.

"*Claro que sí,*" she said, shaking her head. "Ford told me he had medication, but I never dreamed he'd give it to Janusz behind his back."

They exchanged looks with each other and apparently made a nonverbal agreement that I should not be apprised of whatever plan they were about to make.

My dad took the bottle before opening the door and gently pushing me out of it. "Thank you for bringing all of this to us, Sera. Please don't give it another thought. Your mother and I will take care of it. Oh, and don't tell anyone else about this. Okay? Love you, bye!" he said as he closed the door behind me. They didn't even give me the chance to ask about their connection with Jonesy.

I had never seen my parents act this rude to anyone, especially not me or my siblings. But I thought it best to respect their wishes, so I went outside to wait for the farmhand I had previously bribed to fulfill his side of the bargain and return to pick me up. My uncle gave his employees small but frequent breaks, so I knew it wouldn't be that long before I saw the beat-up truck barreling down the street.

Chapter 4 – An Uncomfortable Morning

"Remember, don't tell my uncle about this," I said as I slipped the last few cents I had to my name into the worker's hand after we arrived back at the farm.

I wasn't sure exactly how long I'd been gone, but just like I planned, it was a short enough amount of time for me to reasonably make the excuse that I'd missed breakfast that morning because I had extra work to do in the stables. I thought Jonesy would buy my story because he knew better than anyone how much the horses meant to me. I crept behind the barn and approached him from there. I was right; he barely batted an eye when I met him in the yard and offered the false explanation.

"Oh, okay," he gently said. "Don't worry, I saved some for you." He somberly handed me a massive plate of pancakes.

As I accepted the plate he offered, I realized he wasn't drinking coffee. "Where's Uncle Ford?"

"Oh, he left in a hurry a while ago. He was angry because he couldn't find something. You know how he can be." He shrugged his shoulders.

I nodded as I took a deep breath in. I was pretty sure what my uncle was out getting—another plastic bottle filled with pills to replace the one that I had just left in the hands of my parents to deal with. Naively, I hadn't thought about what I would do once Uncle Ford discovered it missing that morning. He obviously couldn't ask Jonesy about it, so I would be the only one to blame.

My body was practically vibrating from all of the anxiety I was feeling. I was worried about my uncle confronting me about the missing medication and what would happen to Jonesy without the pills. But, more than anything, I was anxious about my parents getting my beloved friend away from the farmhouse. Of course, I wanted him safely away from the control of my uncle. But I was also excited for him to have power once again over his own health. Of course, I desired that for him, but I selfishly wanted it for myself too. I desperately wanted to be free from feeling the responsibility of secretly making decisions on his behalf.

My head throbbed as it processed all these nerves. I rubbed it in an attempt to somehow quiet my mind.

"Are you feeling okay?" Jonesy asked.

"Yeah, I'm fine. Just a little headache. This sometimes happens when I'm around manure for a long time." I let out a small chuckle and stopped massaging my temples with my index and middle fingers.

Perhaps sensing that I was a little on edge, Jonesy's tone became more serious, and he asked, "Is something troubling you? Did something happen . . . last night?"

I was surprised by his lack of subtlety. He was clearly trying to find out if I'd overheard their argument.

Not wanting to reveal my hand, I scrambled to think up yet another believable lie.

"Nothing much. I finished my chores and went right up to bed. I was exhausted, so I fell asleep almost right away."

"Okay," he said with a hint of suspicion.

Wanting to end the conversation, I stuffed the remaining pancakes in my mouth and hurried along to resume my chores. Furthermore, I didn't want to be around when my uncle returned, which I knew could be any minute.

"Okay, well, see you later, *wujek*! I've got more work to do," I said, calling him "uncle" in Polish, which he had previously offered as an additional nickname for me to call him. I walked without turning my head toward him, and my voice was muffled from all of the cooked batter currently resting on my tongue. I tried my best to move as fast as I could without tipping him off that I was trying to get away from him.

When I finally reached the solace of the barn, I stood with my back resting against the cold wooden door and let my heart rate slow down. Then, feeling a little more relaxed, I made a mental list of all the things I could do around the farm to remain invisible and out of the house for the rest of the day.

I was too distracted by my work to hear Uncle Ford's truck pull into the yard. But sure enough, it was there when I emerged from the barn later that afternoon. I hesitated to walk into the house, but I had run out of tasks. Plus, karma had caught up with me, and my head was actually aching from the lengthy exposure to horse droppings.

I was relieved when I paused by the front door and didn't hear any commotion inside. Then, as I had countless times before, after I washed my face and teeth, I tiptoed up to my room, locked the door, crawled into bed, and wrapped a pillow around my head.

I crept down to the kitchen somewhat reluctantly the next morning. To my surprise, I was all alone. This rarely happened. Jonesy or Uncle Ford would usually beat me in there. Questioning whether my solitude was a good or bad thing, I cautiously made some toast, glancing behind my back every few seconds.

After that, I went outside to sit behind a large tree on the very tip of Uncle Ford's plotline. Although its wide trunk concealed me well, I peeked around it several times to scan the farm and check for noise coming from the house. But I saw and heard nothing except for the wind and distant braying in the stables. It was one of the days when the workers didn't need to tend to the fields, so it was extra quiet. Thankful for the moment of peace, I closed my eyes and tried to focus only on the light breeze on my face. I soon fell asleep and didn't wake back up until over an hour later. Once fully awake, I looked across the lawn for any sign of Jonesy or my uncle. But, again, I saw nothing to hint at their presence on the farm.

My brow furrowed in confusion, but I resolved to make at least one aspect of that day seem normal and started working on my daily tasks.

I listened to music on the old radio that Uncle Ford kept in the barn, keeping it at the lowest volume possible. If he confronted me about the missing pills, I didn't want it to be a complete sneak attack. Having just seen her, I was reminded of how much I missed my mom. I desperately wished I could afford a cellphone, so I could text her to get an update on whether or not they'd thought up a plan to help Jonesy. Uncle Ford had a landline, but it was mounted in his room, and it was made very clear to me that I was not allowed to use it.

I suppose I was trying to connect with Mama that morning as I gently swayed to the *folklórico* music ineloquently playing from the dusty speakers. As I moved through the rest of my duties, I occasionally darted a glance toward the farmhouse and the patch of grass where Uncle Ford always parked his truck. To my ever-growing surprise, besides the horses and me, the whole property seemed lifeless. Part of me was worried something terrible had happened to Jonesy and Uncle Ford. The first thing that popped into my head was a car crash. A shiver ran down my spine. But I quickly decided to replace it with a less sensationalized explanation— perhaps they had just gone out to run errands for the day. I hadn't known them to do that in the past, as Uncle Ford usually left by himself, but I figured it was possible.

I continued to make up similar explanations as the sun began to set. Although Uncle Ford almost always came home before it got dark, he occasionally would meet up late with an old buddy at the bar down the street. Still, that didn't explain where Jonesy had been all day.

With nothing else to do, I went inside to make myself some dinner. I opened the fridge and found a leftover piece of pot roast Jonesy had saved for me. I smiled for what felt like the first time that day when I saw my name written in his squiggly handwriting on the Tupperware. He'd also written instructions to place the container in the microwave for one and a half minutes. I did as he suggested.

Then, since my uncle wasn't around, I figured I could bend his rules for one night and eat dinner in the living room. I couldn't remember the last time I had even watched TV. There was a television in the bedroom I stayed in, but it was so old that it only produced static. My laptop was also too outdated to stream anything. Plus, Uncle Ford's less than spectacular Wi-Fi probably would've prevented that even if I did have access to updated technology. I felt a dopamine spike in my brain as I mischievously grabbed the remote and pressed the "on" button.

I wasn't expecting it, but my uncle had cable. Shocked and excited by this revelation, I mindlessly channel surfed before finally settling on one playing *Office Space*, a movie Jonesy had mentioned one morning when telling me about his favorites. I remember he had a certain lightness in his eyes as he recited the best one-liners. He was in a fit of laughter after saying, "That'd be grrrreeaaattt." I had never seen it, but I still laughed along because I loved seeing him so happy.

I watched the screen with the intent to memorize the funniest parts and recite them to Jonesy later. I wanted to make him laugh like he did when he first told them to me. But then, like a smack on the head, I remembered he wasn't there. I changed the channel in anger and walked into the kitchen to discard evidence that I had been disobedient.

When I returned to Uncle Ford's La-Z-Boy, the show *Friends* was on. Oddly enough, Jonesy had also talked to me about this show. He'd said he watched it over and over again when he was first starting to learn English. Annoyed by yet another reminder of him, I switched to a baking competition.

I didn't mean to, but I must have fallen asleep at some point because I was jolted awake by a loud noise near the front door.

That was the beginning of my introduction to "chaos nights," as I referred to them. First, the door slammed shut, shaking the whole house. Then, there was a loud thud as my uncle's large forearm and forehead hit the wall when he attempted to stabilize himself. Next, he muttered something under his breath, but I couldn't make out exactly what he was saying, other than the times he said Mama's name.

While I was still scared because of the stolen medication, I was also concerned for my uncle. I had never seen a heavily intoxicated person before. My only experience with alcohol was when my dad would get a little buzzed after drinking a few beers during the holidays. So, I didn't recognize what was going on. At first, I thought he was having some kind of medical emergency, but the closer I got to the door, the clearer I heard the menace behind his voice.

"Johannaaaaaa, Johannaaaaaaaa!" he said in a low, gravelly tone that was still oddly playful—as if he were playing hide and seek and had just finished counting down from ten.

"Johannaaaa!" he said again, with his forehead still resting on the forearm against the wall. As I inched closer, I looked up to see the odd grimace on his face and his eyes darting back and forth.

"Uncle Ford?" I asked reluctantly. "Wha—" I began as I reached out to him.

Before I could touch his jacket, his still body jerked back to life, matching the intense energy displayed across his face. He grabbed my wrist and twisted it as hard as he could. He then turned my body so that my back was facing him. I was too confused by his actions to say or do anything in response.

He slowly lowered his mouth to my ear and said, "It's all your fault, Jo-ha-nna." He took his time with every syllable, and droplets of his spit sprayed onto me with each one. The saliva burned my skin as if it were turpentine. His breath was equally unnerving; it smelled of vomit and pine needles.

He dragged me up to my room and took off his belt. His last action was too much. I didn't plead with him as we went up the stairs because I figured he was just going to lock me in the room and continue to stew in anger by himself. But the anticipation of the leather striking my skin forced a scream out of my throat, and I yelled, "Uncle Ford. No, please don't! Please!" But he didn't listen to me. He violently shoved me onto the bed and ripped the back of my shirt.

I lost count of how many painful slashes hit my back, but I found it hard to move by the time his frustration was sufficiently expressed. My hands were stuck in fists because I had clasped my sheets to avoid crying out in pain. Unfortunately, I made the mistake of initially letting out a few yelps, and the reactive noises seemed to encourage him to keep going. I hoped if I was silent, he would eventually get bored with it all.

He didn't say anything after he was done. Instead, he simply put his belt back on and slammed my door shut behind him.

I had never been in that amount of pain or shock before, and I was paralyzed with fear. I did, however, manage to crawl my way off the bed and over to the door to lock it. I doubted my uncle's rage could be stopped by such a small barricade, but at least it would make it a little harder for him to get to me.

Unlike my t-shirt, he hadn't bothered moving my long dark hair off my back, which unfortunately didn't seem to lessen the pain of each blow. After I returned to bed, I had to painfully pull the bloody chunks away from the wounds they were stuck to.

I couldn't go to sleep with my hair and body covered in my own blood. So, after I heard my uncle's bedroom door close and lock, I peeked out into the hallway and made my way toward the bathroom. I noted that the spare bedroom door was closed, and I wondered if Jonesy had silently walked into the house before my uncle that night. But, even if he was there, I wasn't in the right headspace to be angry about his failure to help me. I was in such a fog that the thought didn't even cross my mind at the time.

When I reached the bathroom, I turned the shower on the lowest setting possible and carefully climbed inside. I had to muster up the courage to expose my wounds to the water, so I first stood facing the showerhead, and I rinsed my hair. Then I held my breath and clenched my fists as I turned around. It stung for a second, but soon the flowing water actually helped dissipate the pain. It almost felt like I was cleansing my body of the abuse it had just experienced.

I never dared to look down at the water collecting in the tub. The sight of the diluted dark red permeating off my body would only make everything that had just happened to me all that more traumatic.

I had expected him to be mad about the stolen medication, but I'd never dreamed he'd get angry enough to provoke an assault. It was also weird that he'd called me by Mama's name. I didn't know how he could have learned about my parents' possession of the remaining pills. And even if he did know everything, I wondered why he was beating me but calling out her name. Suddenly, I felt grateful that I'd taken the lashes. It would have broken my heart if any harm came to her due to something I had done.

As much as I tried, I couldn't fall asleep that night. My back was in so much pain. But after hours of darkness and silence, I heard two knocks on my door.

"Sera?"

I froze in panic.

"Sera. Please come out. I made you breakfast." Several seconds of silence passed before the voice grew angry and loud. "Sera! Come out, or I'll knock this fucking door down!"

Afraid of a repeat of the night prior, I winced in pain as I rose from the bed. I cowered as I unlocked and slowly opened the door.

Almost instantly, his demeanor changed. He took a breath in and out and smiled with a shake of his head. "Okay, good. I hope you're hungry!" He had a look of relief on his face as he scanned my body, and I could tell he was happy I had cleaned myself up. I assumed he didn't want to see any physical evidence of his abuse. That way, maybe he could convince himself it never happened.

I followed him down into the large dining room. He had taken his time to make the table look as fancy as he could. Even with limited resources, he'd managed to put something presentable together. He'd laid various blankets out to serve as tablecloths, and the old brass candlesticks usually found above the fireplace were placed neatly next to each other in the middle of the table. He'd also

35

brought out the "fancy" plates; they were really just the glass ones he forbade anyone from using because the plastic ones were "cheaper and just as good."

My mind was spinning. *Was this his way of apologizing?* He sort of answered my question when he pulled the head chair out and motioned for me to sit down. Maybe he wasn't blatantly saying sorry, but he was clearly giving me special treatment. It couldn't be a coincidence that the first time he made such an effort came after the night he beat me senselessly with his belt.

He had prepared all the breakfast foods. Buttermilk pancakes, scrambled eggs, omelets, bacon strips, you name it, were on display before me. He stared at me for a minute, and I looked back with a slight smile to express gratitude for his work. This gesture did not serve as a symbol of my genuine forgiveness, but the last thing I wanted to do was make him angry. So, I acted in compliance with the way I thought he expected and wanted me to. When he sat down in his own chair, he wasted no time shoveling food onto his plate.

After cramming several pieces of bacon into his mouth, he looked up at me and said, "Sera? Please eat. I made this all for you." He pushed the plate of bacon closer to me before lowering his head and resuming the grotesque consumption of the food before him. He made weird grunting noises as he shoved the food into his mouth, and he seemed to swallow each bite without chewing. This demonstration made me nauseous and killed any desire I had to eat. But, again, not wanting to make him angry, I slowly filled my plate.

We ate together without speaking for several minutes until he raised his head for air. He then arrogantly said, "You know you can never tell anyone, right?"

I involuntarily dropped the utensils in my hand and asked in a soft voice, "Tell anyone what?"

"What happened last night. You tell anyone—your folks, your friends, teachers, anyone—I will tell your mom's deepest, darkest secret."

"What . . . what are you talking about?" I asked cautiously.

He let out a sinister laugh before saying, "Well, it seems as though your *madre* is undocumented. One word out of your mouth, and the first call I make will be to the authorities. They'll come and take her away, leaving all of your siblings with your dad—who we both know can't take care of them by himself. So, they'll probably be separated and go with different foster parents. But, of course, you wouldn't want that to happen, would you?"

As I was trying to process his words, I swallowed eggs that now tasted like pennies. I didn't notice that I was chewing on my inner cheek so hard that it started bleeding. I choked as the foul-tasting food reached the back of my throat.

"Do you understand me?" He smacked his hand on the table, ensuring he had my full attention.

Trembling in my seat now, I murmured, "I understand." I hadn't had any idea Mama was here illegally. I guess I assumed since she was married to my dad, she had to be a citizen. At least I finally knew why she couldn't get a legitimate job.

As I continued to digest all of that, my mind jumped to another immigrant. I remembered that Jonesy wasn't around. *Is he even in the house?* I wondered again. *If so, why didn't he try to help me last night?* My face burned red with anger at the question I couldn't bring myself to ask before that moment.

I fought off the urge to ask for a while, but the question eventually came spilling out of my mouth. "Where is Jonesy?" The second I finished asking, a fire lit up behind Uncle Ford's eyes, and he clenched his fists so hard that his knuckles turned white. I braced my body for him to strike me. In an unexpected turn of events, however, he didn't remove his belt. Instead, he shoved his chair back, threw his plate against the wall, and then stomped down the hall and out the front door.

His truck engine revved up a few moments later, and I saw the vehicle peel out of the yard and speed down the road.

For what felt like the hundredth time that summer, I was at a loss for words and completely confused by the events transpiring around me.

I figured it would be a good idea to clean up the dining room before my uncle returned home. So, after clearing the table, I carefully picked up the broken glass and wiped the syrup dripping down the wall. I thought for a second about bribing another farmhand to take me to my parents' house to tell them everything. But I had no idea when my uncle would return, and if I was gone when he did, he might follow through on his threat and report my mom.

Once I was satisfied with my work inside, I decided I'd earned a trip to visit Maple. As soon as I reached the barn's door, I could tell that something was off, but I couldn't put my finger on what it was. I brushed off any uneasy feelings I had, chalking the changed energy to the beating I had so recently endured. *Maybe this is just the way I see the world now*, I thought, saddened by the notion that I was somehow permanently changed.

I continued to walk over to Maple but stopped in fear when I heard footsteps behind me.

"Don't be afraid," a voice said. "I'm friends of your parents."

When I turned around, I was surprised by what I saw. The person before me was small in stature but had the voice of a grown woman. Her face and hair were covered in a dirt-like substance, and she smelled like gasoline. She looked like one of Peter Pan's lost boys.

"I'm Kailas." The tiny figure took a step closer and extended her hand.

"Seraphine," I said, shaking it. I tried my best to be discreet as I wiped the transferred dirt off my own hand.

"I know who you are, Sera," she said while lightly chuckling. "Like I said, I'm a friend of your parents. I've known them for a very long time. They asked me to come here and tell you about Janusz . . . or Jonesy, as I'm told you call him—"

"Is he okay?" I said, cutting her off.

"Yes. Your mom and I snuck into the house and got him out to the car your dad was waiting in down the road."

My eyes widened. I fully understood now why Uncle Ford kept ragefully calling me "Johanna." He blamed her for Jonesy's disappearance.

I was flooded with guilt for the anger I'd felt toward my dear friend earlier that day. Even in his weakened state, I knew that he, of course, would've tried to help if he were still in the house during my beating. My hand moved of its own accord and brushed one of the scars developing on my back. It was hard and bumpy, and it hurt when I touched it. A small amount of red residue came with my fingers as I returned them to the front of my body. Again, I tried to wipe my jeans without Kailas noticing.

I followed her eyes as they darted down at my hand and just as quickly back up at my face.

To keep the conversation off of myself, I asked, "Where is he now?"

"He's actually staying with me."

"For how long?"

"Well, for as long as it takes to, you know . . ." My heart panged as the words left her mouth. I had momentarily forgotten the inevitable end to all of this. Jonesy wanted to and was going to die.

"Can I see him?"

"Well, he's in pretty bad shape right now. I'm sure he wouldn't want you to see him like that. Let's meet back here in a few days, and if he feels up to it, I'll help you slip away for an hour or two to see him." She kindly placed her hand on my shoulder.

"Okay. Can you please just tell Jonesy that I miss him?"

"I will. Remember, you can't say anything about this to your uncle. Okay?"

I nodded.

We both flinched at a sound outside. I ran to the window and was relieved when I didn't see Uncle Ford's truck. When I looked back, the small woman had disappeared.

For the rest of the day, I read behind my favorite tree, the same one I had fallen asleep under the day prior. I wished so badly that I could go back in time and warn that innocent girl about what was to come.

I stayed tucked into the comforting roots that protruded from the grass until it got too dark for me to see the words on the pages before me. When Uncle Ford returned, I didn't even notice because I was so engulfed in my book. But after I stood and saw his truck, reels of the night before started running through my head.

When I walked closer to the house and saw that his bedroom window was dark, I let out another sigh of relief. That meant he was likely already asleep. At least that's what I hoped.

I locked my bedroom door—not caring that he'd previously expressed anger over it—and climbed into bed. Kailas hadn't specifically said what day she would return, but I fell asleep while praying it would come sooner rather than late.

Chapter 5 – Cornfields

Luckily for me, I spent the next several nights unharmed. So many nights passed without any disturbance, in fact, that I began to think that night of terror was a one-time thing. In that regard, things were slowly getting back to "normal." As normal as life coexisting with a man like Uncle Ford could be, at least. We settled into a pattern where we rarely ever saw each other. I got up before him, headed out to work and read on the farm, and returned to the house after his bedroom light was already turned off. Each night, I sighed with relief when I saw his darkened window.

I was still counting down the days until I could see Jonesy. Every day when I went to the stables, I silently prayed that I'd find Kailas inside, ready to whisk me away. When it finally reached a whole week since her first visit, I was more hopeful than ever. I even stayed out in the barn longer than usual, just in case. But I lost hope with every minute that passed. Finally, when it was about to turn one o'clock, I decided it was time to give up.

Comfortable with our new schedule, I looked up at the house to see Uncle Ford's dark window. It was black, but I noticed quickly that his truck wasn't parked in the driveway.

Unfortunately, Uncle Ford came home later that night, and I froze in fear as I heard the loud thuds of his work boots coming up the stairs. His belt was already off this time when he entered my room, and he flicked the lights on, apparently wanting to fully see the destruction he was about to cause. I tried to beg and plead again, but it seemed like nothing could stop his rage.

After he was done, I reluctantly assessed the damage he had done in the tiny mirror of my jewelry box. This beating was even more painful than the first because he had not only created new wounds but reopened old ones that were just beginning to scab over.

Due to my fair skin, the areas surrounding the bloodied parts were dark blue and purple. The movie wouldn't be out for several years yet, but when I think back to how my back looked that summer, I'm reminded of a jacked-up version of a character from *Avatar*.

Why was he doing this to me? Hot tears ran down my cheeks when I saw more evidence of his anger forever preserved on my body. I felt mutilated and humiliated. Like most victims of domestic violence, I blamed myself for not trying harder to stop him. I felt so stupid for allowing him to do this to me on two separate occasions. I vowed to myself that I would fight back the next time.

And I did. I managed to get a few jabs in during the next night he came home late. But I learned that, like my cries of desperation for him to stop, fighting back only added gas to his fire. It seemed to only motivate him to hit me harder. Plus, my imprecise and clumsy punches appeared to do little to no damage. It felt like I was smacking a metal statue.

I was slightly vindicated in the morning, though, when I watched from my window as he walked out to his truck. He was unsuccessfully concealing a black eye under his hat. Apparently, my tiny hands were capable of injuring him after all. His foul mouth had since rubbed off on me, and I said, "Ha! Serves you right, you fucking bastard." I gleamed as I thought about him being seen around town with a fresh shiner on his face. Of course, he wouldn't tell anyone that his teenage niece had thrown the blow that caused it, but I knew.

I looked again in my small mirror, and I saw that my punches had invited his boxing-glove-sized fists to make contact with my face as well. I bit down on my swollen lower lip. I winced in pain as I clenched the welt between my teeth.

Later that afternoon, while the horses were out grazing the lawn, I sat in Maple's stall and admired the bruises that now covered my hands. Unlike the scars on my back and the lump on my lip, I considered the blue splotches as badges of honor because they were signs that I had inflicted pain on him as well.

I felt a sudden presence behind me. I whipped my head back and was greeted by a familiar face covered in dirt. It was Kailas.

"Whoa! What happened to you, kid?"

Remembering what Uncle Ford said about going to the authorities with Mama's secret, I lied and said, "Oh. One of the horses knocked me over. No big deal." Then I wasted no time cutting to the chase and asked, "How is Jonesy? Can I see him now?"

She didn't seem to question the explanation surrounding my injuries. "Janusz has been in a much better mental state lately. So, yes, of course. Why else would I be here?" She lightly punched my shoulder. "Come on!"

After securing the horses back in the stables, I gleefully followed her. I could see clear over her head as I was at least five inches taller. Because Uncle Ford was already gone, we didn't need to be that discreet when leaving the farm. A few workers were still busy in the field, but I reassured Kailas that none of them cared enough to concern themselves with my whereabouts.

We walked through the neighboring cornfield until we arrived at what I assumed to be Kailas's car partially concealed under the branches of a willow tree. Just in case my uncle drove by, Kailas suggested I crouch down in the back seat until we got to her house. From my limited vantage point, I couldn't tell where we were going, but it was considerably darker by the time we finally reached our destination. I was filled with two conflicting emotions—the excitement of seeing Jonesy and the fear of the punishment I would receive if Uncle Ford discovered that I was missing.

Kailas eventually pulled into what I recognized as a driveway and closed the garage door once her car was in far enough.

"All right. The coast is clear, kid."

I slowly got up; my knees ached a bit from being contorted behind the driver's seat. But the anticipation of seeing my old friend again made me quickly forget about the pain, and I practically skipped as I followed Kailas's dirty footprints on the garage floor. To my surprise, she took off her dirty jumpsuit and shoes before entering her home.

After we got inside, I was pleasantly shocked by how lovely the house was. I hate to say it, but I'd imagined Kailas's home would match her disgruntled appearance. Instead, it was almost immaculately clean. Kailas smiled as she nodded toward a door and headed up the stairs. Nervously, I walked over to the door and lightly knocked on it.

"Come in," said a quiet voice.

I walked in and saw the Jonesy I had first met and grown close to. This familiar image made me simultaneously happy and sad. He was clearly weaker than he had been the last time I saw him, which I knew meant he was on the road toward death again.

"Don't be scared. I won't break, *mała perła*," Jonesy said, and I realized I'd been standing in the doorway for an awkwardly long amount of time. He was sitting upright in bed, and he stretched his arms out for me to hug him. I sat down next to him and accepted the invite, although we had never embraced like that before. His boney shoulder dug deep into my cheek. Then he suddenly pulled me back up, so my face was close to his. He lifted his slender finger and pointed at my fat lip.

Shit, I thought. I knew Jonesy wouldn't be as amenable to a fabricated excuse as Kailas was. I quickly scooted the sleeves of my sweatshirt over my hands to avoid his detection of the broken capillaries on them. Luckily, that action was kind of a nervous tick for me, so he didn't question it.

"It's no big deal, *wujek*. One of the horses knocked me over yesterday."

"Hm. Which one?" As expected, he pushed back on me. He knew I had ample experience and knew better than to sneak up on them.

"Uh . . . Uncle Ford recently bought a few more mares. They came from a hoarding situation, so they're still extra jumpy." I was both proud and ashamed of myself for becoming the kind of person who could think of a lie so quickly.

"Hm," he said again. "Well, as long as you're okay."

I nodded in reassurance. I was thankful the lashes on my back were hidden. We both knew that a horse, barring a massive stampede, was unlikely to inflict such extensive injuries.

We sat in silence for a moment, not knowing what to say. After a bit, Jonesy addressed the elephant in the room. "What have you told your uncle about where I am?"

"We haven't really talked about it, oddly enough. Before Kailas came to visit me, I asked him where you were, but he just ignored me. He hasn't asked me what I know about your whereabouts. I wouldn't have said anything even if he did."

"I see," he said, looking down at his hands. "Your mom told me that you know about our relationship."

I was slightly uncomfortable with the direction this line of questioning could go. "Yeah. I mean, I came in early one night, and I saw the two of you hugging or something. I'm sorry. I didn't mean to spy on you."

"No need to apologize. I'm glad you know. I wanted to tell you the whole time, but your uncle wanted to keep it from you."

"Oh," I said, internally questioning why Uncle Ford would want to hide something like that from me if my parents already knew about it.

Almost as if reading my thoughts, Jonesy said, "Your uncle is a complicated man. I think he didn't want to reveal too much of himself to you. I think he was afraid you might lose respect for him."

Ha. That certainly isn't a concern anymore, I thought.

Apparently, Jonesy had turned his mindreading skills off because he simply said next, "How is he doing?"

Part of me wanted to tell him everything, but I didn't want to put that burden on him in his already fragile state. I also didn't want to alter his perception of my uncle. It was evident that their memories together brought him comfort and happiness.

"Well, you know we've never been that close. I think I'd be the last person he would want to talk to about something so personal."

"I really do miss him, you know," he said.

"Yeah . . ." I replied awkwardly. I was unable to look him directly in the eye at that moment.

Another few seconds of silence passed before Jonesy gripped my hands with his. I glanced down briefly to make sure the bruised areas were still concealed.

"There's something else I wanted to talk to you about, but your uncle protested against it. Your mother also told me you know about it too—my illness, I mean. I was so foolish for believing you didn't hear that screaming match between Ford and me."

"I'm sorry. I didn't mean to eavesdrop."

"Please stop apologizing. None of this is your fault. We clearly weren't as discreet as we hoped to be, and you are smarter than either one of us anticipated," Jonesy said with a laugh. "I'm the one who should be sorry. I regret underestimating your intelligence—both mentally and emotionally."

"It's okay. I'm just a teenager."

"No. No, it's not okay. The last few months must have been so confusing for you," he said, still holding my hands. "And I know I wouldn't be here without you."

He continued, "I hope you know your uncle isn't a bad guy."

I had to bite my tongue to keep the sarcastic scoff down in my throat. "Mhm." I pretended to agree.

"Things were never supposed to be like this. I was just supposed to stay at the farm until I, well, until I passed." This sent a chill down my spine. "Except over time, your uncle and I developed feelings for each other. After that, he was no longer as accepting of my choice as he was in the beginning. And I do love him for wanting me to stay alive, I do."

I barely listened after he mentioned passing away. The rest sounded like the teacher from *Charlie Brown*. When the "wha wha wha" sounds stopped, I couldn't stop myself from asking, "Why do you want to die, Jonesy?"

He took a deep breath in and replied, "Well . . . that's a complicated question. You almost have to be sick for a long time to understand. You just ultimately get to a point where you don't want to fight against your body anymore. Does that make sense?"

I didn't know how to respond. It didn't make sense to me at all, but I had been relatively healthy all my life.

I wanted to take full advantage of this time with him, so I asked, "When you and Uncle Ford were yelling, I heard you say something about leaving a 'place' to stay on the farm. Where was that? Is that where you met my parents?" I wanted to ask more, but I consciously took a moment to breathe and to allow him to answer the already layered question.

"Uh." He cleared his throat. Before he could continue, however, Kailas walked through the door looking like a completely different person.

She must have seen the surprise on my face. She laughed and said, "You didn't think I was always covered in grease and muck, did you?" I was too embarrassed to admit that I did.

Jonesy interposed and said, "Kailas is a mechanic. I can only imagine what she looked like when she came to visit you after work." He laughed to himself.

Clean or not, she still looked like she belonged in Neverland. I was wondering whether or not she'd be offended by this when she said, "Well, we should probably get you back."

"I wish you could tell Ford that I miss him," Jonesy said as I turned toward the door.

"I know, *wujek*. I wish I could too." I wasn't lying this time, but I couldn't bring myself to turn around to face him. Obviously, I didn't care to make my uncle feel better, but I wished I could relay the message because I knew it would make Jonesy happy.

Before we got into her car, Kailas removed some kind of protective barrier, which I hadn't noticed before, off of the driver's seat. Immediately after she discarded it, the interior smelled less of battery acid and gasoline.

As she drove, Kailas again reiterated the importance of my silence regarding Jonesy's whereabouts. Apparently, she and Uncle Ford were already familiar with one another, and my uncle had come "sniffing" around her house looking for Jonesy several times over the last few days.

Slightly annoyed by her lack of trust in me, I rolled my eyes and said, "I know. I won't say a word."

I contemplated telling Kailas about the beatings several times during that car ride. If I told her, I thought maybe she'd let me come stay with her. But in the end, I concluded that was a lot of pressure and responsibility to put on a relative stranger, so I didn't say anything. I also didn't want her to tell Jonesy. He was going through enough without needing to worry about my well-being. A tinge of anger rushed through me at that moment as I recalled all the nice things he had to say about my uncle. I worried for a moment that even if I did tell him, he wouldn't believe me. I shook the thought out of my mind as I stepped out of the vehicle.

"Will I be able to come over to see him again?"

"We have to take everything day by day. Some days Janusz feels okay, and some days he doesn't even want me to be around him."

I kissed my teeth in disappointment, but I did understand. "Okay, thank you for the ride, Kailas. When the day comes that I can come back, will you meet me at the stables again?"

"You got it, kid."

She did not walk back to the farm with me. Because it was dark, and I was unfamiliar with the layout of the cornfield, it took me a few attempts to reach Uncle Ford's property. As I found my way through the maze, I mentally prepared myself for another beating. I rubbed my bruised and aching hands as I delighted in the thought of using my feet to defend myself this time. I imagined my heels driving hard against his face. Lucky for me and my feet, when I finally reached the farm, his car was in the yard, and his bedroom window light was off. He must have just assumed I was in the barn whenever he returned, which was typical. He never bothered to check up on me before. That night was likely no different.

Careful not to make enough noise to wake him up, I crept up to my bedroom and recapped my short time with Jonesy over and over again in my head. Just the image of his face brought me a great deal of comfort.

I also thought back to my conversations with Kailas. Since I didn't get an answer out of Jonesy, I kicked myself for never asking her how she and Jonesy—and my parents, for that matter—knew each other. I prayed that I'd be able to ask her soon.

The next few days came and went without incident. I rarely even saw my uncle, which was fine by me. I preferred it that way. The sight of him only reminded me of all the horrible things he had done to me. The bruises were fading and were almost unnoticeable, which made me kind of sad. Oddly, even though their appearance was a sign of injury, they made me feel strong.

But inevitably, another "chaos night" would come. It was the same old situation every time. Uncle Ford would be absent most of the day and return in the early morning hours after the bar closed. I thought alcohol was supposed to help make people feel better. I could never wrap my head around why the intoxicating liquid made him so angry. I decided there must be something wrong with him, something that made it affect his body and mind in a different way. In school, we learned that alcoholic beverages make you clumsy and unbalanced. Each precise whack of his belt did not fit that description at all.

That night was particularly horrible. I had, in fact, fulfilled my wish of flipping over and kicking him square in the jaw with the heel of my foot. But, as I should have predicted, my actions made him even angrier. I could see the added flame of vengeance in his eyes.

"You bitch! All right. You asssked for it," he said as he grabbed me and ripped my pajama pants off. His speech was slurred. "I've wanted to do this ever sssince my ssstupid brother married your dirty immigrant asssss!" Again, he must've been imagining that I was Mama. "It's been a while, but I've had my fair share of experience with women as well."

He continued to yell obscenities at me as he vigorously tugged at himself before forcefully entering my body.

"No, no. Uncle Ford! I'm your niece, Sera! I'm not . . . I'm not Johanna. Please, please stop!" I pleaded with him and attempted to kick his hips away from me.

He obviously heard me but didn't internalize what I was saying. Instead, he simply put his massive hand over my face and continued his back-and-forth motion. He covered my nose and my mouth, and I struggled harder as I began to lose oxygen. Eventually, I passed out. I'm thankful for that now because I have no recollection of God knows what else he did to me that night.

I think I woke up three or four hours after the attack. The blanket underneath me felt moist to the touch, and I was horrified when I lifted my hand and saw a thick, red residue on my fingers. It was a harsh reminder that it wasn't all just a bad nightmare. It took me a while to gather the strength to get up. But, finally, I hesitantly started pulling myself out of bed, cautious with each movement because I wasn't sure exactly what parts of my body would hurt the worst.

When I finally managed to slowly walk to the bathroom, I avoided the mirror. I couldn't stand the shame of looking at myself. I considered myself "soiled" after what my uncle had done to me. Like many people from South America, Mama was a devout Catholic. She had preached to me all my life about the importance of remaining pure before marriage. I sat on the toilet to let blood leak out of my body. I lined my underwear with a pad, but I figured the more I could flush down, the less I would need to be reminded of later.

Before I knew it, I was uncontrollably sobbing. I raised my hands to my mouth to muffle the sound. I didn't want him to hear me in case he got some sick satisfaction out of it.

After sufficiently dehydrating my body of every possible tear, I walked back into my room. I slowly peeked over my bedroom window to see if my uncle's truck was there. When I saw that it was missing, I sighed in relief. There was absolutely no way I could have faced him at that moment. *What would I even say? What would I do?* I wondered.

I continued to fear our reunion while I sat on a haystack in Maple's stall. The desire came over me to bite my nails, a habit I had long since abandoned. The last time I could remember doing it was at my grandma's funeral. I was around five or six. As a kid, I gently nibbled at them. But in the barn that day, I furiously bit at each nail until it was shredded down as far as possible. I knew when to stop as soon as I tasted blood. I wasn't surprised that it didn't hurt, but part of me wished that it did. I worried I'd never feel anything ever again.

As I gnawed at my last thumbnail, a small shadow loomed over me. Because I was already in defense mode, I quickly stood up with my hands in fists, raised to my face. Having absolutely no boxing or fighting training, I can only imagine how ridiculous I looked.

"Whoa, kid. What the fuck?" Kailas said, swiftly dodging the punch I never threw out. She softly laughed until she saw the little red rivers pouring down both of my palms. She grabbed my wrists and brought my hands, which instinctively opened upon her touch, closer to her face.

"Jesus, Sera. Did you do this to yourself?" She had genuine concern on her face.

"I'm fine," I said as I ripped my arms away from her and rubbed off the dirty residue her fingers left. "What are you doing here? Can I see Jonesy again?"

"I, uh . . ." she started to say before falling silent for a few seconds. Her eyes were wide. "I'm sorry, kid. I'm just so confused about what's going on with you." She sat down on the haystack I had previously occupied. "First the bloody lip, now this." She looked back down at my hands, which were clumsily folded into one another in front of me. "I know we haven't known each other long, but please know you can confide in me. If you want to, that is. Your parents and Janusz have trusted me to come and check up on you. I promise you can trust me too."

"I said I'm fine!" I barked back at her. I could feel my lip quiver as I struggled to fight back tears. I was ashamed to tell anyone what had happened, but I slowly sat down next to her. I had to turn my face away as tears ran down my cheek. Then, it clicked in my mind that she'd said my parents asked her to look in on me. "Wait, what do you mean? Why can't my mom and dad check on me themselves?"

"Well, they're worried your uncle will somehow find out that you were involved in Janusz's recent disappearance. As much as I'm sure they'd rather do it themselves, they just don't have the time right now. Your dad just got a new job and is working the third shift, so if he isn't at work, he's too tired to get out of bed. Plus, I guess Mrs. Cardoza is having some health problems. So, neither she nor your father are around to help Johanna out with the kids. But, in any case, like I said, I'm here and all ears if you want to talk."

"I—" I forced myself to pause before my entire heart spilled out. I hesitated at that moment because I realized that I didn't really know the person before me. I had trusted her in the past because she claimed to be good friends with my parents. Sure, it was clear they knew each other. The link between them and Jonesy was too strong to just be a coincidence. But if they were *so* close that Mama was comfortable with her looking in on me, I found it strange that I had only met her a few weeks ago. I had recently been betrayed worse than I ever imagined, and I was quickly learning to be more and more skeptical of people. "Like I told you and Jonesy, I split my lip after one of the horses knocked me over. As for my nails, I bite them when I'm nervous. I'm starting college soon. It's normal to have jitters around the end of summer."

"That's more than a nail-biting habit, kid. But fine. If you don't want to talk to me, I understand your skepticism. My history with your parents is complicated. But like I said, they asked me to check up on you, so that's what I'm doing. Without more information, I guess I have to tell them you're fine." She said the last bit like it was a threat.

"Perfect. Because I am," I said with attitude, refusing to take Kailas's bait. Yet, after the words slipped past my lips, I secretly hoped she didn't really know my parents. They would be incredibly disappointed in me for being so rude to anyone, especially one of their friends.

"All right. Well, Janusz is having a bad day. Otherwise, I'd take you to see him. I'll let you get back to your chores. Take care of yourself. I'll be back in the event you want to talk about whatever is going on with you— or if, you know . . ."

I did know. Kailas meant if Jonesy died. I thought about that as I watched her walk away until her figure disappeared in the cornfield.

Chapter 6 – The Truth

Perhaps ashamed of himself for what he had done, Uncle Ford stayed out of my sight again for the next several days. I was more than happy with his constant absence. When he was home, he remained in his room with the door closed. This left me with the sole responsibility to keep the rest of the house in order, but it was a price I was delighted to pay for him to stay away from me.

When I finished tidying inside the house, I buried myself in busy work around the farm. I wanted to stay as distracted as possible to make my last few days there go by faster. I even searched the lawn for blades of grass that were askew that I could put back in their proper positions. Obviously, this was an evergreen task. They could easily be displaced again with the slightest gust of wind, but I did it anyway. I didn't spend as much time in the stables as I usually did out of fear that Kailas would show up out of nowhere and dig into my business again. Of course, I was also worried about her coming around and delivering the news that Jonesy had finally passed. I knew deep down she'd be able to find me anywhere on the property, but I told myself that if I wasn't by the horses, she wouldn't come around, and Jonesy would still be alive. That was one of several coping mechanisms I developed that summer.

It was during those days that the resentment toward my parents grew deeper and deeper. I understood that they were busy. They always were. But if they were that worried about me, I thought they'd make time to ensure I was okay. Part of me wondered if Daddy knew about Uncle Ford's violent side. The thought made me so angry that my head felt like it was going to explode.

To make matters worse, the only person who I knew genuinely cared about me was getting closer and closer to death with each passing day. I knew it was what he wanted, but it still made me unbearably sad to think about a world without him in it.

On one unfortunate day, Uncle Ford walked over to me with his head hung low. Not having anywhere to run, I stood there frozen as his menacing energy got closer and closer to me. He paused when we were about ten feet away and said in a low, monotone voice, "Your folks just called. Clark got tanked again. Guess you're gonna be here a while." He didn't look up from the ground the entire time he was talking. He didn't wait for a response; he just turned and began walking back to the house. I could have sworn his fists were clenched.

The panic set in immediately. Cold droplets began to drip from my scalp, causing the rest of my skin to rise into tiny bumps. I thought I only had a few more days of this hell. I was always back home before the school year started, and Daddy never got fired or laid off in the fall. I never considered that this time would be different.

Then, to distract myself from the reality that I was basically trapped in a house of horrors, I started planning how I'd continue living there and get to school. While Uncle Ford didn't live that far away from my parents, he did live farther away from the community college I was enrolled in. My parents' house was within walking distance, but I would need a car to drive from the farm. I was still wary about getting my license, and even if that wasn't the case, I didn't have the money to purchase a vehicle. I made a mental note to look into the prices of bus passes.

However, when my mind inevitably strayed away from the logistics of my current situation, I would brainstorm ways to get out of it. My first thought was to tell my parents what had happened. However, when I imagined the excruciating look my mom would get on her face upon hearing what Uncle Ford did to me, I dismissed it. I briefly considered calling the police, but I knew I couldn't do that because it would risk prompting Uncle Ford's threat to report my mom for her lack of citizenship.

That left me with one option. I had to tell Kailas. I had hesitated to say anything to her the last time she visited, but I thought I would be going home in a few days. And as much as I wanted to be skeptical, I had no other choice but to trust her good intentions. It's not like she had done anything to make me suspicious of them in the first place.

I spent the rest of the morning planning how I was going to tell my uncle that I was leaving. I knew I had to be careful to make the change seem as nonchalant as possible. I couldn't give any indication that I had told someone about his abuse.

Luckily, I didn't have to perseverate on it long. Kailas came to visit me again in the stables later that afternoon. I had let my duties in there go for as long as I could. I cared about the animals too much to let it get out of hand. The sight of her made me breakout in a cold sweat, and I held my breath in anticipation of bad news as she approached.

"You still mad at me, kid?"

I sighed in relief. If Jonesy had died, that surely would have been the first thing out of her mouth. "No. I'm sorry, Kailas. I was beyond rude to you."

"It's all good. I was a teenager once, ya know? I remember not being able to control my emotions from time to time. Especially during my time of the month."

I scoffed to myself. I wished it were simply a case of PMS.

"Anyway," she continued, "I drove by and saw that your uncle's car was gone, so I thought I'd check in on you again."

"How has Jonesy been doing?" I asked.

"I'm gonna shoot it to you straight. I don't think he has much time left. I've had to take more and more time off at the garage to take care of him."

Right then, I came up with an incentive for her to let me stay with her. It would be a win-win situation. If Kailas let me come live at her house, I could take care of Jonesy, and she could go to work. I was disoriented when I visited her home; it could have been near my school. But even if it wasn't, I would use public transportation—if it was available—or I'd walk there in five feet of snow if it meant I was away from my uncle. It's funny now to think that at one time, walking for hours in wet snow was preferable to just getting my license. But that was my mindset back then. Which, like I said, was completely spawned from my mother's anxiety about driving.

"Maybe I could stay with you and help out. I have a few days before I start school. But even after that, I can come back and forth between classes," I offered bashfully.

"Why would you want to do that? I thought you were going back with your folks soon?" Clearly, she hadn't spoken to them recently. This momentarily caused my suspicion of her to rise once again, but I forced it back down. There wasn't time for it anymore.

"No. Uncle Ford just told me that my dad was laid off again. I guess they don't have the money to provide for me just yet." I was trying to lay it on thick. I flashed her my best puppy eyes and slightly pouted my lip.

"Oh, damn. Is that right? Shit. Your poor parents. Life never seems to give the two of them a break. But I'm still confused. Why can't you just stay here?"

"Well, I can. I just don't want to." I swallowed hard. I knew the moment of truth would need to come at any second.

"Why is that?" She had a genuine look of concern on her face.

I directed her to sit with me on two adjacent hay bales. "If I tell you, you have to promise on your life that you won't tell anyone—not my parents, Jonesy, or the police. Do you promise?"

"I promise," she said as she scooted a few inches closer to me. I offered my pinky out, and she wrapped hers around it.

"I don't really know where to start. Nothing happened until Jonesy was gone. The night you and Mama helped him leave the farm was the first time . . ." From there, I told her everything. I explained every beating in extreme detail. I even showed her the scars on my back.

"Shit. I was worried something like this was happening," Kailas said, staring at the floor. "There's more." I couldn't believe I was about to speak of that night out loud to another human being. "A few nights back . . . he was calling me Johanna again, and he . . . he raped me."

Kailas exhaled in shock. "Jesus. I'm kind of lost for words right now. I'm so sorry all of that has happened to you. I mean, fuck. I kind of suspected the physical abuse, but I never imagined things would have gotten sexual. I think I have to tell someone, Sera. It's like part of my duty as an adult or some shit. At the minimum, I definitely need to tell your parents. They need to know."

"No, Kailas. Please. You promised." I was starting to cry. "My mom is extremely religious. I'm worried what she'll think . . ."

"I know she can be a little old-fashioned at times, but I know she wouldn't hold this against you. It wasn't your fault, Sera. But in any case, what if I told the police without your parents knowing? That way, we could get you some help, and you could wait until you felt comfortable enough to tell them."

"NO!" I screamed. "Uncle Ford threatened me that if he ever found out that I told someone, which the cops banging on his door and arresting him would definitely do, he'd reveal my mom's deepest secret . . . that she's here illegally. He said he'd call the authorities to deport her back to Argentina. Plus, I'm eighteen, so it's not like it was child abuse, right?"

She didn't flinch when I mentioned my mother's illegal status. I guessed that meant she already knew. "Shit. I don't know," Kailas said under her breath. Her hands were on top of her head, and she was staring at the ceiling.

"So, can I please stay with you?" I asked desperately.

There was a long silent pause before she answered. "I wish more than anything that you could. But, unfortunately, Janusz's medical costs and care have made a huge dent in my savings. The time I've had to cut at work doesn't help either. If I had even two extra cents, I'd gladly give them to you. But I don't. I'm so sorry."

"Oh." I was shattered. I felt stupid for ever being optimistic that she'd rescue me.

"You know what? Do you think you can stay out here for an hour or two? I might know of a way to help you, at least for a while. I need to go get something, but I'll come back as soon as I can. Okay?"

"Um, okay. Yeah." My optimism was slowly returning. Her tiny frame hurried out through the back door.

I anxiously waited for her return. As I remained in the darkness, too excited to concentrate on cleaning anything, I watched out the window to make sure my uncle's truck did not return. It would be the worst-case scenario if he found Kailas and me in the barn together. Not only would that give him access to her, but it would also cement my involvement in Jonesy's absence. Even worse, it could ruin any chance I had of disappearing myself.

Thankfully, the truck was nowhere in sight when she reappeared.

"It's my turn to trust you with a secret, Sera," she said as she handed me a piece of paper. I recognized the squiggly handwriting on it as Jonesy's. Upon further inspection, it looked like he had written down instructions for something.

"What is this?"

"I went back to have Janusz write down the steps you need to take to go somewhere, somewhere where you'll be out of harm's way. I would've written everything out myself, but it's been a while since I read them, and I wanted to make sure they were right. Don't worry, I didn't tell him any of the specifics as to why you might need them."

I didn't even know where to start my line of questioning.

"I know. It sounds insane," she continued. "But please trust me. If you follow these steps the next time your uncle tries to hurt you, you'll find yourself in a place even more beautiful than you could ever imagine . . ." I could tell there was more she wanted to explain, but she hurried once more out of the barn. When I looked up, I realized why. My uncle had just pulled up.

Not wanting him to see the paper and confiscate it, I shoved it into my back pocket. Then,
I waited until his bedroom window turned black before I approached the house.

Later that night, I laid out the crinkled paper on my bed and studied the instructions Jonesy had written out for me:

1. Clear your mind of all negative thoughts
2. Take five deep breaths
3. Say, "I submit to Ananda"
Powodzenia (good luck), mała perła -Jonesy

Although I was still terribly confused, I smiled at his handwritten message in Polish, wishing me luck. I wished so badly that I could ask him for clarification. But I decided that if he wanted me to try it, I would.

I'd hoped Kailas only meant it as a suggestion that I should use Jonesy's instructions when my uncle became violent. Like she thought that's when I would need it most, but I could actually go into what I believed to be some kind of meditative state whenever I wanted to. However, after the third or fourth time I tried while alone in my room, I realized it was more of a requirement.

It was strange. Obviously, I didn't want my uncle to attack me again. But I did experience a slight tinge of disappointment each night I saw his truck in the yard and bedroom light off. That's how badly I wanted to uncover the mystery of whatever it was that Kailas and Jonesy had given me. I even got frustrated enough that I tried to provoke a "chaos night."

I wanted to make him angry enough that he would reach for his belt. And the next time he did, I definitely I would not physically fight back. Hopefully that would prevent things from going too far, like they had the last time.

To my dismay, no matter how dirty I left the house or how loudly I stomped up the stairs over the following days, I could never piss him off enough.

When my disobedience to his cleanliness and volume rules didn't work, I set my eyes on a bigger prize. I would go into his room and try to use his phone. He explicitly forbade me from doing both of those things during my first stay with him. All of his other rules were more like unspoken agreements I'd learned to abide by to remain out of his way.

It took all the courage I had left in my damaged body, but I did it one day when I was sure he was in the house. I watched as he parked his truck and walk toward the front door. I had hoped he would come from the back, so he'd see me right away.

But after I heard him walk inside, I clomped my feet against the floor. I wanted to make sure he could hear where I was and quickly discern my location. I paused for a moment before entering his room, something I had never dared to do in the past.

I swung the door open and was shocked by how normal it looked. There was a bed with an intricately quilted comforter laid across it. I marveled at his simplicity. I'd half expected to find a coffin in there, as I thought only monsters were capable of doing the things Uncle Ford had done to me. Similar to the bed, the rest of the room was pretty standard. There was a desk, a set of drawers, and two nightstands, one of which had an old-timey phone on it. Despite its apparent age, I knew it worked because I had overheard him speaking to people on it before.

I carefully listened for his powerful and menacing footsteps as I inched toward it. I picked it up, staring and waiting for his shadow to appear in the doorframe. Because I didn't know how to work the rotary dial and didn't know any other numbers except for my home phone, I had to pretend.

"Hello," I murmured at first. But each time Uncle Ford failed to catch me, my voice grew louder.

"HELLO!" I finally screamed.

"Sera? Is that you?" I barely recognized his voice. It was whiny and breathless. The man who appeared also didn't physically look like my uncle. Instead of his normally strong, stoic stature, his head and shoulders were hanging low. His arms dangled lifelessly in front of his body.

"Uncle Ford?"

To my surprise, he hadn't noticed the phone in my hand. He didn't even seem to care that I was in his room.

He walked sloppily over to his bed and collapsed on it. The earth beneath my feet shook a little from the impact. He was making noises I had never heard come out of a human before. Then, connecting them with his odd demeanor, I realized he was sobbing. In between wails, he tried to say something, but I couldn't quite make out what it was.

A few minutes passed, and the loud cries dissipated. He was lightly whimpering and letting out shallow breaths. It almost sounded like he was hyperventilating. While I felt little sympathy for the man, I wasn't heartless. But I just stood there in the corner, unsure of what to do. That is until I made out what he was saying.

"He's dead. My love. He's gone forever. Janusz. Why?" he eventually screamed, with his head buried in a pillow.

I started convulsing in my own uncontrollable weeping. I knew it would happen sooner or later, but I couldn't believe Jonesy was actually dead.

I left my uncle alone in his room, and I retreated to my own. Tears ran down my face as I clung to his favorite picnic blanket. I had stolen it out of the kitchen a few days after he left. It brought me comfort to have it draped across me as I slept at night. It might have just been in my mind, but I swore I smelled his scent on it. Unfortunately, I'd had to throw it into the wash after one of my uncle's brutal beatings. Luckily, it was already covered in various shades of red checkers, so any remaining stains were relatively unrecognizable.

When the tears had subsided, an enormous flood of guilt washed over me. If it weren't for me, he'd be alive. I closed my eyes and imagined he was in the house at that moment. The cold and dark box that served as my uncle's dwelling felt more like a warm home when Jonesy was in it. Except when the two of them were fighting, of course.

Then, remembering that I would never feel the same light and positive energy that engulfed me when I first met Jonesy, I started to sob again.

In bed that night, memories of the times we spent together flickered in my mind like beloved home movies. I'm not sure when, but they eventually lolled me into a deep sleep. So deep that I didn't hear Uncle Ford's truck leave and return a few hours later.

But before I knew it, my eyes flicked open in terror. I saw nothing but darkness, but I felt the presence of someone behind me.

"Johannnnna," he whispered menacingly in my hair. "Wanna have some fun?"

I stuck to my previous decision and didn't resist or attempt to fight as he berated my body with lashes of his belt. It was hard to hold back this time, though, because he repeatedly hit me with the buckle, something he hadn't done before.

"Johanna. It's all your fault. You took him away from me!" he screamed with each whack of metal against my skin.

Amid the panic and agony, I remembered Jonesy's instructions. I couldn't pull the paper
out of my pocket without Uncle Ford noticing, so I focused hard to remember what it said.

1) Clear my mind of negative thoughts. As hard as that was at that moment, I just thought of Jonesy's face; *2) Take five deep breaths.* It was difficult to get five consecutive breaths in as I was interrupted by my own winces of pain, but I finally did it; and *3) Say, "I submit to Ananda."* I wasn't positive how to say the last word, but I did my best to sound it out in my head.

Chapter 7 – Ananda

Without another thought or breath, I found myself lying face down on the softest grass I had ever felt. I rolled onto my back, delighted with the way its cool droplets numbed my newly created welts. Then, I took the piece of paper out of my pocket to make sure I'd remembered the instructions correctly. Satisfied that I had, I closed my eyes in relief and waited for the meditation to continue.

This tranquil state was interrupted when I heard the sound of other people in the distance. Alarmed, I sat up quickly. I had never tried to meditate before, but I was pretty sure other people weren't supposed to be in your "peaceful place."

An elderly couple approached me. "Welcome to Ananda!"ॐ they chanted in tandem. I sat there in shock.

They smiled sweetly at each other and then glanced back at me. "I'm Matilda, and this old sack of bones is my husband, Ralph," the tall, red-haired lady said."

"I'm Seraphine," I said, hesitantly offering my hand out to her.

She accepted my offering and warmly clasped both of her hands around mine. "What a beautiful name. Isn't that just beautiful?" She looked to her husband for a sign of agreement, and he gave it to her in the form of a small smile and head nod.

"Are you hungry, sweetie? Ralph and I would be happy to have you over for some lunch."

Mama always told me never to trust strangers, but it wasn't like I had anywhere else to go. Plus, my stomach was rumbling. "Are you sure it wouldn't be an imposition?"

"Oh, heavens, no," she said as she wrapped her arm around me. "Don't be silly."

She left her arm draped over my shoulder for the remainder of our walk. The dew from the grass must have camouflaged the dark blood spots on my navy-blue shirt because she didn't say anything about them. It didn't take long for me to notice that she had a slight limp. Each time she stepped off of her right foot, her arm felt a little heavier around my neck. I also quickly learned that Ralph, her husband, had to take frequent breaks. Every few minutes, he crouched with his hands on his knees, took a few deep breaths, whipped out an inhaler, and dispensed the medicine into his lungs with several pumps. Without realizing it, I must have stared back at him for a while because Matilda audibly answered the question in my head.

"Agh. Don't worry." She nodded in her husband's direction. "He's all right. Asthma is all."

Having asthma myself, I found the frequency in which he needed his inhaler a bit surprising. But I reasoned that his condition must be worse than mine. I sure as hell wasn't going to ask follow-up questions. I had already done enough digging into other peoples' lives that summer to learn that it never did me any good.

Kailas was right. This mysterious place was more beautiful than I could have dreamed. I almost felt like I was inside of a Disney movie. The air was clean and crisp, and all the trees were full of leaves that were gorgeous shades of green. I swear I even heard someone whistling a happy tune, but I was only around two people, and their lips weren't pursed when I inspected their faces.

Matilda and Ralph lived in a home right on a beach with the clearest water I had ever seen. Even from a distance, you could see the sand on the bottom.

As we got closer, I reveled in the sounds of the wind chimes that lined the path to their home. They sang in harmony together as the wind blew and reminded me of the beautiful chimes that Mama hung from a tree in our backyard. Daddy crafted it for her after they got married and first moved in together. She told me once that it looked just like the one right outside the window of her childhood bedroom.

"I'll make you a sandwich. Is turkey okay?" Matilda asked.

"Yes, thank you."

Then, she walked into her laundry room and retrieved a sweater for me. I graciously accepted it when she handed it to me. The style of it was a little "old lady" for my taste, but I was grateful for anything that would allow me to get out of my wet shirt.

Without needing to ask, she pointed to where the bathroom on the first floor was so I could change. Not knowing what else to do with my old, dirty t-shirt, I shoved it into their garbage can. I covered it up with a few pieces of tissue.

When I went back out to the kitchen, I sat down at the table while Matilda assembled lunch.

I don't know what made me do it, but I reached into my pocket again and removed the note. I turned it over for the first time and was surprised that Jonesy had written more on it:

Ask for Mattie. If the time comes, look for
the blue reflections to guide you home.

When Matilda brought me my lunch, she sat down across the table with her own food.

"Thank you so much," I said quickly before devouring the food she prepared for me.

"My pleasure, dear," she responded, but to my surprise, she pushed her own plate away from her body. I felt embarrassed at that moment for my lack of table manners. Before I could apologize, she continued, "Do you mind if I ask you a few questions?"

I choked for a moment on the bread in my throat. But I hoped Matilda's questions would shed some light on my behalf as well.

"Sure," I said.

"First things first. Who are you here for?" she asked.

"Uh . . ." I hesitated, not knowing how to answer her.

"Oh, dear. I guess I shouldn't have assumed. You look so healthy. I'm so sorry."

Contrary to my initial hope, this conversation only made me more confused. "What? I'm sorry. I don't understand."

I could tell by the furrow in her brow that I was also confusing her. "Well, this is Ananda," she said. "There are only two reasons people come here. Either because they are like Ralph and me, who were sick in the real world and came here to avoid dying—we're called 'Nirvanas'ॐ—or because they are the chosen visitor of a particular Nirvana. Those people are called 'Samsaras.'ॐ They are allowed to go back and forth between Ananda and the real world. The permanent residents—us Nirvanas—are typically divided by country and region. But there can be exceptions made upon request. For example, most of us who live around here came from the Midwest. Is that where you're from?"

"Yes. Northern Wisconsin. But in terms of the other stuff, I don't fit in either category. I'm not sick either. At least not to my knowledge. I had a clean bill of health the last time I went to the doctor. When the instructions were given to me, I thought they were steps to some kind of meditative exercise. But I'm starting to think I was wrong about that." I looked around and let out an awkward chuckle.

"Ralph!" Matilda screamed as she looked at me with a tinge of terror. When her husband appeared, she said, "Please tell him what you just said."

". . . that I'm not sick?"

"And?"

"I didn't come for anyone who is sick either. I thought I was participating in a meditation . . ."

"What? How? I didn't think unregistered people could even access this world," he said, cutting me off and talking only to his wife.

She shrugged her shoulders. They continued to exchange worried looks with each other before Ralph sat down to join the conversation.

I didn't know exactly what to do, so I just kept asking more questions. "You said this place is called Ananda. What does that mean?"

"That's not the easiest question to answer," he said. "Mattie?"

Recognizing that name, I reached for the crinkled paper next to me on the table. I reread the back:

Ask for Mattie.

"You're Mattie?" I asked as I smoothed the paper out on the table, facing her.

"Well, yes. My close acquaintances call me that." She put on the green-framed glasses hanging around her neck and took a moment to read the handwritten text on both sides. Once she finished, she set it down, looked at me curiously, and said, "What language is the last part in? And who is this Jone . . . Jonesy, is it?" She glanced at the sheet of paper again for clarification.

"It's Polish. He is . . . well, was my friend. Jonesy was just the nickname he let me call him because it was hard for me to say his real name, Jan . . ." I began to slowly pronounce it.

I was interrupted by the audible breaths of excitement I heard come out of the elderly couple as they exchanged hopeful glances.

Ralph left the table but returned shortly after with a picture frame in his hands.

"Show her," his wife urged him. I took the frame in my own hands and recognized the bright blue eyes, beautiful caramel-colored skin, and ginormous smile.

"Oh my gosh. That's him! That's Jonesy!" Tears welled up in my eyes at the sight of his familiar face, although he looked healthier than I had ever seen him in the photograph.

"Janusz was a dear friend of ours. Wait. Did you say he *was* your friend? Does that mean . . .?"

"He recently passed," I said cautiously, bracing for an emotional reaction to the news.

"Oh, thank goodness," Matilda said with a sigh of relief and a smile on her face. "When he disappeared, I figured he'd tried to escape, but I was so worried he had been caught. But the general public isn't allowed to visit the prison, so I had no way of knowing for sure. I'm so happy he was able to go back to the real world. It was clear to everyone that he grew tired of living this life and wanted it all to end."

My forehead creased. "What do you mean, 'go back to the real world?' Why couldn't he die here?"

"Well, sweetie. This is a special place. Are you familiar with hospice care?"

I nodded. I remembered hearing my dad talk about a time when his mom had to be put into hospice care shortly before she passed away.

"This place is like that. It's a secretive realm people who are close to death can come to. Nirvanas are still sick, but we can't die. We also don't age. Samsaras and Nirvanas are all given instructions like these." She picked up the paper I had previously handed to her. "Nirvanas don't need to, but the first time Samsaras come here, they have to put themselves in dangerous environments before reading them out. I don't have confirmation of any kind to back this up, but I think the authorities made that rule as a way for the visitors to prove their loyalty. I assume the logic is that if you're willing to go through that, you're more likely to keep Ananda a secret."

She seemed distracted by her own thoughts. But after a few seconds, she shrugged and let out a sigh. Then she continued,

"Unfortunately, some people, like Janusz, ultimately decide that death is the better option than staying here indefinitely."

I stood still and tried my best to absorb everything she was saying. "So, why can't Nirvanas just leave?"

"Because we agreed not to. If you try to leave and get caught, you could actually go to prison. For many, this threat isn't worth trying to get out because when you're locked up, you can no longer get your medication, and as you can't die, you just sit in a cell and suffer. Getting older and sicker but never getting the release of death."

"Whoa. But what about . . . suicide? Why do you think he didn't just kill himself?" This was a question I'd found myself wondering several times in the real world.

"In an odd way, he had a fear of God in him. I don't think he was devout to any particular religion, but something in him made him cautious about going to hell. Plus, just like leaving, if you try to kill yourself here and fail, you could end up in prison."

"Whoa," I said again.

"Yeah. I used to volunteer at the prison. I saw one man slumped over in his cell who was over 112 years old and suffering from Crohn's Disease. His illness had progressed so much that he couldn't digest food or water anymore. So, he was literally rotting in there and was constantly dehydrated and hungry. He was basically a skeleton with thin, gray skin. I still think about him to this day. The poor man is still suffering. He was bad back then, but that was several years ago. I can't imagine what he looks like now." She again seemed lost in thought for a moment.

Ralph interjected, "Did Janusz ever mention how he was able to leave?"

I jumped a little. I was so engulfed in his wife's story that I was startled when the topic of conversation returned to me. "No. He didn't even tell me about this place. He just wrote out the instructions for me a few days ago."

"Hm," Ralph uttered.

Matilda had apparently snapped out of her imagination because she said, "All right. That's enough questioning for today. I'm sure you're tired, Seraphine. We just gave you *a lot* of information to take in."

"Wait! What about this part?" I pointed to where Jonesy wrote about blue reflections.

She reread it quietly to herself before giving it to Ralph.

"Do you think this means the rumors are true?" Ralph whispered when he had finished reading.

"I mean. It definitely hints toward its true existence." She suddenly seemed to remember my presence and said in a rush, "Oh! Ha. Anyway, would you be comfortable staying with us? Any friend of Janusz is a friend of ours."

I wanted to ask so many more questions, but I was also thankful for the invited break to process everything they had already told me. While the events of that summer had made me generally suspicious of people, I figured if Jonesy trusted them, I could too. Plus, staying in a cozy home was better than sleeping on a park bench somewhere.

Later that night, I followed Matilda up a gorgeous hardwood staircase. Once we reached the top, she pointed to their guest room.

As I walked into the room, she said, "Let me know if there's anything else you need, Seraphine."

I looked around the room and was mesmerized by the bright, clean look of everything. I had grown used to living in a farmhouse that was less than a few yards away from horse stables.

"Oh, Matilda? Please call me Sera. All of my friends do."

She winked at me and started closing the door. "You got it. And you can call me Mattie. Sweet dreams, Sera."

"Good night, Mattie." The second the door closed, I nuzzled into the white, fluffy sheets. The windows were open, and a warm breeze gently blew against my face.

Instinctively, I reached for the pillow to wrap it around my head. But I paused when I remembered that there probably weren't any violent antics in this house that I'd need to shield myself from. I grinned as I placed the fluffy cushion behind the one that I was already resting on. I slept better that night than I had in weeks.

Chapter 8 – Reminder of an Old Friend

"Sera?" Ralph said the next morning as he slowly started opening the bedroom door. In what I assumed to be an effort to protect my privacy, he stopped before he could actually see into the room. "Can I come in?"

"Mhm," I said, sitting up from the bed and stretching.

He caught me mid-yawn and said, "Oh. I'm so sorry. Did I wake you?"

I looked at the alarm clock and saw that it was 7:00 a.m. "No, no. It's fine." It was later than I was used to getting up on the farm.

"Oh, okay. I've heard from other visitors that traveling here can really drain your energy. But then again, you aren't the average Sam . . ." he paused mid-thought. He looked down at the ground and shook his head. Then, he met my eye contact again and continued on with the actual reason he had come up to talk to me. "Anyway, Mattie and I made breakfast if you want to come down and join us."

"Sure! I'll be right down."

"If you want to change, there are clean clothes in the dresser."

After he closed the door, I wandered over and opened a drawer. I dug around for a bit and eventually found a medium-sized white sweatshirt with "*Uniwersytet Jagiellonski*" in black letters across the front. I pulled it over my head, noticed it was a little baggy, but decided it was better than nothing. Upon further discovery, I also found a pair of cute black workout shorts. Unlike the sweatshirt, they were way too small for me. The wide range of sizes confused me a little. In the end, some red pajama pants were my best option. To avoid tripping over the excess fabric that reached well past my feet, I rolled the top part resting on my hips a few times. Then, I threw my long black hair into a messy bun on top of my head and headed downstairs.

When I reached the dining table, I was surprised to see that there were three people sitting there.

"Sera, this is our nephew, Harrison. Harrison, this is the new friend I was telling you about."

The next few moments of my life seemed to go by in slow motion. He was faced away from me, but, after being prompted by Mattie, he stood up and turned around. When his brown eyes finally met mine, one side of his mouth was upturned in a friendly way, and he reached his hand out to me.

Butterflies immediately filled my belly. I nervously looked down and tugged on the oversized clothing I was wearing. I wished I had spent a little more time picking out my outfit that morning.

As I staggered over to him, I tripped a little. Embarrassed, I kept my head down but extended my hand to shake his. I must have looked like some kind of pod person who wasn't used to human interaction.

But he continued his cordiality. "It's nice to meet you, Sera. Please, sit down and join us."

"Um . . . uh . . . wha . . ." I felt each word—or sound, more accurately—leave my lips, but it was almost like they didn't have the momentum to actually reach him. It was as if they'd come out of my mouth but instantly drop to the floor.

He was easily the most gorgeous boy I had ever seen. His face was slim, and his cheeks were slightly sunken in. Not in a sickly way, like Jonesy's were, though. Instead, his long, defined dimples served as shadows to highlight his intricate mouth.

"Thanks," I eventually blurted out before sitting next to him. Our knees touched for a second, and I somehow managed to kick his shin as I was recoiled my legs.

"Sorry," I said awkwardly. *Jeez. Get it together, Sera,* I thought.

"No worries. I didn't even feel anything." I knew he was just being nice because I saw him massaging the bruise I likely caused.

To demonstrate that I was a normal human—not a cyborg—who consumed food, while still maintaining what I now recognize as toxic femininity, I loaded my plate with the fruit set out in front of me. But I was careful to pick around the strawberries; I associated them with my uncle and the farmhouse, and the slightest smell of them made my stomach turn.

"Oh my gosh. I can't remember the last time I saw that sweatshirt," Mattie said and pointed her fork in my direction. "Well, of course you'd pick that one."

"What do you mean?" I asked.

"That belonged to Janusz. That's the university he went to in Poland. I assumed he must have told you about it."

"Oh, no. I had no idea. It just looked comfy." I tugged at the fabric once more, smiling and feeling closer to him than I had in days. But I was also curious why his sweatshirt was in their spare bedroom. *Did he live here?* I wondered.

"What was the nickname you called him again?" Mattie asked.

"Jonesy!" I said enthusiastically. But the second I said it, I realized how childish it sounded.

"That's right. How adorable," Mattie said, only confirming my worry about sounding infantile.

"Jonesy. Ha! That totally fits him!" Harrison commented, which made me feel a little better.

"Yeah," I said with a subtle laugh. It was still hard for me to look directly into his eyes.

Apparently, my presence wasn't at all intimidating to him because he continued talking directly to me. "How did you meet him?"

"I—" I started to answer.

"Now, now. We grilled Sera enough last night. Let's let her eat her breakfast in peace," Mattie said, cutting me off.

"Oh, no. I don't mind." Part of me was excited to talk about my memories of Jonesy. And, although it terrified me, I also wanted an excuse to keep talking with her nephew.

"All right, if you're sure."

"Yeah," I said as I was mustering up the courage to make eye contact with the light brown eyes currently staring at me. "I, um—" I coughed to clear my throat as I looked up. "I met Jonesy when I was sent to stay at my uncle's farm over the summer. He and I became fast friends. Then after time passed, he felt like family. I'm the eldest of my siblings, but I always wished I had an older brother, and he was better than I could have imagined." I looked down at the array of food before me. "It's funny. We actually always ate breakfast together outside. It was the best. Huh," I said with a shrug and laugh. "I mean, as you know, he was the best."

"Definitely," Harrison said, nodding. "He and I did stuff like that too. Janusz always surprised me with adventures. One time, he took me camping in this awesome cave. It was full of crystals that illuminated the entire thing when the sunlight hit them. It was the most beautiful thing I had ever seen."

After he said that, my memories seemed less special. I wished we could have gone on adventures together, but Jonesy was so sick by the time I met him. Our breakfast picnics were probably the best he could do—even when my uncle was slipping him his medication. The affection I had first felt for Harrison turned to intense jealousy. I blamed him for minimizing the time I spent with Jonesy, and I remained quiet for the rest of the meal.

When everyone had finished eating, I helped Mattie clear the table.

"Harry, why don't you show Sera around? She hasn't really had the opportunity to see the beach," Mattie suggested.

"Oh, yeah! That's a great idea," Ralph chimed in.

Ugh, I thought. The last thing I wanted to do was hear more about the fantastic trips Harrison went on with Jonesy. I was also ashamed of the lack of stories I would be able to reciprocate with. I regretted dismissing their previous concerns about him asking me questions.

"Are you down?" he asked me, raising an eyebrow over his caramel eyes.

I didn't want to show any disrespect to Ralph or Mattie, two people who had shown me nothing but kindness since the second I met them. So, reluctantly, I agreed.

As soon as our feet hit the sand, he reached for the hair tie holding up his hair in a small bun at the nape of his neck. I was speechless as I watched his long brown curls unravel and blow in the wind. "Mattie hates when my hair is down at the table," he said as he flashed his subtle but warm smile at me. The curls were frantically flowing over his face. He smoothed them back as he looked away. "So, what is your life like in the real world, Seraphine?"

Hearing him say my full name made shivers rush down my spine. My unwarranted resentment toward him was dissipating by the second, and I was getting a little more comfortable speaking to him. "Well, I guess I'm just a normal teenager. I have a mom, dad, and younger siblings."

"You said you were sent to live with your uncle on his farm during the summer. Is that something you do every year?"

I was flattered he listened to me during breakfast. "No. It's only happened a handful of times as I've gotten older. It only happens when my parents don't have enough money for food and other necessities for my siblings and me. My mom can't really work because she's from Argentina, and she—" I stopped myself before I disclosed the actual reason she couldn't find a stable job. Instead, I faked a slight cough and clumsily changed the focus onto Daddy before completing my previous thought. "Um. Anyway, my dad is significantly older than her and is only qualified for physically demanding mill jobs. And because of his older age, he gets 'laid off' a lot. If you know what I mean."

"Damn. That sucks. It's cool that your mom is from Argentina, though. Do you speak Spanish?"

I laughed and said, "*¡Claro que sí!*"

"The only word I recognized is '*si*'" He was also laughing.

"I said, 'Of course!'"

"Oh, got it. Got it. Ah! This is my favorite spot!" he said as he pointed to a random hill of sand. "Do you wanna sit for a minute?"

"Sure." I was thankful for the chance to rest. It was hard to scoot across the sand in the baggy pajama pants I was currently wearing. After we sat down, I rolled them up to my calves.

We sat in silence and watched the small tides rise and fall. I took Harrison's lead and released my own hair from the scrunchie that held it on top of my head. It felt freeing to let the long black strands chaotically blow around.

He broke the silence by asking, "So, what is your uncle like?"

"He's *complicated*," I answered quickly.

"What do you mean?"

"Well, he and I have never been close. I know that I'm more of a nuisance to him than anything else. So, when I stay with him, I do my best to just get my daily chores done and stay out of his way."

"Hm. That doesn't sound like the warmest environment to be surrounded by."

"No. But it's fine." I didn't want to tell him the whole truth because I didn't want to preemptively turn this handsome stranger off to me.

We fell silent once again and enjoyed the calming sounds around us for several minutes.

"Well, Mattie will probably be worrying about us. Let's get you back there." He jumped up and reached his hand down to assist me. It was the first time I had actually touched him. My hand felt on fire even after he released it.

To my dismay, he didn't stay at the house for very long after we returned. I didn't know what it was about him; it wasn't just about his exquisite looks. I wanted to be around his essence for as long as I could.

"I had a great time getting to know you a little more, Sera. Maybe we can do it again?"

"Sure. I'd like that." I blushed.

"Cool. Well, I gotta get going. Will you tell Mattie thank you for breakfast for me?"

"Are you sure you don't want to come in and tell her yourself?" I said, desperately wanting to spend more time with him.

"Nah, I wish I could, but I made a commitment to be somewhere else in about ten minutes. But I'll see ya, kid!" He said this as he entered the driver's side of his SUV and delicately placed his brown curls back in a ponytail.

My heart sank when he called me "kid." Not that I could blame him. I did look like a child buried in the oversized clothing I was currently wearing. I made a promise to myself that I'd be more prepared the next time he came around. The tight shorts I had found earlier that morning flashed through my mind. I daydreamed about him seeing me cascade down the stairs in them. Then, a low voice brought me back to reality— or whatever state of existence I was currently experiencing.

"Did Harry leave already?" Ralph asked while scanning the driveway for his car.

"Oh. Um, yeah. I guess he had something else to do."

"I see. Anyway, did the two of you have a nice time?"

"Yeah. He seems . . . nice."

"Mhm . . ." Ralph said as he chuckled behind me.

I walked into the house, embarrassed that I might have made my feelings for his nephew too obvious. Mattie greeted me with a smile. She was cleaning the rest of the mess from our breakfast.

"Is there anything I can do to help you?" I asked.

"No, I'm almost finished. Thanks, though, sweetie." Having nothing else to do, I sat down at the island that stood before their sink.

"Oh! Harrison asked me to thank you on his behalf for breakfast. He wanted to come in and say goodbye, but he seemed to be rushing to get somewhere."

She didn't say anything. She just shook her head, smiled, and continued furiously scrubbing the pan in her hands. I couldn't imagine how many girls were probably competing for his time and attention, but I pictured him driving from one of their houses to the next. I assumed that was the life he lived, whether it was in Ananda or in the real world. I then wondered if he was one of the permanent, sick residents or just a visitor. Judging by his healthy-looking appearance, I assumed he was the latter. But I didn't want to demonstrate any more of my interest in him by asking Mattie.

She and I spent the rest of that afternoon chatting and drinking coffee. We never talked about anything too serious, as I assumed she didn't want to continue "drilling me." Part of me wanted to inquire more about this mysterious world I found myself in, but I was also relieved just to talk about normal everyday things. She asked me about my friends in high school and whether or not I had a boyfriend. When I told her that I had never had one, she seemed surprised by my lack of experience in the dating department.

"What? How can those boys stand to stay away from a beautiful young girl like you? That's just ridiculous."

I had never really been described as "beautiful" by anyone. Not out loud, at least. I'm not sure why, but my mom never really commented on my appearance. She never made a fuss about makeup, either. I can't say I ever saw her wearing any, and she certainly never taught me how to apply it. When it came to her and her children's appearances, her sole focus was that we were hygienic and presented to the world as such. Sure, sometimes all of us had to share the same bath water or sneak over to the neighbor's and use their hose as a shower, which she would tell us was a fun game everyone in Argentina played called, "*Ducha Prestada.*" But I have since caught on to that little fib. Nevertheless, she always made sure we were as clean as we could be.

It felt nice to have someone compliment my looks for a change.

"Oh, I don't know. I've always considered myself to be somewhat of a 'plain Jane.'"

"Pfft! Well, judging by the way Harry was looking at you earlier, I beg to differ."

My ears perked up. "Wha—what do you mean?"

"He was hanging on to your every word this morning."

"Oh," I said. My mind was spinning in delight. Never in my wildest dreams did I think someone so attractive could be interested in me.

Mattie got up to prepare lunch and dinner, and Ralph joined us for those meals. But our conversation never stopped. I couldn't remember the last time I'd spent the majority of the day just sitting and talking to someone. Even with Jonesy, our talks were always cut short because I had to start my chores right after breakfast.

She exhausted all of the questions she could think of about my social life, which wasn't particularly interesting. So, we started talking about pop culture—both from way back in the '50s and '60s when Mattie was a young woman and my teenage years in the early 2000s.

Since we were on the subject, Mattie suggested we watch *Paris When It Sizzles,* her favorite Audrey Hepburn movie. Throughout the film, she looked back and forth at me and the screen several times, and she noted the similarities between the famous movie star's face and my own—mostly our wider-set eyes and button noses. She said our mouths were sort of the same, except my upper lip was fuller. I was incredibly flattered to be compared to such a beautiful actress, and I blushed with each compliment Mattie gave me.

Chapter 9 – Connecting the Dots

I heard several loud bangs outside when I was getting ready the following day. When I peeked my head out the bedroom window to see what the source of the noise was, I was pleasantly surprised to see Harrison in the backyard chopping wood.

I was about to go out and talk to him when I saw another girl approach from the beach. I couldn't hear what they were saying, but their body language indicated that they were familiar with each other. I noted in particular that his hand lingered on her lower back for a few seconds after they embraced. He also lightly kissed her on the cheek.

At that moment, I was a little angry with Mattie. It was her fault that I'd even considered his interest in someone like me. The girl in the backyard with him was everything I wasn't. She was blonde, tall, tan, and based on the perfect beach curls surrounding her face, I could tell she was good at doing her hair. Like with makeup, Mama also never taught me how to do anything fancy with my hair aside from putting it up in a ponytail or messy bun. "Practical" hairstyles were all that mattered, according to her.

I ditched my initial plan of looking more presentable in front of him. Instead, I dressed in more oversized clothes I had found the night prior. I didn't care if they really did belong to Jonesy; I'd already decided in my mind that they did, and I felt close to him when I put them on. As funny as it sounds, I developed the habit of giving myself a small hug every time I wore an item of clothing I believed to be his. I reasoned that it was the same as hugging him again.

Apparently, Harrison's conversation with the pretty blonde outside had concluded because shortly after I got into the kitchen, he walked in alone with his arms full of chopped wood.

"Oh! Good morning, Sera. I didn't expect you to be up this early. Did I wake you?"

Still kind of sour, I didn't even bother to look up at him. "No. I always get up early to start chores on the farm."

"Ah . . ." I could tell he was a little taken back by my dismissive tone. "Well, if you want, I have some more stuff I have to do around the yard. Would you want to help?"

I looked up at him now, once again mesmerized by his gorgeous face. His hair was loosely tied back, and smaller curls had sprung up around his face from the sweat of his exertion.

"Okay," I said before actually thinking about it.

"Cool. Do you want to come out and help me after you finish eating?" Harrison said as he unloaded the wood near the fireplace. He then wiped his brow with the V-neck undershirt he wore beneath a red and black plaid button-up that hung open at his sides. I blushed at the small amount of his abdomen he briefly exposed. Hoping he didn't notice, I furiously nodded.

"All right. Take your time. I'll be out back when you're ready."

Even though I was disappointed by what I believed to be a public display of affection toward another girl, I was grateful for the distraction of manual labor. Since the topic didn't come up the day prior, I was obsessing over when I would be able to sit Mattie down and ask all of the questions that had been burning on my mind since I arrived in Ananda. Most importantly, I wanted to ask her how I was going to get home—given that I wasn't a Nirvana or a Samsara. I had enjoyed my time there so far, but I knew my dad would get another job eventually. And when that happened, I could go back home and be safe from more of my Uncle Ford's abuse.

I took Harrison's suggestion, and I slowly finished the rest of the cereal in my bowl. I even put a little extra in when I finished the first one. I didn't want to make it seem like I was super eager to spend time with him. Although, of course, I was.

I reconsidered my plan to look "sexier" in front of him, and I headed upstairs to find something. I knew it was wrong to have these thoughts when I was still unsure of his relationship status. Still, I secretly wanted to prove that I could present myself in that kind of light. I had never really thought about myself like that before.

I ripped through the clothes available to me in the dresser. I found the previously discovered workout shorts, and I struggled to stuff my body into them. But when I looked at myself in the mirror, I was pleasantly surprised by what I saw.

When it came to a shirt, I found a thick strapped tank top. Unfortunately, it was also too small for me. I considered wearing it like a crop top before turning red at the sight of my bare stomach. Instead, I found a black acid-washed t-shirt with the name of a band I didn't recognize printed across it. It was slightly baggy, but I tucked the front of it into the pants that were hugging my curvy thighs. Finally, I folded and wrapped a red bandana around the tight bun on top of my head to finish the look.

I looked at myself one more time. *Good enough*, I thought.

It didn't take long for me to ascertain whether or not he noticed my wardrobe change. When I found him outside by the shed, his eyes were wide, and he said, "Whoa." After that, his pupils scanned my entire body.

Feeling slightly self-conscious but also happy with the success of my plan, I said, "Oh. Yeah, I figured I should change out of the sweats I was wearing. I didn't want to get overheated."

It was clearly a lie, as the sun had since ducked behind a cloud. Plus, my skin was already forming goosebumps in response to the cool breeze.

"Makes sense . . ." he said as he skeptically squinted up at the darkening sky.

I tried to conceal my shivers as I helped him with random tasks around Mattie and Ralph's yard. However, he must have noticed because he told me several times that I could go back into the house if I was cold.

"No, I'm fine. I, uh . . . I run warm." Another stupid lie, but I didn't want him to think I was putting on any kind of display for him. Even though I obviously was.

After a while, he'd clearly had enough of my charade because he strongly suggested we conclude our work, although he had put several other pieces of equipment out in preparation for further tasks.

I wouldn't have been surprised if my lips were blue by that point, so I graciously accepted.

When we reentered the house, I was thankful for the warmth that wrapped around my body.

"Do you drink coffee?" he asked. "I can make us some."

"Yeah. That'd be great. Thanks!" Although I was already more comfortable in the warm environment, the idea of a hot beverage being poured into my body was more than welcome.

He and I sat next to each other and sipped the coffee. At one point, a beeping sound came from his pocket. He took out his cellphone and began pounding on the screen with his thumbs.

"Oh, sorry. Do you mind? One of my friends is going through some stuff, and I'm trying to help her sort it out."

"No, it's totally fine." I wished I had my own phone to whip out. "Is she okay?" I wanted to pry and find out if this "friend" was the pretty blonde I saw him with.

"She'll be fine. She's just seeing a new guy, but it's her first prospective relationship since being in Ananda, so she's a little uneasy about it. We already talked about it a little this morning when she stopped over, but she's going on a date with him tonight, and she's nervous. I don't know why she's coming to me for advice. I'm far from an expert when it comes to Ananda's dating culture. I haven't dated anyone since coming here." His cheeks turned a little pink in embarrassment after he blurted out that last part.

I couldn't help but let out a small chuckle. I was happy that his friendship with the girl I saw him kiss on the cheek that morning was confirmed. But I also felt ridiculous for reading him so incredibly wrong. He wasn't the womanizer I assumed him to be at all.

He cleared his throat and said, "Anyway. I've been meaning to ask you a few follow-up questions about how you got here. If that's all right with you."

"Okay," I said hesitantly. I had planned to seek more information by asking Mattie a series of questions, so I wasn't prepared to learn more through queries posited to me.

"Mattie told me that she gave you a brief rundown of how this place works, right?"

"I mean, yeah. I think I understand the bare minimum."

"And she told me that Janusz gave you the instructions necessary to come here."

"Yes."

"I hope you don't mind me asking, but why would he do that if you didn't have a Nirvana to visit and aren't sick yourself? Especially since he obviously hated it so much here?"

I gulped and felt my heart inside my throat. "Uh, well, Jonesy knew I was going through some stuff at my uncle's, and I had no real way to get out of the situation. That is until he gave me the instructions," I said, trying to be as vague as possible.

"Oh," he murmured, obviously wanting to ask more follow-up questions.

I interjected before he could and said, "Yeah, I think he just wanted to give me some kind of escape. But I have to be honest; I first thought the instructions were part of some meditative exercise. I never imagined it would bring me to . . . well, here."

I think we were both unsure of what to say next because it felt like several minutes passed before either of us spoke again.

"Do you mind if I ask you something?" I finally said.

"Sure. Whatever you want."

"Are you—are you sick?"

"Yes," he answered point-blank.

I was shocked. Harrison appeared to be so physically fit and healthy.

"Oh!" I couldn't hide my surprise. "I figured you were Mattie or Ralph's visitor."

"I know I may not necessarily look sick, but unfortunately, I am. I was diagnosed with hemochromatosis at a young age. Basically, my body absorbs too much iron from the food I eat. Unfortunately, the treatments I needed to undergo in order to survive got too costly, so my family made the decision to send me here," he said with a hint of disdain, leading me to believe he didn't necessarily agree with their choice.

"I'm sorry. I didn't know."

He looked away from me for a moment and lightly sighed before returning my eye contact. "It's fine. Mattie and Ralph aren't actually my aunt and uncle. Not by blood, anyway. The two of them kind of adopted me when I first got here. I was completely unprepared, and they welcomed me into their home with open arms. They've helped a lot of us here. I guess they're doing the same thing for you, even though you're here under . . . unique circumstances."

"So, that's why Jonesy stayed with them?"

"Yep."

"I figured that when Mattie said the sweatshirt I found in the spare room was his. I also found some smaller clothes. Do you know anything about who those belonged to?"

Before he could answer, Mattie walked into the room. "It's nice to see the two of you getting to know one another. What have you been talking about?"

"I've just been trying to clear up some of the confusion I figured Sera was experiencing. For starters, she thought I was your Samsara."

Mattie's chipper demeanor drastically changed before she said, "Oh. No, dear. My Samsara hasn't been back here in almost two decades." Her voice was low and sad. After a few silent seconds, she seemed to shake it out of her mind and said, "What other questions do you have? You can ask us anything."

"Um, I don't mean to be disrespectful at all, and I really have enjoyed my time here. But do you have any idea how I can get home? I don't want to spend *too* much time away from my family."

Harrison and Mattie darted concerned looks at each other before Mattie said, "I'm sorry. I have absolutely no idea how you can get back. Janusz didn't give you any advice on that?"

"No, nothing. He just gave me the instructions and told me to ask for you."

"Huh. So, he probably thought what I've been thinking—I've been considering registering you as my Samsara. That way, you might be able to go back and forth as you want. But—and I want to be completely honest with you—I don't know if it will work for reasons I explained before. I've never heard of another Samsara officially registering while already in Ananda, and I am hesitant to do that. Although my current Samsara hasn't come in a long time, if I officially change it, that's a way of solidifying that she'll never be back."

"I wouldn't want you to make that kind of sacrifice for me, especially if it doesn't work anyway. I couldn't ask you to take that chance. I mean, you barely know me." I was shocked she'd even consider such a thing.

"Maybe not, but I think through your connection with Janusz, I have grown to feel closer to you in a relatively short amount of time."

"Who was she? Your Samsara, I mean. If you don't mind telling me."

"Her name is Johanna. Her father went to college in America, and her family lived next door to us during that time. Her mother and I became fast friends. After her dad finished school, they all moved back to South America. But we made it a point to stay in touch through monthly letters, and I planned a vacation there every other year or so. With Ralph's asthma, extensive travel was pretty hard on him, so he never came with me. Plus, he wasn't as close to the family as I was." She paused momentarily to take a breath. "Anyway, Johanna visited me several times after I came to Ananda. But that all changed when she met and fell in love with Ralph's Samsara here. I've heard that they are married and have kids now in the real world."

I was on high alert by that point. I knew there was always a chance that it was a coincidence that her registered visitor shared the same name as my mom and was also from South America. Plus, my mom had never mentioned anything about living in the United States as a kid. Still, it would make sense—especially given the connection Mama had with Jonesy. *But if this "Johanna" was my mother, that would mean Ralph's Samsara was . . .*

"What about Ralph's visitor?" I uncontrollably blurted out. Then, I braced myself for the answer. Of course, I desperately wanted to know what it was, but I wasn't sure what I would do with the information once I received it. At the same time, the possibility that I might soon understand the link between Jonesy, Mattie, Ralph, my parents, and Ananda in general caused a shiver to rush down my spine.

"Do you want to answer that one, dear?" Mattie asked Ralph as he walked into the room.

"What's that?"

"Sera asked what the name of your Samsara was," she clarified.

"Oh." He took a puff of his inhaler and said in strained voice, "It's Clark."

I gasped. Both of my hands flew up to my mouth in shock. What my parents said about the "random" encounter they had at a grocery stall wasn't true, or at least that wasn't the whole story. The fact that my parents had been to this secretive world made me dizzy with surprise. For one thing, my dad was too afraid to travel outside of the country. *How the hell did he get the courage to cross over to a whole other dimension?* My eyes wandered as my brain continued to conjure up similar thoughts.

"What is it, Sera?" Harrison asked, grounding my gaze by placing his hand lightly on my knee.

"Um . . ." I awkwardly cleared my throat. "I know this might sound crazy, but I think—I think your visitors are my parents. I don't know how that's even possible, but—" My voice was shaking like crazy.

"Oh my God!" All three people around me exclaimed. To my dismay, Harrison removed his hand to bring it up to his own mouth.

The house was quiet for a while as we processed the revelation.

"I can't believe I didn't notice the resemblance right away. You're the spitting image of her . . . I used to tell her all the time that she looked like Audrey too. Your mother, I mean," Mattie said, affectionately stroking my face. "How strange to think of my little Johanna as a mother."

I laughed. "She's a pretty experienced one too. She's had a lot of us."

"Is that right?" Mattie muttered, backing away and staring at me.

"Well, now it makes more sense why Janusz would send her to you, Matts," Harrison eventually said.

"I suppose. But that still doesn't explain why Janusz sent her here if she isn't sick," Ralph muttered.

I knew then I had to tell them the truth, but I self-consciously stared at the floor as the words came out of my mouth. "Uh, I think I know why," I said quietly. Like Kailas, I felt like I could trust these people with Mama's secret. She obviously meant a lot to Mattie, and I couldn't see her husband or "nephew" doing anything to hurt someone she loved so much. I also questioned their ability to relay a message to the real world about her illegal status, even if they wanted to.

"You see, my uncle became increasingly violent toward me, and I had no way of getting away from his farmhouse. I was basically trapped there. And I couldn't tell anyone about the abuse because he told me that if I told anyone, he would report my mom for being an illegal immigrant. With her deportation, my aging father wouldn't be able to take care of my siblings by himself, so they'd all end up in foster care. Or at least that's the scenario my uncle scared me with."

"That's terrible," Mattie commented.

"Yeah. Well, when Jonesy learned that I was in trouble, he had the friend he was staying with slip the handwritten instructions to me."

"I thought he was staying with your uncle?" Ralph said.

"He was but . . ." I stopped talking when Mattie put her hands over mine. I hadn't realized they were shaking.

"It's okay, sweetie. Take your time." She gave me a reassuring look.

Her maternal touch calmed my nerves a little. I shook the errant hairs that had fallen from my bun out of my face before looking up at my eager audience.

Her comforting hands remained over mine as I continued, "Well, I guess I'll have to start from my earliest point of view. I was surprised by his presence on the farm when I arrived at the beginning of the summer. I assumed he was just another worker my uncle hired to help him around the farm. But I had never known him to hire such a frail individual, and, to my knowledge, Jonesy was also the first worker who basically lived at my uncle's house—he didn't even let the others into his home. But I wouldn't dare explicitly question any of this. My uncle didn't like me prying into his business. However, I finished my chores early one night, and I walked in on them, um . . ." I paused.

What if he never came out to them? Sure, he wasn't alive to tell them himself, but it still didn't feel right for me to say anything about it on his behalf.

Mattie, catching on to my hesitation, jumped in and asked, "Are you trying to say that they were a couple? Don't worry. Janusz was very open about his sexuality."

"Oh, okay," I said, relieved. "Well, yeah. I guess something romantic was going on. Anyway, one morning, I caught my uncle secretly crushing up pills and putting them in Jonesy's coffee. Oh, wait. I should go back."

I took another deep breath before continuing, "My parents came over for breakfast one day, and I instantly noticed the familiarity they seemed to have with Jonesy. I wasn't sure how they knew each other; obviously, it makes sense now. Then, a few days after that, I heard Mama and Uncle Ford talking. My mom said something about Jonesy choosing to leave a place because he didn't want to continue suffering. Again, all of this makes a lot more sense to me now. But I was totally in the dark at that point. Then, I heard Jonesy and my uncle loudly arguing. Jonesy basically said he wanted to die and was upset that he was somehow getting better."

"I can imagine that would be incredibly confusing if you didn't understand the background context," Ralph said, with sympathy in his eyes.

"Yes. I put two and two together, and I realized my uncle was giving him medication without his knowledge. I decided the only person I could tell was my mom. So, I paid one of the workers to take me to see her one day. I told her everything, and she and my dad quickly 'shooed' me out of the house as they developed a plan to get Jonesy out of my uncle's care. Jonesy mysteriously disappeared not long after, and that's when my uncle became violent. I don't know how he learned about my mother's involvement, but he blamed her for his disappearance. He didn't have access to her, which I'm thankful for, but due to my resemblance to her, he would call out her name while beating me."

"I'm so sorry that happened to you, Sera," Mattie said, squeezing my hands tighter. "Thank you for being brave enough to tell us that."

I was suddenly aware of Harrison's silence. I looked over at him, but he was absently staring out the kitchen window. I was a little hurt by his lack of concern, but I didn't regret saying all of it. Mattie and Ralph deserved to know everything that came out of my mouth. After all the kindness they had shown me, I owed it to them to provide some clarity and closure.

I didn't know what else to do, so I just kept talking. "I never fully understood why Jonesy had to stay with my uncle and his friend. I often wondered why he didn't just go back to Poland to be with his family. He didn't tell me a lot about his personal life, but he did mention it could be hard at times to be biracial in his country. But I figured he'd want to be around family when he knew he was actively dying."

"Well, I'm sure Janusz would've gone back if he could. From what he shared with me, he was close with his mother and sisters. But they, unfortunately, were led to believe that he had died when he came here. That's the easiest way for most of us to explain our sudden absence from your world. Aside from our own Samsaras, of course, and medical professionals, who are typically the people who first introduce the idea of Ananda to dying patients, we are not allowed to speak about this place with outsiders before arriving."

Mattie clearly did not want to talk about Jonesy's past anymore because she wasted no time asking, "What was the name of this friend he stayed with after leaving the farm?"

"Her name is Kailas. I guess she's an old friend of his and my parents."

"Wait. What did you just say?" Harrison said, his eyes darting back to me.

I was surprised that this was the part of the conversation he wanted to be a part of. But I answered him. "Jonesy was staying with a friend named Kailas. She helped my mom get him out of the farmhouse. She would also sneak onto the farm from time to time to give me updates on his health. She's the one who passed me Jonesy's instruct—"

Before I could finish, Harrison got up from the table. He slammed the door on his way out.

Surprised by his behavior, I quickly said, "I'm so sorry. I didn't mean to upset anyone."   "It isn't your fault, but maybe that's enough for the day," Ralph said as he made his way outside.

Mattie didn't say anything; she just exited the kitchen and headed toward her bedroom. I watched for a while from the window as Ralph attempted to console Harrison. I eventually went upstairs to find a sweatshirt.

When I looked back out the window, Ralph was no longer with Harrison, so I headed out to apologize.

Chapter 10 – A New Adventure

He was sitting on the fence that bordered Mattie and Ralph's property. His back was to me, and he was staring at the horizon. Before I approached him, I paused to watch his hair blow in the breeze. I noted the tint of red that shined in response to the light of the setting sun.

"Hey," I said as I placed my hand on his shoulder to alert him of my presence.

"Hey, uh . . . I'm sorry about that," Harrison said softly. He glanced at me before gazing back toward the water.

"No! I'm sorry. I didn't mean to upset you."

"It's not your fault. You obviously didn't know."

"To be honest, I still don't know what I said to make you angry."

He turned his body around to face me. "Oh!" His eyes were big and focused on the sweatshirt I was wearing. "That's actually mine. I completely forgot about it."

I reached to pull it back over my head. "I'm sorry. I just found it in the spare room. Do you want it back?"

"Nah. You can keep it. You really should ask Mattie to take you shopping, though. I'm surprised she hasn't already." I could tell he was trying to divert the conversation away from himself.

I refused to take his bait and asked, "Do you want to talk about whatever it was I said that made you so upset?"

He took a deep breath. "My Aunt Kailas was my guardian in the real world. She was the one who decided to send me here. In hindsight, I'm kinda glad that she did, but I still resent that I didn't have a choice in the matter. She's also my Samsara but hasn't come in a really long time. Sometimes I wonder if she can't face me because she feels ashamed that she couldn't afford to take care of me."

She had never mentioned having a nephew, and although I had only been in her home once, I'd scanned it as thoroughly as I could and didn't see any evidence of his existence in there.

"Yeah. My medical bills were getting to be too much for her, so she decided to send me here. I suppose she might feel guilty about that? I don't know. I understand why she made the decision that she made, but it does also feel like she kind of abandoned me."

It was nice to see his vulnerable side. It demystified him in a way, and I was able to see him as an actual person—not some kind of intangible, perfect specimen. "I definitely know that feeling. It sucks," I said.

"And now I have confirmation that my aunt can never come back, whether she wants to or not."

"What do you mean?"

"Because she passed the instructions to you. That's part of the agreement Samsaras are required to sign. They have to promise not to tell anyone about this place. If they do, they are permanently banned."

"How does anyone know?"

"When you agree to be a Samsara, you agree to be under surveillance 24/7 while back in the real world."

My heart started racing. "Does that mean the authorities know about me?"

"No. You weren't associated with this place at the time, so they had no business to see or hear you."

"Oh. But wasn't it Jonesy who technically told me?"

"Well, no. I've thought about that. My aunt was already a registered Samsara, so from the higher-up's perspective, Jonesy was just writing the instructions down for her, someone they already knew was aware of Ananda. Nothing against the rules occurred until after she handed them to you."

I never would have accepted the piece of paper if I knew what Kailas was giving up by giving it to me. My stomach panged with guilt that I had selfishly accepted the instructions without inquiring what the repercussions would be for her. "I'm really sorry for digging up some old, painful memories."

"Is she doing okay?" he asked.

"Um, yeah. I think so. When I first met her, she was covered in grease, and I didn't know her profession at the time, so that made me a little concerned."

"Yeah, that sounds like her." He smiled.

"I also went to her house once, and it seemed really nice. Small, but nice and clean. Not at all like her dirty hair and nails when she came to visit me on the farm."

"I'm glad she's doing all right," he said. A smile was still on his face. I thought it was sweet that he still cared for her wellbeing. "I'm also happy that she moved back to Wisconsin. That was always her true home."

I was too distracted to fully hear his last comment. Instead, I said, "I have to be honest with you, though. She did make comments about Jonesy's medical bills draining her savings. So, I can't say for sure what her financial situation is like. But he's obviously gone now, so maybe she can start saving up again?"

"Damn. I still can't believe Janusz is gone."

"I know. I try to remind myself that he's in a better place . . . wherever that might be." I grimaced as the statement left my lips. Mama would be heartbroken if she ever heard me being skeptical about heaven and God. But it dawned on me at that moment—I wondered how and why she was possibly okay with a place like Ananda. Its very existence served as an alternate to the heaven she profusely threatened our "eligibility" into when my siblings and I were acting up.

"Yeah," he said as he faced the water again. My internal line of questioning paused when I saw the reflections of the waves playfully bouncing along his delicate collarbone. The fingers of my right hand instinctively stretched out to touch the silver beams on his skin, but I stopped myself before my arm raised toward him.

When I didn't say anything, he continued telling me about his family. "I never knew my dad, and my mom died when I was little. She also had iron overload disease. For as long as I can remember, she and I lived with Aunt Kailas, who is her sister, in Minneapolis. When she eventually contracted liver cancer, my aunt and I were forced to watch her die a prolonged and painful death. I have wished a thousand times that a doctor would have talked to her about coming here, but I obviously can't change it now. I'm just glad someone mentioned it to my aunt when I got worse, so she didn't have to suffer through watching another loved one rot away. Besides relieving that burden, my absence also allowed her to move back home to Wisconsin a few years ago. Like I said, I've always understood why Aunt Kailas sent me here, especially since she couldn't afford the expensive medications and treatments that I needed. This was the only choice she had."

I was now taking in everything he was saying. Especially that the three of them lived in Minnesota, and that Kailas had only somewhat recently moved back to our home state, since both facts could explain why I hadn't met her before—my parents were obviously busy the last couple of years, so it made sense that they wouldn't have had time to "hang out," even with an old, dear friend.

Although listening intently, part of my mind was still on the big question regarding Mama's acceptance of Ananda. So, in an attempt to see if he had any insight on that matter, I asked, "Have Mattie or Ralph talked to you about my parents?"

"No, not really. But I've seen pictures, and Mattie is right. You look so much like your mom. Same beautiful black hair and alabaster skin."

I blushed at his compliment. "Thanks." I laughed awkwardly. Biting my lip, I looked at the ground.

"I'm serious, Sera," he said as he moved my chin to make me look up at him. "You're gorgeous." His hand lingered on my face for a moment. He was inching toward me, and my heart was racing in anticipation of him kissing me.

Before he could, Mattie yelled from an open window, "Are you two all made up now?"

He and I both jumped a little at the sound of her voice. It was almost like we'd forgotten we weren't the only two people in this world.

"Yeah, Matts. All good!" Harrison softly smiled and yelled back.

"Good," she said as she closed the window. I couldn't clearly see her face, but it looked a little like she winked at me.

He hesitated but reached toward me once more, brushing a few pieces of wind-blown hair behind my ear. He then rested his fingers on my chin for a second time, and he rested his forehead against mine. My hopes were rising again that he was going to kiss me until he quickly pulled away, looked down at his watch, and asked, "Do you want to go somewhere?"

Before I could answer, he jumped off the fence and was facing me with his hand outstretched. I didn't hesitate; I nodded with enthusiasm and grabbed it.

We hopped in his car and took off on our little adventure. We listened to music I recognized from the real world as we drove. The windows were rolled down, and I laughed as I struggled to keep my hair pressed firmly against my head with my hands. He was more prepared and had secured his hair back with a ponytail holder. We engaged in small talk as we drove up a massive canyon. A few times after he switched the gears of his manual vehicle, his hand would linger on the shift, and he'd gently caress my left hand with his pinky. I obviously wasn't familiar with this kind of physical attention, but I acted on instinct. To encourage him and reciprocate my interest, I shuffled as close as possible to his body while still being strapped in my seat.

"We're here!" Harrison said after a while. He abruptly put the car in park and pulled me out of the trance I was currently in, shocked and excited by his small indication of affection.

"Where are we?" I looked around and saw nothing but rocks.

"It's a surprise. Come on!" He grabbed my hand, and I followed as he guided me through twists and turns. He would occasionally stop to feel dents in the sediment. "We left markings the last time we were here together. We wanted to be sure that we could find it again." We walked around for a few moments longer before he exclaimed, "It worked! Here it is!"

I looked at the black hole before us, uncertain what he meant. I didn't see anything special. My emotions must have been written all over my face because Harrison chuckled and motioned toward it. "Trust me."

When we reached the inside of the cave, Harrison got down on his back. Still doubtful but interested in uncovering whatever surprise he had, I sprawled out beside him.

"Wait for it," he said. Within minutes, I realized where we were and gasped. The reflecting light bounced around our faces as the sun hit the crystals.

"I've never seen anything so beautiful," I said, my eyes wide. "This was the cave you and Jonesy camped out in?"

"Yep! I thought you might like to see it."

We continued watching the vibrant blue flecks dancing around the otherwise dark cave in silence. I recognized the specific shade of teal surrounding us. It was the same color as Jonesy's eyes.

I was lost in this thought when I noticed out of my peripheral vision that Harrison had rolled onto his side to face me. I did the same to meet his gaze. He began stroking my face and again tucking unruly pieces of hair behind my ear. My skin burned under his touch.

"Is this okay?" he whispered.

"Mhm," I responded, excited to see what would happen next.

He grabbed the back of my neck and brought his face closer to me.

"And this?" He grazed his soft lips against mine. Again, I answered affirmatively.

Due to my inexperience, I was worried about doing something wrong, but I just mimicked everything he did. When he playfully bit my lower lip, I bit his. When he brushed his tongue on my teeth, I did the same. I was grateful to be learning from such a good teacher. His small moans let me know that I was doing something right. My fingers eventually became tangled in his long hair, which I hadn't noticed fall down before. We continued, and I felt like I had blissfully lost myself until his hand slipped under the back of my shirt.

"Ah!" I flinched away, patting my shirt back down. The last thing I wanted was for him to discover the deformities across my back.

"What? What's the matter?" he asked with genuine concern.

"It's—it's nothing. I just . . ." For the life of me, I couldn't come up with a plausible explanation for my reaction.

"I'm sorry if I did something wrong. I haven't so much as intimately touched a girl since I've been here. I'm sorry if I got carried away and made you uncomfortable."

"No, no. You didn't. I just—can we just go?"

"Yeah, of course."

We drove back to Mattie's without saying anything. I felt him looking at me from time to time, but I couldn't bring myself to look back. I was so embarrassed by my actions. I was also too busy cursing out my uncle inside my head. *Fuck you. Fuck you for ruining this for me.*

I was surprised when he parked in front of the house and got out of the car instead of driving off. "Sera. Can we please talk about this?"

"I told you it has nothing to do with you. It's fine. Thank you for taking me there. I'm just tired, okay?" Without letting him get another word out, I rushed inside to the spare room and closed the door.

He must have stayed to talk with Mattie and Ralph because I didn't hear his car pull away for a few hours. I prayed they weren't talking about what had happened.

My prayers, it seemed, went unanswered. "Sera? Sweetie? Can we talk?" Mattie asked. She was lightly tapping on my bedroom door.

I rolled my eyes but opened the door. "What's up?" I said as if I didn't already know what she was coming to talk about.

"Do you want to tell me about what happened in the cave? Harry is a nice boy. He feels terrible that he might have done something to cross the line with you."

"No, he didn't. I swear."

"Well, what was it then?"

"It's embarrassing."

"I understand. Just know that if you want to talk about it, I'm more than willing to listen."

I realized then that she reminded me of Kailas. Not in appearance, Mattie was over a foot taller than Kailas and had blazing red hair that spiraled around her face—which she swore was naturally curly. But I'm pretty sure I smelled the faint scent of an at-home perming kit when she got close enough to me. It was their energies that matched. They both had their own feminine touches, but, at the same time, they had a lot of masculine qualities as well. It suddenly made sense to me why Harrison would gravitate toward someone who reminded him of his aunt in the real world.

She was about to leave, but I stopped her. "Wait, Mattie?"

"Yes, dear?"

"I—I freaked out because I didn't want Harrison to see…these." I lifted the back of my shirt to reveal my scars.

"Oh, Sera! You poor thing. Does it hurt?"

"Only the ones from the last time." I put my shirt down, and the two of us sat on the bed. She gently touched my shoulder.

"I assume your uncle—"

"Yes." I cut her off before she could ask the full question.

She took a deep breath in and out. "Sweetie, you can't grow closer to Harry if you continue to conceal your insecurities. I guess you have to decide how important he is to you."

"If he wants anything to do with me anymore. I know I really freaked him out."

She kissed her teeth and said, "He'll come around. Especially if you tell him the truth."

"I'll think about it. Thanks, Mattie."

"Anytime. Good night, dear." She turned off the light and shut the door behind her.

Chapter 11 – Matching Scars

I dreamt that night about showing the scars to him, and he wasn't disgusted by the sight of them. Instead, he wrapped me in his arms and apologized that my uncle had done such horrible things to me.

The next morning, Harrison was outside in the yard again, and I hoped my dream had predicted the future. Mattie was right. If I wanted to continue to develop a relationship with him, I'd have to explain myself. I watched him work for a while as I reminisced about how it felt to have his lips against mine. Finally, I took a deep breath and resolved to join him outside and show him what I was so insecure about.

He was wearing headphones, so I cautiously tapped his shoulder, not wanting to startle him. After a few seconds, he paused his music and pulled them down around his neck.

"Hey," I said awkwardly. "Do you mind taking a quick break? I'd like to explain what happened yesterday."

We walked over to the fence he'd sat on the previous day. Before I began speaking, I noticed how intensely my hands were shaking. He must have seen as well because he clutched them in his own.

"What is it?" His light brown eyes were staring deep into my soul, begging for some kind of confession.

"I totally understand if you don't want to continue getting to know me or whatever. But I think you deserve to know the truth." I took a deep breath in and out. I didn't know why, but tears had started forming in the corner of my eyes. "Ugh. Okay. I freaked out because I was scared for you to see these." I lifted my shirt the same way I had in front of Mattie the night prior.

"Jesus, Sera," he said as he pulled the shirt up a little higher to see even more of the scarring. "Did your uncle do this to you?"

"Yes." I pulled it back down and faced him again, wiping away a few tears. "I didn't want you to see my deformities and think less of me."

Just like in my dream, he wrapped me in his arms and lightly kissed the top of my head. "First of all, you are not deformed. And second, I could never think less of you. Especially for something like being the victim in an environment you had no control over."

I continued to weep as he comforted me. I reveled in his wonderful natural scent—a mixture of sandalwood, saltwater, and sweat.

When I had calmed down a little, he released me. "You know, I have scars of my own." He lifted the front of his shirt to reveal markings on his chest.

"What happened?"

"When I was younger, my mom and I got into a really bad car accident. She lost control of the car when she swerved to avoid a deer that appeared out of nowhere. I wasn't wearing a seatbelt, so I went through the windshield. I got stuck in the glass around here." He swiveled his body to show me even more scars on his back. "We all have our own stories and histories, Sera. I want to know everything about you. If you couldn't tell, I kinda like you." He pulled me in and lowered his head to plant a soft kiss on my lips. I was delighted as my fingers once again tangled in his hair.

Now that I allowed him to, his hands were exploring the permanent bumps on my back. "I'm so sorry that happened to you," he said, momentarily pulling away from me. "I'm so glad you're safe and away from that monster."

Not wanting it to end, I eagerly grabbed him and continued kissing him.

Suddenly, we were interrupted by an unfamiliar voice. "Umph!" the stranger coughed to make his presence known.

Harrison and I pulled apart, and he wiped at his mouth with the back of his hand, his cheeks turning red from embarrassment.

"Oh. Hey, dude!" He high-fived the rat-faced person before us. I couldn't help but stare at the overly gelled points that his dark hair formed. "Sera, this is my buddy, Judge. We live in the same apartment complex. He comes to help me around the yard from time to time."

While I was interested to learn more about where Harrison lived, I knew this wasn't the time or place, as it was clear from the weed whacker Judge was carrying that they had work to get done. Instead of inquiring more, I reached out my hand to shake his, which he accepted. "Nice to meet you," I said. "I'll leave you guys alone to finish the yard work."

I left to go back inside, but I turned around before opening the door and playfully blew a kiss in Harrison's direction. He reacted with a wink and smile. My newfound confidence even surprised me.

I was sitting at the dinner table, pondering what I could do to fill up the time it would take them to conclude their duties when Mattie walked in.

"Just the girl I was looking for! Do you wanna go shopping? Harry brought it to my attention that we were making you wear hand-me-down clothes. I'm sorry. I honestly didn't even think about it until he said something."

I looked down at the clothes I had put on that morning. But then I remembered that I didn't have any money. It was the first time that currency came to my mind since I arrived in Ananda. Embarrassed by my lack of fortune, I lied and said, "I don't mind. I'm just grateful that you and Ralph are letting me stay here."

"Come on. We can have a girl's day! It'll be fun."

I kept trying to convince her that it wasn't necessary, but no matter how hard I tried, she wouldn't let it go. Soon she had backed me so far into a corner that I had no other option but to tell her the truth. "Mattie, I don't have any money to buy new clothes."

"Oh, don't worry about that!"

"No. You and Ralph have already been more than gracious to me. I could never ask you—"

She interrupted me. "Things don't necessarily 'cost' us money here. Well, we don't work for it, at least. It's an inducement to come. Each Nirvana gets a certain quota each week downloaded onto this credit card thing." She lifted a small rectangle from her wallet to show me.

I looked carefully at the illustrations on the front of it. There was a word at the top in a language I didn't understand. Also, there was a syringe with flowers and a snake wrapped around it. Three symbols were near the bottom: an eye, an infinity symbol with sun rays coming off it, and two arrows in a circle.

I wanted to ask Mattie what each thing represented, but I was too excited by the idea of going on a shopping spree. "But I'm not a Nirvana. I'm not even officially a Samsara."

"I know. I have plenty left over in my account, and Harrison transferred some for you as well. He has extra now that he no longer has to pay a Samsara fee."

A wave of shame washed over me. No one had ever brought up the fact that the Nirvanas had to give up some of their money for the Samsaras. I was so angry that three of the nicest people I'd ever met were forfeiting funds for visitors that never came. But I didn't want to damper Mattie's mood by bringing this up. "Are you sure?" I eventually asked.

"Yes. Don't give it another thought. Now, let's go!" Mattie grabbed my hand and led me to her minivan.

As we drove, I was surprised by how much Ananda resembled the real world. Except for the almost cartoon-like surroundings I noticed on my first day in this world, of course. The streets were lined with small ranches like I was used to seeing back home. The mall that we eventually arrived at also lacked a certain amount of grandeur. I didn't know why, but I expected a larger-than-life shopping center like the Mall of America. Instead, it was just like the one in my hometown—a mishmash of rectangle buildings that surrounded the food court.

Regardless, I was excited. Mama only took us shopping once a year for Easter. At all other times of the year, I wore her old clothes.

"Where should we go first?" Mattie asked me.

"You pick!" I said back to her. Given the small amount of time I'd actually spent inside a mall, I wasn't familiar with any of the store names.

Mattie clearly did not have the same issue because we had several bags filled to the brim with new clothes before I knew it. I felt slightly guilty, but I tried to remember that we weren't spending money that anyone had worked hard for. Instead, it was given to the residents of Ananda in exchange for their agreement to permanently occupy it.

Recalling that fact, I was confused by all of the people working around the large shopping center.

"Mattie? If you're all given money, why do people work? What's the incentive?"

"That's a good question. Unless you come here over retirement age and/or with a disability that cannot be improved with the medication, you are contractually obligated to work. Which I suppose makes sense. If no one worked, this place wouldn't operate anything like the real world. And that's the whole point."

I had a lot of fun as Mattie dragged me from store to store, but I often got distracted by the other people around us. In addition, I couldn't help but categorize people in my mind as either a Nirvana or a Samsara, which wasn't an easy task because not many people outwardly exuded sickness. When I did see someone who clearly was ill, however, I would get even more lost in thought, trying to guess what they were suffering from.

Mattie had to repeat, "Sera? Sera?" several times to get me out of my own head. I apologized every time and tried harder to keep my focus on her. She was doing me such a kind favor; the least I could do was show her a little attention.

I felt less culpable when she got sidetracked by running into someone she knew, which seemed like almost everyone we passed. The constant stop and go irritated me a little at first. But then I thought back to Harrison and Jonesy, and I reasoned that each person who approached her was someone she and Ralph had helped after arriving for the first time. Obviously, I could empathize with them. I was the most recent "foster" the couple had taken in, after all.

I knew Mattie had officially accepted me as one of her own because she always referred to me as her niece. She introduced whoever was before her the same—as either her niece or nephew. It felt nice to be part of such a large "family."

After experiencing the whirlwind of being around someone as beloved as Mattie, I was grateful for the one-on-one time I had with her as we drove back to her house.

Harrison was still there when we arrived, and he helped bring all of the bags inside.

"I hope you know how much I appreciate all of this," I said after he dropped the last bag onto the living room floor.

"I know you do, Sera! And after everything you've gone through, you deserve to be a little spoiled from time to time," he said as he hugged me with one arm and kissed the top of my head.

"Well, thank you." I looked up and planted a kiss on his cheek.

"You're welcome. Are you going to show me what you got?"

"Oh! Good idea! Fashion show!" Mattie sang as she entered the room.

She and Harrison sat on the couch and watched as I switched outfits and paraded past them. They took turns complimenting each look. Mattie seemed to take extra pride in the ones she had picked out.

After I showed my last ensemble, Harrison invited me over for dinner at his place. I was excited to get a closer glimpse into his life, and I wanted to make our first meal alone, and my first official date, as memorable as possible. So, I laid out all of my new clothes and carefully considered what to wear. I wanted to look dressed up but not *too* dressed up. In the end, I decided to go with a pair of dark blue skinny jeans, a white tank top, and a small silk shawl that was black and covered with little flowers. I tied my hair up and threw on a pair of pink Converse shoes.

As I looked at myself in the mirror, I was reminded of how much I had changed since arriving in Ananda. Being in a supportive, safe home and having positive attention from Harrison had done a lot for my self-esteem. *Maybe I don't even want to return to the real world*, a small voice in the back of my mind started to say.

"You look amazing, Seraphine," Harrison said when I reappeared in the living room. He was still sitting on the couch, but Mattie had since gotten up and left. She returned shortly after and asked us to pose for a picture, which she took with an old Polaroid camera.

When the picture came out from the bottom of it, she fanned it vigorously and then looked at the finished product. "Now, you see that? This rusty old thing has a way of catching everyone's best angle."

She showed it to us, and I had to admit, he and I did look good together. I had never seen myself look so happy and full of life. Harrison, of course, looked as handsome as ever—with his subtle, inconspicuous smile, honey-brown eyes, and long hair hanging past his shoulders.

He held my hand as we walked out to his car, and he continued as he drove—letting go only when he needed it to shift.

I had no idea what to expect when it came to his living situation. He could have lived in a dump, in a lavish penthouse, or somewhere in between. When we pulled up to his building, I was happy to see that it wasn't a trash heap but also not Buckingham Palace. My parents had a little more money before my siblings were born, and they could afford to take me on miniature vacations. On one weekend, we went to visit my cousin at college. I was young, but I still remember that trip vividly.

His building looked a lot like hers did. The outside was covered in dark brick, with vines delicately growing up the walls. It was only five or six floors.

Harrison lived on the second floor, so it wasn't long before we walked up the stairs and stood in front of his door. I took a deep breath, anxious for what I was about to see inside. Remembering he had been raised by Kailas, whose home was immaculately tidy, I had high hopes for his level of cleanliness. I was happy to see that I was right as we walked into his unit. He led me to his large kitchen, and I sat down on a barstool by an island in the middle of the floor.

"What are we having for dinner?" I asked, watching him rummage through his fridge and pantry.

"Well, I remember you telling me that your mom was from Argentina, and I figured you must be at least a little homesick. Therefore, I thought I'd make you a meal that would remind you of her. So, while you and Mattie were shopping, I went out to get the ingredients. I'm going to try my hand at making *empanadas*! I've never made anything like this, so I'm sorry in advance if it turns out inedible." He set a paper bag on the island in front of me. I hadn't noticed him grab it from the car.

I was moved by his thoughtfulness, so I stood up and walked over to him. I grabbed his face between my two hands and softly kissed him. "I'm sure it'll be delicious. It's so sweet of you to put all of that thought into it."

"It's no big deal," he said humbly, but I could tell by the smirk on his face that he was proud of himself.

I often forgot that not everyone grew up with moms who could make such interesting and delicious food. "What kind of food would Kailas typically cook for you?" I asked as I sat back down near the island.

"Well, she always worked long hours down at the garage, so I mainly cooked dinner for myself. And with my condition, I had to be careful about what I ate. I made a lot of plain chicken with a side of vegetables."

"Hm. How flavorful," I joked.

"Yeah." He rolled his eyes and chuckled. While he laughed along with me at first, a slight sorrow washed over his face. And by the way his eyes were darting back and forth, I assumed he was going down a rabbit hole of bad memories, picturing his younger self eating meal after meal alone. "Yeah, those were pretty lonely times."

I felt bad for bringing the mood down, so I changed the subject and said, "Anyway, should we start making dinner? Do you need my help with anything?"

My tactics seemed to have worked because he quickly replied, "Oh. Yeah! Do you want me to show you the ingredients I got?"

As he carefully laid out each item before me, I was impressed to find out that he was actually making *empanadas mendocinas*. A dish specifically from Argentina, not just the run-of-the mill *empanadas* that can be found throughout the world.

"This is exactly how Mama made them!"

"That's right. I've noticed that you call your mom, 'Mama,'" he said, raising an eyebrow. "Is that an Argentinian thing?"

"Um . . . I don't really know." I hung my head in embarrassment. I was ashamed for sounding childish in front of him and not having a definite cultural excuse for it.

He turned away from the mixer in which he was starting to prepare the dough and lifted my chin with his clean hand. Then he "booped" my nose with the hand covered in flour and resumed his work. "I think it's really cute."

I was relieved by his reaction, and I playfully rubbed the flour off with the back of my hand. I had walked over to the mirror hanging on his wall to make sure I'd gotten it all off when, out of the corner of my eye, I saw a large cloud of flour erupt in the kitchen. Upon my return, I assessed the damage.

"Oh, no! What happened?" I couldn't help but laugh.

The figure in front of me covered in white laughed with me. "I don't know! I turned the mixer on, and this happened!"

"Let me help you!" I grabbed a nearby towel and started cleaning him up. After a few failed attempts at getting the residue out of his hair, I suggested that he take a shower. I offered to take over in the meantime. He resisted at first but then gave in.

Once he left, I found a broom and continued to clean up the mess. When the floor and counter were sufficiently clean, I began cooking. I hadn't made food like that in a while, but I tried my hardest to remember the steps Mama took when I would watch her make it.

After the dough was formed, I rolled it out, and, like I had seen my mother do thousands of times, I found a small bowl in the cupboard and used it to form several circles that would eventually be stuffed and sealed in a crescent shape. I then started working on the stuffing.

Apparently, it took Harrison a while to thoroughly wash his hair. I had finished stacking the beef mixture, a sliced hard-boiled egg, and a green olive by the time he reappeared. I was marveling proudly at my creations atop the stove when he snuck up on me. He hugged me from behind, and his damp hair left a pool of water on my shoulder.

"Whoa! That looks amazing!" he said as he embraced me. Then he looked around the kitchen and opened several drawers until he found a piece of paper I had blindly discarded during my cleanup. "And you did all of that without a recipe? Very impressive!"

I shrugged. "It wasn't that hard. I just remembered what Mama did when she made stuff like this. I'm super impressed by how authentic you wanted to be. You even got lard!"

He laughed. "Yeah, I've never cooked with that stuff before. To be honest, it kind of grosses me out. But I didn't want to Americanize it in any way, so I went for that over butter."

"Oh, you'll learn to love it after you have a bite of these babies," I said confidently. I walked over to the fridge to put the food in there while the oven continued to preheat.

When I resumed my position by the stove, he said, "Yeah? Well, right now, I'm craving a taste of something else." He grabbed my face and kissed me. It started as a small peck but became more passionate after I refused to let him pull away. I guess his wet, almost naked body caused me to go crazy. It was almost animalistic. His damp hair was engulfing my face, but I didn't care. I couldn't get enough.

It was evident that he felt similarly because I suddenly felt something hard against my thigh. The feeling of it startled me. Coincidentally, the oven chimed to alert that it was fully preheated.

"What's wrong?" he asked before he saw where I was staring. "Oh, shit. Sorry. I—I'll go change." He quickly used his hands to conceal it and headed toward his bedroom.

I felt slightly dizzy from the intense feelings I had just experienced, but I managed to remove the tray from the fridge, seal the balls of dough, and put them in the oven.

Chapter 12 – There's a First Time for Everything

"I'm sorry, Sera," he said as he walked back into the kitchen, fully clothed this time. He was rubbing a towel against his long curls.

"It's fine," I said, not knowing what else to say.

"Oh! I didn't mean about—well, yeah. I guess about that too. I was going to say that I'm sorry you had to cook everything. I didn't invite you over to make dinner for me!"

"I really don't mind. You accomplished your goal. I really did feel a connection to my mom as I thought back to memories we had together in the kitchen."

A loud *ding* rang out from inside his pocket. He took out his phone and asked, "How much time do we have left before those are ready?" He motioned toward the stove.

"I just put them in. You might want to check the recipe, but I think we leave them in for twenty minutes or so. Why?"

"A few of my buddies live in the apartment next door. You already met Judge, but I want you to meet the others. Is that okay?"

"Yeah, sure!" I was happy that he wanted to show me off to his friends. "But I don't think we should leave with the stove on."

"No, they're gonna come over here for a few minutes."

"Oh, okay. Cool!"

He typed something on his phone, and within a few seconds, there was a series of knocks at his door.

"Come in!" he yelled.

Two men came in carrying large black tarps. They effortlessly pinned the corners so that the ceiling, interior walls, and a majority of the carpet were covered. I shot a confused look at Harrison, but he was too busy helping to secure the blankets in his home. Shortly after that, a woman holding a baby walked in. I hadn't seen such a young child in Ananda before, and I made a mental note to ask Harrison about that later. I thought to myself, *Can you procreate here? Is the baby also sick?*

I could tell that Harrison wasn't as familiar with this procedure as the other two because he was noticeably out of breath when they finished. But he did his best to utter, "Judge, you already met, but Jared and April, this is Sera. She's the one I've been telling you about." I was surprised that he didn't kiss his female friend on the cheek, like he did with the girl on the beach.

Jared was tall and burly. He had long hair like Harrison, but he was strawberry blond, which I didn't notice in the muted apartment until several lamps were turned on.

Jared reached his hand out to me and said, "It's really nice to meet you." I smiled and nodded in agreement.

April, who was fully blonde and had a gnarly piercing in the middle of her lower lip, stepped toward me and offered her hand out. She said nothing as I shook it, and she didn't even bother to look at me.

"And who is this?" I asked her, referring to the baby she was holding. Still, she said nothing.

"This is little Berlin," Harrison responded after a few seconds of silence.

The child had blazing orange hair and, based on what I knew about biology, I figured that meant she belonged to April and Jared. She also had an adorable face and compelling energy. I almost couldn't stop myself from picking her up and giving her a little cuddle. Thankfully, I did resist this urge. To my surprise, it was Judge who grabbed her from April's grasp and said, "Here, baby. Come to daddy!"

I shot another look of confusion at Harrison, but he just nodded as if to say, "I'll explain later."

"Something smells good!" Jared said after taking a deep breath in.

"Sera made it. It's a traditional Argentinian dish," Harrison explained.

"Oh! I don't think I've ever had food from there. Is there any way we could join you? I don't mean to impose . . ." Jared said.

"Well—" Harrison started to say as he looked over at me.

"Sure!" I said, interrupting him. We had plenty to spare. Plus, Jared and Judge seemed nice enough, but April was acting extremely cold toward me. The last thing I wanted to do was reject them and make her hate me even more. I didn't know how close she was to Harrison, but I didn't want to risk ruining anything in case they were super tight. I had no personal experience, but I had seen enough television to know how powerful a female friend's opinion of a potential girlfriend could be.

I suddenly thought to warn the baby's parents, whoever they were. "It might be a little too spicy for her, though."

"She doesn't eat food like that yet," Judge said as he reached into a bag, grabbed a container, and dumped the contents on a plate in front of him. He carefully fed the green mush to the baby, spoonful by spoonful.

"Oh, right." I was never in charge of transitioning the food my siblings ate from one thing to the next when they were babies. But I felt kind of stupid about my ignorance, so I tried to distract them by suggesting that everyone else sit around the tiny dining table. I prepared the unexpected guests' plates in the kitchen. Ignoring my suggestion, Harrison came to join me.

"Are you sure you don't mind?" he whispered.

"I promise. It's totally fine."

"Okay. You're the best. Can I help you?" He helped me serve his friends, and I brought over his plate and mine. I nervously watched as they took their first bites.

"Oh, man. This is delicious!" Jared exclaimed.

"Mhm," Judge uttered and nodded his head.

"Yeah, excellent, Sera!" Harrison agreed. I was offended at first when I saw that he'd cut his serving in half, but I quickly remembered him telling me that he had to limit his red meat intake.

I looked to April to get her reaction. She was picking at her food with a fork, carefully separating the dough and bringing it up to her lips. I tried not to take offense at that; I guessed it might have just been spicier than the food she was used to.

Having assessed everyone else's opinion, I took my first bite, and I was pleasantly surprised by how delicious it was. *Thanks, Mama!* I thought in my head.

Just as we had served the meal, Harrison and I worked together to clean up the table. I was putting one of the last dishes in the sink when Jared came over.

"I can do the dishes!" he said with enthusiasm. He grabbed a towel hanging from the stove's handle and tossed it over his shoulder.

"Oh, no. You don't have to do that."

"It's kind of an unspoken rule in my family that the person who cooks never gets stuck doing the dishes. Please, I insist."

"Okay . . ." I said reluctantly.

He grabbed the two plates that were still full of uneaten food. "I'm sorry about this. I assume you know about Harrison's diet restrictions, and April is just a really picky eater. Please don't take it personally."

"It's okay. I understand." I didn't, however, when it came to April because my parents always taught me to clear my plate at someone else's house, whether I liked the food or not. But she obviously wasn't raised like I was.

Without the task of washing the dirty dishes, I leaned against the wall and watched Harrison as he played with Berlin. He held her with confidence, bouncing her up and down in his lap. She laughed and laughed when he made the funniest faces at her. He was a natural.

April was talking to him and Judge, but she stopped and started staring me down when she became aware of my presence. I tried to ignore her as I walked over to the table.

"Can I hold her?" I asked.

"Yeah, of course," Judge answered.

Unlike the woman I assumed was her mother, Berlin seemed to take a liking to me. I made my own silly faces at her as she was cradled in my arms.

"All right. Dishes are done!" Jared said, emerging from the kitchen.

"Okay, let's go," April said before walking toward me and yanking the baby from my arms.

The two men disassembled the tarps, rolled them up, and followed after her.

Harrison remained seated at the table, and he laughed lightly as he shrugged. Finally, we were alone again, and I sat down next to him.

"I have so many questions," I said.

"I figured you would." He let out another laugh.

"Uh . . ." I struggled to decide which inquiry I wanted to raise first. "Okay, okay. Who does that baby belong to? I figured by her strawberry blonde hair that Jared was the dad. But then, Judge said—"

"Ah. Yeah. That's a very complicated situation. First, I think I should explain a little more about April to you."

"All right."

"She is Judge's Samsara. I guess she was his girlfriend in the real world. Well, one time when she came to visit, Jared got drunk out of his mind and slept with April. He doesn't even remember it happening, but I guess she told him after the fact. Out of respect for Judge, no one has ever brought the question of the baby's paternity up to him. So, it's tough to say who the father is. But, like I said, Judge assumed it was his because he doesn't know about that one night. Oh, I probably should've mentioned that sooner. Yeah, Judge and Jared are brothers."

"Oh, shit!" They looked nothing alike, so I never would have guessed they were so closely related. "Do they both have the same parents?"

"Yeah, as far as I know. Unfortunately, it gets even more complicated because it's kind of against the rules for a Samsara and a Nirvana to produce a child. It's part of the agreement that both parties sign before a Nirvana comes here for the first time. They can engage in sexual activities, but they have to agree to abort it within the first trimester. I guess it goes against the head honchos' purpose to have a bunch of potentially sick, potentially healthy babies running around."

"I was going to ask you about that. When I saw Berlin, I realized that I hadn't seen a baby here before her."

"Yeah, and you likely won't see another one. Some Samsaras and Nirvanas, a group collectively referred to as 'Urvarata' ॐ who have the necessary and fully functional organs to carry a child, must get monthly pregnancy tests. April is one of them, and I still don't know how she was able to simultaneously conceal her pregnancy and secretly provide a urine sample from someone else. Obviously, I've never experienced it, but friends have told me the whole process is pretty invasive. Like a nurse physically watches you provide the . . . well, the . . . the pee." He cleared his throat like he was embarrassed for vaguely talking about female anatomy in front of me. "Anyway," he continued. "What those three are doing is incredibly dangerous. If the authorities found out about Berlin's existence and April's prolonged stay here, they'd probably all go to prison."

"Oh, my God."

"Yeah. That's why they have those big blankets. They surround any apartment the baby is in to conceal her squeals, laughs, and cries."

I wondered about their effectiveness but kept listening as Harrison continued to explain the whole situation to me.

"She doesn't trust you to keep her secret. That's why she was so cold to you."

"What? She thinks I'll rat on her involvement with Jared?"

"Yes, that. But I think April is also worried you'll report her to the authorities."

"That would be pretty hypocritical of me . . ."

"I know. I think she's also a little salty toward you because she's jealous. She has made her advances toward me, but I consistently rejected her. I'm not the kind of person who would betray my friend and do something with his girl."

Suddenly, it made sense why he didn't kiss her on the cheek. He didn't want to give her the wrong idea. The thought of her making a move on him made me burn with anger. "Hmmm . . ."

"I guess she hasn't given up on the possibility of us being together. She's also worried you're going to try to convince me to escape down to the real world."

I pondered for a moment and then said, "I would never ask that of you. Mattie told me all about what happens to the people who get caught trying to escape."

He was quiet for a bit himself before he said, "Plus, you like it here. Right? You're not planning on leaving anytime soon?"

"Oh! Um . . ." I was completely caught off guard, and I didn't know how to answer his questions at first.

Sure, now that a relationship is blooming between us, or at least I hope there is, I have flirted with the idea of staying in Ananda indefinitely. But what about my family? Surely there would come a time when they'd need me. And what about school? Shit. Since arriving here, I've been so concerned about getting back to my family that I haven't even thought about that. I guess I could just start later than I planned. I'd prefer not to do that, but I guess it is what it is. I also know that I'm not ready to part with Harrison just yet. Wait, but we don't even know how I'm going to get back in the first place! Ahhh! The whistle of the panic in my mind made me feel faint.

I had to put my elbow on the table, rest my forehead against my hand, and close my eyes to steady my vision.

"Are you okay?" he asked, rubbing my shoulder to comfort me.

I was so lost in thought that I had forgotten he was even in the room with me. Fortunately, his words and touch caused the high-pitched ringing in my head to stop. I absorbed the welcome silence for few more seconds before I finally collected myself. "Yes. I'm okay. Sorry. There's just a lot to think about. But yes, I do really like it here. I'm not planning to leave anytime soon. For one thing, we don't even know how I can go back. But if we do find a way, there are also things in the real world—like my family and college—"

"We have schools here!" he said, cutting me off. He apparently failed to hear or ignored my first reason for returning home. My first instinct was to be upset with him for this—but I quickly changed my mind and was kind of touched that he wanted to keep me in this alternative world with him. Plus, it would be a win-win for me if I could attend college *and* stay with him a little longer. But that perfect situation wouldn't come without challenges.

"We still don't really know what the rules are about me being here. Wouldn't my enrollment risk the authorities learning of my presence and the unique circumstances surrounding it?"

"Samsaras are allowed to take classes. I know you aren't technically one, but I think you could probably lie. Although, I don't know how that would work since you aren't officially registered to be here. I don't know. We'll have to ask Mattie. She knows more about all that stuff than I do."

"Yeah, let's not worry about any of it right now. I'll talk to Mattie when I get back to her place," I said.

"Speaking of Mattie, she knows you're with me. I don't think she'd worry if you decided to spend the night over here. But no pressure."

"Oh! Well . . ." I was a little dumbfounded that he had managed to throw yet another curve ball into our conversation. And I was hesitant to agree because I had never spent the night with a guy, and I didn't know what that insinuated. I liked him a lot, but I wasn't ready to do *it*.

"I'll sleep on the couch!" he said as if sensing my hesitancy. "Scouts honor!" he shouted while doing the three-finger salute, puffing his chest, and looking up at the wall like he was a soldier speaking to his drill sergeant. Then, he relaxed his body, made eye contact with me again, and smiled innocently.

I felt better after that added clarification. Plus, I wasn't a monster. I couldn't say no to his devastating charm. I don't think anyone could. "Well, all right," I said, lightly giggling and rolling my eyes.

I changed out of my clothes and into his basketball shorts and t-shirt. I didn't have a toothbrush, so I furiously brushed at my teeth with my finger. Then, I joined him in the living room, where he was sitting on the couch and flipping through channels. He stopped when he found a station playing Jonesy's favorite movie, *Office Space*. It had just started.

"Have you ever seen this?" he asked.

"Just once."

"Was that at the recommendation of Janusz?"

I chuckled as I thought back to Jonesy's impressions of the characters. "Yeah! How'd you know?"

"Oh, he was more than a little vocal about his affinity for the film."

I sat on the floor. Within a few seconds, Harrison's fingers were running through my hair, which I had taken down after changing into his clothes.

"Mmm. That feels good."

"Did you have a good day today?" he asked.

"I did. It was fun. Well, except being around April. But I like Judge and Jared!"

"Yeah, they're good dudes. Well, except for the whole infidelity thing."

"But like you said, it sounds like Jared doesn't recall it ever happening. Is it possible April lied?" I lightly inquired.

"It's hard to say with her." Then, he quickly changed the subject and said, "Anyway, the guys seemed to like you as well."

"Oh, I meant to ask. What are Jared and Judge sick with? Is it a genetic thing?"

"You know, I'm actually not sure. They're really private about it. I asked once, but it was clear they didn't want to talk about it. I haven't brought it up since. However, through bits and pieces disclosed over the years, I've concluded that they must have been exposed to some kind of dangerous chemical or drug. They told me that their parents were alcoholics and drug addicts. But that's all I know for sure."

"Huh."

He switched back to his previous topic of conversation. "The two of them can be idiots sometimes, and they have never met a girl I'm interested in before. So, I was worried about how they'd act."

"Oh, you're interested in me, are you?" I said jokingly, laying my head in his lap and looking up at him.

"Well, if you're questioning it, I guess I haven't done a good enough job showing you just how interested I am." He dipped his head to meet mine, facing the opposite direction. He started kissing me, and after a while, I rose to my feet and then sat on his lap. We continued, taking occasional breaks to catch our breath. Eventually, we were both horizontal. The feeling of his heavy body on mine only elevated my desire to ravish him. He went to put his hair back in a ponytail, but I stopped him.

"Uh-uh. I like it," I said as I grabbed his head and brought him back down to me.

I felt the same hardness against my thigh that I had felt earlier that night, but it didn't shock me this time. Before I knew it, his fingers began to slide down the front of my pants.

"Is this okay?" he asked before continuing.

I wasn't sure what was going to happen, but I was excited to find out. "Yeah," I said breathlessly.

"Oh!" I exclaimed as he slipped a finger inside me.

Startled by my reaction, he stopped and said, "You okay? Does it hurt?"

"No, it's good."

He continued moving it back and forth until I felt a fire inside me that I had never experienced before.

The audible pleasure I exuded must have been loud because he covered my mouth with his other hand. I could tell he was smiling as he whispered, "I'm glad you're enjoying yourself. But we don't want the whole apartment complex to know. We don't have the noise-canceling blankets anymore." He lightly kissed my ear. Then, after taking a momentary break, he continued until I felt that explosive fire in my belly again. He left to wash his hands, but we started kissing again when he returned.

That was when I started getting anxious. Of course, I wanted to reciprocate, but I didn't know what to do.

I figured it was better to just ask him rather than embarrass myself through trial and error. So, I pulled my face away from him and admitted, "I . . . I don't know what I'm doing, Harrison."

He looked back at me, puzzled. "What do you mean?"

"Like what to do to you to make you . . . you know."

"Oh! Don't worry about it. I'm perfectly happy to keep doing this," he said as he pulled my face toward his.

"No." I stopped him. "I want to know. Please show me."

He looked at me for a few seconds, waiting for me to change my mind. But, when he was convinced of my sincerity, he got up to get something from his room. When he sat back down, he slowly lowered his underwear and shorts and squirted some kind of lotion onto himself. He took my hand, wrapped it around him, and rubbed it up and down. I repeated the motions he had demonstrated until his back arched, and he let out his own sounds of pleasure. He then asked me to get him a paper towel, which I did. I was sheltered, but my parents had at least briefly told me how a baby was made in a mother's womb, so I knew what liquid he was cleaning off his stomach.

"Did I do it right?"

Instead of audibly answering me, he lightly grabbed my head and pressed his lips once more against mine.

When we came up for air next, the movie was over, and a new one I didn't recognize had started playing. At some point, I must have fallen asleep. But I woke up the following morning alone. I got up slowly, confused for a second about where I was.

"Good morning!" Harrison entered the room with two cups of coffee in his hand. "You know, you sleep like a rock. I was worried that I was going to wake you when I got up to go into my bedroom, but you didn't even flinch."

"Yeah," I said, slightly embarrassed. "My mom used to joke that I could sleep through a hurricane."

"After last night, I'm inclined to agree!" he said as he handed me one of the cups.

"You could have just stayed here with me," I said.

"No. I promised that we'd sleep in separate places. I had intended for you to have the bed, but you seemed comfortable here. Plus, like I said, I don't think I could've woken you up even if I wanted to!"

I took my first sip of the hot beverage before me and made a funny face at him. "Anyway, what are your plans for the day?"

"I—" he started to answer, but I unintentionally cut him off.

"I feel silly that I haven't asked you this yet, but I remember Mattie telling me about how everyone young and fit enough is required to work. Does the yard work you do for her and Ralph count for that?"

"No. I just do that stuff because it's hard for Ralph to be outside for extended amounts of time. All of the pollen makes his asthma even worse than normal. I know he has unlimited access to inhalers, but I figure, why should he have to go through that if he doesn't have to?"

"So, what is your official job then?"

"I don't actually have one. I'm currently enrolled in school, so I'm exempt for the time being."

I felt guilty that I didn't already know that about him. "Oh! You've never mentioned anything about that. I guess that possibility never crossed my mind because it seems like, for the most part, you spend a big chunk of your days at Mattie and Ralph's."

"Well, the seasons here, at least in the Midwest section, are generally the same as in the real world. It's summertime, but classes are starting again soon."

"Oh! Wow. You know, I didn't even think about the possibility of attending school here before yesterday, nevertheless the timeframe we'd be dealing with."

"I think it's normal for this place to scramble your brain a little bit when you're first introduced to it. Especially for someone like you who had no idea where you were going."

"I guess. I still feel a little foolish, though. I've gone through the process of having summer break and then going back to school in the fall for the majority of my life."

"True. But like I said, the seasons *generally* work the same, not completely. If I remember correctly, school would have already started in the real world." Harrison said as he finally sat next to me on the couch. I was comforted when he placed his right arm around me. I gratefully snuggled into it.

"So, what do you study then?" I asked.

"Biology, actually."

"Oh, cool! I've never been good at science. Or math, for that matter. What do you want to do with your degree?"

"I haven't officially decided. Sometimes I think about medical school, maybe vet school."

"Like a veterinarian?"

"Mhm."

Just like when I saw the baby yesterday, I was shocked at that moment because I realized I hadn't seen any animals in Ananda. Not in anyone's home or even in the wild. When I made this confession to him, he did his best to add clarification.

"That's another weird thing we have to agree to. We aren't allowed to have animals. I don't remember exactly what the contract said. But I remember reading something about the potential for allergens being too great. Like the higher-ups feel they are already giving us enough medication. So, they don't want to also give people allergy medicine for exposure to things they don't consider 'necessary.' It's different from the pollen that bothers people like Ralph. That can't really be avoided because trees are essential in cleaning the air. There are animals in the wild, but definitely not as much as in the real world. As far as dogs, cats, and other domestic animals go, there are centers where you can go to hang out with a bunch of them. That's where all of the vets work. Oh! Some officers also have K-9 companions."

"Oh, that's interesting." I had yet to see any police around, but that wasn't what piqued my interest. "What about horses?" I asked.

"I can't say for sure, but I'm guessing there might be some in the wild."

"What about at that center you were talking about?"

"I haven't seen any, but that's something else we can ask Matt—" He abruptly stopped talking.

"Wha—" I started to ask him what the matter was, but he motioned for me to join him in silence with a finger pressed to his lips. Then, I heard the distant hum of some kind of alarm. As the sound grew closer to us, he took my hand and ran to his neighbor's apartment.

Before I could ask what was going on, April, Berlin, and I were crammed into a tiny crate in the back of a closet. It was lined with dozens of layers of the blankets that Judge and Jared had brought into Harrison's apartment.

We sat in darkness, piled on top of each other, for several minutes before there was a knock on the front door. "Jared and Judge Jones?" said a muffled voice I didn't recognize. They responded and confirmed their identities. "All right. Can I please have your diagnosis cards?" the strange voice continued.

They must have complied because the next thing I heard was, "Okay. Good. Show me where you keep your meds, please."

I thought back to a conversation I'd had with Mattie. She told me about the check-ups or inspections they all were subjected to. I guess the leaders of this world wanted to make sure the Nirvanas were taking their medication as the doctor prescribed. And they wanted to study their bodies to see just how they reacted to the medicine. But when she first explained all of this to me, I figured they had to go to clinics like people in the real world did. I was quickly learning that assumption was wrong, or at least partially.

The man, Jared, and Judge exchanged pleasantries, and then I heard him walk over and bang on Harrison's door. The idea of some stranger poking around his body, which I now felt some kind of weird ownership over, made my blood boil.

After several more minutes, the closet door swung open, and Judge quickly picked up Berlin and kissed her on the head.

Harrison walked in with a large bandage around his arm. "Everyone okay?"

"Yeah. All good," Jared replied.

"Sera?" he reached for me, and I nodded to reassure him that I was okay.

"Yeah, it was kind of cramped in here. But I'm good. Just a little confused." I was still staring at his bandaged arm, and I realized it was the first time I had seen him with short sleeves on. I then wondered if the bandage had been there all along.

Jared interrupted my thought pattern. "You didn't warn her about the Ikshana?"ॐ

"I didn't think to before I heard the siren." He grabbed my hand and led me out of the bedroom. I watched as Judge and Jared pulled the soundproof blankets from a separate closet and returned each one to its respective place around their apartment. They then pulled out all of Berlin's things—a crib, highchair, and various toys.

After this process was over, Harrison walked to and opened the brothers' front door. But he made sure I was concealed behind it while he paused and looked cautiously down each end of the hallway. Once he was assured of my safety, we rushed into his apartment.

"I can't believe I was such a fucking idiot. I'm so sorry, Sera," he said. He was sitting on the couch with his head in his hands.

"So, I think I know what just happened, but maybe I'm wrong." I sat down on the coffee table across from him. Slowly, he looked up at me. His hands were then resting together, covering his nose and mouth. "Jared said something about the 'Ikshana.' I remember Mattie telling me about how you Nirvanas have to undergo special inspections and testing by the leaders of Ananda. I'm guessing that's what just happened. Am I right?"

"Yes."

"I wonder why Mattie didn't warn me about these 'raids' or whatever before?"

"That's where I fucked up. The Ikshana don't search the homes of the older ones. They just go to a doctor's office every once in a while. I guess the bodies of us younger Nirvanas show the side effects more clearly or something. So, they are extra invested in us taking our medications as directed. I haven't studied how medications metabolize in the body yet, but I hope to understand it more clearly in the future."

I had no information to add at this point, so I remained silent.

He continued, "They also ensure that Samsaras aren't overstaying their welcome."

"What do you mean?"

"Well, the Ikshana want Samsaras to return to the real world every so often, so people in their lives don't start questioning their prolonged absences. Speaking of Samsaras, that's another reason they don't bother investigating the older peoples' homes—they don't want to waste their time. It's often the case that their Samsaras have come here permanently and become Nirvanas themselves, have chosen to actually die in the real world, or, as sad as this is, just stopped coming."

I thought about my parents, and I felt so sorry for Mattie and Ralph.

Somehow reading my mind, he said, "Oh, sorry. That wasn't a dig at your parents."

I didn't respond to what he said. My eyes were too focused on the large bandage on his arm. "What did that man do to you?"

"Agh." He tried to cover it with his large hand, but there was still visible white on each side of it. "Nothing unusual. Standard bloodwork." I had bloodwork done in the past, and it never required that large of a bandage. But I could tell he didn't want to talk about it, so I didn't ask any more questions.

Instead, I asked, "How do Judge and Jared know that the officers won't look in their closets?"

"They don't. The officers have the right to comb through every inch of our homes if they want to. It's all part of the gamble my friends are taking. I guess this time I was also playing a lottery of sorts by having you hide away . . ." His voice trailed off as he finished that thought. "Anyway, we should probably go find Mattie. I'm sure she heard the siren and is worried sick about you." He started looking around for his keys, so I took that as a sign that he was over answering any more of my inquiries.

Chapter 13 – A Familiar Face

Similar to the time I was in his aunt's car, I crouched awkwardly in the back seat. But unlike every other time I rode with him, the radio remained off the entire drive over to Mattie and Ralph's.

When we pulled up, Harrison stopped me before I got out.

"Let me talk to her first," he said.

He had already stepped out of the car when I saw Mattie's prominent figure storming toward us. Her face was almost as red as her hair. I couldn't make out exactly what she was saying, but I didn't need to hear any actual words to know she was scolding him. But her cheeks turned flush white when she saw the large bandage around his arm. She pointed to it, and after he said whatever he said about it, she pulled him in for a hug. After she released him, she held him at arm's length for a minute to inspect the rest of him. When she was done, he walked over and opened the door for me.

"Sera! I was so worried about you. If anything had happened to you . . ." she said as she now squeezed me. "I could have killed you, Harry, when she didn't come back yesterday."

"I'm sorry. I forgot what day it was."

"I tried calling you several times last night," she said with an eyebrow raised. She also dramatically crossed her arms.

Harrison and I looked at each other and blushed as we remembered what we were preoccupied doing that caused us to miss her calls.

"I'm sorry," Harrison said again.

"Yeah, well. Don't forget again. Promise me."

He nodded slowly and replied, "I promise, Matts."

She had her arms around both of us, and we walked together into the house.

Ralph was seated at the dining table with several photo albums open around him.

"Whatcha doing?" Harrison asked.

Ralph must have been so lost in the pictures that he hadn't even heard us walk in. He was startled by the sound of Harrison's voice.

"Oh! Hi. Sorry. I'm just looking back at some pictures from the real world. Just reminiscing about our old lives and remembering the people we used to know."

"Right," Harrison said dryly. I wondered at that moment if he had any pictures of him and Kailas. From what I had gathered so far, reminders of her only seemed to upset him. But I figured he might have some photos tucked away in an old shoebox or something.

"It is sweet to look back on fond memories, dear." Mattie put her hand on Ralph's shoulder and kissed him on the head. "But it's also important to focus on making new memories here." She gracefully closed the album he was looking at.

Ralph sighed. "I know." He took a puff of his inhaler and got up from the table. Mattie hurried to tidy the mess scattered across it.

"Anyway, I'm glad you're okay, Sera. When we heard the siren, Mattie was so sick to her stomach because you weren't safely under our roof." Ralph shot an angry look at Harrison.

He responded by lifting his hands in the air. "I know, I know. Like I told Mattie, it won't happen again."

"It better not," Ralph said. He lightly punched Harrison's shoulder when he walked by him.

Mattie had organized the photo albums to her satisfaction, and she sat down at the table herself. "I feel like I have to apologize to you as well."

Several seconds of silence passed. "Wait. Who are you talking to?" I looked around before pointing at myself. "Me?" I asked.

"Yes. I should have warned you about the Ikshana. But I didn't want to unnecessarily worry you because I thought you'd never have to deal with it. After all, they don't come to this house."

"I know. Harrison explained everything to me. You have nothing to be sorry for. I appreciate you trying to protect me," I said before sitting down next to her.

"So, how did you manage to stay hidden from them?"

Harrison jumped in at that point. "I took her next door, and she hid in the closet with April and her baby."

"Ugh. I've never liked that girl. Her face is always scrunched in a grimace. And I'm sorry, I know she's your friend, Harry, but she's . . . she's a downright slut!"

Surprised by her language, I had to use my hand to stop my audible, and thankfully dry, spit-take. If I had been eating or drinking something, it would have been all over the table and floor.

"Mattie!" Harrison said, just as surprised as I was. He remained standing behind my chair with his arm resting on the back of it.

"Well, I'm sorry. But it's the truth. Coming in between two brothers like that. It's shameful! Plus, everyone knows she's a crook!"

"Wha—" I started to ask, but Mattie didn't waste any time continuing her gossip.

"She used to volunteer at the Recreation Center where a lot of us seniors go to play bingo, card games, etc. But she was banned after she got caught digging through the pockets of jackets in the coat closet. That's why she isn't welcomed in any of the older Nirvanas' homes during inspections. Well, there's that, but she also can't risk people finding out about the baby. I've offered, and Harrison has let her know, that the poor innocent child could seek refuge here. But I guess she refuses to be separated from her." She shook her head in disapproval and paused a moment as if she was carefully collecting her thoughts. A few seconds later, she continued, "I really only offered because we were already involved in that whole mess."

"Wait, really? How?" I was intrigued.

"Because somehow, they . . . with no help from this one," she shot an evil look toward Harrison, "convinced Ralph to build all of the kid's furniture."

"Oh," I said. I hadn't thought about it before, but it made sense that her parents couldn't simply go out and buy all of her necessities. Babies weren't allowed in Ananda, so there was no need for stores that sold those kinds of things.

"He had to work in secret for weeks, and then he had to carefully deliver it to them. I have no idea how they pulled it off. Frankly, I don't want to know."

Harrison, in a blatant attempt to ignore and move on from Mattie's criticism, butted in and said, "So, the inspections happen on the fourteenth day of each month, but the officers don't come at any specific time. That's why they sound alarms to give us somewhat of a warning that we should be ready for an officer to invade our living spaces within the next few minutes."

"Right. So, if you're planning to stay in Ananda for a while," Mattie added as she smirked toward Harrison, "you need to be in this house during the inspections. Probably from the night of the thirteenth through the morning of the fifteenth. Just to be safe, okay? It's bad enough for the Samsaras who get caught during the inspections. I have no idea what would happen to you, as you aren't one of them or one of us."

"Speaking of that, Mattie," Harrison said. "Sera and I wanted to ask you about the possibility of her extended stay. Besides being with her family," he had apparently heard me say that after all, "she is worried about getting back to the real world because she was supposed to start college. I explained to her that registered visitors are allowed to take certain classes." He turned and looked at me, and I could see the desperation in his eyes. He really wanted me to stay.

"But she isn't technically a Samsara," Mattie said, frowning.

"I know. That's where we need your guidance."

"My concern is that if I register as a student," I said, "I'm basically inviting the Ikshana to learn about my existence here."

Mattie was rubbing at her temples, probably trying to come up with a solution. "Harry . . ." she finally said.

They both paused for a moment. Then, as if they were speaking telepathically, he responded, "Yeah, I know. I think that's the only option."

"What?" I asked, looking back and forth between them.

"I'm going to change it so that you're officially my registered Samsara," Harrison said.

"But what about Kailas?"

"It's like I told you a few days ago; she can't come here anymore. She's banned because she told someone in the real world about Ananda. So, even if she tried to use the instructions, it wouldn't work."

I hung my head in guilt. I hadn't thought about that in days.

Apparently sensing my remorse, he reached from behind the chair and gently put his hand on my shoulder. "It's okay. From everything you've already disclosed to us about your uncle, I completely understand why she and Janusz made the sacrifices they did to send you here. Plus, I'm glad to help keep you here as long as you want to stay—and for you to be as safe as possible." He bent down and kissed my cheek. Mattie beamed as she watched his display of affection.

"Once you're officially registered as his Samsara, I believe you'll be able to attend class without any issue," she said. "Unfortunately, I don't know if you'll be able to come and go as regular visitors do.

Everyone I've ever known has been registered in the real world, not while they're already here. But we'll see."

"Okay, that makes sense." Although I missed my real family, I had grown so close to this alternate one within a short amount of time, and I was happy to spend more time with them.

"But remember, until we know whether or not you can come and go, you need to be careful to be here during the Ikshana inspections."

"I understand. I will, Mattie. Promise."

"Good. Well, Harry, why don't you go downtown to get the paperwork? Tell them you know a Samsara who knows Sera and can bring it to her the next time they go back to the real world. I think they'll buy that and let you bring the papers here, instead of having them go through their official channels. Then, Sera, I'll go to the school with you tomorrow to help you get registered for classes."

"Got it, Matts!" Harrison yelled after her as she left the room. He sat down on the chair next to me.

When we were alone, I wanted to confirm he wasn't being pressured by Mattie's presence. "You promise you're sure about this? I know you're getting a little extra money now that Kailas . . . well, you know. I don't want to take those funds away from you. And What if there's a way for her to come ba—" I whispered.

Before I could finish my thought, he interrupted, "I promise, Sera. Don't worry about the money part. And I know this is what she wanted." He leaned in and kissed me on the lips. "Plus! Now I'll get to keep seeing you throughout the day when the semester starts! Do you have any idea what you want to study?"

"Well, I had considered going into teaching." I bit my lip. "But now, with all the trauma I've recently experienced, I think I might want to be a school counselor instead."

"I think that's a great idea, Sera," Harrison said, flashing his subtle smile.

I grinned back at him, but then I suddenly remembered a potential flaw in my plan. *Are there kids in Ananda?* "Wait! I didn't see any babies, but I definitely saw younger kids when I went to the mall with Mattie. I know what you said about Nirvanas and Samsaras not having kids, but can two Samsaras procreate? Or can sick kids come here?"

Harrison scooted closer to me and grasped my hand. "Kids between the ages of thirteen and seventeen can come here as Nirvanas only if they have family members or someone else who agrees to care for them. Mattie and Ralph have taken countless children in for that very purpose. But they've also taken in people like Janusz and me who were of age but still didn't have anyone to guide them when they first arrived."

"Why can't kids younger than thirteen come if someone dedicates to their care?"

"Well, you know us Nirvanas don't physically age, and we have to work if we're able. So, I believe the Ikshana want to minimize the number of people in Ananda who can't actively contribute to society. Obviously, the younger kids go to school for the first few years they're here. But once they've completed high school, they're required to work or go to college, just like in the real world."

"Oh . . ." I didn't like the idea of seeing someone who outwardly appeared to be a prepubescent kid doing intense physical labor.

"Yeah. It can be hard to get used to seeing ostensibly younger people act like adults. But eventually, you learn to see them for their mental age."

"What about Samsaras? How old do they need to be?"

"I believe above the age of 16."

I knew he was an adult, but I never thought to inquire exactly how old he was, mentally speaking.

"Twenty-one," he said after I finally asked.

"Oh! So, you could drink in the real world!"

He chuckled and said, "Yeah. I'm not a big drinker, though. My condition and meds don't react well with alcohol. Every time I've had drinks with Jared and Judge, I've felt unbearably sick for days. Even if I only have a beer or two."

Due to the interactions I'd had with Uncle Ford when he was drunk, I was overall scared and skeptical of intoxicated people. So, I was relieved when I heard that.

"Anyway. I should probably get going. Mattie will be mad if she comes back and sees that I'm still here. I'm sure you've learned this by now, but in case you haven't, Mattie likes people to do things when she tells them to. As long as you do, she'll welcome you into her home and treat you like family."

I smiled. "Yeah, I've caught on to that."

"I'll come back so we can get everything signed right away." He gave me one more kiss and left through the sliding glass doors that faced the beach.

I considered watching something on TV while I waited for him to return, but my plans changed when I looked at the photo albums. I didn't want to be nosey, but I was curious to see what Mattie and Ralph's lives were like before coming to Ananda. So, after looking around to make sure I was alone, I opened the one on top. I couldn't help but smile when I saw moments in time permanently captured on the glossy squares.

The first ones were younger pictures of Ralph and various other young men. Then, I flipped to a page of photos that included Mattie. The pictures were black and white, but her pronounced bone structure was so unique that I didn't even need to see her red hair to know it was her.

I turned to their wedding pictures and read the invitation that was also included.

Ralph Shepard and Matilda Carrino Joyfully Invite You to Attend Their Wedding on Saturday, August 16, 1958.

I was mindlessly scanning the pictures and the faces in them when I was shocked to see a man—other than Ralph, of course—I recognized.

"What are you looking at?" Mattie asked when she walked back into the kitchen. Then, she leaned over me and answered her own question. "Oh! Can you believe how beautiful I used to be?"

I was still surprised by the unexpected familiar face, and it took me a second to register her presence. But after a few seconds, I moved to close the album in front of me. "I'm sorry. I didn't mean to pry. I was just curious to see what your life in the real world was like." My face was hot from embarrassment, and I tried to conceal the red patches that were inevitably on my cheeks with my palms.

"You don't need to apologize, sweetie." She opened the book back up. "It feels like this was a million years ago," she said, smiling from ear to ear as she reviewed the pictures for herself. "Ah! Look at my hair!"

I removed my hands from my face and laughed along with her. "I also can't get over Ralph's mustache!"

"He got rid of that nasty thing right after the wedding."

"You didn't like it?"

"Heck no! Look at it!" She continued to flip through the pages. "You looked a little bit like you'd seen a ghost when I first walked in. What pictures were you looking at?"

I clumsily turned to the exact photo. "I guess I shouldn't have been that surprised to see my dad, seeing as he was, or is, Ralph's visitor."

Mattie glanced down at it. "Oh, Clark! Of course!"

"My dad doesn't open up much about his past, and he doesn't have a lot of pictures of himself when he was younger. I don't recognize the girl next to him." I pointed at the blonde that stood by his side.

"That's Sarah Faith, Ralph's sister."

I recognized the name at once. "My dad's first wife."

"Oh, yeah. That's right. Wow. That's kind of crazy. They were married for such a short amount of time; I forgot their marriage ever happened."

"Huh." I continued to study her face. "She is one thing he talked about on occasion. He was right; she was beautiful."

"That she was," Mattie agreed. "You know, I never made this connection before. I know your full name is Seraphine, but your parents call you Sera, right?"

"Yeah, most people do."

"I wonder if your parents named you in homage to Sarah Faith. Dang, if that's the case, your mother is a stronger woman than I am. I don't think I could name a child after an ex of Ralph's, dead or alive."

I had never thought about that either. I made a mental note to ask if and when I ever made it back to the real world. Then I continued my line of questioning. "I know Sarah Faith got sick when she was relatively young. Is she here in Ananda?"

Mattie was silent for a while. Then, she glanced around to make sure I was the only one within her earshot. "Unfortunately, no. This place didn't exist when she passed," she said, lowering her voice. "Anyway, after her death, your dad grew incredibly close to Ralph. That's why he's his Samsara."

I felt dizzy as I tried to connect everything in my mind.

"It's actually the anniversary of her death today. That's why Ralph was reminiscing." She turned a few more pages. "Oh! Do you recognize who this is?"

I looked at the stoic lady glaring at the camera, elegantly clutching her very pregnant belly. "No, I don't think so."

"That's your *abuela*! She was one of my bridesmaids and was pregnant with your *tía*, Jackie."

Now I noticed the similarities between the woman in the photograph and my mother. "Wow. I never met her. I was told that she died before I was born. And although I've asked, I've also never seen a picture of her. My mom always said she didn't have any photographs from back in Argentina."

"Do you want to meet her?"

I stared at Mattie. "What do you mean? She's here?"

"Mhm. I didn't mention it before because I wasn't sure how you felt about her, given the turbulent relationship between Elena, your *abuela*, and your mom."

I wasn't aware of any ill will between them, and I wondered what the source of all that was. But, as I didn't have any negative feelings toward her, I agreed to meet her. How could I not?

"Okay, we'll go tomorrow before we get you registered at the school."

Mattie and I continued to talk until Harrison came back with the paperwork.

"Good call, Matts," he said as he walked through the door. "You were right. They let me take the paperwork with me after I said I knew a Samsara who could deliver it to Sera. They barely batted an eye when I suggested it. I guess they allow such a procedure all the time. Of course, I didn't specify which Samsara I was referring to. I didn't want to give them the chance to closely surveil anyone and find out that we're lying. Anyway, I already signed. Now all you need to do is sign on the next line over."

I held the paper closer and read the title of the document.

"Harrison, why does it say this is an 'Intimate' Samsara Contract?" I asked.

"Uh . . ." he said, looking bashfully at Mattie. "Well, there are different labels that are supposed to describe the relationship between a Samsara and their Nirvana. Take your parents, for instance. They are both 'family friends' to Mattie and Ralph. And

Aunt Kailas was my 'family member.' I knew I could honestly register you with the family friend designation, but I thought we should be as honest as possible, given the surrounding circumstances. I know we haven't technically had—I mean . . ." He paused to wipe beads of sweat off his forehead.

I wasn't sure if he was nervous about having this conversation with me or if it was just weird for him to be saying all of this in front of Mattie. I knew she wasn't *technically* his aunt, but still.

"I think that was a wise decision, Harry," Mattie said, reassuring him.

I heard him take a relieved breath in, and he closed his eyes for a moment. "Thanks. That does mean Sera, you have to—"

"You'll have to go in each month and get a pregnancy test," Mattie interjected.

"Oh!" I remembered what Harrison had said about April and other members of a group needing such testing, but I'd never imagined I'd have to be a part of that.

"Obviously, I don't know with utmost certainty about you personally, Sera . . . but judging by a grocery list Mattie has given me, I knew you required *those* products. So . . ." He once again looked to Mattie and inaudibly begged her to continue explaining.

She obliged. "What Harrison is trying to say is that he knows you require feminine products every month, so you obviously get a period. If you didn't, or there was any other indication you couldn't have children, you'd need to be listed in the 'Nisphalata'ॐ group. I know it's a lot, and it seems like the Ikshana have never-ending lists and categories to sort us into. But that's how they keep optimal control over everything in Ananda."

My head was spinning a bit—in part from all of the new information, but I was also incredibly embarrassed that Harrison had purchased tampons for me. But, while I was a little reluctant after hearing about my additional monthly obligation, I knew I wasn't with child, so I figured I had nothing to hide. I delicately wrote my name in cursive: *Seraphine Leonor Acosta Demosey.*

Mattie shuffled over to the scanner next to her computer and made copies of the fully executed document. One for back up, and one to file with the Ikshana, she said.

After giving the original back to Harrison, he examined it. "You have two middle names?"

"Yeah. Mama picked Leonor after an Argentine artist she really likes, and Acosta is her maiden name. Unlike other countries in South America, it isn't as common to include both paternal and maternal surnames in Argentina. But Mama wanted her family represented too. I'm pretty sure all of my siblings have 'Acosta' in their names. Also, she wanted us to conform to American culture, so she made sure our technical last name was my dad's. When traditionally speaking, it should be hers." I took a breath for air; my cheeks burned with embarrassment when I realized that I was rambling.

"Very interesting. So, it's Seraphine Leonor Acosta Dem . . .?"

"Demosey." I helped him pronounce the rest.

"A beautiful name for a beautiful girl." He pulled me in and kissed the top of my head. I took the paper in my own hands and read his scribbled signature: *Harrison Hercules Ellis.*

". . . Hercules?" I was trying but failing to hold in a laugh.

"Shut up!" He tickled my side. "When I was born, my mom was going through a phase."

"What? Was she obsessed with Greek mythology or something?"

"Well, we are Greek. But yes. I guess she was particularly into it at the time."

"I mean, it could have been worse. Harrison Hermes? Harrison Hades?" I joked and poked him in the ribs.

"Very true! I hated it as a kid since everyone at school knew about the Disney movie. I told everyone my middle name was just 'H.'"

"I get that. I got made fun of a lot when I was younger for having two middle names. One kid always said my parents had to give me more than one because they didn't know who my real mom and dad were. So, I guess the implication was that they had to include as many names as possible to ensure all potential parents were included? I don't know. Looking back, it doesn't make any sense. But, nonetheless, it hurt at the time."

"Yeah, kids can be brutal. Even when they're too young to understand just how cruel they're being."

"It's funny we're talking about this," I said.

"What do you mean? Bullies from our childhood?" He was gently rubbing his thumb across the back of my hand, which was in my lap.

"Yeah. It's actually one of the first things Jonesy and I bonded over. I was complaining to him about this guy I went to high school with who always made fun of my fair skin."

He lifted the hand he was already holding. "You mean this beautiful skin?"

"Yeah. The jerk would always comment on my looks and say that I needed to wear blush, so I didn't look like a corpse." I had since remembered exactly what he said after talking with Jonesy about it.

"What an idiot." He kissed my raised hand and brought it back down to rest on my thigh. "I bet he secretly had a crush on you."

I heard what he said, but I didn't fully process it. I was too busy reminiscing about that particular memory with Jonesy. "That was the first time he called me '*mała perła*.'"

"What does that mean?"

"According to Jonesy, it translates to 'little pearl' in Polish."

"*Mała perła*," he repeated. "Do you want to know what he called me?"

"Sure," I said, a little disappointed that Jonesy had given other people nicknames. I naively thought it was just our little thing.

"Since the first day we met, he called me '*brudny hipis*.'"

"What does that mean? I assume it's also Polish?"

"Dirty hippie," he said, laughing as he pointed to his hair and then smoothed a long curl that had fallen in his face behind his ear. I was slightly relieved to know Jonesy had chosen his nickname in jest. Mine seemed to come from a more vulnerable place.

"That's so funny!" I leaned toward him and pretended to take a big whiff. "Well, lucky for me, you don't smell like one!" He made a funny face at me, and we continued to joke around with each other until Mattie aggressively cleared her throat. I think we both had forgotten she was in the room.

"Oh, Matts! I'm sorry—" He cleared his own throat to brush over the awkwardness. "What were you and Sera talking about before I got here?" he asked clumsily.

"We were just looking through Ralph's old photo albums. Do you mind if I show him, Sera?"

"No," I said, slightly confused why she would want my approval. It's not like I was in any of the pictures.

Mattie flipped through the pages until she got to the one with my dad and his then-wife, which was still so weird for me to think about. "See this guy? That's Sera's dad."

Harrison looked at the picture and back up at me several times. "Yeah, I guess I can see the resemblance!"

He and I had gotten up from our seats to get a better look at the photos, so I jokingly bumped my hip into his, although I actually hit closer to his right knee.

"What?" he responded.

I smirked and playfully punched him in the shoulder. I knew why he was making fun of me. Judging from the photo and the appearance of my father now, he certainly grew into his nose and ears since then. Thankfully, I inherited those facial features from my mom.

Mattie, without looking up or acknowledging our interaction, continued, "And that little blonde by him? That's Sarah Faith, his late wife."

"Wait. Your dad's first wife was named Sarah, and your name is Sera . . . well, Seraphine, but—"

"I made the same connection," Mattie said proudly.

I shrugged my shoulders when they both looked to me for a reaction. "I honestly have no idea. It seems too on the nose to be a coincidence, but they never said anything to me about it."

"Interesting—" Harrison began.

"Anyway," Mattie said, cutting him off. She flipped to the photo of my other relatives pictured in the album. "And guess who this beauty is?"

Harrison looked at the picture for a moment and said, "Isn't that Miss Elena from a few houses over?"

"Mhm! She was obviously much younger here."

"You know my *abuela*?" I asked.

"Huh?"

"Oh, sorry. My grandma," I clarified.

"Miss Elena is your grandma? No way!"

"That's what Mattie tells me. I never met her in the real world."

"It's complicated, but Elena's relationship with Sera's mom wasn't the greatest."

"I didn't know anything about that either. My mom just never talked about her. The only things I knew about her before coming here were that she was obviously also from Argentina and died before I was born. But I'm really excited to meet her. I've never had grandparents before!"

"You're going to love her. Miss Elena is the best. She always tips extra when you mow her lawn and invites you in for . . . what are those cookies called again?" he asked, looking at Mattie.

Before she could answer, I interjected, "¿*Alfajores?*"

"Yeah! How'd you know that?" Harrison said.

"Well, it wasn't that hard to guess. They're a popular dessert in Argentina." I smiled, remembering the cookies Mama would make whenever one of us kids did something that deserved a small celebration. The last time she made them for me, I had aced a math test I was really nervous about taking.

I hoped this Elena would have some out when I met her. I was curious to see if they tasted similar to my mom's.

Chapter 14 – An Unexpected Gift

Mattie, Harrison, and I thoroughly mulled over the photo albums, and they took turns telling me stories about my *abuela*. I was so excited to see and talk to her that I could hardly sleep that night.

As I had several mornings prior, I woke up on that special day to the sound of Harrison working on the lawn outside. I showered in a hurry and got dressed for the day before heading outside.

"Whatcha up to, stranger?" I asked as I approached him. He was in Mattie's garden and facing away from me, bending down to secure metal coils around a small plant.

"Oh!" He stood up, faced me, and planted a big kiss on my lips. "Good morning! Um, for some reason, Mattie's tomatoes have had trouble growing this year. I figured they might need some support to flourish."

I noticed that his finger was bleeding a little bit. "Do you want me to go inside and get a bandage? I think I know where they are."

"Agh! No. It's no big deal," he said as he slowly sucked on the blood. "Oh, you know what? I actually have something for you!" He reached with his other hand into his back pocket. "Here." He handed me a small black rectangle.

"Harrison, no!" I couldn't believe he'd get me such a thoughtful and expensive present.

"Sera. It's fine. It's a present for me too, in a way. Now that you have a cellphone, I can talk to you whenever I want!" He smiled at me in a way that made me weak in the knees.

"It's too much—" I started to say as soon as I caught my balance.

"Please. Not another word about it."

I took a deep breath in and said, "Fine. Just two more. Thank you." I wrapped my arms around his torso and squeezed him tight.

"You're welcome!" He hugged me back. "Ralph and I set it all up last night after you went to bed." He continued to show me each function and how it worked.

"So, I know you're going to meet Miss Elena. Then, Mattie is going with you to register for classes, right?" he asked after giving me a full tutorial of my new device.

"Mhm," I said while still marveling at the gadget in front of me.

"Do you have any plans after that?"

"Uh-uh."

He reached toward me and tucked a piece of hair behind my ear to get my attention. It worked. The second I looked into his warm brown eyes, the farthest thing from my mind was some silly cellphone.

When he was confident that I was no longer distracted, he smiled and nodded. "I made a few calls, and there are about a dozen horses at the Sanctuary Center. I was wondering if you'd like to go there with me tonight?"

"Really? Yeah, I'd love that!" I was touched that he remembered my love of horses and had taken the time to follow up on their presence in Ananda. Of course, I was also incredibly excited to interact with another majestic creature like my beloved Maple.

"Sera? Sera?" Mattie called for me from inside the house.

"Sounds like you're needed elsewhere." Harrison grinned and motioned toward the house. "I'll catch up with you later tonight. I'll plan to pick you up around six. Have fun with your *abuela*!" He tried his best to pronounce it correctly.

"Thanks!" I grabbed his face and kissed him deeply. His body responded with similar enthusiasm. I could feel his fingers digging gently into my lower back. After we released each other, he winked and lightly smacked my backside. I playfully bit my lip in response. I gave him one more light peck before turning around and skipping toward the house.

"Mattie! I'm here!" I yelled as I got closer.

"You ready to go?" she asked in her deep but friendly voice.

"Yeah, I think so." The nerves were starting to set in, so I looked outside once more to the handsome boy I couldn't believe I got to kiss whenever I wanted to. He was pouring a small amount of water onto his face and hair. I watched the droplets fall as he shook his head. Then, feeling a little calmer, I followed Mattie out the front door.

As we walked along the sidewalk, Mattie said, "So, I called Elena this morning. She was a little confused by your presence, as we all were. But I tried to explain the bare minimum. I thought I'd leave it up to you to tell her the rest if you want to."

"Okay."

"But she's really excited to meet you."

Before I knew it, we were standing in front of her house. It looked similar to Mattie and Ralph's, but it was a little smaller. The garage door began to open, and with each inch that it rose, I saw more of the tiny woman standing behind it. When her face was finally showing, Mattie and I approached her.

"Elena," Mattie said, grabbing her hand, "this is Johanna's daughter, your granddaughter, Seraphine." She placed Elena's hand and mine together. "Sera, this is your *abuela*." I noticed her glassy eyes right away.

Before I could ask, Mattie offered an explanation. "Elena was slowly losing her sight before she came here. But she can still see shapes and figures."

"*Mi nieta*," she said as she came closer to me. She placed her hand on my cheek. "*Finalmente*." She paused a moment, perhaps realizing that I might not have been able to understand her. Then she asked, "*¿Hablas Español?*"

"*Sí. Mi mamá me enseñó,*" I explained to her that my mom had taught me Spanish.

"Aye. *Bueno,*" she said approvingly.

"Uh, guys?" Mattie said, clearly annoyed at being kept out of the conversation.

"Apologies, Matilda," Elena said in a thick accent. "Would you like to come in?"

When we entered the front door, I was happy to see *alfajores* laid out in a beautiful spread on the coffee table.

"Please, have a seat," Elena said as she gestured toward the couch and rocking chair in her living room. I happily took a cookie when she lifted the plate and offered it to me. I took a bite, and the buttery goodness melted in my mouth. *Just like Mama's*, I thought.

"So, Seraphine," Elena began to say.

"Oh. Um, you can call me Sera."

"Sera," she continued with a slight smile on her face, "you said your mom taught you Spanish?"

"Yeah. Me and all of my younger siblings."

"Oh! There's more of you? How many?"

"Six, including me."

"*¿Seis? ¡Dios mío!*" Abuela seemed stunned, and several seconds passed before Mattie interrupted the silence.

"So, Elena, I told Sera that you were a little confused as to why she was here."

"Yes," Elena said, nodding.

"We all were when she first came to stay with Ralph and me. But, as I explained, we learned that she was Johanna and Clark's daughter, which meant she was your granddaughter. Sera, do you want to fill in the rest?"

"Um." I wasn't sure how to start explaining the circumstances surrounding my arrival in Ananda. "Well, I was staying with my Uncle Ford for the summer."

"Your father's brother?" she asked rhetorically, knowing he wasn't my mom's sibling.

Without answering, I continued, "That's where I met Jonesy, who was also staying on the farm."

Mattie provided clarification. "Sera is talking about Janusz."

"Ah, Janusz," Abuela said, looking up and raising her right hand to her chin.

"Did you know him?" I asked hopefully.

"*Sí*, very well. He came to visit me many times," she answered. It warmed my heart that the two of them had some kind of relationship.

"Well, long story short, Jonesy learned that I was in a bad position that I couldn't get out of, so he sent a friend to give me the instructions. I followed them, and I found myself here."

"Hm . . ." she muttered. I could tell she had more questions, but I wasn't comfortable divulging more than I needed to at that point.

Mattie must have sensed my discomfort because she changed the subject. "Oh, Elena. You will be so proud of your granddaughter. She is going to sign up for classes at the college right after we leave here."

"Is that right? What will you study?"

I shot a thankful glance at Mattie and said, "I'm not one hundred percent positive. Maybe teaching? I heard there are schools for the youngest Samsaras who come here."

"Teaching is a very noble profession. You know, your *abuelo* was a respected teacher in Argentina. He was educated in America but returned to our home country to work."

I remembered what Mattie had said about my mom living in the US as a kid. "No, I didn't know that. Mama never really talked about either one of you." I felt guilty for saying it, but it was the truth.

"I suppose she wouldn't."

Mattie looked down at the watch around her wrist and said, "Well, Sera. We should get going. We don't want to be late; otherwise, the program you want might fill up before we can get you into it."

There was more I wanted to know about Elena, so I asked her, "Is it okay if I come back to see you sometime?"

"*Tú eres bienvenido siempre, mi nieta,*" she said, expressing that I was always welcome to visit. Then, with Mattie's help, she got up from her chair and walked over to me. We embraced in a light hug. She seemed so fragile, and I was afraid to break her.

As Mattie and I walked back to her house, she entertained me by answering more questions about my family. "How long has Abuela lived right down the street from you?"

"A long time. Remember when you first came here, and I told you about exceptions that can be made regarding a Nirvana's location in Ananda? Well, Elena made a request to reside here in the American/Midwestern section. Although she primarily resided in Argentina, her request was granted because of her relationship with me, someone born and bred in Iowa. Did I ever tell you that's where we're from? I don't think so. Anyway, not the point. It also didn't hurt that Elena was my Samsara before your mother was, so she was already fully acclimated to the place."

"Oh. So, what about my mom?"

"What about her?"

"Did she ever visit?"

"With Elena? Well, yes. Since your mother was a teenager, she and Elena have had a complicated relationship. Johanna was hesitant at first for that reason and others, but eventually, she came around and made semi-regular visits. That was before your mom met and decided to marry your dad, though."

I wondered if my dad had anything to do with their bad relationship.

"Anyway. Enough about that for now. On to more positive and exciting things. Let's get you all set up for school!"

We drove to the school in silence, just listening to the soft rock music playing on the radio. As we pulled up to the parking lot, I noted that it said "high school" on the side of the building.

When I asked Mattie about it, she said, "Ah, yes. The whole building is split into two sides—one for college students and one for high school-aged kids. I know Harrison told you about how valuable younger Nirvanas are to the Ikshana. This is just another one of my theories, but I think they lumped both schools into one place to easily and cost-effectively monitor them. It's kind of nice, though. You get a locker and everything, so you don't have to constantly lug your books back and forth. Unless you need them for homework, of course. But don't worry, you won't have any classes with the younger kids. And your teachers are actual college professors."

I felt a pang of disappointment in my gut. Although they wouldn't be in my classes, there would still be younger kids *around*. At least outside before and after school. I dreamed of experiencing a more traditional "college experience," not reliving high school all over again. But I knew being able to stay with Harrison longer was worth it.

Without skipping a beat, Mattie asked me, "So, were you serious back at Elena's when you said you want to potentially pursue a career in teaching?"

"Yeah, I think so." The irony of this statement, after I had just gone down a thought process about my uninterest in engaging with children, was not lost on me. I meant I didn't want younger kids around while I was in college. I didn't have a perpetual disdain for them. Nevertheless, I continued, "But maybe focus more on school counseling? I'd like to help kids who might find themselves in tumultuous situations that they don't fully understand. Obviously, I have some firsthand experience with that."

"I think that's an excellent idea, Sera."

When we walked into the school, I noticed several security officers and dozens of cameras hanging from the ceiling.

"Oh! Look. There's the education department's booth. Of course, you can always change your mind, but we can sign you up to go down that route for now. What do you think?" Mattie inquired.

"Um, yeah. Okay," I said back, still shocked by the amount of surveillance. It was easy to see how and why Mattie developed her theory about the Ikshana's heavy monitoring at the school.

But it didn't seem like a "theory" anymore. It was more like the clear, plain truth of the matter.

But I knew Harrison had filed the paperwork, and I was officially a registered Samsara. So, my appearance in the footage would not be cause for concern. Although, I figured the Ikshana didn't keep pictures of each resident—permanent or not—because Mattie had taken me, before I was somewhat "legitimate," to a shopping mall, one of the most public places you can be. I knew she wasn't aware of *everything* about the inner workings of this alternate world, but surely, she wouldn't have exposed me like that if she questioned my safety.

In any event, I presented the documentation Harrison and I had filled out to the administrators for the education department. After that, I set my class schedule, and Mattie helped me pick out my books in the bookstore.

I was told that lockers weren't assigned yet, so I loaded the heavy books into the trunk of Mattie's van. After getting into the passenger seat, I heard a beep in my pocket. It startled me. I completely forgot about the phone Harrison had given me earlier that day. I took the device out cautiously, still not comfortable using it.

I struggled to remember the passcode he had set but eventually typed in my best guess: 0112. I hadn't known this before, but apparently, Jonesy's birthday was January 12th.

Having successfully unlocked the phone, I read Harrison's message:

Hey, beautiful! How is everything going? All signed up to be an Ananda Agni? ॐ

I slowly typed back, using only my right index finger:

Yep!

Within a few seconds, he responded:

Awesome! Are we still on for tonight?

Still struggling to get used to my new device, I took a few seconds to reply:

Yeah! I'm excited.

I shoved the phone back into my pocket as Mattie approached the car holding a large corndog and some cotton candy. "Dang! You're gonna eat like a queen here!" she commented as she took a massive bite out of the breaded roll and mystery meat. "All set?"

I nodded, and she climbed into the driver's side before handing me her half-eaten food to hold until we got back to her house.

It was only around 2:00 p.m. when we returned home, so I decided to relax by the beach. I went upstairs and changed into the one-piece suit I'd bought at the mall with Mattie. She tried to convince me to get a bikini—but as open as I was becoming to new looks, I had to put my foot down on that one. She said it was a waste not to show off my figure, but I disregarded her opinion and instead picked a modest suit that I felt much more comfortable and concealed in.

I then grabbed a towel and sunscreen and headed outside. I walked to what I thought was Harrison's favorite spot and set up camp near the pile of sand. First, I slathered my fair skin with the sunblock, as any prolonged time of unprotected sun exposure would result in a large, painful burn across my skin. Then, I sprawled out on the towel and closed my eyes. I tried to close out all of my thoughts and instead focus on the calming sounds around me. This must have worked because I was eventually jolted awake by the sound of a shrieking seagull.

I looked at the phone next to me and was horrified when I saw it was already five o'clock. I had no idea how I'd managed to sleep for almost three straight hours. I did have a hard time sleeping the night prior, with all the excitement of meeting Abuela and signing up for classes, but it was still unlike me to take such long naps.

I rushed to pick up everything and get back to the house. I flipped my hair over and tried to shake all of the sand out of it. I then picked my cutest outfit that was still practical for being around a bunch of horses, and I sat by the kitchen island while I waited for him to pick me up. I wasn't sure if dinner was in the plan or not, so I scarfed down half of a PB&J just in case. That way, I'd calm my growling stomach but not be too full to eat later.

Six o'clock came and went, but I didn't think much of it. I figured he was just running late. But when it hit 6:45, I started getting a little concerned. I checked my phone but didn't have any messages from him. So, I sent him one instead:

Everything okay?

After I pressed send, Ralph walked in and was confused by my presence. "Sera? What are you still doing here? I thought you had plans with Harry tonight."

"Yeah, I thought so too. I don't know what happened. I'm kind of worried."

"That is weird. It isn't like him at all to just blow something off."

"I just sent him a message; we'll see if he responds."

"Do you want me to sit with you while you wait?" he offered as he grabbed leftovers from the fridge.

"Are you sure you wouldn't mind? I'd really appreciate the distraction."

"Not at all," he said as he unwrapped the dish and put it in the microwave.

With my mind still wrapped around Harrison, I mistook the beeping of the microwave as an alert from my phone. To my disappointment, I saw nothing on the screen. When I realized where the actual noise came from, I looked up in embarrassment.

I wasn't sure if Ralph saw my mistake, but he quickly tried to distract me. "Mattie told me that you met Miss Elena today. How did that go?"

"It was fine, I guess."

"I can imagine there may have been a weird tension there."

"Kind of. Do you know anything about that whole situation? Did my dad ever mention anything?"

"I've heard pieces and parts, yes. I don't think the two of them ever got along particularly well. After it became clear that Elena was going to turn completely blind if she didn't come to Ananda, your mother was approached to be either Mattie's replacement Samsara or your grandma's first one. Initially, Johanna had an issue with Elena even coming here, seeing as it was built on Hindu and Buddhist principles. I guess she thought of it as a mockery of the whole idea surrounding the existence of God and heaven. But after she learned that everyone has religious freedom here and that your grandmother could still practice Catholicism, she was more comfortable with it. I don't think she would have agreed to be Mattie's Samsara if she still had negative feelings toward Ananda. Anyway, Johanna even got to a point where she started to visit your grandma. That is until . . . well, until she met your dad."

"What do you mean?"

"I don't know how to put this delicately, but your grandma wasn't exactly pleased that her daughter chose to marry someone who wasn't Latino. Which I honestly found odd because I always thought fair-skinned Argentinians, at least some, related to white Europeans on a cultural level. It isn't uncommon for them to be the ancestors of immigrants from Spain and Italy."

I looked down at my light skin. I always thought my mom's side of the family was one-hundred percent Argentine, but I guessed it was possible that we were descendants of the people Ralph just mentioned. This possibility did make Abuela's disapproval of my father's ethnicity seem especially strange.

"Anyway, your parents came to visit once after they got married to show us pictures, and they told us that Elena tried to make amends. Your father was somehow able to forgive her. Your mother, on the other hand . . ."

"Why do you think she couldn't let it go?"

"I don't know exactly. If I had to guess, I'd say your grandma said something about your dad to Johanna, I assume it was related to the fact that he is white, that she considered unforgivable. I'm not sure if you know this already, but your mom's always been extremely protective of your father and their relationship as a whole."

"Hm." I was considering what words might have been exchanged between the two of them when my phone went off.

I rushed to unlock it and read the message:
Yup, why?
Incredibly confused, I wrote back:
?? I thought we had plans to hang out at the Sanctuary Center?
"Is that Harry?" Ralph asked.
"Yeah, it's bizarre. He's acting like he doesn't remember we had plans."
"Really? He even told me about it. He seemed really excited to bring you to see the horses."
The phone went off again.
Can't. w/ friends.
Stunned by his attitude, I showed Ralph the screen.
"None of that even sounds like him," he said. "I've never known him to be dismissive or disrespectful to people like that. And he's usually more eloquent."
Not really listening to his reaction, I sent:
Harrison? What is going on?
I waited for several minutes before receiving his reply:

Talk 2 u tomorrow. K?

Tears started welling up in my eyes. "Um, I'm sorry. I'm just going to go to bed," I said to Ralph and turned away before he could see that I was crying.

I ran up the stairs and closed and locked the door. I sat on the bed and sobbed uncontrollably. I couldn't believe he had blown me off like that. I felt incredibly rejected. I kept reading his messages, and I was in disbelief that he had sent them.

I was so angry that I ripped off my outfit and got ready for bed. I figured out how to turn the sound off, and I placed my phone on the dresser across the room. I guess that was my way to "stick it to him." Even if he had wanted to contact me, he couldn't.

Chapter 15 – A Different Kind of Chaos Night

"Sera? Are you awake?" I heard Mattie knocking at the door. "Can I come in?"

I got up and unlocked the door.

"Morning, sweetie. Ralph told me that you had a bit of a rough night. Do you want to talk about it?"

As she was talking, I walked across the room to check the phone. I had dozens of missed alerts. When I unlocked it, there were messages, videos, and voicemails from Harrison.

"Hold on, Mattie. I'm sorry. Can I meet you downstairs for breakfast? We can talk through everything then."

"All right . . ." she said, frowning a little as she closed the door again.

I scrolled through all of the alerts with my thumb, unsure of which one to open. I decided to watch the videos first. I clicked the oldest one, watched the black screen, and tried to understand the voices in the background. It sounded like they were coming from the TV. That video only lasted a few seconds, so I moved on to the next. This one was clearer, and it looked like it was captured from the ground.

Back then, the quality of cellphone videos wasn't the best, but when I looked closely at the grainy footage, I saw Harrison sitting on a couch in a room I didn't recognize. Suddenly, a blonde female straddled him. He enthusiastically pawed at her as they continued to make out.

A deep rage filled me, the kind I had only felt toward my uncle before. I knew we never technically labeled ourselves as "boyfriend and girlfriend," but I didn't think Harrison would ever be cruel enough to send me a video of him being intimate with another girl. I threw the phone against the wall and stomped downstairs.

Thankfully, I was too angry to cry this time, so I didn't need to conceal any tears.

"Mattie," I said as calmly as I could. "Can I try to go back?"

"What's wrong, sweetie? Your face is bright red."

"I just want to see if I can go back to the real world. I want to go back."

"Does this have to do with what happened between you and Harry last night?"

"No, at least not entirely. I . . . um, I'm just really homesick. I miss my family." This wasn't entirely untrue.

"But what if your dad hasn't found a job—" she started to say.

"I don't know. I'll figure it out. Please." Obviously, I hadn't thought that part out at all. My anger completely clouded my judgment.

Without another word, Mattie went into the laundry room and retrieved a piece of paper.

"Here," she said as she handed it to me.

I unfolded the paper to see instructions similar to the ones Jonesy had provided to me but written in handwriting I didn't recognize:

1.) Clear your mind of negative thoughts
2.) Take five deep breaths in
3.) Say, "I resubmit to life"

Without hesitation, I followed each step. Then, I slowly opened my eyes to see that I was still standing before the same large red-headed woman. It was hard for me to think about anything other than my hatred toward Harrison, but I forced myself to instead picture each member of my family. With clear images of them in my mind, I tried several more times. But the results were never different.

I didn't say anything to her, but I stormed back upstairs. Not only was I upset about everything that had happened with Harrison, but I was also angry that I was seemingly trapped in a world he no longer wanted me in.

As I entered the room, I heard the phone squeak out a distorted beep. I picked it up with the full intention of throwing it again and breaking it, but something inside me told me to listen to the voice message that had just come through. I pressed play.

"Sera. Oh, my God. I'm so—" I could hear him retching in the background. "Ugh. I'm so sorry. Please . . ." he said before he continued to puke. "I didn't—I wasn't—" I heard him groan and continue emptying the contents of his stomach.

Although I was still furious at him, he was obviously sick, and I was concerned for his well-being.

When I walked back into the kitchen, Mattie was still sitting at the table but was noticeably dazed.

"Mattie, I'm sorry. I know my emotions have been all over the place, but I can explain everything later. For now, can you please bring me over to Harrison's apartment? He left me a voicemail." I played the first few seconds of it for her.

Thankfully, she didn't ask me any follow-up questions. She went into her room to get a bag. I was unaware of its contents but wasn't in the mindset to question it. Then, we climbed into her car, and she drove me there in silence.

"Do you mind if I come up with you?" she asked when we pulled up to his building.

"Not at all. I'm not sure what we're going to be walking into. You heard the voicemail. He's obviously sick. He told me that he gets incredibly ill after drinking, and I think he was with friends last night." I didn't want to tell her about the video. I was heavily relying on Mattie's emotional stability, so I didn't want to risk angering her.

We parked the car and headed to his apartment. His door was ajar, so we both quietly stepped inside. As I walked toward his bathroom, I saw his lifeless arm in front of the sink. "Mattie!"

We rushed to him and worked together to lift his heavy body. I furiously wiped his hair out of his face. Underneath it all, I saw that he was pale, and his mouth was dry and cracked.

She immediately started assessing him.

"Well?" I asked in a panic, anxiously waiting to hear if his heart was still beating and forgetting Nirvanas physically couldn't die in this world.

She didn't answer me, she just retrieved a bag full of clear liquid attached to a tube, and she shoved the needle at the end of it into a vein in Harrison's hand. She held the bag up above his head for several seconds.

I held his body against mine and felt the weight of his head resting heavy and limp against my shoulder. It was hard to see someone who was usually so able-bodied in such a vulnerable state.

Mattie soon returned and poured a large amount of the water down his throat.

"What do we do now?" I asked after a few seconds had passed. Nothing about his condition changed.

"Just give it one more—"

She was interrupted by the sound of his loud cough and subsequent release of liquid into the wastebasket Mattie held for him.

"Good job, Harry," she said as she lightly patted his back.

I didn't know how to react, so I just sat there as she continued to clean him up.

"Why don't you go wait in the living room?" she suggested. "I can handle everything from here."

I sat on his couch and tried to work through my conflicting emotions. I was relieved that he was okay, but I was also angry he'd ditched me, even though he knew he would feel like this as a result. Images of the blonde that had bounced around on his lap also flashed through my head.

I don't know how she did it, but Mattie eventually got him up on his feet. At first, I just watched as they moved down the hallway toward his room. His right arm was resting on her shoulders, and she was holding his body upright. The clear bag was in her other hand. After a few moments, given what I knew about her already unstable gait, I stood to help, but she nodded me away.

"All right. I think he'll be okay now. But just in case, let's stick around a bit. At least until I know he can keep liquids down. Is that okay?" Mattie asked. She already knew what my answer was going to be, so she sat down on the couch before she even heard it.

"Yeah, of course. Is there anything you need me to do?"

"Not right now. I got Harry to lie down on his bed. He's still hooked up to an IV. His body needs to be flushed out. I also put a trash can next to him in case he needs it. Thankfully, he doesn't have a fever."

I nodded in silence. I was about to ask her how she knew how to administer an IV, but before I could, we both heard Harrison puking into the basket. Mattie got up and brought him some more water.

When she returned, I abandoned my previous question and asked, "So, what exactly do you think is wrong with him? He told me alcohol makes him incredibly sick, but he didn't make it seem like it was ever this bad."

"Well, the Ikshana warn all of us against abusing alcohol or other drugs. There is a high chance that those substances will react negatively with the large quantities of medicine we take. But Harrison's liver is already damaged because of his disorder, so alcohol makes him particularly ill," she said as she rubbed at her temples. "But I've seen him have a hangover before, and you're right, it has never been like this. If I had to guess, I'd say there was also another substance involved."

I was caught off guard by the nonchalant way she said that last statement. I thought perhaps she wasn't fazed by illicit substances because drugs, although by prescription, were such an essential part of life in Ananda. But I couldn't ask any more questions because we were interrupted by the familiar sounds coming from Harrison's room.

I touched her arm when she started to get up off the couch again. "I can do it, Mattie." I filled another glass up with water and walked to his room. When I first stepped foot through the doorway, I caught the whiff of a familiar smell—the combination of alcohol and vomit. Exactly how Uncle Ford smelled every "chaos night." I started to breathe out of my mouth to avoid being further triggered by the disgusting stench.

I turned my attention to Harrison. He looked so defeated as he lay on his side, clutching his stomach. He had his eyes closed, and for his sake, I hoped he was fast asleep. I set the glass down on his nightstand and clumsily pulled back the wet strains of hair stuck to his face. I had a hair tie on my wrist, so I did the best I could to secure the curls back.

Before I knew it, I was sitting next to his lifeless body and gently stroking his face. Although the anguish he was going through was visible on his face, I still thought he looked incredibly handsome. Any desire I had to scream at him dissipated by the second.

He responded to the touch of my fingertips with a slight grunt. He then opened his eyes and tried to speak.

"Shh," I quickly said. "I'm sorry if I woke you. Do you want some more water?"

He nodded weakly. I lifted his chin to pour the liquid into his mouth. I only gave him half of the glass, and I sat in a chair across the room to observe whether or not his body would reject it. A few minutes passed, and he seemed to keep it down. He had closed his eyes and was breathing deeply. I sat and stared at him a while longer, but once I was satisfied that the water would stay in his body, I walked back out to give Mattie the status report on our patient.

"How's he doing?"

"Well, I gave him half of a glass, and he hasn't puked it up. I think he's asleep now."

"Good." She motioned toward the TV with the remote. "Do you want to watch anything?"

"Sure, whatever you want. But I'm gonna sit here just in case," I said as I pulled one of Harrison's kitchen chairs between the couch and his bedroom door.

"Okay, sweetie," Mattie said, smiling a little. She relaxed into the couch cushions and settled on a show about traveling around Ananda. This program was obviously not terribly interesting to her, however, because she was asleep within the first few minutes of it.

After a while, I went into his room to check on him again. To my surprise, I was desensitized to the foul smell, and I could breathe out of my nose again. I found him lying on his back, staring at the ceiling.

"Oh! You're awake! Here, drink some more water." I carefully lifted his head again so he wouldn't choke. "Okay, good. I'll come back in and check on you again in a little bit. Mattie's outside sleeping, so I don't foresee us leaving anytime soon." As I got up off the bed, he grabbed my arm with a strength I didn't expect him to have at that moment. I turned to face him.

Before I could ask what he wanted, he was on his back and gestured for me to lie with him. I hesitated but eventually snuggled next to him. My heard was on his chest, and I quickly fell asleep to the soothing sound of his heart beating.

I'm not sure how long I was asleep. But when I woke up, Harrison was wide awake and playing with my hair.

"Shit. I'm sorry. I didn't mean to fall asleep!" I tried to get up, but he stopped me. He didn't say anything but kissed the top of my head when I wriggled back into a comfortable position alongside him.

We were both silent until I couldn't stop myself from saying, "I'm still angry with you, you know."

He moaned softly to indicate that he did, in fact, know.

"I can't believe you'd ditch me just to drink with your friends. Especially when you knew—you already knew this is what would happen." I sat up and gestured toward his temporarily disabled body.

Through a scratchy voice, he whispered, "I didn't mean to. I swear, Sera. I don't even know what happened. I just woke up on the ground inside my apartment in a pool of . . . well, you know." He began coughing, so I got up to get him more water.

After I returned and he took a few sips, he said, "I started freaking out when I saw all of the texts you sent me, and I realized I had unintentionally blown you off. I'm so confused. I'm sorry."

"You don't remember anything from last night?" I asked after he took a bigger gulp of the clear liquid.

"Well, I remember texting you to confirm our plans for the night, and then I went over to hang out with Judge and Jared until it was time to pick you up. We usually hang out on Thursday nights and watch whatever game is on. But when I got next door, only April was home. I was going to leave, but she convinced me to stay because she said the guys would be back any minute. After I gave in and sat down on their couch, she handed me a soda."

He coughed a few times before continuing to explain, "When I first took a drink, I thought something didn't taste right. But when I asked her about it, she said it was out of the fridge for a while, so it was probably just flat. I didn't fully believe her, but I took a few more swigs. That's literally all I can remember."

My heartrate rose as everything started to make sense. I had to give it to April; she was calculated. She had intentionally set up his phone to record them fooling around. It was always her intention for me to see it.

"That fucking bitch." I rushed to get my phone in the next room. "Look at this." I held the video above his head and pressed play. I couldn't bring myself to watch it again, so I handed it to him, stood across the room, and waited for his reaction.

"Oh my god. What the fuck?" he yelled. "Where is that? It isn't next door."

I paused for a moment to make sure he hadn't woken Mattie up. But it wasn't long before I heard her loud snoring. So, I continued, "Harrison. This is serious. I think she drugged you."

"But why?"

I rolled my eyes. I couldn't believe how naive he was being. "You said it yourself that she wants you. And she went after me because I'm just another obstacle preventing her from having you. She obviously can't risk exposing herself by reporting me to the Ikshana, so she had to come up with another plan to get me out of the picture."

His head was buried in his hands. I could tell he was struggling to wrap his head around everything. "Is that the only one?" he asked when the video stopped.

"That's all she sent me."

He sighed in relief. "Good. Let's hope that means she didn't take things too far." He was referring to the fact that the video only showed the two of them sloppily making out.

"What if she did, Harrison? From everything you've said so far, it sounds exactly like what she did to Jared. What if . . . "

"We can't worry about things like that without any concrete evidence."

He was right. So, I changed the subject. "I'm ashamed to say that she almost succeeded," I said.

"What do you mean?" He looked up at me, and his light brown eyes pierced my soul.

I had to look away before I could say anything. "I tried to leave this morning."

"Leave Mattie and Ralph's? Where were you planning to go? Your grandma's?"

"No, Harrison. I tried to leave Ananda. Mattie gave me the instructions. I tried several times, but it didn't work."

There was a long pause. Neither one of us knew what to say.

"Well," he said at last, "where do we go from here?"

"I don't know." I was standing by the window, twiddling my hair in between my fingers. I watched the black strands glimmer in the sunlight.

"Sera?" he said, knowing he didn't have my full attention.

"Hm?"

"Come here." He again outstretched his arm, inviting me in. He hugged me tightly. I felt his breath on the top of my head. "I'm so sorry you had to go through that. I can't begin to tell you how sorry I am. I would never do anything like that to you intentionally. Especially after everything that happened with your uncle."

"I know. I know. I'm sorry I got so angry. I should've suspected something else was going on. I saw the blonde in the video, but it didn't register with me at first that it was April."

After several minutes of silence, I asked, "So, what are we going to do about her?"

"What do you mean?" he said, sounding confused.

"Well, she can't just get away with this. I say we turn her over to the Ikshana."

"We can't do that," he murmured.

"Why not? We don't have to tell them about Berlin. She can stay here with you, Judge, and Jared."

"We just can't. I couldn't do that to Judge. We can't tell anyone any of this ever happened, okay?"

I couldn't believe what he was saying. "I get you wanting to be a good friend, but don't you think he deserves to know the truth about her?"

"He does. But I can tell you right now he doesn't want to know. Trust me. He lives and breathes for his family. I couldn't do anything to split any of them up."

I was fuming with anger again. It seemed there was nothing I could do to get my revenge against April. I sat with my arms and legs crossed and my back facing him.

He got up slowly and kissed the back of my neck. "I understand you're upset. But this is the best for everyone, okay? I just won't ever put myself in a position where I'm alone with her again. Promise."

"I don't understand why you aren't more upset. She completely violated you. She sexually abused you!" I started to yell but lowered my voice when I remembered Mattie was asleep in the living room. "You better not expect me to be civil around her," I said, picturing how satisfying it would be to tackle her and pull her hair out, one piece at a time.

"Of course, I'm angry, but it won't do anything but cause problems if we overreact. And Judge and Jared are my best friends. They've done so much for me, so I can't just abandon them altogether. I'm sorry, but I can't say with one hundred percent certainty that you won't ever have to encounter her again."

I heard Mattie stirring. "What about Mattie? We can't even tell her?"

"No. Matts hates April even more than you do."

I snorted, highly doubting that was true.

"I'm serious. She'll also be inclined to report April to the Ikshana. So, we'll just tell her that I did ditch you to drink with my friends. She'll be mad at me, but I think she'll buy it. Will you play along?"

"Ugh."

"Sera. Please? For me? And for Judge and Jared?"

"Fine. But I won't like it."

I was suddenly reminded of the putrid smell emanating from his body. I winced and said, "Now. Do you feel well enough to let me help you wash up a little?" I didn't fully comprehend what I had just offered to do.

"Uh, are you sure?"

Then it clicked. I'd have to see him naked. "Yeah. Yeah, it's fine," I said calmly, but I was freaking out inside. I had seen Harrison partially bare chest and back, and I had seen a more intimate part of him a few nights ago, but I had never seen him fully naked. I double-checked that Mattie was still asleep on the couch when I returned to get him from his room after I turned on the bathwater.

We walked to the bathroom together. He leaned on me the way he did on Mattie, and I held the clear bag attached to his hand like she did.

"Ugh. I definitely needed that," he said as he put his toothbrush back in the medicine cabinet. He started pulling his shirt off but hesitated. "You sure you're comfortable with this?"

"Mhm." It's not that I was uncomfortable; part of me was even excited for him to be totally vulnerable in front of me. But I was still a little scared because I had never seen a man completely exposed before. Regardless, I put on a brave face. We both only had one available arm, and we struggled to get his shirt off.

As I had been in the past, I was almost stunned by the appearance of his body. Given his current state, I wasn't trying to be sexual, but I couldn't help myself. My fingers ran along his chest before clumsily assisting in the removal of his belt and pants. After that, only a thin cotton barrier stood between me and his completely undressed body. I looked away as he removed it. Then, I helped carefully lower him into the water. Fortunately, Mattie had already put tape on the back of the IV bag because I was able to secure it on the wall outside the shower. Then, with all of my attention on his body—I tried my hardest not to look at one specific part for too long. I must have been crossing my eyes or something because he appeared as a big peach-colored blob.

Unfortunately, or fortunately, depending on how you look at it, my vision cleared the moment I heard him softly yelp. "Ah! It's a little hot."

"Oh, shoot. I'm sorry! Here." I turned the faucet on to add some colder water. "Is that better?"

"Yeah, thanks."

My eyes were then drawn to the large bandage that was still wrapped around his elbow.

He saw me staring at it, and he distracted me by saying, "Can you hand me the soap?"

I did as he asked. Then, I lathered up a significant amount of shampoo in my hands, and I covered his hair with it. After I rinsed it all off with the showerhead, he grabbed my chin, so I was focused on his face.

"Thank you for taking care of me. Not every girl would do all of this. Especially after —"

I cut him off. I couldn't think any more about what April had done to him over the course of the night. "It isn't a big deal. I'm happy to help." I reached for the conditioner, but he stopped my hand and instead drew me closer to him. Our lips met, and he began kissing me hard. It was like I was in a trance at first, but I pulled away when I heard him let out a noise indicating he was in pain.

"I don't think you're up for this."

"Maybe you're right. But you seem to be just fine," Harrison said with a mischievous smile on his face. He asked me to grab the showerhead and hand it to him. "Do you trust me?"

"Yes," I said breathlessly. I was surprised he was in the mood to do anything remotely sexual, but I was fine with it. I think I wanted to "reclaim" him in that way from April.

"Take off your pants and come join me in here."

Surprised by this, I said, "Are you crazy? What if Mattie wakes up and comes in here?"

"Don't worry. It'll only take a second." I hesitated, but he looked at me in such a way that I couldn't help but fulfill his request.

I undressed the bottom half of my body and slowly lowered myself so that I was straddling but not actually sitting on his legs. He moved the showerhead and turned it on, so the water was spraying directly under me.

"What? Oh!" Before I could question it, I felt the purpose of what he was doing.

"Just keep doing that," he said as he put my hand around the hose to replace his. I don't know how he did it, but with one hand, he then swiftly removed my t-shirt so that only my bra was showing, and he scooted me on my knees closer to him. I continued as he suggested. For the most part, he just watched me, but he occasionally kissed me lightly on the neck and breasts.

At first, I was self-conscious about doing something like this in front of him, but all concerns dissipated as I got closer to climax. After, he turned the water off, and I opened my eyes to look at his face. I was embarrassed for a second because I'd almost forgotten he was in the room.

"That was incredibly sexy," he said as he gently kissed me. "I wish we could stay in here for the rest of the day, but Mattie might catch us eventually."

I felt the same desire to stay there with him until our fingers and toes turned into disgusting little prunes, but he was right. I got up, dried off my legs, and put my clothes back on. I then continued the task he had just distracted me from, and I covered his curls with conditioner. As I always did with my own hair, I let it sit for a few minutes before rinsing it off.

"Okay, I think you're all set!" I said as I admired his body, which I had helped return to its natural, immaculate state.

"Thank you, Sera. You're the best."

I bent down to lightly kiss him before I helped him stand up. He grabbed the bag attached to the wall and held it above his head this time.

"No problem. Do you feel better now?" I asked.

"Yeah. Much better. Still a little nauseous, but at least I don't smell like trash anymore."

He was probably referring to actual garbage, but I laughed to myself at the thought of April equating to discarded waste. Then I immediately felt nauseous at the reminder of her existence and the video footage I had seen of her taking advantage of him.

I waved the images out of my mind as I walked down the hall to get him some clean clothes. I was happy to see that Mattie was still howling loudly in her sleep. But her neck was in an odd position, so I snuck over to straighten it without waking her up.

After picking a fresh outfit, I walked into the bathroom and got approval from Harrison. Then I helped him as he put them on. When he was fully clothed, he sat on the side of the tub while I dried his hair and secured the long locks back in a low bun.

"You're gonna have to show me how you do that," he said after he examined my work in the mirror. "You do it way better than me."

I used a similar technique that I always used when putting my hair up on top of my head. "Yeah, well, I'm guessing I've had a little more practice. I'll show you how to do it tomorrow. For now, I think you should get some more rest."

"Yeah, you're probably right." We walked back into his room, and he flopped onto his bed. I sat next to him, and he grabbed my hand and planted a kiss on it.

We both heard Mattie's heavy footsteps coming toward us, and her prominent figure crowded the doorframe shortly after.

Chapter 16 – Insecurities

"What did I miss?" she asked through a yawn.

Harrison and I looked at each other and smiled.

"Well, I'm feeling much better, Matts. Sera helped me get cleaned up."

He was still holding my hand, and Mattie noticed. "So, I assume the two of you are on good terms again?"

"Yeah, we're good," I said.

"Hm. Well, as much as I want to know the details of whatever you were up to last night, Harry, I won't ask. As long as Sera is okay with it, I guess I am too. But don't you dare blow her off like that again. You hear me? And you know better than to put yourself in a position like that. That's way too dangerous. If the Ikshana found out—"

"I know, Mattie. I won't let it happen again."

"You better not. If you do, I'll bring Ralph over here to whoop your behind. I don't care that you're technically grown. If you deserve a spanking, you deserve a spanking."

I was stewing in anger because I was reminded that April's actions could have landed him in trouble with the Ikshana. But I couldn't stop myself from audibly laughing at the image of the pudgy, stout Ralph trying to pull Harrison's long body over his knee. It was also kind of cute that Mattie still held Ralph in such high regard. In her mind, I'm sure she believed he was capable of doing such a thing.

"Got it," Harrison said, laughing lightly. He was probably picturing a scene similar to the one that was playing in my head.

"Good. Well, I'm glad you're feeling better, at least. I'm going to get going. Sera, are you coming with me, or are you going to stay?"

I looked at Harrison to gauge what he wanted me to do. He nodded, indicating he wanted me to stick around.

"I think I'll stay, just to make sure he's okay overnight."

"Okay, good idea." Mattie took down the bag I had reattached to his bedroom wall, and she took the needle out of his hand. "Call me, Harry, if you feel like you need this again. See ya later, kids. Be good."

After she closed the door, we looked at each other. He said, "Hey, I never got the chance to ask you. Are you excited to start classes in a few days?"

"Yeah, I guess. It's kind of nerve-wracking too. Just the thought of having to meet all of those new people and everything."

"I get it. But you'll know one person there!" He winked at me.

"True. But I don't know how much we'll see of each other. I was looking at a campus map, and our departments look far away from each other. The science labs are on the opposite side of the building from the education classrooms."

"Hmm . . . if only you knew someone who had some pull with the administrative staff and used a favor to get lockers right next to each other."

"Really?"

"Yep! They're roughly equal distance from both departments, so neither of us has to go too far out of the way from our classes."

"And just what did you do to earn such a favor?"

"Don't worry about it. I have my ways," Harrison said as he gently tickled my sides.

I don't know why I even asked. I already knew he had probably charmed some older lady in the office with that intriguing smile of his.

"Is that all right?" he asked.

"Is what all right?"

"That I did that. I don't want to seem overbearing. I just thought it would be nice for us to have a convenient little meetup spot. I can always have Gladys change the location of yours."

I smiled. I was right about him laying his allure on thick with an elderly administrator. "No, I think it's a good idea. Now I'll have something to look forward to after each class!"

He coughed roughly, and I was reminded of his condition. I retrieved another glass of water for him.

"Why don't you just focus on getting some more rest. Are you hungry? I think having something more substantial in your belly will make you feel even better."

He accepted the cup I offered him. "Yeah, that sounds good." He closed his eyes, and I sat by him for a moment, softly tracing the dark circles that had formed under his eyes and down the bridge of his nose.

When I was sure he was asleep, I quietly escaped to his kitchen. I rummaged through his pantry, fridge, and freezer, and I was happy to find a majority of the ingredients needed.

Whenever I was sick growing up, my dad would always make the biggest pot of chili for me. He said the heartiness of it was the cure to any illness, as long as it was also made with love. I wasn't ready to tell Harrison yet, but I was pretty sure my feelings for him fulfilled that last criterion. I couldn't remember feeling as close to another human being as I did with him. Not even Jonesy, my parents, or younger siblings. And, because he trusted me enough to be as vulnerable as humanly possible in front of me, I hoped he felt the same way.

I finished preparing dinner, and I piled spoonfuls of my concoction into a bowl and set it on the table. Then, not knowing if he would feel up to joining me, I prepared another bowl for him and brought it into his room. He was still sleeping, and I debated whether or not I should wake him. In the end, I opted to because I thought he was in desperate need of sustenance, given everything I had recently seen and heard leave his body.

"Harrison?" I said as I gently shook his weakened form.

"Hm?" he said as he started to regain consciousness.

"I made you some chili. My dad says it's the one meal that's the cure for any ailment. He made it for me all the time when I was a kid. I couldn't find everything, but the important stuff is in here." I helped him sit up a little, and then I handed him the bowl.

"Mm. This smells good. Thank you, Sera. I don't know what I'd do without you."

"Don't mention it. I'll be eating right outside in the dining room if you need me."

He grabbed my hand before I could walk out the door. "I'm serious. I don't know how to thank you enough for everything." I squeezed his hand back and once again headed out of the room. "Wait, Sera? Sorry. One more thing." I turned to face him, resting my body against the doorframe.

"Yeah?"

"This is incredibly selfish of me to ask. But please don't try to leave again. At least not for a while. I'm quickly learning how much I need you here in Ananda."

"I—I won't." My voice cracked as I said this.

"Do you promise?"

As much as I wanted to, I couldn't truthfully make that promise. I still had my family back in the real world to consider. I loved being there with him, but I wasn't oblivious to the fact that there might come a time when I would need to go back.

I knew that my registration as his Samsara wasn't enough to allow me to travel back and forth like the others. But I was determined to find a way to leave just in case I was needed sooner rather than later. Besides, Jonesy, who was a Nirvana, had managed to find a way to escape. So, I knew it was possible.

However, I couldn't bring myself to tell him the truth, so I crossed my fingers behind my back and replied, "Promise."

The guilt I had about lying to him only grew with each passing hour. We didn't talk much the rest of the night. He only muttered a few words to me after he had gotten ready for bed. He walked out of the bathroom, said goodnight, and kissed me on the top of my head.

A while later, when my eyes started growing heavy, I got up to brush my teeth and wash my face. After that, I snuggled under his covers. He seemed to be asleep, so it must have been out of instinct that he turned toward me and wrapped his arms around me. As he did this, I saw the white bandage that surrounded his elbow out of the corner of my eye.

Curiosity got the best of me, and I slowly wriggled out of his embrace. I paused for a few seconds and waited to see if I had woken him up. But his eyes remained closed, and he continued to breathe deeply. So, I pulled the cloth down as gently as I could, and I was horrified by what I saw underneath. There was a large hole in his arm, with deep bruising and spider veins all around it.

"Jesus," I whispered.

He stirred a little, so I rushed to once again conceal the injury he'd so desperately tried to hide from me. Thankfully, he didn't wake up, and I was able to move back under the covers and his arm. I had a hard time understanding why he was so ashamed of that when he was more than comfortable showing me the scars he got after a car accident during his childhood.

I had trouble falling asleep. My mind was going in circles about the bloody hole I had just seen on his arm. He had said it was all part of routine testing by the Ikshana. But how could that be possible? Did the Nirvanas really need to participate in that much pain just to live here? I knew Harrison's pride was too high to tell me the truth. So, instead, I decided to ask Mattie about it the next time I saw her.

I was also beginning to understand another reason why the Ikshana might not want Samsaras to be around during their inspections. They likely didn't want us to witness the abuse they subjected the Nirvanas to.

I spent that night tossing and turning but eventually woke up to the sounds of birds chirping outside. I got out of bed carefully, not wanting to wake him up. After the day he'd just had, I figured his body could benefit from as much rest as possible.

I turned the shower on and stared at myself in the mirror as I waited for the water to heat up. It seemed impossible, but I could have sworn I looked even more mature than I had after my previous evaluation in Ralph and Mattie's spare bedroom. Not only did I look less childlike, but I also felt more like an adult. Possibly because I was now seeing myself as a sexual being for the first time.

Maintaining that state of mind, I removed my pajamas and climbed into the shower. I was letting the water droplets run down all over my body, and I reminisced about what happened in that very bathtub a day prior when I reached for the showerhead. Before I could grab it, however, Harrison knocked on the door.

"Sera? Can I come in?"

I froze in silence. I was scared and excited for him to see me completely naked.

"Yeah, come on in."

"Sorry. I just need to pee. Is that okay?"

"Oh," I said in disappointment.

"Unless?" he said, poking his head around the curtain.

Before I could help myself, I pulled him in to join me. I didn't even give him time to take his clothes off, and they instantly became drenched in water. He apparently didn't care because he started exploring my naked body with his hands as our lips intertwined. I held him close to me, and I helped him climb out of his wet garments.

Holy shit, I suddenly thought, realizing we were both completely naked.

"What's wrong?" he asked.

"Nothing. It's fine. Sorry," I said, shaking my head. I pulled him toward me once more.

He backed me up against the cold wall of the shower, but I was too focused on other things to initially notice the goosebumps that formed on my skin. He apparently took note of them, however, because he gently rubbed my arms. He continued to kiss me, occasionally moving up and down my neck. Then, he propped my left leg onto the lip of the shower, and he lifted my hands above my head with his unbandaged arm.

"Okay?" he whispered into my ear.

"Mhm," I muttered between moans of pleasure, excited to find out what would happen next.

"Stay just like that. I'll be right back." He got out of the shower for a moment, but quickly returned. Then, he maneuvered himself and slowly tried to enter me.

I was not expecting this. I thought he was going to use his fingers like he had in the past. To my horror, the familiar feeling brought me right back to the night Uncle Ford had abused me.

"No, no, no! Please stop!" I yelled. "No!" I pushed him away from me. I heard a loud thud as I ran from the bathroom. I slammed his bedroom door and began to cry.

Slowly, my tunnel vision started to clear, and I started becoming aware of my surroundings. I found myself rocking with my knees against my chest in the middle of the floor.

Harrison must have heard me calming down because he knocked lightly on the door shortly after that. As he entered the room, he had a towel around his waist, and I saw that he had wrapped up his right wrist.

"Shit, Harrison. I'm so sorry, did I do that?"

"It's fine," he said as he covered me with a blanket. In my fit, I'd completely forgotten that I was naked. He helped me to my feet, and we sat together on his bed.

"What was that? I'm sorry if I did something you weren't ready for. That's why I asked before. Don't worry, you can't catch my disease from that. Plus, I was wearing protection. That's what I got out to get."

I was so inexperienced that I didn't even notice. "You didn't do anything wrong," I said.

"Do you mind telling me what happened then?"

Before I could get another word out, I started balling again. "I don't want you to see me any differently," I said between sobs.

He pushed the wet strands of hair out of my face. "Whatever it is, Sera. You can tell me."

I buried my face in my hands, and I was completely hunched over as I continued weeping. "You might not want me anymore," I mumbled, looking back at him briefly. The thought of him being disgusted by me was more than I could handle.

"Sera, you've just seen me in pretty bad shape. I'm not exactly in a place to judge you. Please tell me what's going on." He lightly grabbed my shoulders and guided me to sit up again. Then, he wiped at the tears that remained on my cheeks and grabbed my hands, which he rubbed gently under his thumbs.

"Okay . . ." I took a deep breath in and out. "Well, you know how I told you about the welts on my back?" I had to look away from him as I spoke.

"Yeah?"

"That, unfortunately, wasn't the worst thing my uncle ever did to me."

"Oh my god," he said as he started to put the pieces together. "Sera, did he rape you?"

I couldn't bring myself to answer with an audible response, so I just jerked my head in a nod.

"Jesus. I'm so sorry. I had no idea. If I did, I never would've . . . when did that happen? Was it more than once?"

"No. Just the one time. It happened the night before Kailas gave me the instructions. I told her about it because I was trying to convince her to let me stay with her. But she didn't have any extra money to take in another roommate, so I guess she thought the next best thing would be to get the instructions from Jonesy and send me here."

"Did Janusz also know what happened?"

"No—at least, Kailas told me she didn't go into any detail. I asked her not to. I knew his days were numbered, and I didn't want to add darkness to whatever time he had left. Plus, my uncle meant a lot to him. The last thing I wanted to do was tarnish good memories by revealing the true monster his partner was capable of being."

"Yeah. It isn't often, but sometimes silence is the best gift you can give someone. And you know that my aunt is a good person. If she said she didn't get into specifics, I'd believe her. I don't see what motive she'd have to tell him anyway if he gave her the instructions without any follow-up questions."

"Yeah. But like I said before, if I knew what price she was paying by giving them to me, I never would have accepted them."

He squeezed me in tight. "Please don't apologize for that again. I'm glad she did it. I'm grateful that you're safe here and not in danger of experiencing more abuse from your uncle."

Chapter 17 – Good Luck Charm

I stayed with him cocooned in his apartment over the next few days before classes started. We only left when I needed to get more of my clothes from Mattie and Ralph's.

After I told him about what happened, Harrison was very respectful and avoided going too far with me. He was almost too respectful; in fact, he barely touched me anymore. With each day that passed, I found myself thinking about having sex with him more and more. These thoughts initially made me feel guilty because I could hear Mama in my head. "Sera. It is very important to wait for marriage," she would say.

I eventually managed to quiet her voice. I reasoned that the desire I felt to permanently combine my body with his was only natural. How could God be mad about a feeling he designed us to have?

One night, he was sitting in bed, reading from a large textbook. I walked in, aggressively shoved him down, and straddled him. I flung my shirt and bra off before kissing him.

"Sera? What—"

"Shh. I want to. I promise."

He hesitated, but when I refused to back down, he gave in. He flipped me over, so he was on top and began unbuttoning my pants. I was already pulling his basketball shorts down. We found ourselves naked together once more, but this time, I was ready for what was going to happen next.

He reached into his nightstand and pulled out a condom. He unwrapped it and secured it on. Then, after pausing to look at me to verify my consent, which I expressed with a head nod, he inserted it inside me.

I felt a sharp pain, and I audibly winced.

"Does it hurt? Should I stop?" he asked in reaction to my sounds of discomfort.

"No. It only hurt for a second. I'm okay."

He continued to thrust his body against mine as my legs were crossed behind his back. At one point, he cleared all of the hair out of his eyes and looked deeply into mine. "I love you, Sera," he said before passionately kissing me and continuing the movements he was previously making. Then, like he had in the shower, he raised my hands above my head and tightly intertwined his fingers with mine. He used his other arm to balance himself, careful not to put his whole weight onto me. What came next was a beautiful symphony of our moans until we both finished.

"Did you mean it?" I asked after we both caught our breath. I was resting my head on his chest and tracing his light scars with my fingertips.

"Mean what?"

"That—that you loved me. If it's just something you said in the moment, it's fine . . ."

"I wouldn't have said it if I didn't mean it." He pulled his face away to see mine more clearly.

"I love you too," I said as I stroked his gorgeous face. He went into the bathroom to clean himself up but returned shortly after. After a few minutes, I climbed on top of him again. I bent down to kiss him and was happy to feel that he was ready for a second round.

This time, feeling more comfortable in what I was doing, I pulled out a fresh condom and put it on him. After that, I slowly lowered myself down onto him. I was grateful that I was now replacing memories of this feeling with him, not Uncle Ford.

He guided my hips as I moved back and forth. He stayed lying down until he abruptly jolted up and used his good arm to lift me as he sat up on the side of the bed. His hands soon found their place on each side of my hips.

"God, I love you," he said again right before he finished.

"I love you too," I answered before losing myself completely.

We fell asleep that night with our naked bodies intertwined.

The following day, I woke up to a strange feeling between my legs. When I looked down, I saw Harrison. He grabbed gently at my breasts as he continued.

"I wanted to start your first day of school on a high note," he said after he successfully made me come.

"Hm. I think you definitely achieved that goal," I said, giggling.

He leaned down to kiss my forehead. "We should really start getting ready, though."

I grunted, but I knew he was right. I scampered down the hall into the bathroom and turned on the faucet. I marveled at my naked body as I brushed my teeth. I was proud of how well it seemed to pleasure him. He walked in a few moments later and kissed my neck from behind. I placed the toothbrush back in the cabinet and headed into the shower. He joined me, and we took turns rubbing the soap over each other's bodies.

It wasn't long before we started kissing again and, still covered in bubbles, he lifted me up and pressed my back against the shower wall. Then, as if our bodies were made for each other, he quickly slipped inside of me. I was impressed he could hold me up with only one arm. He bounced me up and down until he lightly put me down and used his hand to finish.

"Jesus. Good thing we have stuff to do today. If we were left to our own devices, I don't think we'd ever get anything done." He laughed as he cleaned himself. After he washed all the suds off his skin, he gave me a quick peck and got out. I did the same and turned the faucet off when I was done. I noticed he had written a message with his finger in the steam on the mirror: *I ♡ Seraphine Leonor Acosta Demosey ☺*.

I wrote with my own finger: *Sera ♡s Harrison Hercules*. I laughed again at the absurdity of his middle name. I wished at that moment that I could have met his mom because, from everything he had told me, she sounded fascinating.

"I saw your message," I mentioned when I joined him in his room. "I wrote one for you too."

After he was dressed, he left to read it.

"You know, I regret telling you my middle name more and more every day," he said, walking back into the room. He chuckled and planted another light kiss on my lips.

I put the final touches on the outfit I had carefully picked out for my first day. Then I read my schedule for the hundredth time and triple checked that I had all the supplies I needed.

I couldn't ignore the butterflies tumbling around in my stomach as we drove to school that morning. Harrison reached over several times to rest his hand on my knees, which were bouncing up and down uncontrollably.

"You're gonna be fine, don't worry," he said.

"Yeah . . ." I audibly agreed, not quite believing it. It was always hard for me to make friends in the real world, and I had no reason to think that would change in Ananda.

"Just remember you can't tell anyone the true story of how you got here. We both need to be consistent in telling people you are just my Samsara. Fortunately, we won't be lying. You legally are, but Mattie still doesn't know what the Ikshana would do if they found out you came here before you were officially registered. Better safe than sorry."

"Mhm," I responded, half-listening to what he was saying.

I must have looked like a deer in the headlights as he held my hand and guided me inside. I had been in the building before, but there were only a few people inside. Now, the hallways were filled to the brim with bodies. At least four backpacks smacked me before we got to our lockers.

Harrison handed me a piece of paper with my combination on it, which happened to be the same four numbers he'd picked to unlock my phone: 0112. When I opened it, I was surprised to see that it wasn't empty. Instead, I found a fuzzy item I didn't recognize connected to a metal clasp. I cautiously picked it up.

"That was Janusz's lucky rabbit foot," Harrison said. "I wanted to surprise you with it. He gave it to me on my first day of college, and I know he'd want you to have it on yours."

I really did appreciate his thoughtfulness, but I must not have been able to hide the disgust I felt about holding the appendage of a dead animal.

He laughed and said, "Don't worry. It's synthetic. But Janusz swore it was just as good as the real thing."

"Oh," I said, relieved. I smiled and secured the keychain to one of the zippers on my backpack. "Thank you," I said, grateful for his thoughtfulness once again.

I closed my locker and secured the lock. Harrison was adamant about walking me to my first class, so he grabbed my hand, and we pushed through the crowd of people together.

We managed to reach the classroom I was supposed to spend my first period in. But the second we got to the doorway, my blood started to boil. I saw the face of the last person I wanted to see—April.

I clenched my jaw and dug my fingernails into Harrison's hand to avoid lunging at her. I had suppressed everything up to that point, but the sight of her face brought it all back to the forefront of my mind. For all we knew, she could be pregnant with *my* Harrison's baby.

"Oww," he whispered before pulling me to the side of the hallway. "I'm sorry. I had no idea she would be in your class. She must have changed her major. Please, please try to be civil. I know it isn't easy. I mean, honestly, the sight of her even spooked me. But we need to stay calm for Judge and Jared's sake, okay?"

I slowly released my talons from his flesh. "Fine. I'll just do my best to pretend she isn't here."

A loud bell rang over our heads.

"Okay, I gotta go. I'll meet up with you in the cafeteria for lunch later, deal?" Before I could answer, he had already disappeared into the sea of students frantically trying to find the rooms they belonged in.

April took a seat in the back row on the other side of the room, and I obviously wanted to sit as far away from her as possible. Luckily, there was an empty desk in the front and close to the door. I might have imagined it, but I swear I could feel laser beams shooting out of her eyes into the back of my head. *I should be the one angrily staring you down, bitch*, I thought.

Fortunately, I didn't have to wait long for a distraction from her evil glares. Another student wasted no time taking the empty seat next to mine. "Hey! I'm Collins," said a short, light-haired guy with gray eyes, extending his hand toward me.

I shook it and said, "Oh, hi! I'm Sera. Nice to meet you."

"You too. Is this your first year?"

"Mhm. What about you?"

"Yeah, same. I've heard this class is kind of hard for freshmen, but at least we'll have each other, right?"

I figured it had to be a good omen that the first new person I met was this charismatic and kind.

The professor began teaching the class, and she paired us into teams of two. When she matched Collins and me together, he had a big smile on his face and gave me a thumbs-up. I was surprised that she didn't waste any time giving us our first assignment. She instructed us to read examples of various behaviors and match them with the appropriate age for children to demonstrate them. I was expecting more of an introductory course. But not being one to give up easily, I buckled in to learn twice as fast as the older students in the class.

Our instructor walked around and checked everyone's work. Collins and I high-fived when she said we had gotten each one right.

To my surprise, this first class flew by, and I had time to kill before my next one. So, Collins and I sat together on a picnic table outside and continued to make small talk. I was happy to hear that I had my following class with him as well.

As we chatted, he seemed to notice my uneasiness about the swarm of security guards hovering around us. To my surprise, he took out his ID and showed it to the next guard who passed by. Upon seeing Collins's name, he motioned to his colleagues to indicate that they should leave us alone.

Without mentioning anything about the special authority he apparently had, he said, "Oh! Hey, awesome keychain. A rabbit's foot for good luck?" He pointed to my backpack when I set it on the ground.

"Yeah. My boyf—" I stopped, unsure whether I could technically call Harrison my boyfriend. We basically lived together and had sex. Plus, we both professed our love for one another, and I was registered as his "Intimate Samsara." But neither of us had explicitly said we were official like that. "My friend gave it to me for my first day," I clarified, not wanting to spend too much time inside my own head.

"Cool." He nodded toward the door to imply that we should head back in.

The morning ended before I knew it, and the bell rang to signify that it was time for lunch. I grabbed the paper bag I'd stuffed with random things I could find in Harrison's pantry, and I headed to sit at one of the large tables in the center of the school. To my dismay, I had beaten Harrison there, so I had to sit down alone. I was anxiously munching on potato chips when my new friend, Collins, slapped his tray across from me.

"Do you mind if I join you?" he asked.

"No, not at all," I said, still scanning the large room for a tall, curly-haired brunette.

"So, are you a Nirvana or Samsara?" he nonchalantly asked me.

"Oh! Um, Samsara." I was surprised by the question, as no one had asked me that since Mattie inquired about it on my first day in Ananda.

"Got it. I used to be one too. I would come up here once in a while to visit my boyfriend from the real world. But then I got really sick myself, and now I'm a permanent resident."

Before I could say anything else, Harrison slid onto the bench and slammed into me so that my body was between his legs. He gave me a hug and kiss on the cheek. When he realized we weren't alone, he backed away a little bit.

"Oh," he said.

"Harrison, this is my new friend, Collins. We have almost all of the same classes together," I said enthusiastically.

"Hey," Harrison said without actually looking at him.

"Hi," Collins responded with similar disinterest.

I was confused by their tones, but I continued, "And Collins, this is Harrison, my—"

"Boyfriend," he said, finishing my sentence. My stomach did a few flips when he confirmed the question I had pondered earlier that morning.

"So, I'm guessing she's your Samsara?" Collins asked with a tinge of sarcasm.

"Yeah, she is." I noticed Harrison's jaw clench tightly.

"Interesting. Well, I gotta get going. I'll probably see you in a class or two this afternoon, Sera."

"Okay, sounds good. See ya, Collins!" I said as he got up and walked away.

My focus now turned to Harrison. "Have the two of you met before?"

Chapter 18 – Layers of Deception

"Unfortunately, yes."

"What do you mean? He seems like such a nice guy."

"He might seem that way, but he's nothing but trouble. I'd stay as far away from him as possible."

I was about to ask why he'd say such a thing, but I was interrupted by the presence of Judge and April. Again, disgusted by the sight of her, I clung to Harrison's knee and squeezed it as hard as I could.

"Ouch!" he muttered so only I could hear.

"Sorry," I mouthed back. He then grabbed my hand and held it in his. He was also squeezing tighter than he usually would. I was happy to finally see some sign of the anger he had toward her.

"Sera! How has your first day as an Ananda Agni been so far?" Judge asked. He and April sat down across from the two of us.

"Um . . . so far so good." I tried my hardest to force a smile. I pulled my hand away from Harrison's, and I looked at it under the table. There were visible indents where his fingers previously rested.

"Cool, cool," Judge said. "April said the two of you have a few classes together."

"Yeah," I said in a monotone voice. I didn't look at April, but I would bet money she was looking at me with a sinister look on her face. She knew that I was aware of what she had done to Harrison. After all, she had sent the video from his phone to me directly. I think she enjoyed how much her presence made me feel uncomfortable.

Wanting to stop giving her the satisfaction of my obvious loathing, I changed the subject. "So, where's 'you know who' while you're both here?" I asked, being extra careful not to divulge too much information about their secret child.

"Jared switched to working nights, so he's got it handled during the day," Judge answered, staying as vague as I was.

Awww. Father/daughter bonding time. The thought made me want to laugh, but when I lowered my head to cover a smile, I was distracted by the sight of April's foot playfully going up and down Harrison's shin.

Before I could say anything, he grabbed me, and we exited the cafeteria together. I looked back, and she was glaring at me maliciously. She seemed happy with herself for making me so upset.

"Harrison, this is ridiculous! We're basically puppets on sticks to her at this point. She's fucking with both of us!" I shouted when we were outside and no longer within their earshot. A few guards looked over at us, but they were mostly distracted by the other students eating outside.

To ease any concern, Harrison smiled and nodded over at them. They seemed to accept his gestures as reassurance that he had the situation under control. "I know. Do you think I like putting up with April's shit?" she asked in a loud whisper.

"So, remind me! Why the fuck are we walking on eggshells around her?"

"Please lower your voice."

"No! I will not continue being disrespected like this!" I fought back the urge to mention the potential pregnancy. I knew it was too great of a risk to say something about it in public like that.

Before I could say anything else, he slammed me, probably a little harder than he intended, against the brick wall. He tried to stop me from screaming anything else by covering my mouth, but I bit his hand.

After he flinched in reaction to the pain I inflicted on him, I quickly squirmed away and walked straight into the women's bathroom. A guard tried to stop me, but I blew right past him. I stayed there until I heard the bell indicating that lunch was over.

I waited until the very last second to exit the stall and walk to my next class. I wanted to avoid contact with Harrison at all costs. I was still fuming with anger at his disregard for my feelings, but I was also a little embarrassed by the way I had acted.

When I found the room I was supposed to be in, I was happy to see an open seat next to Collins and no sign of April anywhere.

"Are you okay?" he asked as I sat down. Harrison had told me to stay away from Collins, but he clearly had no problem being civil to people I didn't want him around. So, I saw it as an act of revenge against him and April to continue getting to know Harrison's apparent nemesis.

"Yeah, I'm fine," I lied. I turned my face away from him and furiously rubbed under my eyes to remove any remaining evidence that I was crying.

Collins and I were again partnered together, and this time our assignment was to be completed after school. He invited me to work on it at his apartment. I didn't want to go to Harrison's place, and I didn't want to bother Mattie and Ralph with more of our drama, so his apartment seemed like the best place for us to go. Plus, he had mentioned during our short conversation at lunch that he previously had a boyfriend.

Of course, I knew that didn't mean he wasn't also attracted to women. But I didn't get any sense that he was interested in *me* specifically. So, I didn't fear that he'd take advantage or try anything. Still, I knew Harrison would worry if I didn't show up by our lockers at the end of the day, so I sent him a text:

Have an assignment. Going to a classmate's house to work on it.

I didn't wait for a response; I just jammed the phone into my backpack.

"All right, we're all good," I said as I walked with Collins toward his car.

Although I was still pretty unfamiliar with Ananda, I swore I recognized most of the scenery as we drove to his place. This was confirmed when we pulled up to the same building that Harrison lived in. Unlike Harrison, however, Collins lived on a higher floor, and we used the elevator to get to his door. When he opened it, I was fascinated by how much larger and fancier his apartment seemed to be than the others I had seen in the building.

"Dang," I couldn't help myself from saying.

"Thanks. I think?"

"Oh, sorry. I was just taken aback by how gorgeous it is in here."

"Well, thank you!" I secretly wondered how a student could afford such a lavish lifestyle. But I didn't want to pry about his financial situation. "Anyway," he continued, "we can probably set up shop there." He motioned toward the enormous table in the middle of the apartment. I continued to marvel as I walked deeper into his unit.

"Is that a hot tub?" I asked, spotting water in a small square receptacle in the corner.

"Mhm! There's also a sauna in the bathroom."

"Wow!"

"Yeah, it helps to know people, he said with a subtle wink. I wasn't sure exactly what he meant by this. *Does he come from a rich family?* I was previously under the impression that the financial situations of every Nirvana were somewhat similar, but I was quickly learning that was not the case.

"Can I get you anything, miss?" an unexpected voice asked from behind me.

I jumped a little. "Jeez! I'm so sorry. You scared me," I said as I turned to face an older man dressed in a butler's uniform. "No. I'm fine, thank you."

"Sir?" he asked Collins.

"Just an energy drink, thanks."

"Sure thing," the butler said before retreating into the large kitchen.

Holy shit. He really is a big shot.

Without acknowledging his apparent wealth, Collins sat down and started reviewing our assignment. I was still scanning his home, mesmerized by the ornate golden decals that adorned the walls.

The butler returned and handed Collins the beverage he requested, and he gave me a bottle of water. "Just in case you want it later," he said. I accepted it with a smile and opened my own textbook to start working.

We worked well into the night. So late, in fact, the butler emerged from the kitchen once more to offer us "menus" to pick our dinner from. I was raised to eat whatever Mama made for dinner or go to bed hungry, so this whole concept was very foreign to me.

Collins must have sensed my discomfort because he said, "Don't worry. None of the food is ever wasted. The staff will take whatever we don't eat back to their families."

That didn't exactly make me feel any better or less pretentious, but I nodded as if it had because I didn't want to seem ungrateful.

I decided to go with the classic chicken tenders and fries. Collins, on the other hand, went with a fancier option. He ordered a dish that, based on the way he said it, I assumed was French. I had never heard of it before.

I had taken my phone and placed it on the table. Suddenly, I heard it violently buzz. When I unlocked it, I saw a message from Harrison:

Everything okay? I thought you'd be home by now.

I texted back:

Yeah. I think we're almost done. Just about to eat dinner. I'm already in your building, so I'll just walk down when we're done.

The bubble to indicate that he was typing back came and went several times before he must have given up on inquiring about my whereabouts further.

Collins and I finished up the small amount of work we had left to do and got to know each other more over dinner.

Then, when the uniformed man came in to take our empty plates away, I started packing my stuff up.

"So, tell me, Sera. When is the next time you plan on returning to the real world?"

Our conversation up to that point had been light and cheerful, so I was taken aback by the serious and inquisitory way he asked that question.

". . . I don't really know. Why do you ask?"

"Just wondering." Collins suspiciously looked me up and down as I stood to leave. "Anyway! Thanks for coming! You're welcome anytime," he said, suddenly bouncing back into the jovial version of himself.

"Okay. Well, thank you for everything. I'll see you at school tomorrow." I walked at a fast clip to the front door. I suddenly felt uneasy. The only other person I knew who could quickly flip between different personalities like that was my Uncle Ford.

"Where were you?" Harrison asked, practically slamming the door shut in front of me after I walked in.

"I told you, I was working on an assignment."

"Yeah, but you said you were in this building. There are only three people I know of who go to school with us and live in this building. Now, I assume you weren't with Judge, and I can't imagine a world in which you voluntarily spent time with April. So, that leaves one other person . . ."

Crap, I thought. I had inaccurately assumed most people in the building were students. It didn't even cross my mind not to tell him that I was already there. "Okay, fine." I threw my arms up in defeat. "I was with Collins."

"I told you to stay away from him," he said. I was still turned toward the door.

"Well, there wasn't much I could do. The teacher paired us together as a team."

"Let me guess. That's because you just happened to be sitting right next to him, right?"

"Uh—" I was about to make up a lie, but he startled me by turning me around and tightly grabbing my shoulders.

"Listen to me. Collins is bad news. He's never involved with anyone who he doesn't think he can mooch something off of."

I shook free from his grasp. "Yeah, well, apparently you haven't even entertained the idea of cutting ties with April, so I'm not going to listen to your judgment about someone when you don't consider mine."

"That isn't the same thing, Sera."

"Why not?"

"Because, and I know this is hard to believe, but even April seems like a decent person when compared to Collins."

I scoffed and rolled my eyes.

"I'm serious," he said, grabbing my shoulders again but with a different intensity than before. His head was lowered closer to mine, and his pupils frantically darted back and forth to make direct contact with both of my eyes. It was like he wanted more than anything for me to understand the seriousness of the situation.

But I wasn't a mind reader, and I wanted the opportunity to form my own opinion. "Okay. But you're gonna have to give me an example of something he's done that makes him such a terrible human being."

He audibly sighed. "You might want to sit down," he said. He then raised one hand to rub at his temples and motioned toward the living room with the other. I took his suggestion, and I sat on the couch.

I watched him pace in the hallway for several minutes before he apparently gathered the courage to join me and continue explaining himself.

"This isn't easy for me to tell you. Honestly, I'd rather be doing just about anything else right now. But it probably is important for you to hear. Even if it ultimately drives you away."

176

He took a few deep breaths in and out before continuing, "You see, um . . . fuck." His hands were trembling, and he tried to settle them by clasping them together and up to his mouth. "So, obviously, you knew Janusz."

My interest was piqued. I had not expected Jonesy to be involved in any part of whatever he was about to disclose to me. "Yes, of course."

"Well, when he first came to Ananda, Collins was his Samsara. The two of them had dated and lived together in Chicago. You see, Collins's grandfather is one of the highest elders involved with the Ikshana. So, when Janusz and Collins both developed AIDS, there wasn't much decision or consideration involved when it came to them coming here. For whatever reason, Janusz's illness progressed faster, so he arrived first. Collins joined him as a permanent resident later on when his condition worsened."

"Oh!" I said in shock. I was surprised in part because Collins didn't look much older than me, when Jonesy clearly did, but I also never dreamed my beloved friend had suffered from such a horrible disease. I didn't know that much about HIV or AIDS, but I read a biography about Freddie Mercury and the end of his life, which was incredibly sad.

Although this information made me mourn for Jonesy even more, I had to admit—I was glad to finally know exactly what illness he had. After a few seconds, however, I realized the implication it may have had on my health. I had every reason to believe Jonesy and my uncle were intimate in that way . . . and considering what my uncle had done to me . . .

Thankfully, Harrison soon interrupted my thought process and silenced my anxiety. "The two of them continued their relationship here, and Janusz made the mistake of thinking he could trust Collins. So, he told him about his plan to escape. I think he was hoping Collins could use some of his privilege to help. Instead, the fucking bastard used this information to blackmail him and everyone around him. He was constantly making Janusz do things by threatening to tell his grandfather about the escape. Collins also warned that he would make up a rumor that Janusz was planning to infect other people."

His jaw was clenched so tightly that he had to pause a moment to calm himself down.

After a few deep breaths, he continued, "The latter part, of course, was completely fabricated. Janusz always told me he was extremely careful to never transmit the virus to anyone else. Of course, it's hard to know for sure whether he gave it to Collins or if Collins gave it to him, but Janusz seemed to assume the guilt of being the one who passed it on. I never knew him to be a religious person, but he apparently feared some kind of higher power. He told me that he even swore to God himself that he would always be protective of his future partners."

I was happy to hear that Jonesy had likely used protection with Uncle Ford. However, now that the topic of conversation was on his "future partners," which Harrison knew included my uncle, I feared he would bring that fact up. I was still uncomfortable talking about my sexual abuse, so I tried to change the subject. "Wait. He told me he was a freshman like me. If he's been here for a while, how is that possible?" I asked.

"Because of his family's high status, he can just keep going to school for as long as he wants. He doesn't have to work like the rest of us. This is probably the fourth time he's started a new program. Anyway, back to what I was saying before—"

"Wha—" I attempted to interject.

But he continued, "He would call Janusz at all hours of the day and night to do random errands for him, and he had no choice but to comply."

Thank God. I sighed in relief when I realized he took my bait to speak more about Collins.

"It got so bad that he barely had any control over his life. When Collins was no longer satisfied in controlling Janusz, he moved on to meddle in our lives. He even started using Mattie and Ralph as pawns in his twisted game. That's when I had enough. So, one day, I set up a meeting with him to ask what I could do to make all of it stop."

"What did he say?" I asked.

"Well—" He abruptly coughed. "He said that he would leave us alone once and for all if—if I would be with him."

"What does that mean?"

"He wanted to have sex with me, Sera."

I wasn't positive I wanted to know the answer, but I asked the question anyway. "Did you?"

"I was fully prepared to, but the night before it was supposed to happen, Jared volunteered to take my place, and Collins accepted."

"Why would Jared do that?"

"I suppose I never told you this. Jared identifies as pansexual."

My confusion must have been clear on my face. He explained that the term described the sexuality of a person who found others attractive based on factors other than their physical make-up.

"It has nothing to do with the gender the other person was assigned at birth or the gender they identify as," he said.

"Oh . . ." I tried to play it off like I understood, but my naive mind was still spinning.

"Yeah. Well, anyway, Jared has been in sexual relationships with all types of people. So, he figured it would be less traumatic for him than it would be for me, as I've only had experience with women. But just because he had relations with men in the past, that obviously doesn't mean Jared was necessarily a willing participant with Collins."

Harrison scoffed and rubbed at his neck. "The crazy thing is that he didn't even really know Janusz, Mattie, or Ralph. He did it purely for me. When I asked him what I could do to repay him, he said it would be payback enough if I made sure to look after his younger brother and make sure he wasn't hurt in Ananda. Like I told you, I've been given hints that they had a tough childhood. He wanted to make sure Judge's life here was filled with nothing but happiness."

Then, it suddenly dawned on me. "So, that's why we can't tell him the truth about you and April?"

"Exactly. Jared gave his body up for me, so I guess I see enduring April's sexual advances as me giving up mine for him."

"Hm." While I didn't like it, I did understand where he was coming from.

"Yeah. Now do you understand why I don't trust that scumbag?"

"Yes."

"I know that if he gets even the slightest idea that you aren't here on a completely legitimate basis, he'll use his connection to the Ikshana against us all over again."

"What am I supposed to do, though? Our teachers assigned us to work together."

"I know. I was going to go down to the office and have someone in administration somehow change that. But the more I thought about it, and especially since you're apparently partners in even more classes now, I decided it would look more suspicious if you stopped working with him altogether. It might be a dead giveaway that we're trying to hide something about you from him. So, I think it might be a good idea for you to suggest doing assignments here or at Mattie and Ralph's."

"Hm," I said absently. Although I was an active participant in the conversation, my mind felt a little scrambled from all of the new information it was processing.

"With one of us around, we'll be able to monitor the questions he asks you. And I'm not accusing you of being unintelligent or gullible. I just know how slimy and sneaky that son of a bitch can be. Plus, the three of us are more familiar with him and his antics."

"I guess that makes sense."

"Obviously, when you're in class, you'll have to be all on your own. Try to divulge as little information about yourself as possible and definitely avoid mentioning your connection to Janusz. That alone might raise suspicion."

"Okay, I won't." I thought back to all of our previous conversations, and I was relieved that Jonesy hadn't already come up.

"Good. Now that you know the truth, can we please make sure this doesn't happen again?" He raised the hand I had previously bit and pointed at it. There were still visible teeth marks on his palm.

I winced at the reminder. "I'm really sorry. I shouldn't have done that. I was just so frustrated with April and with you. Does it hurt?"

"I think it hurt my pride more than anything, but I'll be fine." He chuckled. "You'd think I was a battered man or something. My wrist just fully healed . . . now this."

"I said I was sorry."

"I'm just messing with you, Sera. And it's not like I didn't also lose my temper outside the school. I shouldn't have pushed you like that. I was just angry that you didn't understand why I had to quietly take all of April's bullshit. We're really lucky the guards didn't take too much notice of our scuffle. One of them did ask me why you hurried away so quickly, but I used the age-old excuse that you were having 'lady problems.' Suffice it to say, no further questions were asked. Anyway, I was frustrated because I was afraid to tell you everything about the Collins situation."

"Why were you so scared to tell me about it?"

"Because I was afraid you'd lose respect for me."

"Why? It's not like you did anything wrong. It's clear that Collins is the bad guy in this story."

"I was just worried you might think I was a coward or something for agreeing to sleep with another man."

"Oh! No. Even if you'd gone through with it, I wouldn't think any less of you. You were doing it for friends. Friends I dearly love too, nonetheless."

"I know. It feels good to finally get all of that off my chest. But can we please make a pact to stop doing things to each other that require apologies?"

"Love means never having to say you're sorry," I muttered.

"What is that from?"

"It's a quote from *Love Story*, a book I read in high school."

"Hm. I like it, and I love you," Harrison said as he kissed me.

"I love you, too."

Chapter 19 – Covering Our Tracks

I should have felt the same way about Collins as I did April, as they both had technically sexually exploited the man I loved. But my hatred toward April was still way more intense. Maybe it was because I had seen evidence of her taking advantage of him. Plus, she did it after I was already around, and she purposefully sent me the video to get in between us. On the other hand, Collins hadn't gotten what he wanted, and his stuff occurred way before I was involved. So, I guess her attack was and felt more personal on my part.

It did disgust me, though, how Collins treated Jonesy. For that, I did feel disdain toward him. But I had to act like nothing was wrong because of what Harrison said. If I started avoiding Collins, he'd likely become suspicious, and he might begin his cycle of blackmail all over again.

We received another assignment in class the next day, and I suggested that we work on it after school at Harrison's place. He was reluctant at first but eventually gave in.

"I know we won't have your fancy staff there, but Harrison's a decent cook. I'm sure he can whip up something for us if we get hungry."

I didn't look at his reaction, but I could sense him rolling his eyes.

"So, do you basically live here?" he asked me when we sat down at Harrison's table that evening.

"Um, yeah, I guess. Except for when I go back down into the real world, obviously." I was proud of myself for remembering to keep up the charade that I was just like every other visitor.

"I find it interesting that you just seemed to pop up out of nowhere," he said.

"What do you mean?" I asked, trying to play it cool.

"Well, I've known Harry for a while now . . ." I was instantly annoyed that he referred to Harrison by the affectionate nickname I had only ever heard Mattie and Ralph use. "But I've never seen you until a few days ago."

"Oh. Um . . ." I scrambled to think of a reasonable explanation. *Dammit. Why didn't we rehearse this?* I thought.

"You know us Nirvanas can't leave Ananda, so I'm not sure how he could have met you in the real world."

"We actually met here," Harrison said, emerging from his room.

"Yeah, that's right," I added.

"Sera was the Samsara for her grandma, who I did landscape work for during the summer. She and I became close, and when the two of them had a falling out, I registered her with me, so she could keep coming here. Eventually, our friendship turned into something more, and here we are."

I was impressed. Unlike me, Harrison had clearly prepared and thought up a plausible back story.

"What's your grandma's name, Sera?"

I shot an anxious glance at Harrison, but he nodded at me, which I took to mean that I should tell the truth.

"Elena Acosta," I said.

"Hm," Collins responded. "So, what happened that you don't want to see her anymore?"

Harrison interrupted again. "Oh, that's actually really painful for her to talk about. Right, Sera?"

"Yeah, it's really hard." I sniffled and touched the bottom of my eye like I was wiping a tear away. I was a terrible actor, but he seemed to buy it.

"Oh. Sorry."

"It's fine. We should probably get started on our assignment. What's the first question?" I said, changing the subject. He and I worked, and Harrison retreated once more to his room.

Later that night, Collins was packing up to leave when Mattie walked through the door.

"Harry? Sera? Ralph decided to be adventurous in the kitchen this week, and we have a crazy amount of leftovers. So, I thought I'd bring you some." She stopped dead in her tracks when she saw him standing by the table.

"What are *you* doing here?" she asked, her eyes narrowing.

"Collins and I are in the same program at school," I answered. "We've been matched up as partners in a few classes. We just finished working for the night. He was just about to leave."

He walked past her without saying a word, and she stared him down until he was out of the apartment.

Harrison came out of his room again, and she angrily asked, "How could you let him under your roof?"

"We didn't really have much choice, Matts. I meant to call you about this, but I didn't have time today. But, like Sera said, they're partners and need to work on assignments together."

"But what if he finds out about the unique situation she's in? You know he won't hesitate to repeat what he did to Janusz. He'll be threatening to run to his granddad in no time. I would bet my life on the fact that he has some kind of monetary incentive to turn people in."

"I know. I told Sera all about that. But we figured it would raise more suspicion if she suddenly wasn't working with him at all anymore. So, we're going to try to make sure she's never alone with him. I figured it would be safest to have them work here or at your place, so we can interject if that snake tries to interrogate her."

"Hmph," Mattie uttered. I could tell she wasn't happy with the idea of him being in her house, but she also knew it was the best solution.

"Speaking of Collins and his propensity to play detective," I said, "what happens when he looks up my *abuela's* name? I assume the Ikshana have records of all the Nirvanas and their registered Samsaras?"

Without getting an answer, I turned to Mattie to offer clarification, "We lied and said that I was originally my grandmother's Samsara, but we had a falling out, so I switched to Harrison's."

She let out another auditory sound that wasn't actually a word. But this time, she seemed pleased with the information she was provided.

"I thought of that, and I looked into it. I was at the headquarters for most of the night searching different databases. I already knew Miss Elena never had a Samsara. Mattie told me she was already here when your grandma became a Nirvana, so I guess she figured she didn't need one." From my conversation with Ralph, I knew this wasn't exactly true. My mother actually denied being her Samsara and chose to be Mattie's instead. Of course, I wouldn't correct him. It wasn't the time or place.

He continued, "So, I didn't need to look into that. But when I started researching our names, I was surprised to learn that the Ikshana don't keep a whole lot of information about any of us. They only have two separate lists of all Nirvanas and Samsaras—inactive and current. Both lists include our names, our relationship designations—family friend, family member, intimate partner, etc.—to our respective Nirvanas or Samsaras, and our locations of origin. For Nirvanas, that's where we lived before coming to Ananda, and for Samsaras, it's where you travel back and forth from. Of course, the females listed as intimate partners are also given a symbol to indicate whether or not they're fertile. Oh, and our illnesses are also documented on the Nirvana list . . ."

"But what about the contracts we signed?" I interrupted.

"Very good point. I looked into that too. Besides those agreements, there aren't official documents that match us up in any way. And once a contract is no longer valid, it's completely destroyed. I guess our fabricated story isn't actually uncommon. Samsaras often switch between Nirvanas. I mean, all of this kind of makes sense. If you really think about it, at least. The Ikshana's main goal is to be able to clearly identify who has knowledge about Ananda, and who has the potential of breaking the rules and producing a child here. Since Sera is on the Samsara list already, and there's no paper trail to prove she was never registered with her grandma, there's no cause for suspicion there."

"Oh, wow. I'm sorry I ever doubted you!" I really was impressed and touched that he cared enough about my well-being to do all that background research.

"So that's how you explained her sudden appearance here. Excellent, Harry," Mattie said as she patted his shoulder.

"Thanks. It took me a while to come up with it and fact-check everything, but I'm glad it all came together."

"But how did you explain how the two of you knew each other?"

I jumped in and said, "That was also really smart. Harrison said that we met during one of my visits when he was doing work for my *abuela*. And you actually did work around her property, right?"

"Mhm."

"You clever, clever boy." Mattie tugged on Harrison's cheek. "But he didn't ask follow-up questions about that?"

"Well, that's where my superb acting skills came in," I said, laughing. "I made it seem like it was difficult for me to talk about. It seemed like Collins bought it because he didn't keep pressing me."

"My, my. Aren't you two a good little team?" Mattie said as she hugged us both. "Just be careful to remember your little lies. Even if you slip up once, I'm sure he'll take notice. God, what a terrible human. Seems like he's always trying to stir something up."

Taking Mattie's warning, he and I took the time that evening to memorialize everything we'd told Collins in writing. Then, when we were sure we'd covered every detail, Harrison walked into his closet and took out an old shoebox. When he opened it, I saw a picture of Kailas and him when he was younger inside of it.

"Oh my gosh! When was this taken?" I asked as I grabbed the photo.

"Man, let's see. I think that was my tenth birthday?"

I smiled as I looked at her face. "She hasn't changed at all. Do you want to know something funny? I actually didn't know if she was a man or woman when I first met her."

He chuckled. "That's not surprising. Kids always made fun of me during grade school for having a 'tranny' aunt."

"Well, that's not very nice." I frowned, shaking my head.

"No, but we were all kids. And she didn't seem to get offended by it. I think she liked people to see her in more of a masculine light."

"Given her line of work, I guess that makes sense. I could see ignorant people not taking her as seriously as a man when diagnosing whatever is wrong with their vehicle."

"Exactly." He was holding the picture in his own hand, and I saw the tiniest glimpse of a smile across his face. "Anyway . . ." he said, quickly putting it back in the box and shutting it.

I had learned early on that when he talked about his life with her in the real world, he was only comfortable doing it for a minimal amount of time. I recognized his desire to change the subject, so we got ready for bed and snuggled under the covers together without saying another word about it. We slept soundly, confident we had succeeded in pulling a fast one on Collins.

The following morning, I woke up to a loud alert on my phone.

"What is that?" Harrison asked, half asleep.

I read it carefully. "It says I have until 4:00 p.m. today to take a pregnancy test. I guess I can get it done in the doctor's office near campus."

"Do you want me to go with you?" he offered, a little more awake.

"No, that's okay. I'll just skip out during the lunch period."

"Okay. Like we discussed earlier, I called the clinic ahead and requested that a female nurse help you. You know, because of everything with your uncle. I thought you'd be more comfortable."

"Thank you." Part of me wished he'd allowed me to advocate for myself, but I was also relieved I didn't have to explain the situation to a stranger. Plus, I knew all of his actions were coming from the right place. He just wanted to make sure I felt safe.

I did exactly as I said I would, and I walked to the sketchy clinic in between classes. It was a little awkward to explain to one of the guards why I was leaving campus, but it didn't take more than one mention of a "pregnancy test" for him to let me go.

When I went in, I immediately sensed a darkness in the air. I knew right away that Harrison was truthful about his inexperience when it came to women in Ananda. There weren't any other men in there, and he would have stuck out like a sore thumb if I had accepted his offer to come with me. I tried my best not to stare at the other girls waiting, and I checked in.

"Name?" asked the uninterested receptionist. She was smacking her gum so loudly that it made me want to jump out of a window.

"Seraphine Demosey."

"Samsara or Nirvana?"

"Samsara."

"Okay, Nirvana?"

"No, no. I said I'm—"

"I heard you. What is your Nirvana's name?" she asked sharply.

"Oh, um . . ." I wasn't expecting this question, given what Harrison had just told me about our original contract being the only documentation that linked us together. But it's not like I had anything to hide when it came to our relationship. So, I warily answered, "Harris . . . Harrison Ellis."

She suddenly stopped chewing the wad of gum in her mouth and looked up at me. "Harrison Ellis?"

Worried she somehow trapped me into saying something I wasn't supposed to, I asked, "Yes? Is there a problem?"

She looked me up and down several times before resuming her indifferent demeanor. "No. Just fill out the rest of this form and have a seat. A nurse will call you shortly." She didn't have a computer in front of her, and all the questions she asked me were recorded in her handwriting on the piece of paper she just handed me. I noted quickly that there wasn't a spot for Harrison's name on it. I was relieved that I didn't break any rules, but I was also annoyed. *That nosey bitch. She just asked out of her own personal curiosity.*

I looked around the waiting room and found a seat far away from everyone else. Then, I sat down and further examined the paperwork. As I said, the receptionist filled in most of my basic information for me, but there were more personal questions I had to answer as well. In particular, I was asked to "guess" how many times I had engaged in sexual intercourse within the last month. I just wrote "4 or 5."

Within a few minutes, an intimidating woman appeared in the doorway and said my name. As I was walking toward her, I passed the receptionist. She was now sitting with another woman. Still within my earshot, I heard them say, "That's her? With Harrison Ellis? Lucky bitch. What I would give to have five seconds with that body . . ." My cheeks turned red, but I did my best to follow the brutish nurse's instructions.

As she led me to my examination room, I overheard loud wailing coming from the room next door. I looked to ask the nurse what was going on, but she just shooed me in and gave me a cup. She motioned toward the attached bathroom and told me to deposit a urine sample inside of it. I scurried over to the toilet and did just that. It was embarrassing to be doing something so intimate in front of a stranger, so I pretended she wasn't there. When my bladder was sufficiently drained, I handed the cup back to her. She shut it and left the room.

I could still hear the cries of the woman I had heard before. Even though I had just criticized the receptionist for it, I was also nosey from time to time. I tiptoed over to the door and pressed my ear against it.

"Shut up! This is your fault!" I heard someone yelling within her room.

Before I could listen more, the nurse came back.

"Negative. You're good."

Stunned by the oddity of the entire process, I walked in a daze but exited the building as fast as I could.

During class that afternoon, Collins leaned over to me and asked, "So, your grandma is from Argentina?"

I looked away from him briefly and smiled, knowing Harrison was right, and he had checked his grandpa's records to make sure our stories checked out. "Yeah, so is my mom. Why?"

"No reason. I just think it's cool. I also have South American ancestry."

"Really? From where?"

"Peru, mainly. Have you ever been to your motherland?"

"No, I wish. Although my mom always talked about how badly she wanted all of us kids to see her hometown—" I stopped. I was too embarrassed to admit to someone so wealthy that my family was poor. Plus, I realized I wasn't taking Harrison's advice, and I was about to give him too much information about myself.

"Well, there's always time. Maybe you can go the next time you're in the real world."

"Uh, yeah. Yeah, maybe." I knew that wasn't true for two reasons: 1) I had no idea how to get back home, and 2) I didn't think there was a chance in hell I'd have enough money to travel like that. Not anytime soon, at least. But I couldn't tell him the first part, and like I said, I didn't want to disclose the second.

We weren't given a joint assignment that day, and I was excited to spend an uninterrupted night with Harrison.

This excitement soon dissipated, however, when he told me we would be watching Berlin that night.

"Do we have to?" I asked. It's not that I didn't like her; she seemed like a good kid. But she was still April's, and that fact made her someone I didn't want to associate with more than I absolutely had to.

"It's April and Judge's anniversary, so I offered to watch her so they could go out to celebrate," Harrison said.

"Why can't Jared do it?"

"Sera, he's with her all day, every day. He deserves a break too."

"Ugh, fine."

"By the way, how'd everything go at the clinic?" he asked, lowering his voice.

"Oh. It was so weird." I reduced my voice to a whisper. "My test was negative, so there's obviously nothing to worry about there. But I heard this girl screaming. Like really screaming. Something didn't seem right."

Harrison was apparently uncomfortable with this conversation. He pinched his cheeks together and silently led me to his car.

"Why did it seem to freak you out when I was talking about that girl?" I asked as we drove.

"Remember what I said about women having to get abortions if they get pregnant here?" "Yes. Obviously, I've never witnessed one before, but that didn't sound right."

"I guess the doctors are less than gentle when they perform the procedure." My stomach started to turn. *That poor girl.*

"Apparently, they want to 'teach the girl a lesson' and deter her from getting into that situation again. I had to stop talking about it at school because it makes me blind with rage to think about someone putting their hands on you like that."

I took his hand that was not guiding the steering wheel and kissed it gently. "Well, it's a good thing we're careful. We won't need to worry about that." He turned to look at me for a brief second, with the right side of his mouth upturned into his subtle smile.

I was relieved when we returned to his apartment that Judge, not April, was the one dropping the baby off. He must have had keys to the place because the noise-cancelling tarps were already put up all around the walls.

He handed the child over to Harrison before giving me a bag that felt close to ten pounds. I half-listened as he explained Berlin's nighttime routine. I figured Harrison already knew it, so I entertained Judge with random nods as he went over each step in excruciating detail.

Although I had been less than ecstatic to have her in our care, the three of us actually had a good time that night. Harrison played with Berlin on the floor while I cooked dinner for us and warmed up the gross mush in a jar that Judge packed for her. However, she obviously didn't find it as repulsive as I did. She swallowed each spoonful faster than I could refill it and offer it to her again. It was kind of cute how frustrated she would get when I didn't have more food ready for her to devour. She would express herself with little grunts to show her irritation.

After dinner, we changed her diaper and put her in her pajamas. Then, we sat together on the couch and watched a movie until she fell asleep on Harrison's lap.

I was drifting off myself when someone loudly burst through the door.

"Give me my baby!" April demanded, grabbing the child.

"What the hell?" Harrison exclaimed.

"Just give her to me, dammit!" He complied and lifted her up, so she was within her mother's reach. Judge walked into the apartment shortly after with his brother, who he likely grabbed to help deescalate the situation.

This plan backfired, however. Jared's presence seemed to make her even more agitated. She quickly grabbed Berlin and walked into the kitchen.

"Judge, what is happening?" I asked.

"It all escalated so quickly. April had a few glasses of wine, and she was kind of rude to our waiter and other employees at the restaurant. When I suggested she should change her attitude, she started screaming and causing a scene. We had to leave in a hurry because I was so embarrassed by her behavior."

"Oh, yeah? You're embarrassed by me? Ha! Well, guess what?" she said as she walked back into the room. She was holding her child on one hip with a pair of scissors in the opposite hand. She cut a large tuft of Berlin's hair and blew it into Jared's face. "See that? Whose hair color does she have? That's right. Fuck you. And fuck all of you!" She angrily stomped into the apartment next door and slammed the door.

Harrison and I were frozen. We sat silently on the couch and waited for whatever was going to happen next between the two brothers.

"What is she talking about?" Judge asked, his fists clenched at his sides.

"Judge. I'm so sorry," Jared pleaded. He was still trying to brush off the small pieces of hair that were stuck to his face.

"Are you saying that Berlin isn't mine? How . . . how could you do that to me?"

"I was drunk. I honestly don't even remember it happening. April told me a few days after. I swear I'd never do anything like that intentionally to you."

Judge raised his fist, but Harrison jumped up and held it back before he could throw it toward his brother.

"Judge, wait—" Harrison started to say.

"Did you know?" Judge asked as he turned to face him. "Answer me! Did you know about this?"

"Don't bring him into this," I said, hurrying to get between the two of them. "This is between you and your brother."

"This isn't any of your fucking business, spic!"

I was about to react to the racist slur he just called me. But before I could, he raised his fist again, and I cowered in anticipation of being struck. However, a hand pushed me out of the way to avoid his punch. Instead, his clenched hand slammed into Harrison's face.

After being shoved out of the way, I stumbled into the wall and knocked down several decorative art pieces. In reaction to the blow to his face, Harrison's body made a similar trajectory as mine, and he ended up ramming into me. I didn't feel any pain right away, but I felt the warm, sticky blood pouring down my face after his shoulder hit it.

Jared somehow managed to swoop Judge up over his shoulder, and they were both out of the apartment before I realized what had happened.

Harrison rushed into the kitchen to grab paper towels. He handed me a few pieces and told me to keep my nose upright.

"We need to get out of here," he said after taking down all of the tarps around the apartment and stuffing them into a closet. In all the excitement, his friends didn't take them when they left.

"Why? Aren't we better off just staying here?" I was confused because I figured the black cloth would've concealed all the noise. But I blindly followed him as he shut off all of the lights and went outside to his car.

"I'm sure someone who was at the restaurant called the Ikshana. Jared works there, and someone easily could have recognized Judge. If we're here when they come, and they catch April and Berlin, we might somehow be found guilty by association. I don't know. I just don't want to be around to find out what happens next." The engine of his car revved loudly as he pulled out of his parking spot.

"Where are we going?" I was starting to feel intense pain in the center of my face.

"Mattie and Ralph's. We'll be safe there."

We pulled up and hurried into the house. Luckily, Harrison knew their garage code, and they left the front door attached to it unlocked. So, we didn't need to waste time by wake anyone up to let us in. We must not have been as quiet as we thought, though, because Mattie came barreling into the kitchen within seconds. "What's going on?" she asked, still half asleep but holding a baseball bat.

"It's okay, Mattie. It's just Sera and me." He grabbed the makeshift weapon in her hands.

She rubbed her eyes and then looked at us in shock as she assessed our current conditions. "What in the world?"

"It's a long story. There was an altercation between Judge, Jared, and April. Sera and I managed to find our way in the crossfire."

"Come here, both of you. Let me look at you." She evaluated Harrison first, lifting his shirt to look for signs of internal bruising. I watched as she did this, and I noticed a large pool of blood on his shirt I hadn't seen before. It was by his right shoulder. When she discovered there wasn't a scratch or cut underneath, he explained that my nose was the source of the large red stain. He also had a black eye and a large gash on his hand. It must have hit the sharp edge of one of the broken pieces of glass on the wall.

"That's going to need a few stitches, I'm afraid," she said. Ralph was also awake by this point, and she ordered him to get ice packs and her medical bag.

Her efforts then turned to me, and she slowly removed the soaked paper towel I had draped over my nose. Very calmly, she asked me, "Did you hear a loud crunch when this happened?"

When I told her that I couldn't remember hearing anything, and Harrison said the same, she sighed with relief. "Good, then it probably isn't broken. A little ice should bring the swelling down." She retrieved a clean towel for me.

Ralph returned with her medical bag, and Mattie quickly gathered a needle with some kind of thread. I noticed that she struggled to put the string through the tiny hole at the top. After several unsuccessful attempts, she was finally able to do it. But her hands still shook violently when she lifted it to Harrison's hand.

"I really don't know if I'm going to be able to do this. If I can't, you'll need to go to the hospital, Harry."

"No! Mattie, I can't. If I show up injured, the Ikshana might piece together our involvement in the situation. We had the special blankets up in our apartment during the scuffle, but Judge made it clear that April had already caused a scene at the restaurant."

"Agh. Good point. I'm just not confident enough to do this anymore. I'm too old. I haven't needed to stitch anyone up in years."

"What if Sera did it?" Ralph suggested.

"Me?" I reluctantly said when all three heads turned to look at me.

"Do you think you'd be able to do it? I'll guide you through each step," Mattie said.

". . . I guess I can try." I took the covering off my nose and was happy to feel that blood was no longer pouring out of it. Mattie handed the threaded needle to me, and I crouched down to get a better look at his hand. She pulled up a chair next to me.

Ralph was behind Harrison, holding his shoulders in a showing of support. My own hand shook a little, and my stomach panged with guilt again when I saw that the new cut was extremely close to the teeth marks I had left on his palm. But I tried my best to dismiss all thoughts from my brain and focus.

"Okay, so puncture the skin from this side, thread it through, and then go at it from the other side." I did as she said, trying not to notice Harrison wincing from the pain I was causing him. "Okay, perfect. Now, tie it off. Good." She bent down and used her teeth to cut the remaining thread.

"How do you know how to do that, Mattie?" This was the second time I saw her demonstrate medical skill.

"She was a nurse in the real world," Ralph answered for her while she was busy continuing to clean Harrison up.

Of course she was, I thought to myself. I felt stupid for failing to reach that conclusion sooner.

Mattie walked to the freezer, pulled out an ice pack, and brought it over to me. "Here, sweetie." She turned toward Harrison. "Now that the two of you aren't bleeding all over my kitchen floor, do you want to tell me exactly what happened tonight?"

Harrison recounted the best he could, and I jumped in to fill in details when I thought it was necessary.

"So, I don't really understand. What do you think set April off in the first place?" Mattie asked.

"It's hard to say. Judge said she was kind of belligerent and was acting rude to the wait staff. He said she freaked out after he suggested she should be kinder to them."

"She risked everything just for that?" Mattie made a *tsk* sound. "I always knew that girl was mentally unstable, but this is next level. I can't even think about what might happen to those boys if the Ikshana find out about her and the baby."

I pictured both of them locked in a damp, dark cell, and my skin crawled at the thought.

"I also don't get why she felt compelled to tell Judge the truth about the baby's real father," Ralph chimed in.

"I think she was hurt by the fact that Judge was apparently embarrassed by her, so she wanted to hurt him back?" I guessed. "If that's the case, she clearly overreacted. But we all know she's crazy."

"Well, in any regard. I'm glad you were smart enough to come here. You'll stay here for the night, yeah?"

"Yeah," Harrison and I said in tandem.

"Good. Well, unless you need me for anything else, I'm going to go back to bed," Mattie said before heading into her bedroom.

"I think we're good. Thanks for everything," Harrison said.

Ralph followed his wife but briefly raised his hand to acknowledge Harrison's words of gratitude.

When the two of us got into the room, we rifled through the dresser and found clothes to wear to bed, as we obviously didn't want to stay in the bloodied garments we were currently in.

We changed, found the extra toiletries Mattie and Ralph always had on hand, got ready for bed, and snuggled in under the covers together. I was on my back, and he was on his side, facing me with his head resting in his hand. He wasn't looking at me, though. Instead, he was staring out the window across the room.

"What are you thinking about?" I asked.

"I'm just worried about my friends," he said.

"I know. But to be fair, they did get themselves into this mess."

"True. But that doesn't mean they deserve whatever might happen to them. You know the prisons here are brutal places to be. And I have no idea what they'll do with Berlin."

"She can't be the only secret 'love child' conceived here, surely. Do you know what happened to any of them?"

"No, that stuff just isn't talked about."

"Well, let's try to think positively. It's possible no one called the Ikshana, right?"

"Sure. But people are usually pretty quick to report noise disturbances. Since we've all waived so many human rights to be here, most people want to be rewarded for that with a peaceful and quiet environment."

He was looking at me now and gently rubbing the bruised area around my nose. "Sera, I'm so sorr—" he started to say.

"Uh-uh!" I stopped him by pressing my fingers to his lips. "We don't say that to each other anymore, right? Especially not for something that wasn't either of our faults."

"You're right. I just feel bad that you were involved in any of this."

"I know. But I'm fine. My nose isn't even broken. It honestly doesn't even hurt that much anymore."

He lowered his head down to kiss me. When he moved to release me, I grabbed his head and continued to kiss him deeply. I wanted to keep distracting him from worrying about his friends, and honestly, I wanted a little distraction myself. Obviously, I couldn't have cared less about what happened to April, but I'd grown to really like Judge and Jared—despite the things Judge said to me earlier that night. And, of course, I didn't want anything bad to happen to Berlin. She was just a baby, and she didn't choose to exist illegally in Ananda.

"Ouch!" I said when his nose knocked against mine.

"Oh, shit!" he said like he'd momentarily forgotten about my injury. "Maybe we should just stop?"

As much as I didn't want to agree with him, the small pond of blood circulating around my nose did kill the mood. He quickly retrieved some toilet paper from the bathroom for me to hold up to my face.

"Let me see," he said after a few minutes. "It looks like the bleeding stopped. But you should probably keep pressure on it for a little longer, just in case."

I was recalling the events of that night as I tried to fall asleep when something occurred to me. If April was actually pregnant with Harrison's baby, she likely wouldn't have been drinking. She was a horrible person, but I figured that not even she would risk hurting an unborn child like that. Plus, she likely would have exposed that during her rant.

Unless she doesn't know she's pregnant yet. The thought caused my body to uncontrollably shiver, and I had to get up to grab an additional blanket to cover myself.

Chapter 20 – The Betrayer is Always Discovered

We woke up early the next morning, but I think we both tried to pretend to be asleep for several hours because we knew what harsh truth we would need to face once fully awake.

Around 10:30, Harrison couldn't take it anymore, and he got up and hopped into the shower. I followed his lead, but instead of heading into the bathroom, I went downstairs, hoping that Mattie would be there.

I was in luck because I found her sitting and reading at the dining table.

She must have heard me coming because she had already bent a corner of her newspaper in anticipation.

"Morning, sweetie. How'd you sleep?" she asked as she pulled her green-colored eyeglasses off her face.

"Harrison and I both tossed and turned a lot. We obviously had a lot on our minds," I answered before grabbing one of the bagels she had carefully arranged on a plate.

"Yes . . . yes, I know," she said.

I paused and listened to make sure I could still hear the shower on upstairs. I was worried about Jared, Judge, and Berlin, but I had waited several days to get alone time with Mattie. So, I wasn't going to waste this opportunity to ask her about Harrison's secretive injury inflicted by the Ikshana.

After I heard the confirming sound of water spraying onto the floor upstairs, I sat down in the chair next to her. "Mattie, I've been meaning to ask you about something."

"What's that, dear?"

"Well, after the Ikshana inspection, I noticed that Harrison had a white bandage on his arm. I don't know if it was there before, and I just didn't notice or . . . Anyway, whenever I asked him about what happened, he always dismissed me and said it was nothing. Just 'standard bloodwork.'" I raised my hands and emphasized the quotations around his words. "But it oddly seemed to get worse, not better, over time. My curiosity got the best of me the other night, and I peeked at it while he was sleeping."

"Hm," she said as she listened to me.

"I couldn't believe what I saw. There's a huge hole in the center of his arm surrounded by deep bruising. Do you have any idea what caused that?"

She went over to the old-fashioned desktop computer in the corner of the living room. She motioned for me to join her.

She typed:

You can't tell him I told you any of this.

I don't know if you're aware, but it's kind of rare to have hereditary hemochromatosis. That's what Harrison suffers from. I believe he is the only person currently in this part of Ananda who has it. That, coupled with the fact that he's very young and fit, makes him particularly interesting to the Ikshana. Every inspection, they order tons of blood to be taken from his body. This is a way to treat his disease, but they also want it to run tests on it. I don't know why they always use the same vein, but they do. His arm now looks like the appendage of someone who has abused intravenous drugs for a long time. He's very embarrassed by that.

"Why?" I asked in a low voice after reading her lengthy note.

She continued:

He doesn't tell many people this, but his mom was a heroin addict for several years while he was young. He's mortified that his arm looks like hers did.

The thought of him being ashamed of any part of his body made me sad. I knew that he and his mother lived with Kailas, but I figured it had to do with their lack of money. I never even considered it was because his mom had a drug problem. I didn't think it was possible, but I respected Kailas even more at that moment. She'd stepped up and raised an amazing young man.

"What are you two talking about?" Harrison asked from behind us a few seconds later.

Mattie deleted the document and shut the computer down.

"Um, nothing much. Mattie was just showing me something," I answered quickly. She and I both rose to join him in the kitchen.

He looked skeptical, but he brushed past it and asked, "Do you want to hop in the shower real quick so we can go back to my apartment and assess the damage?"

By the emphasis he added to "damage," I knew he was talking about the physical harm to his unit but also the situation his friends currently found themselves in.

As I showered, I pondered the condition of his personal belongings and Judge, Jared, and Berlin. I kept picturing the worst-case scenario: we'd find his apartment and the unit next door completely ransacked with no sign of anyone.

Even if that was the scene we were about to walk into, I didn't want to put it off any longer. We needed answers to start developing a plan. And the sooner we could do that, the better. With that in mind, I hurried to get dressed—I threw on Jonesy's old university sweatshirt and the pants I had worn the night prior. I gathered my wet hair and secured it on the top of my head.

"You ready for this?" I asked Harrison before we got into his car.

"Not really, but . . ."

"Yeah, I know." I grabbed his hand. "Whatever we find, we'll process it together, okay?"

We drove in silence, and while I did my best to remain calm in front of him, I was terrified to see the aftermath of whatever happened after we fled the building last night. I attempted to soothe myself by kicking my shoes off and hugging my knees up to my chest as I sat in the passenger side of his SUV.

To my initial relief, the exterior of the apartment complex looked unscathed as we pulled into the lot and parked in Harrison's designated spot.

He and I stood for a second in front of the building. Then, he grabbed my hand, squeezed it tightly, and we walked together through the main door. The beat of my heart grew faster and faster with each step we took up the staircase.

Once we reached the second floor, we noted a small trail of blood on the carpet in the hallway. We decided to inspect his apartment first, and we both let out tiny sighs of relief when he jiggled the handle of his door and found that it was still locked. Inside, the interior appeared undisturbed—aside from the damage that Judge and Jared's scuffle had already caused.

"Why don't you stay here." Harrison suggested. "I'll go over and assess the situation next door."

"Are you sure you don't want me to come with you?"

"No. I have no idea what I'm going to find. For all I know, he might still want to beat our faces in. You've experienced enough trauma already. Plus, if the Ikshana did show up, and there was even the slightest resistance to arrest . . . I mean, I know you saw the blood out there. I've heard about Nirvanas getting horrifically brutalized before being handcuffed and hauled away. I can't imagine what they'd do to a Samsara who so egregiously disobeyed their rules."

Despite my disgust toward April, a chill ran down my spine. I sort of felt sorry for her, but I was also worried for myself, as I technically also fit into the category he had just described.

Without saying another word, Harrison left to inspect the other apartment. I grabbed a broom and started to clean the glass shards covering a section of his floor. Before I could begin sweeping, I heard the faintest sounds of conversation between Harrison and someone else. I set the broom down and crept over into his bedroom. I placed my ear against the wall to hear them more clearly.

The deeper voice responding to him sounded like a man. So, logically, I assumed it was either Judge or Jared. But I couldn't distinguish between their voices well enough to discern which brother it was.

When I heard the door shut, I rushed back over and resumed sweeping. Harrison entered his apartment again seconds later.

"Well?" I asked.

"It isn't good," he said before flopping onto the couch. I walked over and sat down beside him. His forehead was resting in his hands, and I cautiously put a hand on his back.

"What happened?"

"Well, we were right to leave. Someone at the restaurant called the Ikshana. A few officers showed up to the apartment and arrested April on the spot. Then, when they asked who the father was, Judge was about to say it was him, but Jared stepped in and took responsibility. Jared told the officers that Judge had no prior knowledge of the baby, and the argument started because he had just found out about her existence and their affair."

"So, Jared and April were arrested. Is Judge still in the apartment then?"

"Yeah, I was just talking to him. He's in bad shape. I could tell the second I walked in that he's been up all night and day drinking. He can hardly stand up straight, and both of his eyes are completely bloodshot."

"Where is the baby?"

"Judge doesn't have any idea. The officers took her, but they wouldn't say anything about where she was going. I guess April lunged at them when an officer first grabbed Berlin, and that's when the others started beating her with their clubs." He paused for a moment but continued, "I just wish we knew where Berlin was now. Remember I told you babies aren't commonplace here, so it's not like we have child protective services like in the real world."

"So, what do we do next?"

"I don't know. We definitely can't leave Judge alone. I think the best course of action would be to bring him back to Mattie and Ralph's and ask for their opinion on what to do in terms of finding Berlin."

I felt terrible for constantly dumping more baggage onto them. But if Judge was in as bad of shape as Harrison said, I figured there wasn't anyone better than Mattie to take care of and monitor him for the time being.

Harrison went to the medicine cabinet, took all of the bottles with Judge's name on them, and shoved them into a backpack before slinging it on his back. Then, I helped him the best I could as we dragged Judge out of the apartment to the car. We put one of Judge's arms over my shoulder and the other over Harrison's.

By the smell coming from Judge's mouth, I could tell that Harrison was right about him drinking too much. It was also evident he had thrown some of it up. I tried to breathe through my mouth to avoid smelling the foul combination of odors as he rambled nonsense. But, when he spoke in my direction, my stomach turned into knots. The whiffs of the stench accompanying his breath were all too familiar. It got so bad a few times that I had to stop walking for a few seconds to avoid retching myself.

I felt the instinct to apologize to Harrison for each pause, as I knew I was slowing all of us down, but he never seemed fazed by it. I assumed he was also feeling the nauseating effects of the rancid aroma emanating from his friend.

We managed to shove him into the back seat as gently as we could.

"What happens if he gets sick again while we're driving?" I whispered to Harrison as I climbed into the front seat.

"There's a small trash can—it might be under one of our seats. Do you mind finding it and putting it near him?"

I dug around under the seats before locating it. "Here you go, buddy," I said as I moved it closer to Judge. Now that I didn't need the use of both arms, I was able to evade his scent by pinching my nose. So, without thinking about it, I gently patted his arm a few times to comfort him.

It was clear that he felt awful physically. But with all of the events that had just transpired, I couldn't begin to imagine what mental anguish he was also enduring. His whole world had turned upside down within a matter of twenty-four hours. I turned to check on him several times as we traveled to Mattie and Ralph's.

On occasion, I brushed longer pieces of his hair, which were usually gelled into pointed tips, that had fallen onto his face when Harrison took faster turns. It wasn't sensual at all; I think it was more of a maternal instinct. I also offered him sips from a water bottle in the car.

When we pulled up to the house, Harrison went inside while I stepped out of the vehicle and opened one of the back doors. I continued my best to comfort and care for Judge. He needed to drink more water. So, I hoisted his body upright and poured a small amount of liquid down his throat.

"Which one is it?" I heard Mattie asking Harrison as she walked outside. She sounded kind of annoyed by the situation.

"Judge," Harrison answered. "The one who thought he was the dad. His girlfriend and brother were arrested last night, and the baby was taken," he continued to say in a hushed voice.

Ralph came out as well, and he and Harrison worked to wrangle Judge's incapacitated body into the house and up to the spare room.

Mattie followed to assess her newest patient. When she finished, she came back downstairs, where the three of us were gathered near the dining table.

"He'll be fine. As far as the hangover goes, that is. Poor lad. I can't say I have the cure for his heartache in my medical bag," she said. She took a magazine off the table and fanned herself with it. "As for you," she said, looking at Harrison. "You're lucky I love you, kid. All the riff-raff you involve me with."

"I know, Matts. I'm incredibly grateful for your kindness and generosity. I didn't know where else to bring him, and I didn't trust him to be alone."

I chimed in at that point. "We do need one more favor, Mattie."

She put the papers down and let out a deep sigh before focusing her attention on me.

"We were wondering if you have any idea where the officers might have taken the baby?" I asked.

She let another loud sigh out before uttering, "Hm." Her eyes darted from one side of the ceiling to the other while she thought about it.

"If I had to guess, I'd say that the Ikshana will try to contact someone from April's family in the real world to see if they can find a home for her," Ralph said. "Harry, do you know if she has dependable family members?"

"I honestly have no idea."

"Would they risk doing that, though? Contacting people in the real world, I mean. Wouldn't that just invite questions and inquiries about where the baby came from? From everything you've told me about the Ikshana, it seems like they don't want more people to know about Ananda than necessary."

"That's a good point, Sera," Mattie said. "I wonder what would happen if you went downtown and asked around, Harrison. Ugh, no. That might implicate you. It would prove that you knew about her and were aiding and abetting Jared and April. Shoot, I really don't know what to do here."

The landline phone started ringing, and she got up to answer it.

We continued to brainstorm until she returned a few minutes later.

"You're never going to believe who that was," she said. "It was an officer. He asked if Ralph and I would be interested in committing to the care of an infant they had recently found living here illegally. He said her parents were no longer in a position to take care of her because they were incarcerated because of her existence . . ."

Harrison and I looked at each other with wide and hopeful eyes.

"What did you tell them?" Harrison asked.

"I told them the truth. Ralph and I are in no position to take in an infant. We wouldn't be able to keep up with her. It wouldn't be fair to her to be raised by two old fogies." She then looked at Ralph and said, "Sorry, honey. But you know it's true."

Ralph looked angry at first, but then he conceded and nodded in agreement.

"Anyway." She glanced at Harrison again. "I did mention that I had a young nephew who was in a committed relationship to his female Samsara who might be interested . . ."

It took me a few seconds to process that she was talking about Harrison and me. "Oh!" I said as I made the connection. "Um?"

"What do you think, Sera?" he asked me.

"I mean, I'm not sure. That's a huge responsibility. Shouldn't Judge be the first person they consider? They obviously don't know that he has raised her as her father, but they know he's her uncle by blood."

"Unfortunately, just like in the real world, the authorities here are wary about awarding the care of children to single dads. I don't think it's right, but that's just the way it is," Mattie said.

"If we agree to take care of her, Berlin can stay in Judge's life," Harrison added.

Judge had been through so much, and I did want to help reunite him with the baby he'd raised. Plus, I knew that Harrison had a strong connection with her. "Okay, Let's do it," I finally said. Looking back, it's insane how little convincing it took for me to agree to this. I clearly hadn't thought through all of the implications motherhood would have on me.

"Thank you so much, Sera!" Harrison sprang up and gave me the biggest hug. "Will you please call them, Mattie, and let them know we agreed to take care of her?"

"Of course. I'll call now."

Harrison ran up the stairs to tell Judge the news.

"Is he happy?" I asked when he came back down.

"Yeah, I think so. I think his mind is still reeling from the revelation that he isn't her biological father, but I could tell he was relieved that she would stay in his life. He smiled and weakly lifted his thumb up in the air. In his current state, I think that's the most excitement he can exert right now."

"Did you call, Mattie?"

"Yep. The baby is ready whenever you are. Sera, I was asked to remind you that this doesn't change your status as a Samsara. They acknowledged that this is a unique situation, as they don't often deal with the adoption of babies. Especially not to a Nirvana and Samsara, but you will still need to be here every month to avoid detection during the inspections. Oh, and I went to the drugstore while you were gone, and I did my best to find your shades." She held up two bottles of foundation. I never had any, but I'd seen similar containers in the hands of girls at school.

I knew which one was meant for me, as it was much lighter—almost stark white—than the other one.

Due to both of our inexperience with the product, Mattie had to show us how to apply it on our faces. Surprisingly, she did a great job of matching our skin tones, and it was shocking how well our injuries were covered underneath the makeup.

Harrison seemed to be focused on one thing, and that was getting Berlin back. "Okay, Sera. Let's go over to their apartment and pick up her car seat and other stuff," he said after assessing the successful cover-up around his bruised eye.

I took his hand and followed him to his car. My mind was running wild with questions that this new responsibility would present.

I asked Harrison a few of them as we drove. My main concern was who would watch her while the three of us were in school.

"That's a good question. I know that when Mattie and Ralph took on another person to support, they got extra money from the Ikshana. So, I assume that will also happen for us. Well . . . me, at least. In any case, maybe we'll be able to find someone to watch her during the day in exchange for some of that additional money I receive. I'm sure Judge will also chip in."

We continued to talk about what our new life would look like. After we arrived at the apartment building, we wasted no time packing up everything we could discreetly carry in our hands. We were unlikely to get the crib out of the building without anyone noticing, so we left it. We planned to move it into Harrison's apartment later, but I was worried about where she would sleep that night at Mattie and Ralph's. We wanted to stay with them for at least our first night as parents just in case we needed help.

Harrison seemed less concerned about Berlin's sleeping situation, and he assured me that we would figure it out. We covered and brought everything else we thought we'd need for the next twenty-four hours or so down to his car with the large blankets lying around the empty apartment. Once satisfied with the content's anonymity, we shut the trunk, climbed into the car, and headed downtown to go get her.

Chapter 21 – Maternal Instincts

I knew what building we were headed to when I saw the same logo that I had previously seen on Mattie's credit card on the front of it. When we got inside the Ikshana's headquarters, the secretary hurried us into a large board room. It was lined with the same soundproof material that was currently covering her things in Harrison's car. The space was empty when we first arrived, but three men in suits entered soon after.

"Please, have a seat," one of the men said to us. "We wanted to sit down with the two of you and discuss a few caveats before you officially sign the paperwork."

Another one of the men cut in. "As you know, this is a very unique situation that we haven't encountered before. Having said that, we had a board of directors meeting to decide on a few terms and conditions. First, ma'am, you will not be given any special treatment. You are to have the same rights as all the other Samsaras. We will not hesitate to ban you if you tell anyone about this place. If that happens, sir, you will be under an obligation to find another woman to help you raise the child within sixty days. If you fail to do so, we will reevaluate the best home for her to be placed in.

"Second, we tested her and found that she does not have any disease or illness, so she cannot qualify as a Nirvana. As Matilda Shepard suggested, we've contacted your grandma, ma'am, and she agreed to have the child be her Samsara. As I'm sure you've been told, we don't usually allow younger children, nonetheless infants, to be visitors, but we are making an exception this time. She will age normally and can travel between Ananda and the real world with you. You do not need to conceal her when you're home. But you must lead your family and friends to believe she is your biological child. We think this is the best way to conceal the fact that this world exists. If you kept returning with a random child, especially one who didn't age, people would obviously ask questions. Clearly, you're also going to need to impress the importance of keeping this place a secret onto her once she starts talking. We'll leave that up to your discretion when the time comes.

"Third, unlike you, the child can remain in Ananda during the inspections. She isn't required to be, but until she reaches the age of fourteen, neither she nor you, sir, will be penalized in any way if she is around during inspections. Fourth, you will need to agree to keep the child away from the public while in Ananda until she reaches the age of the youngest Samsaras. Having said that, you two, along with your grandma, the child's uncle, and the Shepards, are absolutely prohibited from telling anyone here about her existence. Fifth, in all aspects, you are to operate as her parents. You shall represent Judge Jones to be a family friend. You are not to tell her about her actual parents. You shall raise her to believe she is Miss Elena's Samsara and your daughter, nothing else. Okay, I think that's it. Any questions?"

Harrison and I were both processing everything that was just said to us, and I'm sure both of our mouths were agape. Suddenly, my mind filled with dread. Like a typical teenager, I hadn't considered all the potential ramifications of my actions. *What would happen when I did eventually go back to the real world?* I couldn't imagine Mama's reaction when she was under the impression that I 1) had unprotected sex and 2) had gotten pregnant. I was already so worried about her finding out about the sexual abuse I'd endured, nevertheless being forced to tell her that I had consensually engaged in premarital intercourse.

Would I just leave her here with him? I wondered. *Maybe once we find a way for me to leave, we'll also find a way for me to come back and forth like the others? But what if I couldn't return? Well, like the man said, Harrison would need to find another woman to help raise her.* While I didn't like that idea, I had to accept that it was a possible, and potentially necessary, option. The men before us seemed to have answers for almost everything, and I so badly wanted to ask them for clarification on all of this.

My mind raced a little more, but I eventually came to terms with my decision. I reasoned that it was in her best interest to be with us for the time being, and I determined that I wouldn't get too close or attached to her.

"Well," Harrison loudly cleared his throat, "Sera and I both attend college right now. So, we will need to find someone to watch her during the day. Her uncle, Judge, is also in school. Plus, Mattie and Ralph have already expressed concern about taking care of a child for long periods of time. And Sera's grandma is legally blind, so she can't care for a baby. So, we're going to need to find someone outside that group of people to watch her. Obviously, that person will need to know about her existence."

The only suited man that hadn't spoken yet chimed in. "We did discuss that. We're going to find someone suitable who will agree to remain silent and watch her in our offices every day. This person shall be fully vetted by us, but you will need to pay them a weekly fee in exchange for the child's care. Sir, you know you'll receive additional funds because you agreed to take on this extra responsibility."

"Yes," Harrison said.

"We expect you to use a portion of that money to pay for the childcare."

"Understood," he responded.

"Good. Anything else?"

Harrison and I glanced at each other and shrugged. "Not that we can think of right now," I said.

We carefully read the contract, and we both signed our names at the bottom. This particular agreement I assumed would not be publicly accessible.

One of the men pressed a button to speak to the secretary, and he directed her to retrieve the child.

Both my face and Harrison's lit up when we saw her sweet face again, but we were both careful not to make our familiarity with her too obvious.

"Hi, baby!" Harrison said as he grabbed her and hugged her tightly.

I offered her my hand, and she wrapped her tiny fingers around my pointer finger. I bounced it up and down playfully and made silly faces at her. I was still in disbelief that I had just agreed to basically be her mother.

"If you think of anything else, please feel free to call us," one of the men said as he handed us business cards. "We'll call you and set up a meeting between you and the caregiver we find. Now, if you don't mind, sir, can you pull the car up in the back? Ma'am, you can stay with the baby and meet him back there. But remember, from here on out, you need to get used to being as discreet as possible."

Harrison did as he was asked, and he rushed back inside with the empty car seat. I was thankful for all the experience I had with my younger siblings. Because I had done the same thing hundreds of times before, I was able to promptly secure her in the back of Harrison's SUV. I then got myself situated in the back with her. Harrison looked back at me before he started the vehicle and asked, "Are you ready?"

"Ready as I'll ever be," I said, referring to the current situation at hand and to being a motherly figure as a whole.

When we were far enough away from the headquarters, I removed the blanket I had previously draped over her. I was pleasantly surprised that she was sleeping peacefully. I had only ever associated her with April, so I never took the time to *truly* look at her. Now that she was legally mine, I couldn't help myself from staring and taking in all of her beauty. I gently stroked her strawberry blonde hair. My will to remain detached from her was already crumbling.

"You know it's going to kill Judge," Harrison said out of nowhere.

His statement snapped me out of the trance I was in. "Huh?"

"Remember, it's a part of the agreement that we have to tell her that we're her parents."

I laughed to myself as I looked at my reflection in the mirror. It was almost preposterous to think about me, with my fair skin and jet-black hair, as the natural birth mother of this child, with tan skin and red hair.

"Sera?" Harrison said, getting my attention again. "What I was saying is that that will be really hard on Judge. He's been her dad from the day she was born."

"Yeah, but I think it's a small price to pay for her to stay in his life."

"I guess. I still feel bad. And it's going to be strange adjusting to us being Berlin's primary caregivers. It will be hard not to just defer to him to change her, feed her, and all that. I'm sure that's going to be tough for him too."

"I know. We're all going to have a lot of adjustments." I was sympathetic toward Judge. But I was also kind of annoyed that Harrison was acting like he was the only one making sacrifices in this situation.

He must have caught on to my frustration because he didn't say anything else about it.

When we passed Abuela's house, I made a mental note to go over to visit and thank her for everything she had just done for us. Of course, I knew it didn't make much of a difference to her daily life, but I still appreciated that she'd acknowledged Berlin as her Samsara for my benefit.

Plus, I hoped the two of them would maintain a close relationship. That way, the tiny baby would always have a connection to me, even if I wasn't physically around. I can't say for sure what it was about Berlin, but the thought of leaving her already made me incredibly sad. It was like she put a spell on me or something.

Then, another option, that I had not considered in the office, came to me. "Do you think that maybe the Ikshana would be okay with the truth about me?" I asked Harrison. "Berlin was here on an illegitimate basis and didn't intentionally reside here illegally. Just like me. And they let her become a run-of-the-mill Samsara while she was already in Ananda."

"I thought about that too. It would be great to be released from the secret. But I think it's too risky to say anything. You could be banished forever. Sure, they were lenient on her, but she's a baby."

I sighed a little in defeat, knowing that he was probably right.

"Oh, one more thing," he said. "With all this 'keeping her in hiding' business, if we do ever find a way for you to return to the real world safely, I want you to take her with you."

I was speechless. I had just convinced myself I wouldn't bring her back.

"But, Harr—"

"Please. Promise me, Sera. She'll have a much better life that way. She can be a normal kid."

". . . Okay. Fine. I promise." The sincerity in his brown eyes made it impossible for me to say anything other than that. It would take all the courage in the world to give my mom the impression that I had a baby, but I had just made two vows—one to the Ikshana, and one to Harrison—that I would do just that.

When we reached the house, Harrison grabbed the copy of the agreement he'd asked the secretary to make for him and walked ahead of me inside. He and Ralph went back and forth to the car several times. Then, when I went to grab the heavy blankets, Harrison stopped me.

"We won't need all of those here. The houses are so far apart. No one will hear her once we're inside. Why don't you get her settled in?" He turned away and said over his shoulder, "I'm going to go explain everything to Judge."

I carefully unlatched Berlin's car seat, placed a single blanket over her, and got into the house as fast as I could.

Mattie snapped the buckles on the car seat open and cuddled Berlin to her shoulder. "Hello, beautiful girl. I've heard so much about you!" she said as she rocked her gently. "Welcome to the family!"

It warmed my heart to see Berlin take an instant liking to her new "aunt." She had the brightest smile on her face as Mattie continued to talk to her.

A few minutes later, Harrison came walking down the stairs slowly.

"How's Judge doing?" I asked.

"Well, I think he's feeling better physically. But he was less than enthused about all of the terms and conditions we had to agree to," Harrison answered.

"That was to be expected," I said. "But is he actually angry with us?"

"No, I don't think so. He again expressed gratitude that we agreed to care for her. I think he's just angry about the situation as a whole . . . and as we predicted, he isn't particularly comfortable with Berlin calling us 'mom and dad.'"

I rolled my eyes at the fact that he, once again, seemed to only consider Judge's feelings.

Mattie must have sensed the tension between us. She interrupted by saying, "Well, I'm just happy this gorgeous girl is safe with people who already love her." She planted a big kiss on Berlin's cheek and then handed the baby over to me. I bounced her on my hip.

At that moment, Judge emerged from the lair he had been hiding in for several hours. I was shocked by the sight of him, and I wasn't sure how to react. I might have been projecting, but it sure looked like he was resisting every urge to raise his fist toward me again. Even if I just imagined it, I thought it was best to hand the baby over to Harrison. I assumed it was easier for Judge to see his friend holding and cuddling the child he, until very recently, thought was his.

Always the helpful hand, Ralph assembled her chair that clung to the lip of the table. He awkwardly smiled at me as he shook it to test its stability.

"Well, the three of you have a lot to talk about. We'll leave you to it. Holler if you need anything," Mattie said before linking arms with Ralph and walking away.

I could tell that Berlin recognized Judge, and she raised her hands as if to ask him to pick her up. He must have been trying to distance himself from her because he did not accept, despite the fact that Harrison was clearly offering her to him.

Harrison then secured Berlin in the chair. Instinctively assuming my motherly duties, I went into the fridge to find some applesauce.

Before putting a bowl of it on her tray, I glanced up at Judge and asked, "Uh, she isn't able to feed herself yet, right?"

Looking defeated, he answered, "No."

He and Harrison were already seated, and I pulled an empty chair over to help Berlin eat her food. I was thankful that I had a task and didn't need to make eye contact with Judge, but I still wanted to be a part of the conversation. However, I waited for one of them to start it. I didn't feel like it was my place because I was clearly the odd man out.

"So, Judge. I know we went over the contract that Sera and I signed, but if you have any other questions you want to ask us, please feel free to do so."

Judge continued to look down at the floor until he snapped his head up with the most sinister expression on his face. He practically snarled as he spat, "I just want to know why you didn't tell me." Then he darted a look toward Berlin.

Harrison, keeping his composure, said, "It isn't that simple. For one thing, I was never definitively told that Jared was her biological father. I only knew that it was possible."

"After Jared took my place with the whole Collins situation, I promised him I would try my best to ensure you had a happy life here in Ananda. Unfortunately, that meant I could never tell you about his accidental one-night stand with April."

Judge scoffed. "Well, you sure kept your promise, didn't you? Can't you tell? I'm so fucking happy right now!"

"You really shouldn't use that language in front of her," I said without thinking.

"Don't even get me started with you, bitch," Judge snapped back.

"Excuse me?" I said in a calm voice, not wanting to scare Berlin. "How dare you. You have no idea what Harrison and I have had to put up with to keep you naive about everyone and everything around you."

Harrison gently put his hand on my knee, nonverbally telling me to back off. I brushed it away and continued without raising my voice, "No. Now he needs to know the truth. I'm done hiding his own reality from him."

I pulled out my phone, started playing the video April had sent to me of her straddling Harrison, and pushed it toward him. Judge watched it out of the corner of his eye. When the video ended, I grabbed it and said, "See? That's who your girlfriend really is. She drugged and took advantage of your friend. She probably did the same exact thing to your brother."

He shoved his chair away from the table. "I need some air."

Once he was outside, Harrison turned to scold me. "You didn't need to do that. He's clearly processing a lot right now. The only thing you accomplished was adding a large storage box on top of an already seven-story pile of shit accumulating in his mind." He was careful to mouth the expletive, so the baby didn't hear it. He then got up and headed out the front door to tend to his friend.

I shifted in my seat, but I didn't regret what I had said or showed to Judge. Enough was enough. I was tired of everyone coddling him. I had already put up with so much for him, and I guess I'd reached my breaking point.

Berlin had finished her small snack, and the opening and closing of her eyes told me she was tired and ready for bed. I took her upstairs to the spare bathroom and gently wiped the two or three teeth she had with a warm washcloth.

After that, I brought her to the bedroom. A smile spread across my face. The air was clean, so it was evident that Mattie had flipped Judge's sheets out for fresh ones. Ralph had also made his own changes to the room. He must have worked with superhuman speed to make a crib for us that day. It was beautifully assembled against the wall.

He'd also whittled her a few wooden toys. I used to read *Little House on the Prairie,* and I laughed at the thought of Berlin having the kind of toys Laura Ingalls probably played with.

I gently placed her in the crib, and I softly sang a lullaby I remembered Mama singing to me.

"*Esta nena linda, que nació de noche . . .*"

"I didn't know you could sing," Harrison said behind me. I glanced over my shoulder and saw him leaning against the doorframe.

"It's nothing. Just a song my mom sang to help me fall asleep."

He walked over to the crib. "Well, it looks like it worked. She's out like a light."

I smiled weakly up at him from my seated position on the floor. He sat down next to me and grabbed my hand. "I was able to cool Judge down. He's going to stay at his apartment for the night."

We were silent for the next few seconds before Harrison sighed. "Look, I realize I haven't been doing a great job being your partner. I've been looking at the situation from Judge's eyes, not yours. I should have had your back before with him. Especially with the way he was talking to you. You were right to react the way you did."

Damn right I was, I thought to myself.

"And I just want to say thank you so much for everything you're doing for her and me," he said, looking down at Berlin. "I know you were just getting used to being here, and then I went and threw motherhood at you."

I had to chuckle. My life had changed in almost every respect within a very short amount of time. In that way, I could identify with Judge. "It is crazy," I said as I reached through the bars of the crib and smoothed an orange curl that was standing up on Berlin's head. "But she's already worked her magic on me. I don't even see April's face when I look at her anymore."

"Yeah, she is something special, isn't she?" he said as we stared at her together. "Anyway, it's getting late. We should probably get some sleep ourselves."

He rose to his feet, and I yawned before grabbing the hand he offered to help me up.

That night, I dreamt that it was Berlin's fifth birthday. She was sitting at the table, her eyes sparkling from the candles on her cake.

Harrison and I were standing at either side of her. Beautiful balloons and streamers were hung up all over the place, and everyone we loved was singing happy birthday to her: Mattie, Ralph, Abuela, Jonesy, and my parents.

Just as she took a deep breath in to blow the candles out, a large gust of wind from out of nowhere blew as all the lights in the house went out. All that remained on top of her cake were small clouds of smoke. I grabbed her in my arms to protect her, and she dug her head into my chest.

My mom's face suddenly started to contort. It looked like her skin was made of wax, and it started melting from the top of her head all the way down her face. She reached up to touch it, looking panicked. "Clark?" she cried. "What is happening?"

I jolted awake with a gasp, sitting straight up in bed with sweat pouring down my face.

"Sera?" Harrison asked. "Everything okay?"

I didn't answer him before heading over to Berlin's crib to ensure she was all right. I was happy to see that she was still sleeping on her back with her tiny arms stretched out on the sheets.

I returned to bed and told Harrison, "I'm fine. Go back to sleep. It was just a bad dream."

"Okay," he murmured. He was knocked out again and breathing deeply within seconds. I snuggled in next to him and stroked his long hair that was sprawled across his pillow as I lulled myself back to sleep.

Chapter 22 – The Exchange of an Illegal Child

When I woke up, I reached my hand toward Harrison's side of the bed, but he wasn't there. I soon heard a low voice coming from outside, and I looked out and saw him on the grass. His speech was calm, but by the way his heel was furiously bouncing up and down off the ground, I could tell he was a little agitated.

"Who were you talking to?" I asked him later when he came back inside.

He took Berlin from my arms and slid her into the highchair. I got up to retrieve a jar of food to feed her.

"It was the secretary from the Ikshana's headquarters. I guess they've found someone to watch Berlin while we're at school. We're supposed to go in to meet her before our first class today."

I hadn't calculated for this additional task, so I hurried to get myself and Berlin ready for the day. Since I didn't have time to shower, I swooped my hair tightly in a bun on top of my head and then threw on a pair of jeans and a floral blouse. There was still a little bruising near my nose, so I applied a thin layer of concealer on my face.

I didn't look my best, but I was presentable enough not to be embarrassed in front of this potential caregiver. The last thing I wanted to do was appear like a dirty teenager who wasn't responsible enough to keep up her appearance, let alone care for a child.

As I had the day before, I buckled her in the car seat and placed a blanket over her. Then, I hurried to get her snapped into the back seat of Harrison's car.

I was bouncing my knees in the front seat while I waited for him to come out and drive us downtown. Even though she'd only been in my care for a day, I felt a strong bond with her. And now that I knew she was permanently going to be in my life, whether in Ananda or in the real world, I allowed myself to actually feel like her mother. So, I was anxious to meet whoever the Ikshana had decided was suitable enough to care for her while Harrison and I couldn't.

He tapped the steering wheel with his thumbs as he drove, something I had never seen him do before. I think he was just as anxious as I was.

He pulled up to the back of the building, and we rushed inside. After we got into the office, we were once again led into the large conference room.

I put the car seat on the chair next to mine, and I lifted the blanket to check on Berlin.

Shortly after, the same suited men entered the room.

"Good morning. Thanks for coming in on such short notice. We understand you have a limited amount of time, so we'll cut to the chase," one of the men said. He pressed a button and asked his secretary to bring the caregiver in.

Within a few seconds, a tiny Asian girl appeared in the room.

"This is Hai Rong."

She didn't look a day over twelve years old.

"Uh—" I started to say, sharing a look of concern with Harrison.

"No need to worry, ma'am. She has been a Nirvana for many years; she's technically twenty. She's also very experienced in childcare."

Although I was reluctant, I offered my hand to shake the child-like figure before me. "I'm Sera. This is Harrison," I said as he also shook her hand.

"And this, I assume this is the little miss—" she said before taking Berlin out of the car seat.

"Yes, her name is Berlin." I stood up to follow her as she walked around the room.

I stopped dead in my tracks when one of the men shot a look of intense disapproval at me. I raised my arms in surrender and sat back down.

"So, what do we do now? We have about fifteen minutes to get to school," Harrison said.

"You're free to go," one of the suits said.

"Just like that? We don't have any say on whether or not we're comfortable with this setup?" I asked. As hesitant as Mattie was to watch Berlin alone, she'd agreed to do so until we were satisfied with the Ikshana's pick—as long as Harrison and I took turns checking in throughout the day. We weren't sure what we would tell

218

the security guards when we left each time, but we knew we'd figure it out.

"I don't see how you have a choice, ma'am. Unless you want to drop out of your classes—"

"No, that isn't going to happen," Harrison said before the man could finish. "Is it okay if we call in to check up on her throughout the day?"

"Hai Rong, would that be okay?" a man asked.

"Sure, whenever you want!" she said enthusiastically.

"Okay, I'll have my secretary give you the number."

I rose from the chair and walked across the room to say goodbye to Berlin, not caring what dirty looks the men might throw my way. I hugged her and said we would be back soon. Harrison followed me and did the same before we both walked out.

We got a slip of paper with Hai Rong's cellphone number on it from the secretary, and we headed down the stairs and jumped into Harrison's car. I placed the piece of paper in the front pocket of my backpack for safekeeping.

"I don't know how I'm going to concentrate on anything today," I said to Harrison. "I'm going to be too worried."

"I know. I was thinking the same thing. But let's try our best to get through the day. Apparently, we don't have any other choice but to trust the Ikshana's judgment on this one."

"Yeah," I said before calling Mattie to let her know that her babysitting services wouldn't be required. She sounded relieved.

We didn't say anything else before pulling up to the school, and our silence continued as we walked silently to our lockers. Then, we parted ways and headed to our respective classrooms.

My mind was still clouded with worries when Collins sat down at the desk next to me.

"Hey, so rumor has it you and your boy toy had a pretty crazy weekend."

His presence startled me, but I said, "Wha—what are you talking about?"

"Well, I assume you heard about all of the shit that went down on the second floor of our building."

I remembered the warnings I had received from both Mattie and Harrison about Collins's less than pure intentions, so I was extra careful responding to his inquiries. "Yeah, a little. We heard about it after the fact. It was in the apartment next to Harrison's, but we weren't around when it happened."

"Mhm," he said, looking me up and down as if to observe my body language. "It just seems a little suspicious."

"I don't know what you're insinuating."

"I'm not insinuating anything. I just find it all a little fishy . . ."

I was grateful for the distraction when the professor walked in and announced what page we should turn to in our textbooks.

After class, I carefully ducked out before Collins could ask me any more questions. Then, while I waited for my next class, I made my way to the one place I knew he couldn't go—the women's bathroom.

I took out my phone to text Harrison:

Can we leave campus for lunch today? Collins has been sniffing around asking about our involvement with April and Jared's arrests. I don't want to sit through another interrogation session.

He quickly responded:

Definitely.

I successfully avoided Collins for the rest of the morning, and Harrison and I darted outside at lunchtime.

I took out the piece of paper I had received earlier and dialed the number on it.

"Hello?" Hai Rong answered after a few rings.

"Hi, this is Sera. I'm just calling to check on her—"

"Oh, she's fine. We're having a great time. No need to worry."

"Okay . . ." I said. Collins, like the snake he was, suddenly appeared in front of our faces. I snapped the phone shut and hung up.

"Who were you talking about?" he asked.

"I'm not sure that's any of your business," Harrison said coldly.

Collins grimaced at him before looking back at me with a raised eyebrow.

I figured it was better to offer up an explanation rather than leave him to his own devices. "I was on the phone with Mattie. My *abuela* fell yesterday, and she's taking care of her." Then I added, "She didn't go to the hospital or anything. She just sprained her wrist pretty badly." I wasn't sure how deep his connections ran, and I didn't want to give the impression that there were witnesses—

doctors, nurses, etc.—that could deny my story. Given everything I'd been told about him, I tried to cover all of my tracks.

"I thought you and your grandma had a bad relationship?" Collins asked.

"Just because we don't get along doesn't mean I'm heartless. I still care about her well-being." I was proud of myself for coming up with this so quickly.

"Well, we gotta get going. Right, Ser?" Harrison gently guided me with his arm on my lower back toward his car. I glanced back at Collins once, and I saw that his index finger was up, and his mouth was open like he wanted to continue questioning us. Luckily, we were able to shuffle into the car without another word.

"God, I hate that guy," Harrison said as he put his keys in the ignition. He discreetly moved his left hand down and pressed the button to lock all four doors of his car.

"Good thinking," I said.

"You can never be too careful with that one. I could see him just hopping in the car and inviting himself to come with us."

He and I drove to his apartment, where we prepared and ate ham and cheese sandwiches. After eating, we had time to spare, so I asked if we could go downtown to check on Berlin in person.

"I don't think that would be a good idea," Harrison said.

"Why not?"

"Sera, we're lucky they're even letting us keep her in the first place. They could have easily sent her back to the real world to live with God knows who. The less we step on their toes and risk pushing their buttons, the better. Trust me."

"Fine." I crossed my arms and exaggerated a deep sigh. Like a lot of his opinions, I understood where he was coming from, but I didn't like it. Defeated, I sat on the couch and flipped the TV on to waste time before we needed to be back at school. I flipped to a cringey soap opera, which I knew Harrison hated. I think I wanted to get under his skin as revenge for him denying my request to go check on Berlin.

My plan worked; he sat down but got irritated within seconds. "Ugh!" he said in disgust as he got up and went into his room. I smiled a little as he walked away.

I didn't particularly like those kinds of shows either. So, with him safely away, I turned the channel to a light-hearted comedy that I had watched on my parents' tiny television. It was supposed to get more channels, but the antenna was so old and falling apart that we only managed to get three or four. Even then, you usually couldn't get a clear picture without experimenting with the placement of the long silver sticks.

I was engulfed in nostalgia as I watched it. Before I knew it, Harrison emerged from his bedroom and indicated that we needed to leave in order to make it in time for our classes.

We parted at our lockers with a light peck and walked in opposite directions to our respective classrooms.

When I entered the doorway, the first person I saw was Collins. He enthusiastically moved his backpack from the desk next to him, and then he pointed at it to indicate that he had been saving the seat for me. I tried my best not to roll my eyes as I walked over and sat down. Glancing up at the clock, I was filled with immense dread when I realized we had several more minutes before the class would start.

Taking full advantage of this time, Collins leaned over and said, "So, I had some extra time during the lunch hour." I leaned my head an inch or so closer to him to show that I was listening, but my focus remained on my backpack as I stalled by slowly taking the items I needed out of it. "I went down to the police station and found the most interesting little report from this past weekend."

My heart sank, but I continued to act distracted. "Huh? What did you say?"

"I happened to get my hands on the report the police wrote up after arresting your friends April and Jared . . ."

I didn't know where he was going with this. But knowing him, I knew it couldn't be good.

"There was a large chunk of the report that was completely blacked out. So, I asked the police chief what was redacted. He was too worried about losing his job to give me the straight answer, but he hinted that I should check out the latest list of Samsaras."

"Okay?" I continued to play dumb.

"Well, wouldn't cha know it? There was only one new addition. Does the name 'Berlin Jones' mean anything to you?"

I shuddered as he said her name, but I did my best to keep my cool. "Per usual, Collins. I honestly have no idea what you're trying to get at." *What the fuck? Did he have to entire list memorized? If so, why didn't he notice when my name was added? Maybe it was a new hobby?*

"Sure, you don't," he said as I looked at him for the first time since I sat down. He had the evilest grin on his face. I took it as I'm sure he intended, as a warning that he would keep digging until he found more answers.

I tried stuffing any thought of Collins down in my mind, and I watched the clock like a hawk the rest of the afternoon. I was anxious for the time to come when we could pick up Berlin.

When the day was finally over, I arrived at our lockers before Harrison. I impatiently stomped my foot and bit at my lower lip while I waited for him. The hallways were almost empty by the time he made his way toward me.

"Where were you?" I asked.

"It was mine and my lab partner's turn to stay behind to clean all of the equipment."

Even though I had asked the question, I only half-listened to his answer. After he finished stuffing belongings into his backpack and zipped it up, I grabbed his arm and guided him out to the parking lot.

It felt like a lifetime before we actually pulled up to the back corner of the Ikshana's headquarters. It kind of scared me how quickly my "mama bear" instincts kicked in, but with Collins on the hunt to discover who she was, I was even more anxious about her being in someone else's care. I continued to drag Harrison behind me as we went up the stairs to the conference room.

Like she had on previous occasions, the secretary led us into the large conference room. I was pleased to see a nice little play area set up in there. Berlin and Hai Rong were both giggling.

"Hi, baby!" Harrison said as he bent down and opened his arms to pick her up. Her face lit up even more when she saw him. "Did you have a good day?" He softly kissed her on the cheek.

"Was everything okay?" I asked Berlin's new babysitter as Harrison handed her to me. I gave her a squeeze and kissed her on top of the head.

"Oh, yes. She was a perfect angel."

Neither Harrison nor I wasted any time getting her concealed in the car seat and into the car. Again, I sat in the back with her.

"See?" Harrison said, looking back at me from the rearview mirror. "I told you everything would be okay."

"Yeah, except we have a little more to worry about when it comes to Collins. The jerk went snooping around in the police records over lunch today. He noticed they had heavily redacted the report from the weekend. I assume those were all the spots that mentioned Berlin. He also told me that he used his influence to get the chief to hint that he should look at the list of Samsaras. Apparently, he has the whole thing memorized because he noticed there was only one new addition to it."

"Are you serious? I guess I figured they wouldn't list her. Do you know where it said she came from?"

I addressed his questions in the order he asked them. "Unfortunately, they did. Maybe they thought no one would know who she was? And no, I have no idea what location they listed for her. Obviously, I would guess in the Midwest somewhere. But in any event, Collins found her name, and he asked me if I knew her."

"What did you say?"

"Nothing, really. I just tried to keep my cool and act like I had no idea what he was talking about."

"I just don't understand what his end game is."

"Honestly, I think Mattie's right, and he gets monetary rewards from his grandpa for busting people violating the Ikshana's rules. I don't see any other reason why he'd be so invested. I know some people are just nosey, but he goes very, very far out of his way to dig up stuff."

I noticed Harrison was gripping the steering wheel so tightly that his knuckles were white. I leaned forward to gently rub his right shoulder. "Let's just hope the Ikshana stop his quest for information soon. Even though he does have connections with them, I don't see why anyone would want him, of all people, to find out about her. They're bending the rules by keeping her in Ananda, and we're just following the terms and conditions they set for us by keeping her existence a secret. So, if you think about it, he's the one fighting against them here, not us."

"I suppose that's a good point," he said as we pulled up to Mattie and Ralph's. We wanted to get all of Berlin's things, so we could take them to his place. We had considered staying with them, as they lived in a stand-alone house that could conceal the sounds of

Berlin's crying and cooing, but we ultimately decided against that for two main reasons. First, April and Judge had already lived in an apartment with her, and not even we, as the next-door neighbors, ever heard her make any noise. Second, we didn't want to raise any suspicion by going missing from the building altogether.

Ralph, Harrison, and I took turns taking trips to the car and stuffing things into the trunk. Then, after we were sure we had everything, we drove to Harrison's to set up what would be our new reality.

Being mindful that Collins lived in the same building, we were extra careful to smuggle each item up to Harrison's apartment. We both sighed in relief when he hauled the last thing up and safely behind his door.

Ralph had thought ahead and made the crib extra easy to tear down and reassemble. He must have anticipated that we'd need to transport it frequently. While Harrison put it back together, I unpacked Berlin's clothes and arranged them in drawers and closets. Luckily, Harrison was a simple guy who had a minimal wardrobe, and I kept all of my stuff in two pieces of luggage that Mattie had bought for me. So, there was plenty of space around the apartment for her things.

I was folding one of her last onesies when Harrison came into the room after securing the sound-proof blankets around the ceiling, floor, and interior walls. "I'm going to check in on Judge," he said.

"Oh, yeah. Good idea. I didn't see him at school. Did you?" I remarked.

"No, that's what worries me. Judge isn't one to miss classes, even when he's sick."

"Hm. Well, while you're gone, I'll blend some carrots up for Berlin, and I'll make dinner for the two of us."

"Sounds good. I love you, Sera. You know? This whole motherhood thing looks really great on you," he said as he bent down to kiss me.

"Thanks! And I love you too."

I did as I said I would, and I took the blender out of the cupboard and peeled three large carrots. Before I could do anything else, however, Harrison returned, holding a piece of paper as white as the color of his face.

"What is it?"

"He's gone," he said as he handed the crumpled note to me.

"Wha—" I started before trying to read Judge's messy handwriting. "I can't read any of this. What does it say?"

"It says he thinks it's best for Berlin if he isn't involved in her life going forward. He trusts that we will give her an even better home than he could, and he packed up all of his stuff and left."

"Does it say where he went?"

"No. Judge probably didn't want us to try to find him and convince him to stay."

Chapter 23 – The Cynicism of Shadows

Harrison and I did our best to adjust to our new life as parents—going along with the same schedule every school day: wake up, get Berlin ready, organize supplies for class, drive to drop off Berlin at the Ikshana headquarters, go to school, leave for lunch to avoid Collins, go back to school for afternoon classes, pick up Berlin, go back to Harrison's apartment, prepare dinner for all three of us, get Berlin ready for bed, do homework, get ready for bed ourselves, sleep, and repeat.

Of course, this routine changed when I had assignments to complete with Collins, which thankfully seemed to happen less as the school year progressed, and during the Ikshana inspections every month. I did as Mattie said, and I made sure that I was always safely concealed under her and Ralph's or my *abuela's* roof during those days. For the first couple of inspections, we decided it was best to keep Berlin with Harrison. We initially thought that was a good way to prove we weren't doing anything outside of their terms and conditions when it came to her.

But we quickly learned that it was a better idea to have her hide with me. When she was with him, the officers would excessively poke and prod at her. That made Harrison and me uncomfortable, so we made the unanimous decision to stop that from happening.

Thankfully, it seemed as though my prediction that the Ikshana was going to actively pause Collins's investigation was correct. He generally stayed away from both Harrison and me unless we had a project we had to work on. When that happened, we would go to Mattie and Ralph's.

I didn't want the hassle of carefully hiding all of Berlin's stuff around our apartment. So, I'd lie and say that we couldn't go there because Harrison was working on this or that experiment with his lab partner. Obviously, that wasn't true. It would've been incredibly unsafe for them to work with such dangerous chemicals outside of the lab. Fortunately, Collins had never pursued a science degree, so he never seemed to question it.

Eventually, I think both Harrison and I were lulled into a false sense of security after a few weeks went by without Collins prying into our personal lives. This caused us to get sloppy.

Abuela and I had grown close, and although she was mostly blind, it didn't seem to stop her from seeing the undeniable and contagious brightness that exuded from Berlin. She would call and practically beg me to bring her over to visit.

"She *is* my Samsara, after all," she'd say through what I could tell was a smile on her face. She knew that no matter how busy I was, she'd always successfully guilt me into visiting.

It was the fourteenth of that month, so I had packed up our things the morning before and was careful to stay inside her house for the next few days. Berlin and I were playing with blocks in the living room. Although the Ikshana never went into the older Nirvana's neighborhood during the inspections, I still usually would have closed the large bay window, just to be safe. However, without thinking about it, I left it wide open.

As we were playing, out of the corner of my eye, I noticed a dark shadow move outside. I got up right away to check what was out there, but I didn't see anyone or anything out of the ordinary. I reasoned that it must have just been a tree branch or something.

That night, I had a nightmare like the one I'd had at Mattie and Ralph's after our first day with Berlin. It had already become a prominent recurring dream of mine. It was always placed at Berlin's fifth birthday, my mom's face always started melting off from the top of her head down, and I always woke up from it startled.

We stayed at Abuela's for the rest of the inspection. Then, on the morning of the fifteenth, Harrison picked us up to drop Berlin off downtown, and I noticed he wasn't acting like himself. He was quiet and seemed distracted by something. His forehead was covered in sweat, but I didn't feel any warmth when I raised my hand to check his temperature. Instead, his skin was cold and clammy.

"What's going on with you?" I asked that morning when we were both standing by our lockers. He didn't say anything in response; he just handed me a piece of paper.

"What? Is this Judge's note?" When I opened it, I answered my own question because the words were typed, not handwritten like Judge's was. I was confused why the people in this realm had modern technology but seemed to opt for the dramatic flair of leaving notes instead of simply sending texts.

Nevertheless, I carefully read it:

*I saw Sera and the baby at her grandmother's house
during the inspection. Clearly, the two of you lied about
their bad relationship. I also found a report about your aunt.
I know she gave someone in the real world the instructions . . .*

*Your little girlfriend's sudden appearance makes a lot more
sense now. I will not hesitate to tell the Ikshana about underline everything.*

That is unless—you know what will keep me quiet.
-C

"I don't understand."

"I found it under my door this morning. It's from Collins. Remember what he wanted in exchange for keeping Janusz's secret?"

"No . . ." My stomach flipped, and I started feeling queasy. My mind raced to think of a way for us to get out of this. "Harrison, no. No. There has to be something else. I'll talk to him—"

"It won't make a difference. Trust me. He wants what he wants. Collins won't accept a negotiation."

"But he let Jared stand in for you last time. Maybe we can find someone—"

"No, Sera. This is my karma for letting someone else pay off a debt that I owed."

"Harris—" I started, but he slammed his locker shut and headed to class before I could say anything else.

With no other choice, I went to my next class. Thankfully, Collins wasn't in that one. I don't think I would've been able to resist my intense desire to pounce on him and pummel his face until his flesh turned from its natural peach color to dark red. I pictured this encounter in gory detail while I sat in my seat and waited for the professor to come in.

When she finally walked in and zapped me back to reality, my hands were in such tight fists that my nails left deep indentations on my palms. I rubbed at the marks as I looked around, embarrassed and unsure of the other movements I might've made to mimic the scene inside my head.

Luckily, I had calmed myself down throughout the morning because as I waited for Harrison by our lockers before lunch, I saw Collins sitting in the cafeteria. Despite Harrison's skepticism that he could be negotiated with, I decided it was at least worth a try to talk to him.

I sent a quick text to Harrison and lied that I had to stay and finish a project during the lunch hour, and I calmly walked over to my newest enemy. First, it was Uncle Ford, then April, now this blond-haired, gray-eyed snake of a human.

He was looking down at his phone when I approached. A sinister smile crossed his face the second he looked up from it and saw that it was me standing in front of him. I sat down, put up the hood of my sweatshirt, and turned my body so that Harrison wouldn't be able to easily recognize me if he walked by.

"We need to talk," I said.

He licked his lips, put his elbows on the table, and inched his face closer to mine. He then briefly looked around to make sure no one else was close enough to hear him and said, "Let me guess. Harry showed you the little note I left for him this morning."

My fists started clenching again, but I took a deep breath and flattened them on the top of my thighs. "Yes."

"The Ikshana tried to stop my investigation, but people can always be bought," he said. "It didn't take me long to find a schmuck who was more than willing to spill the beans. After I promised to give him a sizable chunk of my monthly allowance, he told me everything I wanted to know."

"I—"

"Let me finish. I'm also guessing you're here to try and convince me to accept another 'payment' to stay quiet. Am I right?"

I couldn't bring myself to answer him. I just clenched my jaw and let out a loud sigh.

"That's what I thought. Well, save your breath. My note clearly indicated what I want to keep my mouth shut. I will not accept a substitution like I did last time. It's your hunky boy toy . . . or nothing." He laughed to himself and clarified, "Well, not nothing. It's either that, or I'll happily tell my grandfather that you purposefully broke your agreement and told me about the baby. Your choice." He placed his hands around his mouth and only mouthed the word "baby."

"Collins, please," I said after he got up and started walking away.

He was standing right next to me by that point, and he bent down to whisper in my ear, "Don't say another word. I will not change my mind. In fact, as punishment for the time you just made me waste, I'm going to add another condition to my offer. You have to watch while Harry's body and mine combine, and I get to finally hear the sweet sounds of his pleasure. Hmm." He seemed to relish in the thought as he scampered away.

The thought of him violating Harrison was enough to make me feel nauseous. But the realization of that taking place in front of my eyes was more than I could handle. It was as if I had to expel the whole conversation I'd just had from my body. In response, I put my hand over my mouth and rushed to the bathroom to avoid throwing up in the lunchroom.

I spent the rest of lunch standing by the sink and splashing my face with water. But apparently, that wasn't enough because Harrison noticed right away that I didn't look like I was feeling well.

"What's wrong?" he asked as we stood by our lockers and prepared for the afternoon.

I was so ashamed that I had not taken his advice and left Collins alone. He was right. Trying to talk to that soulless monster only made things worse.

But, like ripping a Band-Aid off, I figured the truth would sting less if I let it out quickly.

"Harrison, I really fucked up," I whispered.

"What do you mean?"

"I didn't listen to you, and I tried talking to Collins."

"Sera . . . no. Please tell me you didn't."

"I was just trying to help, but—but I made it worse. I made him so angry that he's now demanding that I watch when—"

Harrison slammed his locker shut and punched it loudly.

"Harris—" I tried to pull on his arm, but he ripped it away.

I figured all of the eyes in the hallway were on me at that moment, so I stupidly raised the folder I was holding to my face in an attempt to sneak into my next class.

I was physically at school for the rest of the afternoon, but my brain was far, far away. I couldn't think about anything other than how to make things better with Harrison. I'd screwed up, and I knew it.

To my surprise, he was waiting for me at the end of the day. I figured he would have just left to pick up Berlin and go back to his apartment without me. Frankly, I wouldn't have blamed him if he did just that.

"Harris—" I attempted again to talk to him, but he just shook his head and started walking out to his car. I didn't know what else to do, so I followed him.

We were silent in the car as we drove to the headquarters, but I did look at his face a few times to try to read his mind. It never worked. All I saw was his stern facial expression. His eyes were fixed on the road, and his teeth were grinding together.

"Just stay here," he said when he pulled up in the back of the building. He slammed the door shut before I could say anything. When he returned to the vehicle with Berlin, however, he had much more poise. He gently lifted her car seat inside the car and buckled it in. He then calmly shut the door, opened his own, and climbed inside. I continued to look toward him every so often, but I didn't say anything as we drove home.

Once inside the apartment, I carried on with the tasks I did every day. I heated more mush I had blended for Berlin, and I prepared dinner for us adults. I was stirring a pan of pasta sauce when I heard a faint knock on the door. My blood turned cold. Now that Judge was gone, no one ever came over to visit, except for Mattie, but she usually just barged in.

Harrison swiftly emerged from the bedroom, closed the door to conceal the things inside it, and whispered, "Get her and hide in the pantry."

I turned the burner off, picked up Berlin and several of her handmade toys, and concealed us in the small room. I hadn't seen him do this, but at some point, he took the time to carefully hang noise-cancelling blankets along the walls, behind the wooden racks that stored our food. He must have anticipated that the exact situation we were currently in would happen. *The boy thinks of everything*, I thought.

I put my ear to the door, but I didn't hear any voices. After a few minutes, I heard the front door close, and Harrison opened the partition we were hiding behind.

"Who was it?" I asked.

"Guess," he answered without looking at me.

Based on his labored breathing and clenched fists, I knew it wasn't a welcome guest. "Collins?"

"Yes."

"What did he want?"

"Let's wait until she goes to bed, then we'll talk about it."

He grabbed Berlin from my arms, picked up her heated bowl of food, strapped her safely in her highchair, and started feeding her. I turned the burner back on and continued to make dinner for him and myself. My heart was beating fast as I worried about what *else* Collins had wanted.

After we all finished eating, I gave Berlin a bath, put her in her pajamas, and read her a bedtime story before she closed her sweet little eyes. I looked at her for a second while she peacefully drifted off to sleep, and I bent over to kiss her on the forehead. "Sleep tight."

I walked into the dining room, where Harrison was already seated at the table.

"She's down," I said. "So, what did Collins say?"

He was quiet for a while but finally looked up at me and said, "It was a scheduling conference, of sorts."

"What does that mean?"

"He wanted to set a date and time . . . for *it* to happen."

My saliva felt like it was made of tiny, sharp-edged stones as it slid down my throat. "When will that be?"

"Tomorrow night. 8:00 p.m. He also gave me this." He slid a small box across the table toward me.

I grabbed it and read what it was. My mother had warned me about using such products, as she said women used to in the old days, but they were actually terrible for you. Sure, I was admittedly naive, but I had since worked out how homosexual intercourse worked, and I reasoned what the contraption was intended to clean out. My hands had concealed my initial gasp, and they lingered there as I reread the words.

It was bad enough that Collins wanted to humiliate Harrison by forcing him to perform sex on him. I never fathomed he'd take it a step further and invade Harrison's body.

Without saying anything else, he asked me to stand up, and he picked me up and cradled me against his body. Confused by all of this, I opened my mouth to ask what he was doing. But he engulfed it with his before I could say anything. He led me over to the couch and gently set me down. He pulled my shirt and pants off before removing his own. Then, with one hand, he unlatched my bra, and I quickly scooted out of my underwear.

I was so lost in passion that I no longer cared why this was happening. I was just grateful that it was. I brought my hands to his face and delicately tangled my fingers in his hair. He kissed at my wrist, and we continued to make love. He stood up quickly and dressed after that.

"I just wanted to do that one last time," he said before grabbing Berlin's diaper bag and starting to fill it.

"Harrison. What are you doing?"

"I'm getting her ready to stay with Ralph and Mattie tomorrow night."

"We can do that later. Do you want to talk some more about your conversation with Collins?"

"Well, you'll be happy to know that he confirmed that he—that he would use protection."

"Oh!" I was stunned. I'd completely forgotten about Collins's diagnosis and hadn't considered its potential consequence on their interaction.

Harrison was still frantically placing items inside Berlin's bag. I got dressed, walked over to him, and put my hands on his. "I can do all that. Please, talk to me."

Reluctantly, he stopped and sat down. I looked at him as he wiped tears off his cheek. In an attempt to soothe him, I placed a hand on his shoulder. He grabbed and held it.

"I just feel so ashamed, Sera," he eventually said.

"I know. But you shouldn't. Think about it this way. You're doing it to keep all of us safe, right?"

"Yes, but—"

"But?"

"Nothing will be the same after. You'll never be able to look at me without thinking about what you're going to witness tomorrow. And then I'm sure you'll never feel the desire to be intimate with me again . . ."

"That is so far from the truth, Harrison. I love you. Nothing can change that."

"I love you too. I just don't know if I can live with myself knowing that you had to witness me being forced to engage in sex with another person. Especially a man. I've honestly even started thinking about escap—"

I pushed my finger against his lips before he could finish his sentence. "Don't you dare say that. You mentioned worrying about what you can live with. Well, I'm not worried. I can live with whatever happens tomorrow. What I wouldn't be able to handle is you rotting away in prison, getting sicker and sicker, without anything I could do to help you. We will get through this. I promise."

We clung tightly to each other's bodies in bed that night. Then, when I was sure he had fallen asleep, I let myself cry a few tears of my own. For the sake of the man I loved, I pretended to be strong. But I knew deep down that I wasn't, and I was grateful for the time to finally express the weakness I'd felt since the moment I saw Collins's note.

Chapter 24 – A Snake's Ultimate Bait

We didn't have school the next day, so I didn't bother setting the alarm. I figured Berlin would wake us up. Harrison, however, must not have been able to sleep in. When I got up, he was already up and feeding Berlin breakfast.

"Good morning," I said as I went over and kissed his cheek. "And good morning to you, sweet girl," I said to Berlin. I looked around and saw that he had cleaned the entire apartment. "Why didn't you wake me? I could've helped you."

"Nah. You looked so peaceful. Plus, I figured you deserved a little extra sleep."

I felt a sudden pain in my stomach as I was reminded what day it was. I tried my best not to think about what was to come as I packed the rest of Berlin's bag.

Harrison and I took turns showering and supervising the baby before heading out to Mattie and Ralph's. Harrison, in what I figured was his way of distracting his mind, was determined to get a bunch of yard work done around their house.

When we arrived, Mattie burst out excitedly from the screen doors. She reached for the car seat covered with a blanket in my hand, and she hurried back inside. She had already taken Berlin out and was holding her on her hip by the time I walked in.

"Well, I guess we're chop liver now," I said and smiled toward Harrison. He acknowledged what I said with only a slight smirk. *Okay, message received. No jokes today*, I thought.

He didn't even touch the spread of food Mattie had prepared before heading out to start his work.

"What's wrong with him?" Mattie asked.

"He had a disagreement with his lab partner. I guess they had an argument over the best way to dissect a dead pig." I knew the second it left my lips that it was a weird lie to make up. But for some reason, it was the only one I could develop at the time.

Mattie grimaced in disgust. "Hm. Anyway, help yourself. I made plenty!" She pushed the plate of bacon away from herself. "Did this little princess eat breakfast yet?"

"Yeah, Harrison woke up early to feed her. But she might still be hungry. Let's see." I looked at the table and saw several slices of avocado. I grabbed them and placed them in front of Berlin on a small plate. She had just started showing an interest in feeding herself.

She did her best to pick up the slimy pieces and shove them into her mouth. Mattie and I both laughed as we watched her. She seemed to like them because she kept eating, and she giggled back at us.

After breakfast, I put Berlin in the car seat again and walked to my *abuela's* for a short visit. "*¡Hola!*" she happily said when we walked into her house. I held her arm as she slowly got out of her chair, and then I brought Berlin over to her. She briefly looked toward the door and, after failing to see his shadow, she asked, "*¿Dónde está tu guapo novio?*"

"Harrison is busy doing yardwork over at Mattie and Ralph's."

"Oh, if he has time, could you ask him to trim the rose bushes out back?"

"Sure, I'm sure he'd be happy to do that," I said. I figured the more work he had to busy his mind and body that day, the better.

I stayed and chatted with her until lunchtime. Then, around noon, I started to make *choripán* in the driveway while she stayed inside and played with the baby.

"I didn't know you knew how to use a grill," Harrison said, suddenly appearing from behind me. "What are you making? It smells so good. I could smell it from Mattie and Ralph's."

"It's nothing too complicated. I'm just grilling some chorizo. I'm making enough if you want to join us."

He agreed, and I was happy to see him acting somewhat normal. He helped me bring the grilled sausages inside, and I showed him how to prepare the bun and *chimichurri*, a mixture of herbs and spices that I had prepared earlier.

"*¡Abuela, esta listo!*" I called, letting her know the food was ready. She appeared moments later, with Berlin crawling next to her.

"Oh my God! I've never seen her do that. Have you?" I asked Harrison.

"No, I can't say that I have."

"Good job, big girl!" I said before wrapping her up in my arms.

"What are you, Abuela? Some kind of baby whisperer?" I joked.

237

She was too busy hugging Harrison to answer me. "*¡Que bonito!*" she said as she embraced him. He later told me that she never talked to him affectionately like that before I came around.

"I'm hoping that's a compliment?" he whispered after she released him.

I laughed and translated, "She's just saying that you're handsome."

"Isn't she blind?" he mouthed.

"Mostly. But I think she means that your energy as a whole is nice," I said back in a soft voice, but I could tell Abuela heard me because she smiled and gave my explanation a thumb's up.

His cheeks turned red. "Oh. Um. *¡Gracias!*" he said, almost shouting in her direction.

"She isn't also deaf!" I laughed. At that point, his face turned an even deeper shade of red from embarrassment.

I took one of the sausages, and I mashed it into small pieces for Berlin to eat. She sat in my lap and clumsily brought the meat up to her face while I struggled to maneuver my own food around her wiggly head.

"Dang, this is really good," Harrison said after taking his first and only bite.

"*¡Gracias!*" I yelled, poking fun at him. To my delight, he smiled softly in response. *There's my Harrison*, I thought.

Out of the corner of my eye, I noticed a picture in the small curio cabinet that was in the dining room. It was black and white and showed a young woman next to a horse. I got up to look at it more closely, and I gave Harrison the baby.

"Is this you?" I took it out and described what I saw to Abuela.

"Ah. *¡Si!*"

"I didn't know you liked horses. I can't believe we haven't talked about that. That's so cool. I do too!"

"You must get your love of them from her," Harrison chimed in.

"Yeah, I think you're right. I didn't get it from my parents, that's for sure. Daddy is allergic, and Mama was always deathly afraid of them."

"Even as a young girl, Johanna was terrified of them. I tried to get her on one, but she cried and cried," Abuela said. "One of the many differences between the two of us . . ."

She and I never talked about her issues with my mom, and I was starting to get uncomfortable. So, I interrupted. "Harrison, would you mind trimming the rose bushes in the back? Abuela wanted me to ask you if you had time to help her out with that."

"Sure, no problem."

I can't say I ever looked at her rose bushes, but they must have been pretty out of control because it took him several hours to cut all of the rebellious branches off.

The sun was starting to set, but I successfully ignored just what the darkening sky meant that night. Until, of course, he came back into the house. The significance of nightfall was not lost on him; he looked defeated and nervous.

We didn't say anything to each other at first. He just pulled me in for a hug.

The sound of Berlin's happy shriek distracted us. We both looked over at her playing on the ground while Abuela watched from her chair.

"Are you sure there isn't any way out of this?" I asked as I looked up at him.

He let out yet another sigh. He didn't look at me; he just stared blankly ahead. "I've spent hours racking my brain trying to think of one. But no. Like you saw, Collins will not be bargained with. Not this time. This is the only way."

He clenched his jaw tightly, and I responded by kissing him on the cheek before nuzzling back into his embrace.

"If it helps, just keep reminding yourself that you're doing it for us. For Berlin and me."

I didn't look back up at him, but I felt a warm tear fall from his eye onto the top of my head. "Believe me. That's what has kept me going the last few days. And I know that's the only thing that will save me from dying from the humiliation of being taken advantage of . . . especially since it will be in front of you." I could tell by the sharp breaths he was taking that he was choking back more tears.

"Abuela, we're going to go outside for a few minutes. Are you okay with Berlin?" I asked.

"*Sí*. Just leave the door open a crack. I'll call you if I need something."

I hugged him even tighter before we released each other and headed outside to sit on the porch swing in the backyard. I did as my *abuela* instructed and left the sliding glass door open a little bit. We sat on the same side, and I lightly rested my head on his shoulder. We didn't say anything. We didn't need to. We both knew this was the last time we would be the same. Regardless of what I was about to see, I knew my love for him wouldn't change. But I knew the whole event would change Harrison in some way.

I'm not sure how long we stayed out there, just swinging in silence. We were both pulled back to reality when we heard my name being called from inside the house.

We went back into the house, and my *abuela* handed her to me.

"Everything okay?"

"She was just starting to get a little restless. I think she was getting bored of being around such an old lady." She smiled.

"I'm sure that isn't true. But *gracias,* Abuela."

She responded with a nod but yawned and quickly returned to her chair.

"Well?" I asked Harrison while I bounced the baby on my hip.

"Yeah, let's get this over with," he said back in a tone of voice I didn't recognize. I didn't know it at the time, but now when I look back, I figure this was the beginning of his dissociation from himself. It was like he had to be someone else in order to make it through such a traumatic event.

I packed up all of Berlin's things, and Harrison got her situated in her car seat. Abuela had drifted off to sleep, so I quietly kissed her goodbye on her forehead and covered her with a blanket before we walked back to Mattie and Ralph's.

After successfully transferring the baby, Mattie yelled after us, "Have fun on your date!"

We obviously had to lie to her about our plans for the night, and neither of us could bring ourselves to audibly respond. So instead, I did my best to smile and wave back in her direction.

We continued our silence as we drove to his apartment. Once we got inside, I looked around, and the darkness was immediately apparent. It felt like I was walking into Uncle Ford's house again. Shivers ran down my spine, and I tried to shake them off.

Harrison was already in the kitchen, and I slowly walked over to join him. He was ominously looking at something on the table, and once I got closer, I could see what it was.

I picked it up and hesitantly asked, "Do you want me to help with this?"

"No!" he yelled before grabbing the instrument intended to clean his insides in preparation for intercourse. Then, without saying another word, he stomped to the bathroom and slammed the door shut. I heard the toilet flush, and I assumed he was using the device as intended.

When he came out, he looked at the clock and said, "He'll be here anytime. Are you sure you're ready for this?"

"I—I don't really have a choice, Harrison." I involuntarily snarled.

"I know." His head was hung low.

I walked over to him, grabbed his face, and said in a calmer voice, "I'm sorry. No matter what happens, I will love you. We will get through this. You have nothing to be ashamed of now or after. You're doing this for people you love, and that is honorable." I kissed him on the lips tenderly before we heard villainous knocking on the door.

Harrison went to open it, and I was left alone in the living room. I tried my best to slow the rapid thumping occurring in my chest. *You can do this; you can do this*, I told myself.

"Heyyyyy!" Collins said as he burst into the apartment. He was holding two bottles of champagne in his hands. "Why so glum, Ser? This is a party!"

It took all the strength I had not to tackle him.

"Can you grab us some cups, babe?" he asked me.

I clenched my fists once more as I walked into the kitchen to grab him a glass out of the cupboard. I thought for a moment about different substances I could secretly slip into his drink—but then I remembered that Nirvanas couldn't die. Instead, I put on my best fake smile. I figured the more pleasant I was toward him, the better. I didn't want to stir up anger in him that he would later take out on Harrison.

"Here you go," I said sweetly through clenched teeth.

"Thanks, doll," he said as he popped one of the bottles open. After a significant amount of the alcohol had flowed onto the floor, he filled his glass. "Why didn't you grab any for the two of you? It'll help loosen you up." His eyebrow was raised, and he was looking at Harrison like he was a piece of meat.

"We don't drink," Harrison answered with the flattest look on his face. He was pale, and he was staring at the wooden table in front of him.

"Hmph. Well, more for me!"

He finished a few glasses off and said, "Well? Shall we get at it?" He clapped his hands together in excitement.

My stomach dropped, and as the two men walked into the bedroom, I grabbed the bottle on the table and chugged a large amount of the liquor inside. I still didn't like alcohol consumption in general, but I knew watching their interaction through foggy eyes would be preferable to my normal 20/20 vision. After I emptied it, I put the bottle down and walked down the hall.

The alcohol wasn't kicking in as quickly as I hoped it would, and I clearly saw Harrison naked and on all fours on the bed. Collins was touching himself and putting a condom on. I looked away from the scene in embarrassment.

"No, no," Collins said. "We don't have a deal if you don't watch."

To comply, I looked in their direction as much as I could without actually looking at them. Instead, I watched cautiously out of my peripheral vision.

When Collins eventually inserted himself, Harrison let out a yelp in pain.

"Shut up and take it," Collins yelled and pushed harder into Harrison's body.

I could hear Harrison holding back tears. And I don't know if it was in reaction to that or because of the alcohol I had just dumped in my body, but I felt uncontrollably nauseous. I threw up a little in my mouth, but I choked it back down—afraid Collins would insist on starting again if I left to go to the bathroom.

Like Harrison's cries of pain, I tried to tune out the disgusting sounds coming from Collins with each thrust. It didn't work. At one point, it sounded like he was almost howling like a wolf.

When it was finally over, Collins ripped his used condom off and threw it in my direction. It hit my sleeve but bounced off onto the floor. He also grabbed one of the blankets hanging from Berlin's crib to further clean himself with. He looked up at me and smiled, obviously happy with all the control he had over us at that moment. *Sinister bastard,* I thought. I also made a mental note to burn the small piece of fabric after he left. Luckily, her favorite blanket was safe with her at Mattie and Ralph's. So, this one would not be missed.

Collins got dressed and sauntered through the front door. Harrison lay face down on his bed. Now that the devil was gone, I went to the front door to securely lock him out. Then, I carefully picked up the used contraception and cleaned its contents that had spilled onto the floor. Once in the bathroom, I inspected it to make sure it had not broken. Thankfully, the whole thing appeared to be intact. I threw everything away and shimmied out of my soiled shirt. I still felt sick, and the overall smell of him on me did not help.

I walked into his room and sat down next to his lifeless body. Unsure what to do, I softly laid my hand on his shoulder.

"Don't touch me!" he said. "Leave me the fuck alone!" he continued to scream in the same unrecognizable voice he had developed earlier that day.

And just like that, I saw the aftermath of Collins's wrath. The new Harrison introduced himself to me. He was still shouting a little, so I left and closed the door to his bedroom. I knew there was no chance that I'd be able to go to sleep that night, so I turned the TV on and watched cheesy infomercials until the sun rose.

I thought maybe seeing Berlin would help him, so after leaving his apartment, I started the long but manageable walk over to Mattie's to get her. I knew she would give us a ride back.

When I reached their house, however, I was greeted by a face I'd only ever dreamed of seeing in Ananda.

Chapter 25 – Spiritual Guidance

"Dad?"

"Sera!" He outstretched his arms to embrace me in a hug.

"What? Why?" My mind was flooded with questions about his sudden appearance.

"Your father came back to relay a few messages to you, sweetie," Mattie said before pulling one of the chairs away from the dining table. "I think you should sit down."

I did as she suggested but remained looking dumbfounded at my dad.

He cleared his throat and started to speak. "Well, you see, Kailas came to us shortly after you came here. She told us that Janusz had written the instructions for you to escape abuse Ford was inflicting upon you . . ."

I was angry for a second with Kailas for telling my parents, even though she'd promised she wouldn't. But I knew she was right to do so. What else could she have done to explain my absence over the past few months? Let my parents spend their already low income on a massive missing person's search?

He continued, "I'm so, so sorry, Sera. Neither your mother nor I knew he was physically hurting you like that. I wish you'd said something—"

Ralph cut him off. "Clark . . ."

"You're right. Not the time. After Janusz died, Kailas was cleaning out his room and found this journal." He pulled it out of his pocket and handed it to me. "Turn to the page that has been dog-eared," he instructed me.

I turned to the page and saw brightly highlighted in yellow:

Attempt #3 - Escape through mysterious blue hole rumored to be in the center of the prison.

"Does this mean . . .?" I looked curiously up at Mattie, Ralph, and my dad, who were now surrounding me.

"Yeah," Mattie said. "We think that's the way he got back home, Sera. And since we know you can't get back through the normal Samsara instructions, we think this might work for you too. But if

244

you notice the date of the entry, it was written around a year ago today. He wrote farther down that he believes the portal only stays open for a few days. So, we are losing time with each second that passes."

I heard a faint cry in the distance, and Mattie left the room to attend to Berlin.

"What was that?" my dad asked.

"We must have left the television in our room on." Ralph jumped in and offered a reasonable explanation for the noise. I was grateful for this because I'd completely forgotten that I couldn't tell him about her, at least not while we were still in Ananda.

A sudden feeling of dread washed over me. "Wait. What about Harrison and—?" I motioned my eyes upstairs to reference to Ralph and Mattie, who had since returned, that I was talking about the baby. "I can't just leave."

"Wait. Now, who is Harrison?" my dad asked.

"Would you mind giving us a few minutes? Just a little girl time?" Mattie asked the two gentlemen in the room.

Ralph nodded and lightly guided my dad outside with him.

"Ralph and I figured you'd say that," Mattie said as she scooted her chair closer to me. "The baby should be able to travel with you— just like the contract with the Ikshana stated. Although they thought you could come and go like every other Samsara, we don't see why she couldn't leave with you this way."

"Do you think I would be able to come back? Through the same instructions Jonesy left for me?"

"I don't see why not. As long as you don't tell anyone about this place. But you might have to go through the danger of secretly leaving without the Ikshana's detection again. It's already bad enough that you have to do this once. But that's for you to decide someday down the road. Besides, think about it. That little girl will no longer need to live a life in hiding."

She was right, and that was exactly what Harrison said to me after we first got Berlin. I made a promise to him that I would take her with me if I ever figured a way back.

But how can we leave after everything he just did for us? I suppose his actions will keep us safe in the real world as well, and it hopefully prevented our banishment. But . . .

245

Mattie got up to signal to Ralph and my dad that it was safe for them to come back.

"Go ahead, Clark. Tell her," Ralph said encouragingly.

"Tell me what?"

"Ma—Mama is sick."

"What do you mean 'sick?'" I asked in a demanding tone. Mattie put a supportive hand on my shoulder.

"Well, the migraines started a few months ago. Our initial healthcare options weren't great since your mother is undocumented. Oh, yeah. Kailas mentioned that Ford told you about that too. Don't worry. Ford won't be reporting her anytime soon. Anyway, we had to basically go from one back-alley doctor to the next. They didn't have the proper equipment to scan her brain or anything, so it seemed like they would just guess and throw a different prescription our way. That was until . . ."

"Until what?" I inquired for more information.

"Dammit, Ser. I'm so ashamed to even say this in front of you. Please just remember that we had to. Mama needed professional help from someone who would also agree to keep her illegal status a secret . . . and that secrecy comes with added costs. We had no other choice but to ask him for the money. He rejected us at first, so we had to bribe him."

He didn't need to say anything else about this mysterious donor. I knew it was Uncle Ford. It also wasn't hard for me to guess what information they'd threatened to disseminate if he didn't give them the money. My blood boiled, but I braced myself and attempted to focus the best I could on the rest of my dad's story.

"So, we were finally able to see a neurologist, and she diagnosed Mama as having a brain aneurysm. Luckily, it hasn't ruptured. But the doctor suggested that we get permanent care for the twins, as the simple act of lifting them up could cause it to burst, and if that happened, we'd be in real trouble. The stress your little brother and sister cause could also be a problem, as a spike in blood pressure is also dangerous for her now. Obviously, we don't have access to care like that. Unless it comes from you. We need you, Ser. Please. For Mama and me."

My mind flashed back to the recurring dream I'd been having about Mama's face melting from the top of her head down. It was like my own mind had sent me a warning.

"But you couldn't afford to take care of me before," I said as I also wondered how I'd be able to provide for Berlin.

"Well, that's the thing. Kailas set me up with a job at a consultation company. It pays much more than factory work, and it's much less physically demanding. Plus, Janusz left a sizeable amount in his will for you. I guess he knew you'd always find your way back to us."

Mattie interjected. "I really think this is what is best for everyone. I know it will be hard. Like I said, this is a decision that needs to be made quickly."

With the news of my mom's deteriorating health, I knew I had to go back. I had a duty to help her raise my younger siblings and to give Berlin the best life possible.

Like when I agreed to adopt her, I was forced to make a life-changing decision in a very short amount of time. I swallowed hard and nodded. "Okay, I'm going to do it."

"Thank you so much, sweetie." He hugged me and kissed the top of my head before he and Ralph went back outside, so I was able to talk freely with Mattie again.

"Before we leave, if I write a note to Harrison, will you please make sure he gets it?"

"Of course."

She handed me a piece of paper, and I wrote:

Love means never having to say you're sorry.
Please remember that I promised you to do this.
I love you, Harrison Hercules Ellis.
~Sera Leonor Acosta Demosey ♡

I folded it up as neatly as my shaking hands would allow me to, and I gave it to Mattie. "Okay. You don't have any more time to waste. Let's get you packed up and on your way to the prison," she said.

I didn't think to say goodbye to my dad, and I felt instantly guilty when we walked outside and didn't see him standing next to Ralph.

"Don't worry. Clark used the Samsara instructions to get back. You'll be with him before you know it," Ralph said as he hugged me goodbye.

247

Mattie soon followed me down the stairs with Berlin. "Are we all set?" she asked me.

"I think so," I said before putting the blanket over the baby in her car seat for what I hoped was the last time. I wanted to bring more blankets, as one was much less effective in concealing noise. But Mattie talked me out of it by pointing out the nuisance that numerous layers of cloth would be as I tried to secretly navigate the prison.

"All right. I'll drive you as close to the prison as I can, but the rest will be up to you. I did rip this poorly drawn map out of Janusz's journal. I think he drew it based off of memory for you, but he died before he could give it to Kailas. It's kind of a mess, so I don't know how much help it will be to you, but at least it's something." She handed me the crinkled paper, and I stuffed it into my back pocket.

"You'll explain everything to him, Mattie?" I asked as we drove.

"I will. I promise."

"I just don't want him to feel abandoned . . . again." I also didn't want him to think it had anything to do with what I witnessed him and Collins doing. "And I'll spare you the details, but something happened last night. He made a huge sacrifice for Berlin and me. I don't want him to think we left because of that." I was full-on weeping at that point. I hated that the last image I would have of him was his humiliated and broken body lying face down in his bed.

Mattie grabbed my hand and squeezed it. "Well, now it's your turn to make a sacrifice for Berlin. I'll tell him everything. I won't leave his apartment until he knows just how much you and that little girl love him. I don't care if it takes so long that I completely lose my voice."

I sighed a breath of relief but was overcome with dismay when I again considered the fact that I might not be able to return. I hated to ask Mattie for yet another favor, but I had to. "I know he will resist, but if he ever finds someone to replace me as his Samsara, will you please convince him to do it. I hate the idea of him being all alone forever."

"I will. But, like you said, I doubt he'll listen. I know him too well. He's stubborn. He'll probably never give up hope that you'll come back."

After she agreed to my request, I kind of stopped listening. Instead, I was intently studying and trying to make sense of the map Jonesy had drawn out.

He hadn't actually written any words on the paper; he only used stick figures, hand-drawn clocks, and other symbols to illustrate his escape.

I'd never been inside the prison before and had no idea of its layout. But luckily, I had Mattie, who was somewhat acquainted with it due to her years of volunteer work. She was able to identify some of the key "landmarks" within the building itself. However, she hadn't been inside for several years. So, we knew there was always the possibility that things had been remodeled, and her memory wasn't accurate anymore.

Together we were able to guess Jonesy's path to the large porthole, which he indicated by placing a large X and circling it several times. It was smack dab in the middle of the first floor.

"Is that the blue hole he mentioned in his diary?" I asked Mattie.

"Yes, I think so. I heard rumors about it while I was volunteering, but I've never actually seen it myself. I don't know if you remember this, but the first time you showed us the note, Ralph and I both thought it hinted toward its actual existence. But since we didn't have any actual proof, we didn't want to get your hopes up."

I did remember that. I nodded in response but kept my eyes on the map.

Suddenly, another feeling of dread washed over me.

"Mattie?"

"Yes?"

"What if this doesn't work?" I asked.

"Well, that's why I brought this for you," she said before handing me a strange looking pill.

"Wha—"

"It's arsenic. Trust me, if you get caught, death is optimal to suffering inside that hell hole."

Jesus Christ, I thought. I remember learning about North Korean refugees who brought similar pills with them when they escaped their country. Chills ran down my spine. As my teacher talked about it, I felt so bad for them. To be put in a position that death was the optimal choice over being captured and punished. I never thought I'd ever face a similar situation.

Jonesy, I really need your help on this one, I said in my head as I looked up at the sky. There was no way my life would end this way. I had more to live for than that.

"But what about Berlin? I'm not going to murder—" I started to say.

"You won't have to. Harrison still has rights over her," she quickly said. "Legally, she will need to be returned to him. He didn't break any of their terms."

A little relieved by that, I looked back down at the map. If I had any hope of succeeding, I'd need to study every last inch of it. Near the large X, Jonesy had drawn a box full of stick figures with hats on their heads. I figured this was supposed to represent a guard post. He'd drawn a large rectangle to the right of that station but added bars along the interior walls. He'd also placed several circles with lines across them.

We couldn't know for sure, but Mattie thought she remembered a cell of Nirvana betrayers there. Based on the symbols Jonesy had drawn, that also made sense to me. There was a clock pointed to what we guessed was six o'clock. Whether it was a.m. or p.m., we had no idea.

Another box in the lower left-hand corner had bars and circles. There was a clock above it that pointed to five. He had drawn yet another large rectangle to the right with bones inside it. I was happy when Mattie dispelled my fear that they were supposed to indicate human remains. Instead, she said that was where the K-9-unit dogs were kept when they weren't on patrol or in their cage.

Based on his drawing, it looked like the animals had a large play yard outside, and he had drawn a clock pointing to four, and an arrow to what I assumed was the doggy door they were let out of. There were also little lightning bolts along the yard, which I took to mean they were kept in there by an electric fence.

After looking at the map for a while, Mattie and I deciphered that the dogs were let back in at 4:00. At which point, Jonesy had disguised himself as one of them, climbed through the doggy door, and hid in a dark corner in their cage until after 5:00. That was when the guards would do their rounds in the next cell, apparently full of Nirvana betrayers. After they were satisfied with their inspection, he'd planned to sneak into the cell of prisoners.

Then, it appeared as though he'd crept to the porthole once the guards had moved on to check the cell in the far-right corner.

The only thing we couldn't understand was how he'd gotten in and out of the cage and cells, as we assumed they'd be tightly locked to keep the animals and humans in them. At least, that's how it worked when Mattie was there last.

But of course, there wasn't anyone we could run our previous conclusion by for accuracy. So, I had no other choice but to trust what Mattie had said about the layout of the prison and my own gut instinct.

I hadn't believed in God for a while by that point, but I continued to silently pray to Jonesy. If heaven did exist, I knew he'd be there, and he'd be able to hear me.

Please, Jonesy. Please guide us so we can return back to the real world safely. Please, I repeated over and over in my head.

Then, as clear as day, I heard his voice. "You'll make it, *mała perła.* I promise."

"Did you hear that?" I asked Mattie.

"Hear what?"

Even though I was the only one who heard it, I knew it was actually him. I felt it in my bones. The thought of him being some type of guardian angel gave me the hope I needed to attempt such a dangerous escape.

Before I knew it, Mattie had pulled off into a dark corner and parked her minivan.

"This is as far as I can go, sweetie." I was surprised to see that she had tears in her eyes. I had seen all kinds of emotions come out of her during my stay in Ananda. But I'd never seen her full-on cry before. "Please, be careful," she said as she pulled me in for a hug. She embraced me for several seconds and kissed the top of my head. "Okay, you better go. It's almost 4:00."

I was just about to open the door when she grabbed my arm. "Wait, Sera. Take this. You might need it if she starts crying," she said as she handed me a tiny bottle of rum.

"Mattie! I could never . . ." I said, surprised that she would ever suggest giving alcohol to a child.

"I know, I know. But her slight inebriation, which will wear off, is better than being discovered and you needing to ingest that pill."

I knew she was right, and I begrudgingly accepted it and concealed it in the small bag of essentials I was bringing with me.

I hugged her one more time and profusely thanked her for everything she had done for me. I was starting to get teary-eyed again as I got out of the car and grabbed Berlin from her car seat.

Mattie and I both reasoned that I shouldn't try to take it with me. It was too cumbersome and would make it harder to escape. Her van soon sped off, leaving us in a storm of dust. When it settled, I hid behind the nearest building. I peeked around it and saw the side of the prison and the play yard Jonesy had indicated was used by the K-9 dogs.

I didn't have a watch of my own, and I'd decided my cellphone was not one of the "essentials" to take with me, for I feared it would go off and blow our entire cover. Because of all that, and the strict timeline we had to abide by, Mattie had graciously given me one of her old watches. The face was small, but the long silver band was way too big for my wrist, so I had to be careful not to let it slip off. To ensure its security, I pushed it up onto my left forearm.

I looked down at the watch and saw that it was 3:45. I didn't have much time to plan, so I pulled my large green cloak over the both of us and hurried toward the prison without another thought.

I wasn't sure how, but I knew I had to sneak inside with the pack of canines that were playing and rolling around in each other's feces. At least, that's what I thought they were doing, as a putrid smell grew stronger and stronger with each step I took toward the small doggy door. I had no way of knowing if there were guards above. So, I walked as slowly as possible, hoping that the moss-colored fabric around us would blend in with the ill-cared-for patches of grass.

I was grateful to feel the coolness of the bricks on my back when I successfully reached the side of the building. However, that moment of solace was cut short when Berlin started stirring. It was clear that she was detecting the same foul smell invading my nostrils. When her quiet cries became loud enough that the dogs began to take notice, I panicked and did something I never thought I'd do. I reached into my pocket, pulled out the bottle Mattie had given me, and sprinkled a tiny amount of it on her top gums.

I felt sick with guilt for my actions, but within a few minutes, it seemed to work because she was fast asleep.

Someone blew a whistle nearby, and the dogs darted toward the door. I followed their lead but stayed close to the building to conceal myself and Berlin in the shadows. I quickly bent down and began my ascent through the tiny door.

I entered backward so that my dark clothing would hopefully blend in with the dirty animals that had just rushed through it. In doing this, however, I failed to notice a thin rubber lip—which presumably stopped the door from flapping—jutting out of the floor. I stumbled over it, losing my balance for a second, and inadvertently put all of my weight on my left wrist. Luckily, I didn't drop the baby, and my adrenaline was so high by that point that I didn't feel any pain.

Finally, I rose to my feet and once again felt the cold brick against my back as I scurried deeper into the cell.

To my surprise, the smell inside the prison was even worse. Reaching the darkest corner, I pulled up some of my cloak's fabric to cover my mouth and nose. I looked around frantically to make my escape route into the next cell. Unfortunately, the darkness concealing us was also hindering my vision, and I couldn't see more than two or three feet away in every direction. I couldn't even see the watch Mattie had given me, so I did my best to guess how much time had passed and count each minute after that.

After standing in silence for what I believed to be half an hour or so, I started to creep closer to the other side of the rectangular enclosure I was in. I guessed the guards would make another whistling noise when it was time for the Nirvana betrayers' cell to be inspected. But I figured the closer I was to the next cell, the better. I would be less likely to get caught because I'd only have a few steps to travel. As I inched closer to the human enclosure, I was shocked to see there weren't any bars between one section and the next.

Just as I expected, the whistle did blow again. I remained hidden for several more minutes before stepping into the next cell. It appeared empty. As I continued to walk across it, though, I stumbled over something big and fleshy. A body. This time, I lost my footing, but by some miracle, I managed to fall on my back, and Berlin remained secured in my arms.

I must have let out some kind of noise when I fell because I soon heard a guard yell, "Oy! Quiet in there!" He then spit in my direction. I felt the body beneath me shift slightly, and they responded with a weak groan.

After the guard walked away, I tried to get up, but I found myself stuck in some kind of spongey matter. It was soon abundantly clear to me where the horrible stench was coming from. These people were living in their own filth. I managed to get back on my feet, with some effort, and I wrinkled my nose in disgust with each squish I felt beneath my feet as I walked.

I walked past several other bodies that were just as lifeless as the one I had tripped over. They were silent except for the chilling rattle their lungs made with each breath, which seemed to occur in dissonant and stagnant turns. One person, however, was more vocal and obvious about their distress. He was slumped in the corner, coughing, and gasping for breath. Without thinking, I leaned over to inspect him further.

I swatted away rats and dozens of flies that were crowding him, and I bent down to rest a supportive hand on the poor soul. Then, as I got closer to his rotting body, my eyes widened in shock.

"Jared?"

Chapter 26 – The Kid Comes Home

I whispered his name as quietly as I could. He moaned, lifting his weak head to get a better look at me.

I don't think I would've recognized him if it weren't for the small ray of light bouncing off his strawberry blond hair. Once I cleared the dirty strands that hung over his face, I noticed how much his appearance had changed. What once was a strong, handsome man was now an emaciated skeleton. His once sparkling white teeth were reduced to brown stumps, and his eyes that used to be a mesmerizing blue appeared black and deeply sunken into his head.

A spark of recognition filled his gaze, and he opened his mouth to say something but was stopped by the sound of a loud buzz. His skeletal hands grasped at the white collar around his neck. I hadn't noticed it before, but as I looked around, I saw that all of the bodies had similar ones resting on their scrawny clavicles.

I covered my mouth to hide my gasp of realization. I'd reasoned that the lightning bolts Jonesy had drawn around the dog's playpen meant that they were confined by an electronic fence, but I'd never dreamed the humans would be reduced to such cruelty as shock collars.

And then it hit me—that was why there weren't any visible barriers outside of the cells. All entities who were not allowed to leave the building, or its surrounding areas, were kept inside by strong electric currents. My stomach rumbled as I continued to witness how much pain Jared and the rest of the prisoners were experiencing. I tenderly stroked his face until I heard the next whistle blow.

Then, I did the only thing I could to bring some kind of happiness into his world: I quickly revealed the tiny baby cuddled in my arm. His eyes brightened immediately, and he raised his hand toward the porthole. I nodded, and he smiled.

A few minutes had passed, and I didn't want to risk any more time going by before I reached the location Jonesy had marked on his drawing. I gave Jared's hand one more gentle squeeze before rising to my feet and beginning my journey toward the middle of the large room.

As I had before, I clung to the wall as I slowly inched forward. My heart was beating out of my chest, and my hands were trembling. But I was in too deep to give up.

When I got closer, Berlin started to rustle a bit, but she seemed to be stunned into a state of calm when she saw the dazzling blue reflections coming from a small slit in the weighted tarp covering the gateway to her new life. The beauty soon lulled her to sleep.

I was able to shuffle the tarp off just enough for the two of us to fit under it, but instead of jumping right in, I stood still for a few seconds. I was mesmerized by the sight myself, and it instantly comforted me.

"Thank you, Jonesy," I murmured, looking up as if I was praying to him again. I then closed my eyes and muttered, "Reflections of blue guide us home."

After a few seconds, I opened my eyes enough to see two or three guards turning in my direction. They had large masks covering their faces, likely to avoid the horrid smell. Before their eyes could focus on us, I took another few steps into the hole.

A cold feeling enveloped me. It wasn't abrasive, however; it was actually a satisfying feeling. It was like the tingling feeling that washes across your leg after kicking it out from under your comforter on a warm night, except it was all over my body. At the same time, I also felt as weightless as a feather. I closed my eyes to enjoy all of the sensations—but my mind was suddenly filled with memories, good and bad, I had acquired in Ananda:

Mattie and Ralph first approaching me on the grassy field.

Seeing Harrison look up from the dining table that first morning, warmly upturning one side of his mouth and introducing himself.

The feeling of guilt I felt when I upset him by bringing up his aunt.

His pinky finger gently grazing my hand as we drove to the cave. His lips pressing against mine for the first time.

Deeply breathing his smell in.

His head helplessly resting against mine after April drugged him.

Feeling him deep inside me during the first time we made love.

Tangling my fingers in his long hair when we kissed.

The sympathy I felt watching Collins take advantage of him.

His body lying lifeless and damaged on his bed.

Suddenly, I felt like I was physically in Harrison's apartment again. I reached my arms out to comfort him, but as I got closer, he transformed into Jonesy. I was overcome with the feeling of desperation I felt toward both of them. The two people I loved most in this world but couldn't save. I tried to scream; instead, I woke up in a room I vaguely recognized. I jumped up and pressed my fingertips against my cheeks to absorb the tears falling from my eyes.

"Sera?" I heard a familiar voice call my name.

"Where am I?" I asked.

Kailas soon appeared in the doorway, holding Berlin on her hip. "You're home, kid.

Key Terms ॐ

(Americanized spellings of Sanskrit and Hindi words rooted in Hinduism and Buddhism philosophies)

Agni: Fire-God of Hinduism.

Ananda: State of eternal bliss and the ending of the rebirth cycle.

Ikshana: Eye, sight, viewing, etc.

Nirvana: State of perfect happiness where there is no suffering; release from the cycle of death and rebirth.

Nisphalata: Infertility.

Samsara: The cyclical life process.

Urvarata: Fertility.

Made in the USA
Monee, IL
13 January 2022

88855162R00148